THE WITCH AT RIVERMOUTH

STEPHEN P. O'CONNOR

merrimack
press

An imprint of 512 Media Inc.

512
media inc.

Methuen, Massachusetts

Edited by Emilie-Noelle Provost
Line Edited by Steve Wilder, Media-Pro Enterprises, Canton Center, Conn.
Cover Photo by Deb Venuti, Haverhill, Mass.
Author Photo by Adrien Bisson Photography, Lowell, Mass.
Design by Brenda Riddell and Jaimie Knapp, Graphic Details, Portsmouth, N.H.

Published by Merrimack Press
An Imprint of 512 Media Inc.
Glenn J. Prezzano, Publisher
P.O. Box 867
Methuen, MA 01844
MerrimackPress.com

Printed in the United States of America

First Printing in March 2015

10 9 8 7 6 5 4 3 2

TABLE OF CONTENTS

I was given a thorn in my flesh, an angel of Satan, to torment me. Three times I pleaded with the Lord to take it away from me. But he said to me, "My grace is sufficient for you, for my power is made perfect in weakness." That is why I delight in weaknesses, in insults, in hardships, in persecutions, in difficulties. For when I am weak, then I am strong.

Paul, *Second Letter to the Corinthians*

I gave up the church to ease my horrors—too much candlelight, too much wax—I prefer rivers in my death, or seas ...

Jack Kerouac, *Doctor Sax*

Alas, how is't with you,
That you do bend your eye on vacancy
And with th' incorporal air do hold discourse?

William Shakespeare, *Hamlet*

For Olga,

As Brel wrote, "De l'aube claire jusqu'à la fin du jour."

PRELUDE

N one of them wanted to admit that they were afraid. That would ruin the adventure. The older of the two girls was the least afraid; she was nervous, yes, because her parents had told her never to take the harbor skiff out of the estuary into the open sea. And she never had until today, when, seeking to impress her younger sister and her little cousin, Skipper, with something grander than moored boats, marshy islands and the echoing undersides of bridges, she had motored out of the rivermouth and left the shoreline behind, intent on the view of the coast they now had—a grand view indeed—from out on the wide expanse of Plum Island Sound.

"Look!" She pointed off to where a pair of gannets, brilliant white, tucked their black-tipped wings and missiled into the sea. One of them rose, working its wings and stretching its long neck as a fish disappeared down its gullet. "A school of mackerel," she said. Her hair streamed out like a golden banner in the westerly breeze. She kept one hand on the throttle; with the other, from time to time, she pulled a few wayward strands from her face, revealing a broad smile and shining eyes.

The eyes of the younger sister, whose dark hair was clipped short, were apprehensive. The sea was not rough, but it was a small boat, low in the water with a freight of three—"full to the gunnels," as her father would say, and it seemed to her that the sun was declining too quickly toward the dark, uneven outline of the land. Skipper had ceased his usual chatter; he sat erect and moved his body continually, trying to compensate for every shift of the vessel as it rode the easy swells.

"Let's head back," the younger sister said finally, casting a longing look at the rich shadows of the shore. She didn't trust the sea. "Come on, it's getting late."

The older sister nodded. She shifted the tiller handle so that the boat banked for a wide turn. The boy leaned far to the high side, eyes wide, gripping the sideboard tightly with both hands. "Tomorrow," she said, "we could get our rods and go out early to the Speckled Apron."

"That's four miles out," the dark-haired girl said, "and you don't know the marks." Their father knew all the marks; when he brought them out fishing in his Parker Sport Cabin, he'd gaze landward, lining up the water tower with the lighthouse, or the lights from the ballpark with some buoy, and follow a compass from there to set the boat right over the lump in the ocean floor known as the Speckled Apron.

They all felt better with the land before the bow. The westerly swept their faces now, and with her free hand, the girl at the tiller touched the heavy, silver miraculous medal that shone in her open collar. It had belonged to Uncle Mike, her mother's brother, and had been returned in a crumpled packet by a friend who was with him when he was killed near the end of the war at the Battle of Luzon.

At first it was no louder than the drone of a cicada in the garden, but the whine grew, and looking backward they saw another boat heading into port. The girls knew the yacht; it was *Victor*, a 25-ton Sea Ray, more than fifty feet from stem to stern, owned by some real estate magnate who lived in a mansion up on Green Street. They could see a few people stretched on the raised bow behind a silver railing, and a few more under an awning at the stern. A woman held down a floppy sun hat with one hand and waved a drink at them with the other.

There were miles of open water, but *Victor* cruised along at half throttle within an eighth of a mile of their skiff, double 800 horsepower engines churning. The yacht and its merry excursionists faded into the distance, but its roiling wake now ran across the water toward them in three great swells.

The girl in the stern shifted the tiller handle sharply to turn the bow into the waves—too sharply—the boat lurched sideways. In a panic, she shoved the tiller back and wrung the throttle, but before the craft could answer, the first wave struck the port bow.

The skiff reared up and was flung backward, coming down crookedly on its starboard side. A rush of foam rolled over the gunwale as the second wave struck them, spinning the foundering boat and sweeping the three into the sea.

The younger sister surfaced screaming, "Bastards!" in the direction of the yacht, which was now a light dot against the darker shore. They were swamped and found themselves clinging to a boat that was upright but had settled just under the water. The flotation foam in the hull kept the boat from sinking completely, but they could not bail out a vessel that had no freeboard.

"The water is cold," Skipper said, and when neither of the girls responded he said, "Wha—what are we gonna do?" A faint plume of oily smoke wafted away from the spot where the outboard had sputtered and died as it sank below the wave.

"Just let me think, Skipper," said the girl who had been steering the boat a moment before. Don't let those oars float away! Hold onto them!"

"What can we do with them?" he cried, but he reached out and grabbed the oars, tucking them under one arm.

The water *was* cold, and the older girl already suspected that they would drift with the current farther out to the open sea as darkness fell and hypothermia set in. The sun was low over the shore now, and there was no one. No one. *What have I done? Jesus, I've killed us.* And despite her efforts to hold the panic in check, she heard the cries of her forlorn parents when the news reached them that the skiff and their children had vanished in the sea.

Skipper, taking in the vast emptiness around them, began to cry. "Are we gonna die?"

"Don't be stupid, Skipper," the younger sister said, but they all heard the wavering in her voice. Scanning the horrible, vacant, long, curving horizon, she shuddered. She was thirteen years old, and she was going to die. She imagined their bicycles in the morning, still chained to the apple tree at the marina—dew-dripping and ownerless.

Her older sister was thrashing about the submerged boat, trying hopelessly to raise the vessel above the water, searching for something, for some way out. All at once she stopped and looked at the sky and then at her sister and younger cousin. "I don't know. Let me pray," she said. "Let me pray to the Virgin and she'll help us."

"Pray," her sister echoed, and she whispered, in a voice so low that neither of the others heard, "We're dead."

The older girl clutched the miraculous medal in her right fist. The others watched her lips moving as she prayed, her eyes tightly closed, her fist in motion as if she were getting ready to cast a pair of dice. "*I promise,*" she concluded softly, and opened her eyes, which were unclouded, lucid, the color of the sea. She began to scan the swamped boat desperately, and after a minute she moved toward the submersed stern, feeling for something. She stopped and looked at her sister, her wet hair flat against her skull. Wordlessly, she pulled over her head the black string on which the medal hung.

The outboard was attached to the motor mount with four flat-cap screws. "Yes," she whispered as the edge of the medal slid into the first slotted screw head. The boy stopped sobbing and watched her as she loosened the screws and pulled them out one by one. She called her sister around to the stern, and together they managed to lift the motor off the transom and drop it.

The boat immediately came up in the water. There were a few inches of freeboard now, and they pulled out the cut Clorox bottle that was wedged under a seat. The girls took turns bailing while the boy splashed water out with his hands. They worked wildly for their lives—the boat steadily rising in the water. Skipper got back in first, and balancing carefully, one on each side, the two girls pulled themselves into the skiff.

Wasting no time, the older girl set the oarlocks, slid the oars in up to the leather collars, and began to row for shore. "You saved our lives, Gretta," the boy said.

"After I nearly got us killed," she said. "Listen, we'll have to say the motor was on the skiff when we left it—that someone stole it. If our parents knew the truth, my God, they'd die."

The boy nodded gravely. "What if you weren't wearing the medal?" he asked. His lips were blue, and he held his elbows in his hands. The oars knocked about in the oarlocks as the older girl rowed. The boat lunged shoreward and the blades rose, dripping.

She ignored the question because she did not want to think about that. "Look at you. You're shivering like a luffing sail. Anyway, you'll be home in time to watch *Happy Days*." They both laughed, while the younger sister, silent as a shroud of fog, stared hard at the shore.

The girl at the oars looked over her shoulder, keeping the bow lined up with High Sandy, the great dune that rose from the shore behind Camp Sea Haven, the polio camp. Turning back, she grew serious and said to her sister, "My life can never be the same now."

"What does that mean, Gretta?" her sister asked.

"I made a promise. A solemn promise."

"What kind of promise?"

"A promise to the Virgin Mary. *She* showed me the way, and now I owe her my life—our lives."

Her younger sister didn't try to understand; her thoughts had turned elsewhere. The shore was deep in shadow when they hailed a lobsterman setting the last of his traps just off Newburyport Light. He threw them a line and towed them upriver. When the boat was tied up at a dock at Bridge Marina, the dark-haired girl told the others that she would be along after them. "Hurry," her older sister said, "if Mom and Dad get back from Maine and you're not there…"

"I'll be along," she repeated. Their gas can had gone overboard, but she slipped onto the deck of a cabin cruiser tied up nearby and found a reserve can, nearly full. The cabin was unlocked, and she picked up a pack of cigarettes, a book of matches, and a *Record American* newspaper.

She stowed the gas at the stern of the skiff and put the other things on the bench beside her. The boat rowed easily with a freight of one as she moved across the black water to the spot where *Victor* was moored.

She tied the boat to the side ladder and climbed aboard with the gas can. Without hesitation, she unscrewed the cap and spilled the gasoline across the deck. Then she lit a cigarette and folded the pack of matches over it. When the cigarette burned down, the matches would flare. She tucked the homemade fuse into the balled-up newspaper and set it on the puddled gasoline. She was already on her bicycle when *Victor* burst into flames.

PART I:
LOVE COMES IN AT THE EYES

CHAPTER ONE

I look back at those days and wonder. How does it begin? You walk out one evening, young and full of hope and a reservoir of love that's yet to be tapped. One night like so many other nights of your youth, crowded with revelers, the spirit lifted on a swelling tide of music and laughter, and freed from every care with glasses of summer ale. No black cat crossed your path; no red moon hung above the cityscape. There were no portents at all, nor any of the foreboding that Romeo felt as he made his way toward the home of the Capulets that first evening. And yet you will meet her. Happy fool, your ship is even now cresting the dark waters while an unseen storm gathers beyond the horizon.

from Nestor McCorley's Journal, August, 2014

JULY 2007

It was carnival time in the city. The Lowell Folk Festival drew eighty-thousand visitors for a weekend of music from around the globe, performed on six stages throughout the downtown. Nestor McCorley stepped out of the Old Court, well-wrapped in the glow of a couple of pints of Harpoon ale and the golden warmth of a Jameson chaser. A street vendor stood beside a cart that anchored an enormous cloud of balloons: SpongeBob, Elmo, Mickey Mouse and Batman stirred gently above him, their painted eyes watching. The vendor hawked his airy goods to the passing crowds while waving a fistful of flexible phosphorescent wands that traced glowing circles of green, pink and blue in the night.

Nestor paused to watch a performer in a fool's cap and bells balance a wine glass on a long wooden spoon that projected horizontally from his mouth. The spectators who encircled him cheered as he pulled a tin whistle from his pocket and tucked it into the corner of his mouth. His fingers flew over the silver barrel, and as the whistle sounded an Irish jig, the fool tossed his hips from side to side; the wine glass still perched on the spoon before his bulging eyes.

An amplified voice floated over Merrimack Street. "Check, one, two. Check. Check." A bass guitar essayed a few syncopated scales while a drummer pedaled throbbing booms out of the bass drum and rapped out terse rolls on snare and toms. "Vocal check one zero one."

Nestor had decided to catch the Red Stick Ramblers, a Cajun gypsy swing band over at City Hall Plaza, but as he walked past John Street he heard, from the direction of an illuminated soundstage, a button accordion plying some riffs that piqued his interest. He passed a smoky grill, dodging couples with strollers and tourists with backpacks, still wearing the wide-brimmed hats that had shielded them from the sun hours before. A barker standing beside a spinning wheel, hands tucked in a change pouch, cried: "Round and round the wheel goes, where it lands no one knows! You spin it you win it!" A pack of teenage girls, eyes bright with the enchantment that night and music cast over the city, giggled as they waved phosphorescent wands before one another's faces.

A whiteboard announced: FENÓMENO VALLENATO WITH DIEGO ORTIZ, 9:00–10:00. Nestor picked his way through the throng to the open side of the tent, where he was able to find a seat near a foldout wooden dance floor that had been set up in front of the band. The air was rich with a mélange of spices, a bouquet of ethnic cooking that wafted from the food tents nearby and hung in the humid air.

The stage was crowded. There were four percussionists, extra vocals, guitars and, standing in the center of it all, a middle-aged man in an embroidered white shirt and straw cowboy hat of ornate design. An accordion hung over his broad chest. Diego Ortiz.

The band opened with a rolling wave of congas and smaller, handheld percussive instruments, a churning Caribbean beat that seemed to undulate through the air like a living thing, a crawling snake of sound. A cheer rose from the crowd as a voice called over the rhythm, "*Colom-biaaaaaaaaa! Que linda eres!*" The accordion wove its high, clear notes into the throbbing cadence and the dance floor filled.

This was why Nestor loved the city. The world was here in its infinite variety, in its various cultures and languages, all the ways of seeing and feeling. He had spent a couple of years working for the Peace Corps in a village in Bolivia, where he learned Spanish, and now he caught phrases that rode on the notes of the accordion. *La hechicería de tu sonrisa.* The witchcraft of your smile. *Mi mujer divina.* My divine woman.

Most of the Americans on the dance floor bounced or swayed stiffly, as Nestor knew he would, but the Latinos moved as though their bodies were extensions of the rhythm. Amid those moving bodies he caught a glimpse of a dancer.

Her arms were raised and her hips, through a long white cotton skirt, marked a lovely time. Dark curls swung across her back, and he saw an Indian beauty in her profile. As she turned with the music, a smile flashed in his direction. Had she smiled at him? A gap in the dancers closed and she was lost.

He rose and peered through the crowd, trying to see her again, the radiance of that smile, the luster of those eyes. The *lux aeterna* of feminine beauty. He watched a man leading a woman effortlessly, one hand on the small of her back, turning her, guiding her through the pulsing cadence of the accordion's note-stream. The couple understood each other perfectly; no movement was wasted.

Nestor wished he could dance like that. To move with her to this music, feeling her in his arms, pliant, complicit—inhaling the scent of her hair, her body. When he saw her again, he realized that she was not dancing with a man, but moving to the music with a couple of her girlfriends. The song ended, but they stayed on the floor, laughing and talking. He could not make out the words she spoke, but he sensed somehow—her gestures or the movement of her mouth, that the language was Spanish. Diego Ortiz introduced the members of the band and said that they would begin with an old *vallenato* called "El Camino de Amor," or "The Road of Love."

There was nothing for it but to ask her to dance and risk the rejection that was the fear of every suitor. He stepped across the sidewalk and peered at his reflection in the window of the Union National Bank. *Shit.* He'd forgotten to use a comb before he went out. He ran his fingers rapidly through his dark hair, smoothing it and pushing it back. He needed a haircut. Could use a shave, too. He smoothed his mustache with his index finger and thumb, and straightened his dungaree jacket. *Right. Can't wait until the song ends, or some other guy spots her while I stand here preening.*

As he walked back under the tent, he ran over various dance invitations in Spanish, searching for the most polite, mulling over combinations of words. He saw as he approached that she was about to leave the floor with her friends. He recalled Shakespeare's words:

> *Our doubts are traitors,*
> *And make us lose the good we oft might win*
> *By fearing to attempt.*

His father, Eamon McCorley, had put it more succinctly: "Faint heart never won fair maid." He took a deep breath, stepped in front of her, and asked in English, "Would you like to dance?"

The smile reached her eyes and kindled them in warm light. *La hechicería de tu sonrisa.* She said something to her friends, then nodded and held out her arms; at her throat, a silver crucifix on a thin chain shone against her bronzed skin. "I'll follow you," he said, and he did his best to do so, watching the movements of other dancers and listening hard to the rhythm. Unfortunately, that took so much of his concentration that he was unable to think of anything to say to her.

She rescued him. "Ah, these *vallenatos* are sad. He says, 'The road of love is like the road the… *el nómada,* the…' "

" '… the road the wanderer takes.' "

"Yes! 'It is steep and, full of… *las vueltas peligrosas*… dangerous turnings.' "

Nestor continued, " 'The wisest man does not know where it leads.' "

She leaned back, looking into his eyes. "How do you know Spanish?"

"I was in the Peace Corps in Bolivia for two years. *Vallenato* music is even popular there."

When the song ended, they applauded and stood for a moment at the edge of the dance floor. "I thought I read that the Peace Corps—that they ask them to leave Bolivia," she said.

"That's right. For about twenty years. They were invited back in 1990, and I went in '96. There are people who want them… us… out again. I could never follow the politics. I just thought it would be good to do something like that, but it's very complicated—who's going to control the resources of the Eastern provinces. They have a lot of natural gas. I'm sorry, what's your name?"

"Minerva Herrera."

Minerva. *Mujer divina*, divine woman, the singer had cried. The name brought an image to mind: the Greeks called her Athena, the long spear held upright, war helmet pushed back on her head, gray eyes, aquiline nose.

"A beautiful name," he said. "I'm Nestor McCorley."

"I know Latinos called Nestor, but no Americans."

"My mother is from Greece. My father was from Ireland."

"That's an interesting combination."

"The sun of the Mediterranean and the fog of the North."

"And which ancestors do you... how do you say... which are like you?"

"Whom do I take after? Well, I guess I look Greek, but I feel more Irish. Anyway, as the Irish say, 'What's bred in the bone will out.' You know, whatever you grow up with comes out in your character somehow."

"Yes. I think that is true."

She invited him to sit with her sister, Marina, and her sister's friend. He learned that she was visiting from Miami (his heart sank), and was thinking of moving up to Lowell (his heart rose). When he said that he regretted not being a better dancer, she took him by the hand and said, "Come on, I will really teach you." She did her best, but he knew it was a matter that would require time, and perhaps professional help.

"You have to move your hips!" she said, stepping back so that he could see her move, so gracefully, so effortlessly with the music. Ah, the Latin soul. He wondered if it really was in the blood—bred in the bone. If that were the case, there was little hope for him.

"Damned Irish genes. You're supposed to dance..." He almost said "as if you have a stick up your arse," but amended that to: "You know, with your back straight."

"But they have beautiful... *baile folklorico*... traditional dances. I bought the DVD of *Riverdance*."

"Yes, it's beautiful, but... why are you laughing?"

"I'm sorry. I just remember, I was watching that with my father, and he said, "*Dios mio*, those *Irlandeses* kill a lot of cockroaches!" Even as she laughed, she guided him in the dance, unconsciously, but when he did not laugh, she leaned back and looked into his eyes. "Did I offend you?"

"No, not at all. It's just that I'm concentrating on not stepping on your feet."

"You are doing fine," she said.

When the song ended, Minerva blew a breath and fanned her face with her hand. She said she was thirsty, and they made their way through the crowd toward the concession stands, leaning into each other to speak. He learned that she'd moved from Colombia to Florida at the age of fourteen; she had a green card and a degree in business, and worked at an insurance company, helping customers, mainly Hispanic, with claims. Her English was not bad, though she thought it was. Nestor told her he was a high school teacher, which he always felt was respectable, though hardly impressive.

He bought her a lemonade, still trying to discover more about her without seeming to interrogate her. She enjoyed nature, loved canoeing, hiking and reading in her spare time.

"What do you read?"

"García Márquez, Ernesto Sábato…"

"*El Túnel?*"

"I read that book three times!"

"Rather depressing, isn't it?"

"Hmmmm." Her head tilted in thought; her eyes lost their focus and seemed to search for a moment among those obscure interior pages where our feelings are written in the ink of culture, experience and the unique electrical firestorm that flashes among neurons. "The story is an… *afirmación* of great love. *Un amor grande.* A great love story, like *Romeo and Juliet*. It's sad that they die, yes… but it makes you feel joy that there is love like that. Stronger than death."

"I don't know about that Romeo. Come on, Minerva. Any guy who asks you to marry him on the first night—wouldn't you wonder about him? After a half hour he's jealous of the glove that touches your cheek? That's crazy. Not only that, but he was a damned Montague! Maybe she should have listened to her parents."

Her face was aglow with an amiable light that indicated to Nestor an engagement in the conversation. "Maybe I would think, yes, he's crazy," she said. "I don't know." She twirled the straw in her lemonade and added in a serious tone, "But Nestor, if you are in love and you're not a little jealous and crazy, are you really in love?" Her lips formed a kiss at the end of the straw, her dark eyes full of the question, shoulders still swaying slightly to the music, like a tree stirring in a summer breeze.

"Spoken like a true Latina. Life without passion is not worth living, right? Don Juan, *matadores*, guitars under the balcony, eyes flashing over a hand-held fan, a duel to the death for love, a crime of passion…" He wanted to keep the discussion light, but the words his own heart whispered were: *I could be a little crazy for you.*

She nodded. "That's our heritage…"

"Well, I suppose it's better than what people think about the Irish—that they just like to get drunk and fight."

"And that is not true?"

"Hell, no. We also like to sing sad songs and go to wakes."

"You are joking. What do you like to do?"

"I've always liked old stuff for some reason… old movies, old books, antiques. Baroque music. I like running. I do some acting. I got into it at UMass, and continued… with small local theater companies. You know, just for fun."

"I'd like to see you sometime."

"I'd like to see *you* sometime."

First meetings like this were rife with trials and missteps, the thousand nonverbal cues the mind tried to interpret and respond to. The smile she bestowed, reserved yet inviting, led him further into that intimate space where feelings flourished, but the rapid glance in the direction of her sister recalled him to the sense that he really didn't understand her feelings or how to read all the signals he was receiving.

They made their way back to the seats, and when the *Fenómeno Vallenato* finished their set, Minerva's sister and her friend stood and began to sling the straps of their handbags over their shoulders. "We are going," she said. Nestor knew it was time to roll the dice. "Could I buy you, and the others of course, a drink at the Irish bar across the street?"

She spoke with the other two girls, who politely declined. "I'm sorry, they say they have to go, but it was very nice talking with you. Really."

He was wary of transgressing the line from friendliness into boorishness, and so rather than press his case, he took her hand. "Best of luck, Minerva. Maybe I'll see you around the city if you do move up here." He turned away, wanting to say more, knowing he would later regret his reticence. Still, one person he never wanted to be was the guy who could not take a hint.

He walked back up John Street, hearing her voice in his mind, feeling the movement of her body under his hand, inhaling the memory of the fragrance of her hair.

Though the encounter was brief, he suspected that he'd remember her for a long time, maybe all his life. *File under: the one that got away.*

No, he would probably never see her again—but for tonight, and maybe for a while, something of her would remain close to him. As he passed the back of the stage he saw one of the roadies wearing a T-shirt bearing the motto, "Beer Kicks Ass." He smiled and told himself, "Ah what the hell. It's still a good night in the city."

A light tap on his shoulder made him turn, and Minerva was there, a little out of breath, pushing back strands of her dark hair. "Wait." She wrote on a piece of paper in her palm and handed it to him, saying, "I leave Monday. You can call me before then if you want. I would like you to."

"I'll call you tomorrow."

"I don't usually run after men," she added, almost apologetically, touching the silver cross at her neck.

"Then I'm lucky."

She disappeared into the crowd. He wandered up John Street, studying the script of her name, trying to read more about her in the rounded numbers, clutching the small square of paper like a piece of the Holy Rood.

Nestor found Declan Prendeville leaning against the bar at the Old Court, where a raspy-throated guitarist with a scraggly beard stood in the corner amid amps and mikes, crooning a mournful ballad:

O make my grave both wide and deep
Put a marble slab all at my feet
And at my head a turtle dove
That the world might know that I died for love

Nestor slapped his back and said, "Ah, the Butcher Boy. Brings a tear to your eye."

"Brings a tear to your eye, maybe." With his neatly trimmed beard, Declan resembled Kris Kringle in *Miracle on 34th Street*, except that his white hair was tied back in a ponytail, and he was wearing thick eyeglasses set in tortoise shell frames. A native of Dublin, Prendeville was the only man Nestor had ever met who could wear an ascot without looking ridiculous. He was a dealer in paintings, antiques, rare books. A scholar and a cynic.

Being still in a transcendent mood, Nestor ordered a Guinness and another Jameson on the rocks for his friend. "Butcher Boy, my arse. The most depressing race of whore's gits on the planet," the Irishman grumbled.

Nestor ignored the complaint and said, "Have you ever met a woman who just, what's the word, inspires you immediately?"

"You mean who gives you a towering erection? Consult your physician if it lasts more than four hours." He snorted, "Four hours! Jasus, I'm goyn to call the fuckin' Guinness Book of World Records."

"Beyond sexual attraction," Nestor said, "almost like, well, for lack of a better term, love at first sight."

"Aw, Christ, please, stop. I'm beggin' ye. I'm goyn to be fuckin' ill."

The barman arrived with their drinks and rang them onto the tab. "Higgs, when you close it out, give it to me," Nestor said. "It's a big night."

A big night. A red-letter night. He couldn't say that he was in love, like some woeful Romeo; not yet, but some kind of strong magnetism had drawn him to her. "All right, maybe love is too strong a word…"

"Not at all, and I'll put a turtle dove on your grave so the world might know what fuckin' killed ye."

Nestor laughed, as much at the other man's accent as at his words. *"So the wurrult moyt know whot fookin'...* So what, you don't believe in love?"

"Love is codology. I believe in Pavlov's fuckin' dog. Now here's a good aul' Dubbalin song, 'The Waxies' Dargle,' and no fuckin' turtle doves about it."

"Surely, at some point, you must have felt love? Been just knocked off your feet by some woman?"

"Chemical reactions," he said, and he enjoyed Nestor's frustrated expression so much that he continued. "Tubes and pumps, Nestor boy! All we are is tubes and pumps!" He picked up his Jameson and said, "Thanks for that. Cheers." He took a sip and began to bawl along with the balladeer.

> *What'll you have I'll have a pint*
> *I will have a pint with you sir,*
> *And if one of you doesn't order soon*
> *We'll be chucked out of the boozer*

Leaving Declan to enjoy his song, Nestor slipped through the crowd to the men's room, considering the Dubliner's philosophy. In the mirror above the urinal, he noticed again that he needed a shave. The door opened behind him, and a blast of music resounded through the tiled room. Nestor smiled, listening to the old Irish song, so familiar, a part of some part of him.

> *Says my aul' wan to your aul' wan*
> *Will ye go to the Waxies' dargle?*

The "waxies," he recalled, were shoemakers, and the "dargle" some kind of annual outing. After a few seconds, these idle thoughts fell away as he noticed that the figure that had entered the men's room after him had not moved, but stood still by the door. Looking into the corner of the mirror, he saw the dark hair slicked back, the square face, and the overhanging brows of a man of vengeance.

"Enjoying yourself tonight, Coach McCorley?"

Nestor said nothing. He zipped his fly and went to the sink to wash his hands. A series of images, like a horrible newsreel one tries to forget, was already playing itself out in his mind for the thousandth time. A young man dashing along the black asphalt of the track, graceful, fast and strong—then stumbling. It seems he's tripped or pulled a muscle, knees wobbling, body swaying drunkenly, somehow grotesque, as if Frankenstein were trying to turn his plodding steps into a sprint, trying to tame the wild and disparate parts of his anatomy into a purposeful whole under the direction of a single will, but young Ian Casey is unable to keep up with the impetus of his own body. And then he falls, tipping forward, headlong, crashing hard into the long September shadows of the pines that stand beyond the empty bleachers. The distance closes as Nestor flies toward the fallen runner, shouting for the others to call 911, realizing with horror as he tries to lift him that the young man is already dead.

"I asked you a question, McCorley. Are you enjoying yourself?"

"The judge told you to stay away from me, Casey."

"You're out here enjoying yourself while my son is lying in the ground. You should be in jail, you bastard."

"Mr. Casey, we've been over this so many times. I had no way of knowing—*no one* knew that Ian had a defective heart. They don't give an MRI to every kid who runs track."

"I don't believe there was anything wrong with his heart." His voice was low and hard, and his mouth curved with hatred. "I don't believe anything you say. He played sports all his life. You killed him. It was the beginning of the season and you pushed him too hard. He wasn't in shape yet, and you drove him into the ground."

"Why would I do that?"

"Maybe because you don't know what the fuck you're doing, and you don't care."

"That's just not true. I didn't push him hard. Look, I have to go."

Tears of rage welled in the other man's eyes. He nodded slowly. "Oh yeah, go. Go, you bastard! And I hope someday you find out what it feels like to lose a child."

Nestor stopped at the door and looked at the broken man. "And how would that help you? Ian was a great kid. It was a freak thing, a horrible thing. I lost a lot of sleep over it. It was hard for me. But in my... heart I know I was not responsible. I'm sorry."

"Oh, you lost sleep. Poor you. My son is dead!" He lunged at Nestor and drove him back against the wall, clutching at his throat. Instinctively, Nestor threw his hands up between the man's outstretched arms, knocking them away, and raised his fists. "I'm sorry about Ian! But leave me the fuck alone!" Someone opened the door, but seeing what looked like a brawl, closed it again.

"Don't even say his name, you prick!" He slapped at one of Nestor's raised fists, daring him to swing, but Nestor wanted no part of a fight with the dead boy's father, though he would not take a beating to avoid it.

"Stay away from me, Casey," he said. Frank Heslin, the bouncer, threw the door open and stood there eyeing Nestor, whom he knew, questioningly, and Casey, whom he did not, suspiciously.

When Nestor got back to the bar, Declan said, "What did you do, clean the jacks?"

Nestor threw back his beer and took a deep breath, as his heart began to resume its normal pace. He told Declan what had happened in the men's room, and the backstory, as briefly as he could, because he was tired of it. "It was the spring training season for track and field two years ago."

"I know what track is, but what the hell is field exactly? Sport is not my..."

"Let's just say the full range of jumps and throws." Seeing the puzzled expression on his friend's face, he continued, "Shot put, discus, javelin..."

"Oh yes, of course. Classical Greek stuff."

"Well, I was just getting the runners in shape, stopping them for frequent breaks, water breaks especially, because it was getting warm. Ian Casey was pretty good, and the pace was easy for him, I thought. Toward the end of practice we did a sort of cool-down mile jog on the track, but as we were finishing, Ian kicked out on us and started to sprint around the track. I think he wanted to impress me with his speed in the 400 meters, and he was flying, too, fast for a sophomore. And then, he just stumbled and went down. Defective heart, they said. An artery had thinned somehow, and finally burst. Could have been repaired if they had known, but…"

"And the aul' fella blames yerself."

"Yes. Robert Casey, he sued me. Personally. The school got me a lawyer, thank God, and I was found not to be responsible."

"But you feel responsible?"

"I really don't feel responsible. But for a long time I felt… I don't know, I just felt bad, Declan. I even saw a shrink. I'll never coach again, that's for sure. Because to win, at some point you do have to push the kids hard, and I'm afraid to do it now."

"Does this sort of thing happen often?"

"No, it's very rare. We all hear about it on the news when it happens, especially to celebrity athletes like Hank Gathers or Reggie Lewis, but nothing like that has happened before to me or any coach I know."

"Damned shite luck for him and you."

"Especially for him." He raised his glass. "Well, God bless him and keep him, as your people say." They drank, and he continued. "But I'm done with it. I can't go back over it, Declan. I won't." They were quiet for a moment as Nestor tried to regain the mood he'd been in before he saw Casey. He recalled the bewitching smile of Minerva, and told himself firmly that he would be happy tonight.

"Where were we in our theoretical discussion?"

"I was saying that love is a load of shite."

"Right." He cleared his throat and tried to think while Declan swirled the ice in his Jameson, gazing into the glass as if he might find some profundity lurking there.

"Well, let me ask you this, Dec. Isn't all of literature, from the Greeks on, full of examples of real love, of a sympathetic and deep connection between two beings, beyond the physical."

He grimaced and recoiled as if Nestor had struck him, his beard splayed over his barrel chest. "Sure and that's why they call it fuckin' mythology and fiction."

"But…"

"Listen to me, McCorley. You're inhabited by the worst kind of romanticism. Sure ye must be Irish. Next thing you'll be wantin' to die for Cathleen ni Houlihan. Tubes and pumps. Pavlov's dog. End of fuckin' story."

"Will you forget the dog? Humans are far more complex."

"Oh, I see." He leaned back, the squat glass of whiskey like a votive before his bemused smile. "*But we are spirits of another sort,*" he said to the air above Nestor's head. "Nevertheless, boy," he continued offhandedly, "I'll wager that this woman, for all her sympathetic soul, and her deep connections, has the shapely little arse and the beguilin' smile known to elicit Pavlovian salivation in the male *homo sapiens.*" He paused and added, "I hear no retort from young Master Montague."

Nestor sighed. *Romeo and Juliet* again. "I didn't say sexual attraction had *nothing* to do with it."

"And by the way, you left out the last word. The one you didn't want to say."

"What word?"

"Animals. Humans are more complex *animals.*" His white eyebrows rose over the speckled brown frames of his glasses as if he'd caught the younger man in deliberate disingenuousness. "You know," he continued, "I have an engraving by Gustave Doré from an old French translation of *Don Quixote.* The French call him Don Quichote. I had it framed. There is the Man of La Mancha, sitting in a grand chair, a throne of sorts, a book in one hand, a rapier in the other, while all around him in the air swirl visions of visored knights, fuckin' winged dragons, and ladies pleading for rescue from brawny brigands. *Son imagination se remplit de tout ce qu'il avait lu,* reads the inscription. 'His imagination filled with everything he had read.'

See, that says it all. That's what education is, Nestor. They fill your mind with all their nonsense, the teachers—I call them *blackboard terrorists*—they fill you with their world views, their prejudices, their ideas about love and redemption, romanticism, and the worst poison of all—religion. Fill you right up like an oul' garbage can, and then when they have done with ye, they slap the tin hat on. Graduation. And you go through the rest of your life full of all their pie-in-the-sky illusions."

"Jesus, you're a depressing bastard."

"Ah, you had it comin' with your inspirations, and your love at first sight. For fuck's sake, be grateful I didn't vomit on ye."

The younger man squinted skeptically. "Have you never been in love, Declan?"

"When I was young and still full of their nonsense. I left it all behind long ago. Fare thee fuckin' well." He spoke like a stalwart and tossed back his whiskey as if toasting his liberation from the illusions of love, but Nestor was sure he detected the shadow of pain as it crossed his face.

The bar was getting more crowded. A young blonde standing near them leaned in front of Declan to take her drink from the bartender. "Sorry," she said. His eyes, slightly magnified under the glasses, widened as he found his nose an inch away from her ample cleavage. When she had retrieved her drink and turned away, Declan said, "That reminds me. I have to pick up a quart of milk on the way home."

"You do know how to kill the romance," Nestor said. His heart was light again; he had not allowed himself to watch the door to see when Casey left. He wanted to put all that behind him—in the past, where Declan had left his love-dream. "A quart of milk!" He let himself laugh broadly, while Declan laughed begrudgingly, for in spite of the past and of the dire prognostications of the surly Irishman, Nestor was aware of Minerva's number in his pocket—a talisman of ineffable power.

There was nothing but the woodland path before his feet and the air in his lungs, and, of course, the thoughts that passed through Nestor's mind as he ran. Out here in the woods surrounding Walden Pond, they were never small thoughts; what bills had to be paid, what appointments kept, what work to be done. Often the thoughts were nearly wordless: images, feelings, the primal alertness awakened by the scent of the woods or the squawk of a great egret sounding from a rushy wetland—like a door opening on rusty hinges. Sometimes the heart startled at the sight of a white-tailed deer bounding across the path and disappearing beneath a cathedral ceiling of pine boughs.

This morning, he held another image in his mind: the woman he had met the previous evening. He saw the dark, curling hair, the bright smile, the silver crucifix on her brown, radiant skin, and her words came back to him. *You can call me before then if you want. I would like you to.*

The path widened, and the sliver of light that appeared through the trees broadened as he neared a ridge above the pond. He slowed, breathed deeply, and descended a path toward the shore. At this early hour, a solitary swimmer made her way across Walden Pond, trailing a low, rippling wake of brightened water. Nestor trotted along the bank of an inlet and up an incline to the site where Thoreau had built his cabin. He read the line that had been inscribed on the flat stone set in the ground, the hearthstone marker of Thoreau's cabin:

Go thou, my incense, upward from this hearth

From memory, he called up the line that followed:

And ask the gods to pardon this clear flame.

He ran on through the woods, feeling the clear flame in his own heart, and remembering the question that Thoreau, his old mentor, had posed a century and a half earlier, "What pill is there to leave one, serene, content?" And he answered, "Morning air."

CHAPTER TWO

T
hree weeks later, Nestor McCorley rapped on the door at the rear of the Acropolis Construction warehouse, and stepped into the so-called office, little more than a broom closet. It could barely contain the dented metal desk littered with binders and notepads, and the stout balding man sitting behind it. This was his summer job, a welcome change from standing in front of a class of bewildered and disinterested honors high school seniors with textbooks open to *Paradise Lost*. For six weeks a year he became once again the drywall man he had been when he worked with his father through the summers of his own high school years.

Nestor sat in a foldout chair facing the desk and the man behind it, Nick Betsis, the middle-aged nephew of the locally famous George Betsis, the founder of Acropolis Construction, the old patriarch and rags-to-riches contractor who had given Nestor's father, a Clare man, a job when he stopped in Lowell on his way from Chicago to Ireland via Boston, a stop that lasted the rest of his life.

"When you think you gonna finish hangin' the house on Curtis Drive?" Nick fumbled among piles of trade journals, invoices and Dunkin' Donuts napkins covered with figures and telephone numbers. He fished a soft pack of Winstons out of the mess.

"We'll be ready for the tapers on Friday. They can do the downstairs now if they want."

"They finishin' up on Campbell anyway. Friday's good."

Nick tapped the filtered end of the cigarette on the desk and ran a hand over his bald head thoughtfully while he looked over some figures scrawled on the back of an envelope. Nestor looked past him to the photo of the Greek island of Santorini on the Acropolis Construction calendar. He could not imagine living in such a place: a honeycomb of whitewashed habitations set into an island cliff above a sea of startling blue. The whole scene was a medley of blue and white, blue window frames and doors cut into the white of the abodes.

There were white tables and blue chairs on the sunlit terrace of the—Nestor leaned closer to read—the Porto Fira Hotel, where a few people took coffee or a glass of retsina. From the narrow streets where roses splashed crimson against the alabaster walls, winding stairs led to a chapel, its blue dome topped with a white cross. A single bell hung in an arched campanile. Nestor imagined its tolling voice rolling over the open sea to resound against the volcanic cliffs of the neighboring islands, where white towns on mountain ridges appeared like foam on the crest of a great wave. The islands of the Cyclades stood in the Aegean like dark giants: rising out of blue, into blue. *Hellas*. His mother's home. One day he would have to go.

Nick swiveled in his chair and looked not at the photo of Santorini, but at the days of July blocked out beneath it. The unlit cigarette dangled from his lips while he ran a thick finger over the numbers. "Foster's done. The painters are in. Finish Campbell. Start Curtis on Friday. The framers are working on the two in Andover. We're in good shape."

"Listen, Nick, I need to take off Monday and Tuesday. I'm flying to Miami for a couple of days on Saturday."

"What's in Miami, Nestor?" He pulled a lighter from the desk drawer, sparked the cigarette and leaned back, getting comfortable, examining the nicotine stains on his fingers.

"What do you think? A woman."

"What's wrong with the women in Lowell, eh? Why you gotta go to Miami? Plenty of nice girls here. Pretty girls."

"This one's special." When he'd returned from his early run at Walden he called her, and spent that Saturday with her, listening to a Greek band at the Folk Festival, showing her some of the historic points of the downtown, becoming progressively more bewitched as the day went on. They had lunch at *El Rincon Paisa*, a Colombian restaurant in Centralville, where Minerva explained the subtleties of the menu.

"Oh, special." Nick sniffed dismissively and took a drag. "What's her name?"

"Minerva."

As they'd passed the granite enclave of St. Joseph the Worker Shrine, she took his arm and led him inside. "Are you Catholic?" she asked.

"Twelve years of Catholic school, but I'm not a very good one now." In those twelve years he'd come to know all the exemplars of the faith; the good ones, and they were many, patient and kind and true, and the others, who hid their iniquity behind black cloth and a crucifix.

"My faith is important to me. Do you mind if I light a candle?"

"Certainly not." It may have been at that moment, as he watched her hold the flaming wick above the sacred candle, her face glowing, her head bowed before the blue-robed Virgin, that Nestor began to feel the first stirrings of a some great tenderness toward her, a feeling that was not just infatuation, he thought, but akin to love. Was it somehow connected with the intense religious devotion of his own youth? He didn't know, but the image of the beautiful woman kneeling in humility before the queen of heaven was one that he knew would stay with him for a very long time.

More than their brief time together, it was the letters they exchanged—he had four of hers already in three weeks—that sealed a bond between them. Not emails, but handwritten letters that he imagined her writing by the light of a bedside lamp, describing, in the aftermath of a downpour, while the air was still heavy and moist, the croak—which she said was more like a quack—of the green tree frogs in a neighboring pond.

Nestor began to know her in the simple stories she recounted of a funny girl at work, a family problem, a book she was reading. She quoted poetry, the amazing, and to Nestor unknown, "Primero Sueño," or "First Sleep," of Sor Juana Inés de la Cruz, a seventeenth century Mexican poet, and he imagined Minerva there at the edge of her own first sleep, a cotton camisole so white against her brown skin, her dark hair sweeping the page, the silver rings on her fingers moving across the page as drowsily she wrote out the words of good night—words that he translated as he read: *Sleep, finally, all possessed/ All, finally, did silence take/ Even the robber fell into dreams/ And the lover did not wake.*

"So," Nick continued, "you gonna have a little Puerto Greecan with her?" He tried not to laugh at his own joke, but a smoky chuckle escaped.

"First of all, I'm half Irish."

He nodded. "The dangerous half."

"And she's not Puerto Rican."

"Cuban, right?"

"Colombian."

"Colombian. Hmmm. I don't know any Colombian girls." He tapped the cigarette ash into an empty Coke can on his desk and continued in a tone that indicated he had given the matter some thought. "What I'm gonna do, I'm gonna send my son back to the village in Greece to find a nice girl."

Attempting irony, Nestor asked, "What's wrong with the Greek girls in Lowell?"

Irony was wasted on Nick. "The Greek girls in Lowell? The young ones are too wild, and the old ones are too ugly. Minerva, eh? That's what the Romans called Athena."

"There you go showing off your Greek school education again."

"Damn right. And Athena was a good god, or goddess, to have on your side. The best. What the hell, you're a smart guy, right? But all the way to Miami?" He shook his head and smiled as if such an expedition was beyond the comprehension of any sensible man.

"When you meet the right one, you gotta make a move, Nick."

"Well, you know what they say..." Losing his condescending smile and putting on the blank face of the tragic chorus, he uttered a sentence in Greek, a cascade of staccato syllables. Nestor had a smattering of the language from his mother—not enough to follow him.

"Translation?"

The smoke rose up in front of the portly man like incense before a Buddha. He nodded sagely and repeated it for him in English. "The power of a pussy could pull a boat." Nestor smiled and got up to go.

"What a philosopher."

He nodded sagely. "Aristotle never said anything truer, my friend. You be ready to go on Wednesday?"

"Right."

The phone on Nick's desk rang. He picked it up. "Hold on!" He put a hand over the mouthpiece. "I leave a check for Curtis Drive with Teddy. If you can't be good be careful."

"Yeah, yeah. *Yiá sou.*"

"*Kaló taksídi!*"

He heard Nick launch into an animated discussion in Greek as he closed the door. Discussion, argument—it was hard to tell with the Greeks.

Nestor opened the door to his room on the eighth floor of El Olympico Sports Hotel in Carol City, Miami, and tossed his single suitcase onto the king-sized bed. He changed into his bathing suit and pulled back the curtains on the glass doors that opened onto a small balcony. The view was wonderful for a two-and-a-half-star hotel. He could make out a green tractor dragging a rake over the mile long oval of sandy clay at Calder Race Course. Beyond that, Dolphin Stadium hunched in the middle of its gray expanse of parking lots, and on the horizon, the Miami skyline rose before a ribbon of blue sea.

And this is the way that life happens, he thought. The sound of an accordion draws you down a street, and a few weeks later you find yourself on a balcony in Miami waiting for a woman. About fifteen minutes later, he saw a red Honda Civic pull into the parking lot.

His father used to have a saying, "My heart leapt up like a cat to milk," and that was the phrase that came to him as he saw her get out of her car. He called out and waved, and she leaned back, looking upward, a hand held up to shield her eyes while she pulled sunglasses from her bag. She returned his wave, and even from here he could see the smile. Minerva came up to see the view, but seemed a little uncomfortable in the hotel room, where the oversized bed seemed to offer itself indiscreetly. She waited by the door as he rifled through his suitcase. "I brought you something," he said, handing her a small bag.

"It's beautiful," she said, holding up the T-shirt, on which the words "Lowell Folk Festival" were printed above a colorful image of a traditional Cambodian dancer wearing a high golden crown. "Ah, you are very... *detallista*... what is the word... *thoughtful*."

Poolside, she unbuttoned her short-sleeve cotton blouse and slipped out of her jean shorts. Her bathing suit was black, two triangles at the top and a bikini bottom, with a black and white checked waistband. His eyes wandered the length of her legs, her hips, up to the hint of paler flesh at her cleavage, and he looked away for fear that he would have to throw himself into the pool before they had a chance to talk. Nestor pushed a pair of chaise lounges close together, and stretched out. "God, this is relaxing after the brouhaha of airports and traffic."

"The what?"

"Brouhaha. Craziness."

"That's a funny word. It sounds like *bruja*—like a witch."

"Yeah, it is a funny word."

"You know what I think is a horrible expression in English?"

"What?"

"I want to 'pick your brain.' I hate that expression."

"Now that you mention it, it is kind of disgusting."

A woman pulled orange water wings over the pudgy arms of a four-year-old and slid into the water, her arms outstretched, calling him. Outside the fence that surrounded the pool, palm trees splashed leafy fronds against a blue sky, reminding him of Cochabamba, where the Peace Corps had its headquarters in Bolivia. He recalled palm trees rising from a cobbled plaza before an ornate colonial Spanish mission with curving gambrels on each side of an old bell tower. He had worked farther out, in the nearly treeless mountains, where the descendants of the Incas scratched out an existence from the depleted soil. What had Pádraig Pearse written of the Irish? *No treasure but hope. No riches laid up but the memory of an ancient glory.*

"Why do you want to leave Miami?" he asked.

She leaned closer, her head at the edge of the chaise lounge, close to his. For him, a woman's scent was always important, and he thought hers was like some wonderful rare flower he had never been near. "Well, there are two reasons really. First, is my mother doesn't like my sister to be alone in Lowell."

"I love the way you say that: Low-well. I'm used to hearing people say: Lole."

"Are you… *burlando de mi?*" She slapped his arm half-heartedly. "That is the way is the spelling."

"Teasing me. No, you're pronouncing it correctly. But we Americans talk lazy. Lazily. So why did your sister come to Low-well?"

"My sister want to open a restaurant. A small restaurant, with a few tables, and anyway, she is really good cook, my sister Marina, much better than me. So she is working there now, and planning to do this. She has a place picked out and is talking with the owner, trying to get the permits and all that. But my mother would prefer if I'm there to… you know, help her, and give her the support."

"And the second reason?"

"The second reason is Marquis Alicea."

"Who is he?"

"He is my fiancé."

He sat up as if a jolt of electricity had run through him. "What?" The little boy plunged into the water, gasping out giggles as he paddled toward his mother.

She put her hand on his chest, instinctively, to calm him. "I'm sorry! I still sometimes mix up the verbs—I mean the, what's the word, the *tenses*. I mean he was… Marquis Alicea *was* my fiancé."

He sat back and took a breath. "Colombian?"

"Venezuelan."

"What happened, if you don't mind me asking?"

"Oh, I don't know. He had a lot of money. A lot of money."

"Oh yeah, that's a turnoff. What business was he in?"

"Everything. His family was in oil before they nationalize the industry in the seventies. And now he is running a company is call Sea Horse Shipping. It's import-export in the … *mercado de productos básicos…*"

"The commodity market."

She nodded. "They have private airplanes. And he's taking me here and there, all the time. Parties, discotheques, and this racetrack you can see, Calder, he spent a lot of money there. But really I don't like it. I mean, I start to get tired of the people he's with, of the business dinners, and I felt just like, how do you say…"

"*En Español?*"

"*Como un trofeo.*"

"Like a trophy… a trophy girlfriend."

"Yes, he just want a good-looking girl with him." She said it without arrogance. There was no point in pretending that she didn't know she was good looking. "Maybe he has other girlfriends, too, because, you know, I was the good girl, the one you marry, but while you wait to get married, and probably after, you have other girlfriends. It's a *machismo* thing."

"So you broke up?"

"Yes."

"How did he take it?"

"He doesn't like it when he doesn't get what he wants. He called for a while. Sometimes he find me, he found me, in different places and try to change my mind."

"So should I expect to be shot?"

"No, he's not crazy or violent with guns. He's a businessman. The matrimony that we planned, I think for him was like a business deal that fell down, and maybe that bothered him more than anything."

"I see."

"But he won't make a big scene. That's for the low-class people, and his family is very high-class people. So you see it's another reason I want to get away from here, so he will forget me." She shrugged and added, "Maybe already he has, really. He's not so insistent recently. Anyway, he can have plenty of women."

There was something disquieting in all this. Not that other men had been in love with her, or that she'd had other boyfriends. He expected that. "I confess I feel a little inadequate. How am I going to impress you on a teacher's salary? Sure you're not too accustomed to the high life?"

"No, I don't care about it. With money comes other things. He was always talking like... well, he read, about five times, that book *The Art of War*, by some ancient Chinese general."

"I know who you mean. Sun something. Sun... anyway, go on."

"Yes, and he says, 'Minerva, business is like the war.' " He smiled as she imitated the gruff voice of a man. She shook her head and made a face as though she were suddenly tired. "Please, isn't there enough war in the world without turning your work into a war? And he want to talk about his strategy, you know, he's in love with strategy, to buy this company, and ruin this other guy that competes with him. *Aye, no, por favor.*"

"So you're not impressed with money. What do you want?"

"Do you know what I used to think about? What I wanted for a while?"

"Tell me."

"I imagined a quiet convent, just praying and reading the holy books and working in a garden, away from the world, to live in peace and grow old there."

Nestor shook his head. "I have bad memories of nuns."

"That's too bad."

"Well, there were good ones, too. And I can understand the attraction to the ascetic life."

"*Aset... ? Oh, la vida ascética.* Yes, that is what I used to think about, sometimes."

"I would come and steal you away."

She laughed. "Now I want something else, I think."

"And what is that?" he asked, touching her hand.

"A kind man, a good man, who really loves me, and if I have a child, will love my child and be a good husband and father."

"Where do I fill out an application?" She laughed and rose, dropping her sunglasses on the lounge chair. "Come on," she said. He followed her across the concrete apron to the pool, memorizing her curves and smiling slightly as he remembered Nick's words, "The power of a pussy could pull a boat."

Later, they drove along streets full of one-story bungalows painted in pale pastels behind neatly manicured lawns. Palms, rising singly or in stands of three or four, obscured their facades. At Northwest 170, Minerva turned and pulled into the driveway of a neat little stucco. It was pale orange, a color, Nestor reflected, that would never suit one of Lowell's stolid New England colonials, but which seemed natural in this tropical environment. "Here goes," he said, because he saw her mother in the garden, trimming a rose bush. She stood when she saw Minerva's car, and pushed the hair from her face with her wrist. She pulled off one of her gloves and shook Nestor's hand, a plump woman with a broad face, wearing a flowered gardener's apron over a simple blue cotton dress.

"My mother, Doña Barbara. Nestor McCorley."

"*Bienvenido a Miami,*" she said.

"*Hola Papá!*" Minerva said. "My father, Don Andres." He was shorter than Nestor, but lean and well-built, in a white T-shirt, his weathered face still handsome, mustache and temples gone gray. He set down a wheelbarrow from which protruded a shovel, an iron rake, and a tamper. Minerva must have told them that Nestor spoke Spanish, because her father addressed him in his own language, saying, "Three days up there in Lowell, and she says, 'A young man is coming to visit me!' *Ave María!*"

"Ah, you know how it is with the young people..." her mother began.

Don Andres raised his hands innocently, palms outward, and said, "I'm not saying anything, but... three days?" He took Nestor's hand in his, laughing softly and repeating, *"Ave María!* The young people."

While her parents went inside to wash up and change, Minerva brought Nestor to a badminton net, where they played while the guests arrived. He loved to watch how her eyes gladdened every time she got a point, and how she shook her fist at him when he got a point. "Oh," she said, dropping the racket as a big Buick pulled up. "Let me introduce you to our priest."

Minerva ran up to him. Nestor saw the priest whisper something to her before he looked up and smiled in his direction. "Nestor, this is Father Solano."

"Just call me Father Felix," he said. Nestor asked if he was Colombian. "No, my parents are Cuban, but I was raised here in Florida. In fact, I attended the College of the Holy Cross, not far from... Lowell."

Nestor didn't like the way he said "Lowell." As if someone at Holy Cross had told him to stay far away from the city.

When Minerva excused herself to help in the kitchen, the priest said, "Let me show you Don Andres' garden," and they walked together toward the far end of the yard. Father Felix wore a dark gray fedora with a black band, as though he were Karl Malden playing Father Barry in *On the Waterfront*; his visible hair was white, as was his mustache. He wiped the lenses of his wire-rimmed glasses with a handkerchief as he walked a few steps ahead of Nestor; apparently he was accustomed to being followed.

When they arrived at the garden, a rectangle the size of the end zone of a football field set off by posts and enclosed with rabbit wire, the priest opened the gate and walked in as if he owned it. There were rows of plants neatly spaced and supported by stakes. He pointed to the ripening toma-toes, naming the varieties: "St. Pierre, Big Boy,... those yellow ones are Brandywine Heirlooms, and the ones I like best in a salad are over there, the Arkansas Travelers."

He paused near a raised bed of leafy plants covered in bird netting. "Southern highbush blueberries," he said. He reached under the netting, plucked some, and handed them to Nestor.

"They're good," Nestor said, "kind of..."

"Tangy."

Nestor nodded, and the priest asked, "So, are you sleeping with Minerva?"

He coughed on the last of the tangy blueberries. "Excuse me?"

"I think you heard my question."

"With all due respect, Father, I didn't mean, excuse me, I didn't hear you. I meant, excuse me, you have a lot of damned gall."

The priest removed his hat, unfolded his handkerchief and dabbed at his brow. He shrugged innocently. "Well, I suppose you might think it forward of me, but I am her confessor. I do care about her. I care about her soul. I know that it's natural for you two to want to have a carnal relationship..." He pocketed the handkerchief, smoothed his thinning hair and replaced his hat.

Nestor shook his head, "Hey listen, Padre..."

"And I would have to warn her against that. That's all. I'm not condemning you. But I have to advise her and you, if you are in a relation-ship. That's my duty. You are a Catholic, aren't you?"

Nestor took a deep breath. He knew that his temper was a weakness. Working with high school kids had been good for him. It forced him to control that temper and deal calmly with difficult students. But this priest's attitude brought back memories of old injustices; he loathed the smug air of superiority that some put on along with the black habit or the Roman collar.

With deliberate calm, he said, "This is not a confessional."

"Well," the priest responded, eyes wide as if he were shocked at such a reaction, "I'm sorry if I've offended you, Nestor. I'm just trying to have a frank discussion of spiritual matters concerning a member of my flock. I would have thought you owe that much..."

"No, I don't. I don't owe you anything."

"Are you upset?"

"On the contrary. Like you, I'm just trying to be 'frank.' Thanks for the tour. I'm going to get a beer."

Other aunts and uncles were arriving, trailing lines of cousins. Nestor hoped that they had not all been invited to see him. Probably not. He had the feeling that these weekend get-togethers were not unusual.

Don Andres and Doña Barbara were good hosts. Her father showed off the extended stone patio he'd been working on. He lit the grill, and his wife came out with two platters and began to lay out marinated chicken and steak, along with some sort of thick sausages. When the grill was crammed with sizzling meats, she handed Don Andres the barbecue tongs and hurried back into the house.

"*Chorizo*," Don Andres said to Nestor, waving a fork over the sausages.

"What's in *chorizo*?"

"It's about ninety percent cholesterol and ten percent rocket fuel."

The guests brought bowls of pork rinds, rice, and small fried banana pancakes called *patacones*. Minerva came back out. She had changed out of her shorts into a white linen summer dress. She handed Nestor a beer, but the Colombian men, and some of the women, reached toward the tray on the picnic table and picked up shot glasses filled with a clear liquor. "*Aguardiente*," she said. "It's not a good idea to mix it with beer."

"Sound advice, no doubt," he said, but when her father handed him one, he tossed it back all the same. It tasted of anisette, smoother than the *singani* of Bolivia. Her father was telling a funny story about something that had happened where he worked as a supervisor loading cargo onto UPS planes at the Opa-locka Airport. One of the women put on some *cumbia* music, and soon Minerva was dancing with a cousin. She winked at Nestor as she danced, and flashed the smile. Once again he admired the grace, the ease with which they moved to the music. Just then the cousin twirled her, and when he saw her face again, the smile had faded, and her eyes had lost their light.

He looked around and saw a newcomer at the cookout. When she had spoken of Marquis Alicea, Nestor had imagined a celebrity smile in a bronzed face, a gold chain glittering in an open-collar sport shirt, an impeccable white suit jacket and alligator loafers. A young Julio Iglesias following the progress of his container ships on a vast digital map in an oak-paneled boardroom. The man who was shaking hands with Don Andres and chatting with the aunts and uncles looked nothing like the one he had imagined. His hair was long and somewhat unkempt. He was wearing jeans, and a blue T-shirt that was not loose enough to conceal a slight paunch—yet somehow he was sure that this was the man to whom Minerva had been engaged. His guess was confirmed as he read the print on the T-shirt: Sea Horse Shipping.

Minerva came and stood beside Nestor. "Marquis Alicea," she whispered as he stepped up to them with outstretched hands. He and Minerva exchanged greetings in Spanish, but he switched smoothly to English as he turned toward Nestor. "My name is Marquis. You are Minerva's friend from Massachusetts?" Like the priest, his English was fluent and nearly without accent.

"Nestor McCorley." They shook hands, and Nestor noticed that he lacked the firm grip that he had expected from a man who viewed business as war. The handshake did not convey the alpha male's desire to impress a competitor with his confidence and strength.

"Can I get you something?" Minerva asked him. He glanced at the Corona in Nestor's hand and said, "I'll have a beer, thank you."

As soon as she had stepped away, Marquis said, "I hope I haven't made you feel awkward by coming here. I suppose you know that Minerva and I were engaged..."

"Yes, she did mention that." He was surprised by the directness of the man's address.

"I'm afraid I didn't take the rejection well at first. Sometimes, frankly, I behaved like a spoiled child. You know, he demands the very thing he cannot have and maybe wants it all the more for that reason. Minerva is a wonderful woman, and I know now that what I really want is for her to be happy. I could not have made her happy."

Nestor felt a genuine sympathy for this jilted lover, and an admiration for his honesty. "We've all been there," he said.

Marquis nodded. "Yes, but then my brother told me, 'She'd hold you back,' and I knew that was true. You know why? She's too honest for that life. She would not have wanted to play the part of the CEO's wife, going to cocktail parties and pretending to like all the other wives, and laughing at the jokes and flattering the old men. And in some way I would have held her back, too, from what she really wants to become."

He shook his head, a little wistfully, and added, "I had to fall for the one woman in Miami who doesn't care about money. And I'm afraid I don't have much else to offer a woman. I'm really very boring, and look at me. I'm getting fat from sitting talking on the phone all day and the endless business dinners." He patted his stomach sadly and said, "I need to start working out, lose twenty pounds."

"Don't be so hard on yourself. You're not what I'd call fat by any means. And from what I hear, you've accomplished a lot. Success in any business is nothing to scoff at."

"Well, that is very kind of you. Anyway, I'm telling you all this because I do still care about her, and her family—very much."

"They seem to be great people."

"Oh, they are the best."

Nestor saw Father Felix talking to Don Andres, who was nodding respectfully, as if he agreed wholeheartedly with whatever it was the priest was propounding. He wanted to ask Marquis about him, but the question the priest had put to him was not something he wanted to share with Minerva's former fiancé, even though the truth was that, no, he was not sleeping with her.

"Minerva will be back in a minute," Marquis said. "Here." He slipped a business card into Nestor's hand. "If ever I can help you and Minerva, don't hesitate to call me. If you need money, whatever... advice... I mean, you know, on some business matter. You never know. You don't need to tell Minerva. I don't want you or her to feel any obligation to me, and I certainly don't want to put you in a compromising position. Just between you and me."

"It's very kind of you to offer, Marquis, but I really don't think..."

"I understand. But the offer is there. That's all. Here she is." He changed the topic immediately as Minerva handed him the beer. "So where are you staying, Nestor?"

"The Olympico."

"It's not bad, eh?"

"No, great view." Nestor was certain that Marquis was being polite. He was sure that his friends stayed at one of the luxury hotels he'd seen online, Delano, the Viceroy or the Epic Hotel.

"No, there's nothing wrong with El Olympico," Marquis continued. "You could have done a lot worse." As they spoke, Nestor tried to imagine these two together. The pensive beauty who took a melancholy delight in Ernesto Sábato's tragic tale of love, and the businessman who was ever rereading *The Art of War*. He could not see them together, and that was something of a relief.

When Marquis finished his beer, he said, "I have to go. This crazy Arab in Abu Dhabi needs some price quotations and... well, I won't bore you with all that. I'm glad I had a chance to meet you, Nestor."

When he had gone, Nestor said, "Not a bad guy, if I'm any judge of character. I like him."

Minerva smiled once more, and pushed a strand of hair behind her ear. "I suppose he's all right," she said, somewhat grudgingly, Nestor thought, which pleased him, since he did not want her to like him too much.

Back in the hotel that evening, Nestor became more certain that Marquis had been generous in his praise of El Olympico Sports Hotel. The view was about the only good thing. The air conditioner that he'd left on low had leaked water onto the carpet, filling the room with a musty smell. There seemed to be little or no sound insulation, and the surrounding rooms flooded after midnight with drunken racetrack gamblers and a couple of mariachis. He was thirsty, but had forgotten to bring a bottle of water. He grimaced as he drank a glass of metallic-tasting tap water, listening to the chorus of drunkards singing along with the mariachis, *La De La Mochila Azul*, the song of the boy who can no longer concentrate on his studies because the girl with the blue schoolbag and the sleepy eyes has not been in school.

He put on his earphones, tuned the radio to a Marlins game, and finally began to doze, but was awakened after 2 a.m. by a pounding at his door. "What the hell," he muttered. He took off the earphones and got out of bed in his gym shorts and T-shirt. There was no one at his door, though there were people singing and drinking outside of their open rooms. A woman holding a red plastic cup peeked out of one of the doorways, laughing. She stepped into the corridor, a petite brunette with big boobs, followed by two other young women. "You wanna party with us?"

"No, I don't."

"You're not gay, are you?" The three burst into laughter. Nestor saw the thin tan lines on her shoulders, and imagined for a moment the soft pale breasts. Tempting, but he held the reins.

"Whatever. Good night."

The music began again. "Come on, we wanna dance!" The brunette threw herself at him. He took a step backward, and she was in his room, kissing his neck, her hands under his T-shirt. Her drink spilled over his back as he pushed her away, toward the open door. The woman turned when he released her and lifted her halter top to display two firm, perfect breasts. "You like them?" she asked. "They're real."

"Ah, Christ," he said. He closed the door and locked it, ignoring a very insistent voice in his head that told him to open it again. He took off the wet T-shirt and pulled a dry one out of his suitcase. He heard more loud laughter in the hallway, and some bits of conversations in Spanish; he put the earphones back on and turned up the volume.

Some late-night sports show hosts were dissecting the Marlins' loss to the Braves. His imagination dallied with the party girl outside his door, but soon turned back to Minerva. So she had considered becoming a nun. The question men always asked about a beautiful nun—could God be so jealous of mortals as to keep a woman like that for Himself? He could understand the appeal of that life, the tranquility of serene withdrawal from this world—living moments of mystical transcendence in the silence of some quiet chapel where frozen saints held folded or outstretched hands above a tray of flickering candles.

In twelve years of Catholic school he had heard every tenet of the faith, said all the prayers, sought out the plenary indulgences, taken five of the sacraments, mumbled rosaries at wakes, fasted, made novenas, served on the altar and sang in the choir. The Sisters of the Holy Faith, devoted lay teachers—and later, the Brothers of the Sacred Heart.

As an altar boy he'd rung the bells and swung the censer, standing in the sickeningly sweet smoke; he'd studied the priests in the vestibule as they prepared for Mass, often seeming to inhabit a world apart as they donned the vestments, looped the rope belt, kissed the stole, and put on all their mysterious power. In those days he'd felt himself full of the Holy Spirit at times, but as a young man he laughed irreverently at Bob Frenier's jokes during Forty Hours Devotion, and the mystery of the Mass began to seem a dolorous cultural practice rather than a union with God.

There was something strange, too, at times, about being in the sacristy with the priests, not that any of them had ever tried to abuse him, but they were different when you got to know them—not the "Christ on Earth" figures the nuns and his parents made them out to be, but real humans.

Nestor recalled Father Ferguson, a man who seemed, in the pulpit, like Moses come down from the mountain: stentorian, righteous, and uncompromising in his call to the Catholic way of life. And yet, if Nestor arrived early for the Mass he would find him slumped in a chair behind the altar smoking a cigarette and reading the sports section of the *Herald*. Once, he shocked the naive young altar boy by emerging from the lavatory and commenting, "When you get to my age, Nestor, about the only pleasure left in life is a good shit."

But Ferguson was all right, and if the difference between the two personas had given Nestor the feeling that the man was living a lie, he now saw that the expectations he had of priestly behavior were unrealistic, like imagining that a comedian is funny all the time, or that a doctor would never indulge an unhealthy habit. In twelve years of Catholic school, Nestor had seen all the faces of the Church: the saintly Sister Winifred, the sadistic Sister St. Michael, the manipulative Sister Theresa; Father Grenville whispering his obscene questions in the confessional, and Father Leahy, ready to suffer all for the least of his brothers.

Lying in this strange hotel room so many years later, he recalled his introduction to Catholic education, the day he was brought to the nuns. Half drowsing, he saw himself in his white shirt and little polished saddle shoes. He had told his father he didn't want to go to school, but his father said that if he didn't go to school he would never amount to anything in life. "If you don't study, Nestor, you don't *know*."

They were late getting to St. Brigid's because "the Bomber," which was what his father called the old station wagon full of his drywall tools, would not turn over. He called Wally Drew, a friend who owned a gas station on Broadway, and a while later he showed up with a new battery. The Bomber jolted to life, and they set off for the Catholic school that sat like a brick shoe box at the edge of the North Common, Nestor warmly ensconced in the front seat between his parents. The children were already in their classes when he arrived. His parents apologized to an old woman in black robes who said her name was Sister Winifred; his father filled out a paper. Nestor's lips moved as he read the black letters painted on the open door: PRINCIPAL.

She stood up and came around her desk and looked him over and said, "He'll be all right." His father signed the paper and paid the sister his milk money, while his mother knelt down and told him to be good; she wet her fingers on her tongue and patted his cowlick, and then she handed him the lunch bag that contained a peanut butter and jelly sandwich and a Twinkie. "You study hard now." She said words in a different way, and with his aunts she used all different words, strange words, because she came here from Greece. His father said words in another way because he was from Ireland, and he called the stove "the cooker" and a cookie a "biscuit."

"Ma, do I have to stay here, Ma?" he whispered. She squeezed his hands in hers and said, "We will have *baklava* when you come home," and for an instant his mind considered gratefully an image of the golden leaves of pastry and their filling of minced walnuts, cinnamon and honey. His mother seemed about to cry, but his father said, "He'll be fine, Daphne." Then he clapped Nestor on the back and winked at him and said, "Keep your nose clean."

They left him in the corridor that smelled of strong floor cleaner with the old woman dressed all in black like the witch in *The Wizard of Oz*, except that her forehead was covered in white and her ears, too, and even under her chin. Instead of a cone-shaped hat she wore a black veil. You could only see her eyes and nose and mouth; the rest of her was wrapped in black and white. Her face was wrinkled like a dried-up apple.

Over his shoulder, he watched his parents go down the stairs. At the door, his mother smiled and waved, but her eyes looked wet. He didn't want to follow the woman in black, and he hung back, still looking after his departing parents, inhaling the strange smells. "It's all right," the sister said, bending over him. "You'll see them right after school, there's a big boy." She told him that he would start first grade with Sister St. Michael. "She's strict,

Nestor, but you just do your work and you'll be fine."

They walked the green tiles of the long corridor together, every step opening up the distance between his old life and this new one. She knocked on a door at the end of the corridor and waited with hands tucked into her sleeves. Another mass of black clothing darkened the window and the door opened. She was much younger than Sister Winifred, and taller. The old nun put a hand on his shoulder and gently pushed him into the room. He heard his name and smelled what he thought was desk polish and something strong that came from the black robes of the nuns, like the mothballs his mother put in the clothes she stored in the attic.

The class sat staring at him silently, hands folded with fingers interlaced as though they were all about to say grace, while he stood in the doorway with the two nuns behind him. The windows that ran along the opposite wall looked out on the North Common, and he wished he was out there, walking down to Lulu's Variety with his father to buy some Gold Rocks bubble gum or a Sky Bar.

The door closed, and Sister St. Michael stretched out the pointer, indicating an empty seat. "Sit over there, Mr. Nestor McCorley," and he watched as she wrote his name in her book within a little square that he knew represented his desk. All the squares had names in them, and his name was in that square now. She addressed the class. "I can see right away that the student who just came in, late, on the first day, has not been taught good manners." Nestor cringed at those words, and his shoulders slumped as he approached the empty desk. The sister continued, "When I told him to take his seat, what did he say?" The class was quiet. "What did he say?" she asked again, now with an edge to her voice. "Nothing, Sister," a few students mumbled.

"Not a word. Very rude. And what should he have said?"

"Yes, Sister," the class said.

"Yes, Sister," she repeated. Nestor, hurt and ashamed at having been singled out for rude behavior, ducked into his seat. He wasn't sure if he should say anything now, or just accept his scolding quietly. He wanted to say, "Sorry, Sister," but he was quiet. The black robes frightened him, the black tie shoes with their thick heels, and when she moved the glimpse of black stocking, the crucifix swinging on the long string of beads. God, the school, the Church, they were all on her side, a mighty army, and no one could question her or disobey her. When he raised his head, he saw her white-encircled face, a small U behind silver-rimmed glasses, looking angrily in his direction. "Sit up straight and fold your hands! Put your lunch in your desk!" He heard a loud, sharp click as she rapped the blackboard with the pointer.

Sister St. Michael was written at the top of the board, and below it, printed neatly, a prayer. "We will recite this prayer every morning, and you will learn it by heart. There is a notebook in your desk. Put your name on the front and copy the prayer into it."

Desks creaked open and the students took out the notebooks. "We will begin…" She paused. Without warning, the pointer slammed down on the desk of a skinny boy in front. Nestor, and all the others, flinched. "Don't you dare look out the window when I'm talking, boy!" She glared at him for a moment, letting him feel his smallness, and then continued. She placed the pointer under the first word, and read it over once by herself, moving the pointer from word to word. "Now we will say the prayer together." The tiny chorus of voices droned out the prayer.

Saint Michael, Archangel, defend us. Be our protection against the wickedness and snares of the devil; may God rebuke him, we humbly pray. O Prince of the heavenly host, by the power of God, thrust back into hell Satan and all the evil spirits who wander through the world for the ruin of souls. Amen.

"That was awful!" the sister said. "What an insult to poor Saint Michael. Are you all *stupid*? I hope I don't have a class of stupid children because I know what to do with stupid and willful and stubborn children." She put the pointer down on her desk and picked up a flat piece of wood with a handle. "I warm their backsides with the paddle! That's what I do with stupid children who refuse to learn!"

She took a deep breath as if she were trying to control a swelling anger. She said, very quietly, "Now, repeat after me... Saint Michael the Archangel..."

"Saint Michael the Archangel..."

They sat with backs straight and hands folded. They bowed their heads at the mention of the holy name of Jesus. The pointer rapped the board, slammed on desks, swished through the air and at times lifted a student's chin so that his eyes met the piercing eyes of Sister St. Michael. The warm September air moved the venetian blinds, and Nestor McCorley longed to be out of this room. The nun had two boys pass out the worn textbooks, *Stories for Catholic Children*, and told the students to open to page 52. Nestor tried to read the title. "Our Lady of..." The last word was hard. "Our Lady of Guadalupe," Sister St. Michael announced.

He read along while a boy with a bad haircut two seats in front of him slowly deciphered the large print. In 1531, such a long time ago, Nestor thought, on the Feast of the..."Immaculate Conception," Sister St. Michael pronounced, the Indian Juan Diego was walking through the desert of Te... pe... yak, Tepeyak, when he heard the most heavenly music, like choirs of birds and angels. A lovely lady called his name, "Juanito! Juanito!" The lady was clothed in light, and Juan Diego shielded his eyes. There was a colored drawing in the book of the Indian, all amazed, and his little donkey and the Lady clothed in light, who was, of course, Our Lady. She spoke in his Indian language and she instructed him to go tell the bishop she wanted a church built on that spot, but Juan Diego said, "I am just a poor Indian. He will not listen to me. You must choose someone more important." She told him, "No, my Juanito. I have chosen you."

Nestor was entranced with the beauty of the colors, imagining the instant devotion that the Indian must have felt. He wished more than anything that Our Lady would choose him and appear like that before him somewhere. Clothed in light. Those words almost brought tears to his eyes. He lost himself in the picture, imagining the desert path cut into the mountainside, and the sudden appearance of the bright Lady, her outstretched hands and loving eyes, the light. His father had told him that the Virgin had appeared to a whole crowd of people in Ireland at a place called Knock. Funny name. *Knock knock. Who's there?* Well, Saint Joseph and Saint John were there, with Our Lady. Each night at bedtime for weeks his father recited the prayer to Our Lady of Knock. He remembered the words as he stared at the image of Our Lady of Guadalupe. They were the same saint, really.

> *Great Mary Greatest of Marys,*
> *Greatest of Women,*
> *Mother of Eternal Glory,*
> *Mother of the Golden Light,*
> *Honor of the Sky,*
> *Temple of the Divinity,*
> *Fountain of the Gardens,*
> *Serene as the Moon,*
> *Bright as the Sun,*
> *Garden Enclosed,*
> *Temple of the Living God,*
> *Light of Nazareth,*
> *Beauty of the World,*
> *Queen of Life,*
> *Ladder of Heaven,*
> *Mother of God.*
> *Pray for us.*

"Mr. McCorley, continue from there."

The words jolted him from his reverie and filled him with dread. He scanned the page, feeling as though he were suddenly thrashing in deep water, searching for something to hold. The last words he had heard were "some proof."

"Mr. McCorley?"

He turned the page and with some relief saw the words at the end of a paragraph, *I will need some proof.* "The next day... Juan Diego returned to the spot..."

Sister St. Michael interrupted. "Were you on the wrong page, young man?"

He knew it was no use explaining that he had been admiring the beauty of Our Lady of Guadalupe, or that he would remember the drawing of poor Juan Diego and the bright Lady forever.

She rose and took a step toward him, pronouncing each word as though it had hard, cutting edges. "I asked you a question, boy. Were you on the wrong page?"

The entire class seemed to hold its breath. "Yes," he whispered.

"Yes, *Sister*! You rude boy!" He cowered as he felt the blow coming; she caught him hard on the side of the head, rocking him in his seat so that he nearly fell off his chair. He knew that she could see he was afraid of her. There was a ringing in his ear. He trembled, but tried not to cry, though tears had begun to leak from the corner of his left eye, which he dabbed quickly with his finger.

"Yes, Sister," he said.

"Go stand with your face in the corner! Go! Get! Leave your book, it does you no good, daydreamer!"

He stood in the corner, looking at the wall, remembering his mother smiling at him as she went away. No adult had ever been mean to him like this. His stomach began to turn as he imagined the days ahead, years and years of days with these women in their black clothes, and suddenly he felt as though he wanted to pee, but he was afraid to ask. He tried to listen to the story, how Our Lady had told Juan that for proof he should go pick flowers on the mountain, but he said it was winter and there were no flowers on the mountain or anywhere. Of course when he went there, he saw roses and flowers of every kind, and he lay his poncho on the ground and bundled the flowers into it. He brought them to the bishop, and when he poured them out, they saw the sacred image of the Virgin Mary that had miraculously appeared on the inside of the poncho.

He tried to forget about being in the corner and to think about Our Lady again, but he couldn't, and he stopped listening and imagined being bigger so that he could take Sister St. Michael's stick away from her and break it and throw it on the ground. One day he swore he would.

Just before lunch, everyone began to whisper and turn to look at a boy in the back row. Nestor, too, stole a glance at him. His face and hands were covered with blue ink. He'd been sucking on a pen, and covered the tiny hole in its plastic side with his finger. The ink had gushed up into his mouth. A hush fell over the class as Sister St. Michael raised her head like a wolf getting a scent in the air. She saw the boy. She rose. "Go wash your face, *baby*!"

Slowly, he got up, head hanging low, and walked toward the door, nearly shrinking as he stepped by the nun. Before he could pass, her hand shot out of the black sleeve, clutched him by the hair and slammed his head against the blackboard. The class gasped at the suddenness and violence of the assault, staring at their books in silence as the boy staggered out of the room whimpering, his blue fingers rubbing his skull.

Nestor ate his lunch standing in the corner, and when the recess bell rang, Sister St. Michael told them to rise by row and form a single file line. She called to Nestor, "You too, boy. I don't trust you alone in here."

He wondered why she didn't trust him. As he passed her he asked, carefully, "Sister, may I go to the bathroom?"

"Everyone will go after recess. Get back in line."

Once outside, the nun told them they could play, but that when she rang the handbell, they were to stop whatever they were doing immediately and form a line at the steps, silent with fingers over their lips.

Nestor didn't know anyone yet, but out in the schoolyard the skinny kid with the bad haircut sidled up and said, "Sorry you got sent to the corner. That stinks."

"What's your name?"

"Roger Shea."

"I'm Nestor McCorley. I don't like this school."

"No, it stinks, really."

"She's wicked mean."

"Real mean. Mean as anything. That kid whose head she smashed on the blackboard, I don't think he's too smart. That ain't his fault."

Some boys were playing tag and running wildly around them. There was a tangle of bodies, shirttails pulled out, red faces, and then, before Nestor could step out of the way, a sweaty kid with blond hair slapped him across the face and said, "You're it, corner boy." He ran away laughing, but Nestor was on his heels, full of the anger that he could not show to Sister St. Michael.

He caught up with the laughing boy and grabbed him by his shirt. Pulling him back, he slapped him twice in the face and said, "You're it, stupid!"

The other boy turned to strike back, but Nestor stepped in close, throwing his arm around his neck. They grappled, each trying to throw the other down when one of the other nuns came and split them apart. "What grade are you in?" she asked.

She delivered them to Sister St. Michael, who looked at Nestor and nodded scornfully, "You again." The two boys stood, heads hanging, on either side of the tall, dark figure, waiting for the recess to end.

A minute later, she drew the brass handbell from the great folds of her sleeve and swung it vigorously. One other nun began to do the same, and the classes formed in lines, fingers over lips. Nestor looked up the steps at the arched doorway that was about to swallow him once again into its polished and hateful interior. The boys stood in one line at their bathroom, the girls at theirs. Four boys at a time went in, standing at the porcelain urinals. "If I hear you talking in there, I'll come in and drag you out!" Sister St. Michael warned.

Before he could take his place back in the corner of the classroom, because she had not yet said that he could sit down, Sister St. Michael announced, "Luca Pavia and Nestor McCorley, come to the front of the room." She stood beside her desk, rapping her pointer against her dark robes. As the two boys approached, she stretched out the pointer to indicate the open area before the blackboard where they should stand. Nestor guessed that she would make them shake hands in front of the class, or apologize for fighting, but when they had taken up their positions at the front of the class, she lowered her pointer and said, "All right, you want to fight? Go ahead, fight."

Luca shook his head apologetically, sweat still running down his red face, and Nestor said, "No, we don't want to fight, Sister."

"I don't believe you. You wanted to fight a minute ago. You will fight now!"

"But Sister…"

"Fight!"

Nestor couldn't believe that she really wanted them to fight. It must be a test. It must be. Surely she would tell them to sit down soon.

"Fight!"

"Sister, I…"

"Shut your mouth! I told you to fight!"

Nestor stood immobile, confused, trying to think what his father would tell him to do, surely not to hit another boy in front of a class. But the sister shouted her command once more, and while Nestor waited, paralyzed with doubt, Luca hit him in the face, and he knew that his father would not tell him that he should stand there and let the other boy beat him. He flew at Luca, swinging furiously. He heard the shouts of the class and of the sister without hearing what they were saying. Both he and Luca Pavia were bleeding, he from the mouth and Luca from the nose. Their faces were bruised and their shirts torn, but neither would stop swinging until they heard another voice close by, a voice with authority, "Stop this minute! Sister, what in the name of all that's holy is going on here?" It was Sister Winifred. The old nun told them to take their seats and said she would like to talk to Sister St. Michael. She spoke to her in the same tone that Sister St. Michael spoke to the students.

Nestor McCorley and Luca Pavia and all the rest of the class smiled because they could see that the principal was not angry at them, but at their teacher. A minute later, another young nun came in, and he heard someone whisper that her name was Sister Theresa. She handed a Kleenex to the two bleeding boys and told them to go to the bathroom and wash up, one at a time. Nestor let Luca go first because his nose was dripping all over his shirt. When he came back, Nestor set out. Drifting along the hall, he stopped near the lobby and peeked around the statue of Saint Brigid into the principal's office, where he saw Sister Winifred talking to Sister St. Michael. She was leaning forward, shaking her head and tapping her index finger on her desk, and Nestor heard the phrases, "I've told you repeatedly," and "the last straw."

Sensing that she was being watched, Sister St. Michael glanced suddenly in his direction, and before Nestor could turn and run, she gave him a look—a cold, hard look. That was the last time he saw her, and when he returned to the class, the door was opened to the adjoining room, and the sister next door was watching both classes. She told him to sit down and finish the story of the Virgin.

A little while later, the principal came in and erased the name of Sister St. Michael and wrote "Sister Winifred." She stood back for a moment, reading the prayer to Saint Michael on the blackboard, and then she erased that, too. Roger Shea turned in his seat and gave Nestor the thumbs up. She took drawing paper and boxes of crayons out of the cabinet and told the students to draw their own pictures of Our Blessed Mother. And while the students bent over their drawing paper, she asked, "Can you imagine, boys and girls, what a beautiful sight it must have been for that Indian, Juan Diego?"

The old nun continued, "Wouldn't you love to see Our Lady like Juan Diego did?" The children looked up and nodded their heads vigorously. "Well, one day you will, I'm sure. And what was the Virgin wearing when she appeared in Mexico?" she asked.

Her voice was kind, and now, without fear, Nestor raised his hand.

"Yes, young man? Nestor?"

"Sister, it says Our Lady was clothed in light, Sister."

She smiled warmly. Her old eyes shone and she said, "Yes. Clothed in light. How beautiful that must have been."

And Nestor felt at once that he loved this old woman, and he looked from her face to the double row of crayons, wondering which one was the color of light. It must be yellow or white. When he raised his head again, the room was quiet; the students chose colors and tried to convey their own visions of Our Lady.

At the front of the room, Sister Winifred chalked a new prayer where the prayer to Saint Michael had been. Nestor's heart was full as he read it: *Dear Mother, we love you. We thank you for your promise to help us in our need. We trust in your love that dries our tears and comforts us. Teach us to find peace through your son Jesus, and bless us every day of our lives.*

CHAPTER THREE

When he awoke, he wasn't sure where he was. The curtains glowed in the morning light and the face of Sister Winifred shone on him for a moment while the name *Olympico* came to him. He pulled off the earphones, now crackling with static. All was quiet. It was as if the wild party people of a few hours before had been a dream. He turned and slept again, until 9 a.m., when the desk called to inform him that Minerva was waiting downstairs.

He brushed his teeth, splashed his face with cold water and was ready to go, his father's voice in his head. "There'll be sleeping enough in the grave," Eamon McCorley had been fond of saying. Nestor stepped onto the elevator while his mind wandered the quiet paths of St. Patrick's Cemetery. There, in the moving shade of maples, his father slept under the stone on which were inscribed the words he'd loved: "He's gone and God be with him, the Rambler from Clare."

Minerva was wearing her jean shorts and the Lowell Folk Festival T-shirt, and Nestor thought she could not have been more beautiful in a sequined gown. They stopped for coffee and a croissant at the Havana Spice Café, and she said she had a plan for their day together. She wanted him to see some of the natural beauty of Florida.

"Great," he said. "By the way, what's the story with that Father Felix?"

The coffee cup paused in front of her lips. "Why? What do you mean?"

"I mean, does he always inquire about people's sex lives?"

She took a sharp breath and her hand rose to her mouth; her cup came down hard on the saucer. "Did he ask you about that?"

"Yes, he asked if we were sleeping together."

"What did you say?"

"I told him I didn't want to talk about that with him."

"Why didn't you just say no?"

"Why should I do that? It's none of his business."

"Well, he is a priest. They think they have to warn you against... you know, falling into sin before you're married. I mean, Nestor, you are a Catholic, right? Even if you're not a strong one?"

"God, that's what he asked me. Minerva, listen, I'm a good person. I try to be. But I'm not a good Catholic. I believe in what Henry Thoreau said about the afterlife: 'One world at a time.'"

He caught a fleeting look of indecision in her eyes, the way a woman might look at a dress when she couldn't decide whether it was suitable or not quite her style. "If you had a child," she said, "if we had a child, ever, would you object to that child being, how do you say, *criada...* ?"

"Brought up as a Catholic? Of course not," he said, gripping her hand. He leaned toward her. "I believe you could do a lot worse than to follow the teachings of Jesus and pray to the Virgin."

She smiled. "Anyway, Father Felix just wants to make sure we're staying on the right path. Oh, *mi amor*, let's don't worry about it now. I think he means well. He is our family priest for a long time and he worries about us."

"I just don't like being interrogated at a cookout."

"I understand." She wrapped his hand in both of hers, and smiled with that light in her eyes that melted resentment, anger, everything but love. *The witchcraft of your smile.*

On the way out to Biscayne National Park, he told her about the party girl of the previous night. "You didn't do anything with her?"

"No, I didn't."

"Did you want to?"

"Did I want to? Well, I'm a man. Of course I wanted to."

"Why didn't you?"

"Do you have to ask?"

She kept her eyes on the road, and one hand on the wheel, but with the other she reached out and stroked his unshaven jaw, and now it seemed that all of her gestures bound him to her.

At Biscayne National Park, they rented a canoe, and soon they were gliding among the mangroves of Caesar Creek in water too shallow for motorized boats, watching the skimming swallows and the wading pelicans. And in the dappled sunlight of a narrow channel where blue dragonflies hung lazily in the air, she laid her paddle on the bottom of the canoe and turned in her seat to face him at the stern. Wordlessly, they leaned toward each other, and Nestor felt the soft warmth of her lips and the electric rush as their tongues touched. He felt that if he lived another hundred years, he would recall this moment at the hour of his death.

But a better memory was to come at the airport the next day, when they embraced. He felt her warm moist breath in his ear as she whispered, "I love you, Nestor." The anguish of their parting was relieved by the sincerity in her voice. He only needed to know that she would miss him.

"I'll call you every day until we see each other again," he promised.

"No," she said, "write to me."

He put down his suitcase and they embraced amid the clamor, one still pair in the milling stream of travelers, but while he inhaled the fragrance of her dark curls, a metallic voice filled the air: "Flight 2207 for Boston now boarding at Gate 9."

And as he watched her walking out the door, he remembered the old Doors song. Yes, he loved her madly. She turned as the sliding glass closed behind her and waved once more, mouthing again the words that had thrilled him. *Te amo.* I love you.

Minerva was in Lowell a month later. Marina was finally ready to open her Colombian restaurant on Merrimack Street, which she would call "La Aguacatala," after a restaurant she liked in Medellín. One Saturday, Nestor and Minerva helped to paint the walls with colors the women had chosen after long deliberation: burnt ochre and sea blue. A large mirror at the back made the room seem deeper, but it was a small restaurant, two booths near the front windows and five small tables, a couple of which could be brought outside when the weather was fine.

Across the street stood Page's Clock, the ornate four-faced street clock under which a young Eamon McCorley had often rendezvoused with Nestor's mother, the dark-eyed Daphne Laganis, after she completed her shift at the counter of Scott's Jewelers. The old clock read 1:10 when they finished painting, and the two sisters stood admiring the room and talking excitedly in a Spanish so rapid that Nestor had to listen hard to follow. He descended the narrow stairs to the cool basement to clean the rollers in the sink.

"I'll make for us lunch at Marina's apartment," Minerva called down the stairs a minute later. "Come there when you are done."

Alone in the apartment, Minerva wasn't sure if she should do it, but then what harm could there be, really? She had asked her mother once if it was a sin to practice the little enchantments that her grandmother, her *abuelita*, had described to her throughout her childhood during engrossing conversations in the garden or at the kitchen table. *Mamá* had responded that it was only a sin if you really believed in it, and Minerva didn't think she did, any more than she believed all the other things her *abuela* had attested, that a man who saw his shadow without the hat he was wearing would soon be dead, or that a white mark on a nail of the right hand brought good fortune, on a nail of the left hand, misfortune. She smiled as she remembered all the wild prognostications and superstitions that the old woman had tried to pass on to her. It was all nonsense, of course, but one stood in her memory, and she thought she would try it, just for luck.

She knew that Nestor would arrive soon. Hurriedly, she took a bowl from the cupboard and the kettle from the stove and went into the bathroom. She removed her paint-stained tunic and reached behind her back to unclasp her bra. Leaning over the sink, she washed her face and breasts in warm water. Then she put the bowl in the sink and began to pour the cool water from the kettle over the paler flesh of her breasts and over her rising nipples into the bowl, and for good measure she scooped the water in her hands and let it flow again over her breasts, thinking of Nestor and saying simply, "Let him love only me. Let him love only me." With this water she would now make tea for the man she loved.

"Come in," she called a little while later in answer to his brisk, distinctive knock. When Nestor opened the back door, he saw her standing in a column of vapor, pouring him a cup of tea from a silver kettle. "Have this while I make you a sandwich," she said, placing the cup of tea in front of him beside a small pitcher of milk and a spoon.

"Tea in the afternoon," he mused. "Just like in Ireland."

"You don't want sugar?"

"No thanks. I don't put sugar in anything." He picked at a spot of sea-blue paint on his knuckle as the tea steeped. "Those back stairs are dangerous. They're way too steep. It's like climbing a ladder. The railing is a bit loose, too. Tell your sister to get the landlord to fix them."

"Yes, they're awful. I will tell Marina." As he sipped the tea, Minerva prepared *arepa con queso*, a sort of corn tortilla with white cheese, a staple of the Colombian diet, and heated up some rice and beans. He loved to watch her preparing the food. So intent, he knew, on pleasing him.

"Excellent!" he said after swallowing his first mouthful.

"As we say in Colombia, you would make a good poor person, *muy bien pobre*, since you are so easily pleased." But Nestor could see that it was she who was pleased with his heartfelt compliment for the meal she'd prepared. "This is *ají picante*," she said, uncovering a bowl. "Very popular salsa in Antioquia, my state in Colombia, for soups, stews, *empanadas...*"

And as he watched her spoon the *ají* onto his plate, he was seized with a tender longing for her, a desire to protect her, to cherish her, to touch her face and kiss her, a feeling that he knew was love. For this, he realized, was a sort of preview of their married life. They were alone in the apartment, and this thought increased the intensity of his longing and his desire to kiss her, though he knew the timing, in the middle of a meal, was poor. He mastered these desires, thinking it better to show appreciation for her cooking, but he could not quell the feeling that they were playing house, and that what he wanted was the reality. With some shock, he realized that this was unlike the dalliances, affairs, and even heated romances of the past. He wanted to marry Minerva.

In any case, he knew her well enough to know that she would not consent to a sexual affair. Father Felix had no worries on that score. To her, sex was no light matter. A truly serious relationship with Minerva would require a ring and a priest. They had kissed, often passionately, but she resisted anything more, and he did not insist because he knew what it meant to her. When she lit her candles to Our Lady, he was reminded of a priestess of Diana, a virgin offering tribute to the Virgin.

"What's in the *ají?*"

"Oh, *dejáme pensar.*" She counted off the ingredients on her fingers. "Peppers, vinegar, tomato, cilantro, parsley, lemon… the green one…"

"Lime."

"Yes, lime, and how do you say *cebolleta?*"

"Little onions? Scallions?"

"That's it."

And all the time, he was thinking. *I want to ask her to marry me, but when I say the words, I can never take them back. Marriage. The life sentence of love. Until death do you part. Not years, but decades.* He could not imagine Minerva's luminous dark eyes faded and watery, set in a thin and wizened face encircled with coarse white hair, and himself with sagging biceps and stooped shoulders, eyes sunken into the sockets, telling her a story she'd heard before.

All the veils long torn asunder, the walls knocked down; they would know each other in all their nobility and in all their pettiness. The years would charge onward with their triumphs and defeats, harmonies and misunderstandings, pain and joy—the two of them bound together by vow and law, and maybe children. Until death! And yet if he didn't ask her, if he let her go, to be remembered through wakeful nights in some distant future when perhaps a different woman slept beside him. When finally he fell into a troubled sleep, whose image would come to him, what voice would whisper to him, what eyes would still search his? Regret is another thing from which only death parts us.

He recalled the feeling he'd had on the high diving board at summer camp as a boy. Not wanting to jump, and yet knowing he could not shame himself by climbing back down the ladder. There was only one way.

"It's very good," he said, nervously.

"Yes, Marina makes it very good."

He swallowed hard and stepped to the edge of the diving platform. It was not the twinkling blue of the pool that stretched out below him, but all the misty valley of life. "Minerva, listen, I don't know if this is really a good time. I mean maybe there should be candlelight and Frank Sinatra…"

She put down her fork and looked at him, almost afraid to comprehend, sensing something in his voice. He continued. "But what I want to tell you…" Yes, her eyes told him, go on. "Not tell you. I mean what I want to ask you…" He blew a deep breath, frustrated with his own inarticulateness. He stepped from the edge and felt himself falling through air. "Will you marry me, Minerva?"

She stood, and he rose to touch her. "*Sí, mi amor.* I will be your wife." Entwined in her arms, inhaling her scent, feeling the wet of her tears on his neck, he was full of joy, and empty of doubt. He had surfaced in the cool water, and gazing up at the platform, he wondered why he'd ever been afraid of the leap.

Five months later, she and Nestor were back in Miami, together with their families at the Church of the Visitation of the Blessed Virgin Mary, where Father Felix Solano, looking somehow less than pleased, pronounced them man and wife.

Outside the church, they mingled for a few moments with the guests before going to the reception. When Minerva was called for a picture with her family, Nestor saw Marquis Alicea amid a circle of friends. He watched him whisper something to his date, a shapely blonde in a royal blue dress, and then come toward him. He wore a dark double-breasted suit that made him look rather pale.

"Congratulations to the groom, Nestor. I think she got a good man."

"That's very kind of you, Marquis."

"Good luck, and remember what I said. Anything I can do."

"Thank you," Nestor said, and nodding toward the blonde he added, "You seem to have landed on your feet. She's a knockout."

"Well, I can't tell if she really likes me," he said.

"I think I saw her giving you looks of ill-concealed lust," Nestor confided with a conspiratorial wink.

Marquis Alicea shrugged. "Well-concealed contempt can look an awful lot like ill-concealed lust," he said.

Nestor put his hand on the other man's shoulder and the two of them laughed.

PART II:
AN ANGEL OF SATAN

CHAPTER FOUR

When she heard the back door close, Minerva Herrera was dreaming of eating a mango in her grandmother's garden. With a small knife, she'd peeled back the thick green skin stained with red like a blushing girl, and bit into the sweet yellow-orange fruit. The closing door startled her and she was drawn out of the drowsy garden where bees droned about the *azucenas*, and where mangoes, carambola, and papaya hung amid the sun-drenched leaves. She threw back the quilt and sat up, rejoining this gray world of the North, listening for a moment to the icy rain falling through the barren trees. *Dios mio*, the climate up here was hard after the trees shed their leaves.

Their November wedding in Miami had been lovely... the week in San Andrés, drinking wine in the dory out on the turquoise water of Sound Bay, reading the poems of Neruda in a chaise lounge on the beach until she dozed in the delicious warmth of the sun... and in their little cottage, wrapped in her husband's arms, naked for the first time together as the gentle breath of the Caribbean stirred the curtains and they heard the waves languidly slapping the shore on the beach below, the way she sometimes slapped Nestor, not angrily, but playfully, as if she wanted him to stop, but not really.

She had feared that her inexperience in bed would frustrate Nestor, but she gained confidence as she let nature, desire and love guide her, and she smiled remembering the words he'd said: "You learn fast."

A spark of that desire kindled as she recalled their sexual play, the eager request in his eyes—a midnight walk and a fervent kiss on the starlit sands. But the flame flickered into smoke as a burst of wind-driven rain rattled the windows of the old house. Oh, this winter raged on—it seemed that it would never end, though Nestor assured her that the worst was over and that spring was just around the corner. The creaking boughs reached out like dark, gnarled hands, almost touching their bedroom window. She heard her husband's car starting in the driveway as her honeymoon, her dream, and the taste of mango faded from her thoughts. Last night, on the way home from Marina's, she had asked Nestor to stop at CVS, and now she recalled the small box in her drawer, and what she had to do this morning. She slid out of bed and onto her knees, her elbows on the mattress, her head against her clasped hands. Her eyes closed and her lips moved soundlessly.

A moment later she was standing in her cotton camisole in front of the mirror in the bathroom, feeling the warmth on her fingers of her urine in the Dixie cup. She held the test kit over the toilet bowl, and let fall a few drops into the plastic apertures. She poured the rest of the urine into the toilet, and set the kit down on the counter. She bit her thumb, staring intently into the tiny plastic wells. Her breath caught and a hand involuntarily rose over her mouth as a pale blue positive sign appeared in the base of each tester. Her other hand moved slowly under her camisole, feeling the belly, beneath which new life was growing, gaining strength. She swallowed and picked up the slim box the kit had come in. She read, not for the first time, "Smart Start Pregnancy Testing Kit gives a correct diagnosis 99% of the time."

Nestor came up the stairs holding two coffees in a cardboard tray in one hand and a soggy bag of croissants in the other. "Beautiful all week," he grumbled as he pushed open the door to the apartment. "Well, March is coming on like a lion."

He saw his wife standing immobile in her housecoat by the kitchen table. "Here's breakfast," he said. But as he set the coffees on the table and pulled the newspaper out from where he'd held it under his arm beneath his jacket, he saw that she was crying.

"What's wrong, Min?"

"Nestor!" she cried. Though he'd always had ambiguous feelings about his name, the way she said it made him smile. Nay-store.

"*Si, mi amor.*"

She threw her arms around him and began to kiss his neck. He clutched her tightly and ran his fingers through her dark curls, wondering, then seeing for the first time the testing kit on the table and the two blue positive signs. He felt the hot tears on his neck as something welled around his heart that he knew was love. A child. Their child. A perfectly ordinary event, yes, and yet… a child born of their bodies, their love. "Don't cry, Minerva," he said as the wind blew sheets of rain against the windows. "You're going to be a great mother."

"Oh, I don't know anything!"

"No one does at first."

"*Te amo*, Nestor."

"I love you, too."

She wiped her eyes and opened the cupboard. She took out a long blue candle in a cylinder of glass. The label bore a picture of a crowned Virgin Mary praying over an infant. She wore a white mantle and a blue, starry cloak. An archway behind her gave way to a sky from which a perfect star shone rays of light that haloed her inclined head. *Nuestra Señora de los Milagros*. Our Lady of Miracles.

She lit the candle and pressed her palms together at her breast: "*Oh Madre querida, Virgen dulcisima de los Milagros, patrona nuestra! Miranos aqui…*"

Nestor stood in respectful silence. Though this was not his religion, or was no longer his religion, the words soothed him in some way, like the sound of water flowing in a shallow brook: "... *a los innumerable favores que de tus manos hemos recibidos.*" He watched the flame, which lent luster to the Virgin's golden crown, the goddess to whom he had once sung with the young boys in the choir loft of St. Brigid's Church. *Immaculate Mary, our hearts are on fire.*

His heart had been on fire with an emotion he'd felt was divinely inspired back then, but now he suspected that it was the beautiful words of the hymn that had ignited it, rather than the presence of God's mother. More than the religious feelings it intended to foster, school had kindled in him an appreciation of the power of poetry, particularly poetry coupled with music: the church hymns and the other songs the sisters taught them in the squat brick building beside the Acre housing projects.

The minstrel boy to the war has gone
In the ranks of death you will find him.
His father's sword he has girded on,
And his wild harp slung behind him.

He remembered the illustration of the minstrel boy in the enormous tome his father kept in the bookcase beside his reading chair, *The Poetry and Song of Ireland*. The wounded minstrel boy gazed heavenward, his hands tearing at the harp's strings. The dying words he spoke so bravely. "Thy songs were made for the pure and free, they shall never be sounded in slavery."

The power of words was one thing the Irish knew, just as the Greeks knew the power of myth. He had grown up with both. It was his mother who had saddled him with the name of Nestor, the ancient king of Pylos, and the adviser to the Greek forces at Troy. He smiled as he watched his wife finish her prayer, and bless herself. Maybe the Church knew better than anyone the power of word and myth.

She took a deep breath, content to have finished the first order of business. "Nestor, I know it doesn't mean so much to you as it does to me, but would you come to Mass with me tomorrow, just this Sunday, to pray for the child."

"Sure, Min," he said. He handed her a coffee, the way she liked it, one sugar and extra cream.

"It's the way I was brought up," she said, as if she had to explain.

"I understand. It's the way I was brought up, too. I just kind of lost it."

"I know," she sighed. "That's the only thing I wish was different about you." She sipped her coffee and looked at him—perplexed, the two small vertical creases between her eyebrows deepening in her consternation. "How can you 'kind of lose God,' like you lose the keys of your car?"

This was a discussion he didn't really want to involve himself in right now, but he tried again to explain himself simply. "Faith can grow in a person, and I guess doubt can, too. It may all be true, for all I know. It's just that I don't know, and for me, believing is knowing."

She shrugged off this elucidation. "You will come back to Him someday. I do pray for you." Her tone was hopeful, and in some way he regretted that he was a disappointment to her. He knew that she loved him, but that she envied the women whose men stood devotedly beside them at Mass, missals open to the proper hymn, singing, rather than looking alternately at the stained glass windows and their watches.

He didn't think it was likely that he would go back, but out of some kind of pity or to avoid the issue he uttered the dishonest reply, "Maybe. You never know. But thank you for your prayers. That's very sweet." They sat at the table and he pushed back the sleeve of her housecoat and caressed her arm. Her dark almond eyes peered over the coffee cup at him. Ah, but he did love her. "Life is going to be different," he said.

"Yes. There will be three of us, *si Dios quiere*. We will not be alone again." It was so obvious, yet that simple truth struck him with the weight of a revelation. *We will not be alone again*; his feelings touched for a moment the edge of sadness because this carefree portion of their married life was about to end. And yet a child would open a new world, and forge new bonds between them. He remembered how another woman had told him years ago that she had never experienced such pain, such love, such worry or such joy until she became a mother. The same must be true for a father. Without fatherhood, a man's experience of life was incomplete.

"Are you going to call Doña Barbara?"

"I think I'm going to wait until I talk to the doctor, just so I can tell her for sure. But I am sure. I feel it."

"What do you feel?"

"I feel something inside me that's not me. Well, it's me, but…" Her eyes were touched fleetingly with a new emotion, as if a cloud had passed over her mind. "Are you happy?" she asked.

"Yes, of course. I'm very happy, *mi amor*."

"You didn't say so."

He should have known that she would want that reassurance. "I am happy, believe me, but you're right. I should have told you. I'm very happy to be having a child with the woman I love."

She swiped at an eye with her little finger and raised a pleading face toward him. "Have patience, Nestor. I'm going to be very emotional. They say your hormones go crazy. You know how sure of myself I was when I met you. Now I feel… so sensible."

"Sensitive," he said, suppressing a smile, but she smiled and the two of them laughed. "I'll get over it," she said.

"That's all right. Don't worry."

"Strange. Even now, I feel my body protecting this baby. There's a perfume I use from South America, called Jasmine. I always loved it."

"Yeah, me too."

"But yesterday the smell of it made me sick. It's as if my body can sense the toxics…" She was intent on her thoughts, so he didn't interrupt her to say *toxins*. "And," she said, "I'm getting *antojos*."

He didn't know the word. *"Antojos?"*

"Those strange desires pregnant women get."

"Ah, like pickles and ice cream?"

Her nose crinkled. "Pickles and ice cream, ugh, no. I have this *antojo* for a mango. Oh, I was dreaming about eating a mango."

"I'll go to the market and see if I can get you one," he said.

"No, no, later. And I had the most strange *antojo* yesterday! Marina was smoking a cigarette. She left it in the ashtray for a minute, and I don't know why, but I had to flick the ash of the cigarette on my tongue."

"That is strange. Was it good?"

"There was something there that my body... what is the word?"

"Craved. Your body was craving."

"Crav-ed. Let's drink our coffee in bed and read the newspaper."

"Ash. Strange. Wonder what's in it?" Can't be good, he thought.

"Anyway, my mother said that she had no sickness in the morning. She was very healthy, and I hope I am so that I can keep working. We need to save." She had found a job surprisingly quickly at the Fred Temple Insurance Agency, dealing primarily with Hispanic customers.

"Well, we'll see how you feel," he said.

They propped pillows and Nestor kicked off his shoes, and they sat close to each other. He read the news while she looked at the *Lifestyles* section, but a part of their minds dwelled in new knowledge, and wandered the mysterious paths of altered circumstance, and when he finished reading an article he looked at her and saw that she was looking at him and they laughed. He let fall the paper and wrapped her in his arms and kissed her warm mouth. Loosening her housecoat, his hand slid under the cotton to her breasts. "Nice mangoes," he said. She smiled and rolled her dear weight over him. "They're yours," she said. The temperature had dropped and now the rain was freezing and making a sound that reminded him of James Joyce's forlorn Michael Furey tossing gravel at the bedroom window of his beloved.

On Mount Olympus, far above the rain-charged clouds, the Lord of Storm had seen his daughter's namesake in her perfect joy. No god pleaded for her, even uselessly, as Apollo had for Hektor. He called for a scale to weigh that joy against a debt he owed the Furies, and her lot sank low. That was how Nestor imagined that moment, later, when it came to him in memory, as it so often did, for what he had known as the happy part of their marriage was drawing to a close.

Seven months pregnant, on another Saturday, in October, Minerva left Nestor at the Brew'd Awakening coffee shop. She was going to light a candle at the St. Joseph the Worker Shrine. "I'll meet you back here in a half hour," she said. He ordered his usual, 100 percent Colombian. The young woman behind the counter wore a sleeveless black tube top with spaghetti straps. Her beauty was marred, sadly, in Nestor's eyes, by the numerous tattoos of astrological signs and mystical symbols, as if her young body were some old necromancer's parchment.

You really have to know when you have enough tattoos, he thought, but then wondered whether he was old fashioned. He saw on her wrist as she handed him his coffee a crescent above a cross. "What does that represent?" he asked, nodding toward it.

"The half circle represents the mind, above the cross, which is the material world."

"Mind over matter."

"Yeah."

Nestor could see that she had probably spent more time than she cared to explaining her tattoos to people, so he thanked her and dropped his change in the tip jar. He took his coffee to a table by the window, where he sat and pulled a book from his jacket pocket.

St. Joseph the Worker Shrine was constructed in a masterful blend of granite blocks—like those that walled in the city's canals and some of its older churches—and the signature red brick of its famous "miles of mills." Brick ran in crenulated columns up the corners of the edifice and edged its windows in red frames. A double parallel line of red brick ran horizontally through the waist of the granite blocks, too, and another capped them just below the roof. Minerva had never seen a design quite like it, and she sometimes wished it were not tucked away so, almost hidden on Lee Street between an old company row house and the back of the Bon Marché building. Then again, that was part of its charm, like a grotto discovered in a remote glade.

Throughout her pregnancy, she had come here every Saturday to light a candle for the child growing within her. Nestor came sometimes, but she could see that he was bored, so she urged him to read his book and drink a coffee nearby while she prayed; he was happy there. He had no faith, but he was a good man, and he would be a good father. She must have faith enough for both of them.

Inside the silent shrine, a plaster Christ hung on a cross suspended from the vaulted ceiling on wire so thin that the crucifixion seemed a vision in air, framed in a gilded hemisphere laced with stained glass. Above the cross, also suspended from the ceiling, the Holy Ghost in the image of a white dove shed brilliant rays of golden grace over Jesus' thorn-crowned head.

Minerva Herrera bowed before this image and walked to the far wall, where statues of the saints stood at intervals above dark glass boxes of flickering candles. This quiet space, a place apart from the world outside, seemed to share a border with some other reality, some holier dimension. The church was nearly empty, but Minerva felt as though it were, paradoxically, a vacancy of presence. The God and saints of her faith would listen attentively to prayers made here.

The only people she saw were old, she thought sadly. At a side altar at the front of the shrine, she saw a replica of the Pietà; Mary held her dead and broken son in her arms. An old woman, her head covered in a kerchief, knelt before the sculpture, holding the feet of the Christ, her lips moving rapidly. Minerva wondered what it was that the old woman prayed for with such devotion.

Reverently, Minerva approached the blue-robed statue of Our Lady, astride the starry globe, her hands showering grace over Earth. She slid two dollars into the metal box, and another into the box for the souls in purgatory, opened the glass door and took a long wick from the tray. She lit a candle in a small blood-colored cup, blew out the flaming wick, and closed the door. Folding her hands before the sacred image, she began her prayer: "*Oh Madre querida…*"

A tall woman with steel gray hair came up and nodded to her. Minerva stepped aside to give her room to open the glass door. The woman lit a candle and stood near her, her head bowed in silent supplication. When Minerva had finished, the woman smiled at her and said, "I see you're pregnant."

"Yes," she said. "I come here for the child, to pray to the Virgin."

"Oh, that's so very nice. I pray to the one under her feet."

Minerva's eyes shot to the long serpent, its mottled length coiled under the bare feet of the Virgin, eyes red, forked tongue flicking between curved fangs. Her stomach turned, but she thought she must not have heard correctly. "I'm sorry?"

"You heard me, dearie. The snake. He's my master, and he hears all my prayers." With one raised hand she pointed toward heaven, and with the other she pointed to the floor. "*So mote it be, says he!*"

The young woman recoiled, turning her head as if the words stung her face like wind-driven hail. "You should not say such a thing!" she cried.

"Do you know what I prayed for, you little candle-lighting bitch? I prayed that your baby would die!"

"No! God forgive you!" The awful malediction entwined about her lungs like a living thing, like the snake beneath Our Lady's feet, constricting her breath. She ran for the exit, sobbing, choking and suffocating under the terrible weight of those words.

At her back the fiendish salvo continued as the shrieking woman followed her. "Glowing, they say! Isn't she glowing! Ha! Your heart will be torn in half, dearie! Torn in half!"

A bent old man, a rosary hanging from one hand, stood and cried, "She must be crazy! Pay no attention to her!" The woman who had been praying at the Pietà hurried toward Minerva. She caught her by the elbows at the back of the church, supporting her sagging weight and guiding her toward the doors. "I'm so sorry," she whispered to Minerva. Then she shouted fiercely over her shoulder at the other, "Shame on you! How dare you defile Our Blessed Mother!"

"Defile this, bitch!" the woman shot back, pulling her dress up to show pale flesh and a gray triangle of hair. A priest appeared from the sacristy and ran down the center aisle, his mouth gaping, stunned at the sudden apparition of this hellish figure that had shattered the tranquility of his shrine. He blocked her way, wrestling her backward, shouting over his shoulder, "Help that poor woman out to the street!"

Minerva did not understand her shrill parting cries. She did not want to understand. Breathlessly, she thanked the woman who helped her, but pushed her away and burst through the swinging doors at the rear of the church and out the glass door to the street, where she fell to her knees and vomited.

At the coffee shop, Nestor was in a meditative mood. He was reading "On the Road," not the novel by Lowell's favorite son, Jack Kerouac, but a short story by Anton Chekhov. "Faith is a faculty of the spirit. It is just the same as a talent, one must be born with it."

He pondered the statement. One must be born with faith. And yet he'd had great faith once. Minerva's question ran through his mind. How do you lose it? A creeping cynicism? Some bad experiences with the exemplars of the faith? Was that enough? And having lost it, why was it that he still admired its expression in his wife? In some way, he was almost jealous of the simplicity of her world view: *This is what I believe, all evidence to the contrary notwithstanding.* It was this simplicity, in part, that had drawn him to Minerva, the sense that her love, like her faith, would be unbreakable and unwavering.

"Hey, Nestor!" It was Eddie Saitz, a local actor and impresario with a long résumé of theatrical roles and play productions to his credit. He managed a small theater company that had met with critical and popular success by performing original plays, though he usually set his productions in venues of limited capacity, such as the stage upstairs at the Old Court, around the corner from the coffee house where he now greeted his friend. Nestor had done some college and amateur acting, and had appeared in a couple of Saitz's productions.

Eddie sat, rubbing his hands together in satisfaction. "I just planted my bulbs," he said.

"I didn't know you were a horticulturalist."

"You kidding me? Planting bulbs is one of the best things you can do! You put the fuckin' bulbs in the fuckin' ground, right? About six inches down, and then you forget about 'em, and in the spring all this colorful shit pops out of the earth! And you can plant 'em so they bloom different times—you got the early daffodils and snow crocuses, blastin' right out of the fuckin' snow, then the hyacinths and tulips, the fuckin' English bluebells in late spring, dahlias and gladiolus in midsummer, begonias in late summer. They got little fucking timers inside 'em! It's amazing! Hey, lemme tell you, anyone who says there's no God is full of shit."

"That's what the nuns told me, in so many words."

Eddie wiped a scattering of crumbs off the table and leaned forward, his eyes narrowing intently like a quarterback about to call the play in the huddle. "Hey Dude, listen. I was gonna call you today. I want you to audition for the part of Hamlet."

"Hamlet? That may be a bit ambitious."

"I'm gonna show the big theater companies that we got the talent to do anything right here in Lowell. I got the idea when I heard you doing that 'O what a rogue and peasant slave am I' soliloquy at the theater Christmas party a few years ago. That was great, man."

"It sounded great because we were both half in the bag."

"Come on. You've done Shakespeare before, right?"

"I played Theseus in *A Midsummer Night's Dream* out in Amherst. A good part, but nothing like Hamlet. You need pros to play parts like Lear and Othello and Hamlet."

"Ah, that's bullshit. Everyone thinks you need pros for everything. You think Shakespeare's actors got degrees from the Academy of Dramatic Arts? Audition, man, it won't kill ya. If Ann picks you, I'll work with you. The play will be abridged for the shorter attention span of the MTV generation. Anyway, the way you played Joe Megessy when we put on *Strange Snow*? Trust me. You can play Hamlet."

"Don't *you* want to play Hamlet? I mean it's your company."

"I'm gonna take Horatio. I'm in *A Funny Thing Happened on the Way to the Forum* at the Concord Theater in June."

"That's a funny play. You have a big part?"

"Dude, are you kidding me? It's a great script! Sondheim is a fucking genius! I'm Pseudolus. I gotta learn a shitload of lines and songs, you know, 'Comedy Tonight,' and 'Free,' and 'Everybody Ought to Have a Maid.' Anyway, it's a big commitment. Take a shot at the Prince!" When Nestor hesitated, looking skeptical, he continued.

"Everybody's afraid of Shakespeare. For Chrissakes, when it was written they had a guy playing Ophelia! We gotta beat that production!" His laugh was loud, spontaneous and uninhibited.

"It does sound interesting." He already knew most of Hamlet's lines from having taught it so many times in Honors English at the high school.

"Listen to me, it'll be fucking fantastic. Shakespeare at the Old Court. It will knock your socks off. People are going to love it. I got Ann Whitmore to direct it, and I got this amazing Brazilian lighting guy—Wellington, like the fucking British general."

"Irish."

"All right, Irish general in the British army. Anyway, he will turn that fucking stage into a parapet of Elsinore. I can't wait! Lemme grab a coffee."

"Yeah, you need one."

Eddie Saitz saw the world in two categories: things he absolutely loved, and things he absolutely hated. His energy and his self-confidence were boundless. He'd put on a one-man show the previous winter called *A Path to the Sea*, based on the life and works of Herman Melville. He had thousands of lines, and yet he was drinking beer and eating fish and chips with Nestor downstairs at the Old Court forty-five minutes before curtain call. They were swapping jokes when Eddie looked at his watch and jumped up, "Shit, I gotta get rollin', put on the old grease paint and costume. My fuckin' beard!" He guzzled the rest of his beer.

"You'd better make sure you take a leak before you go on."

Eddie leaned forward and said, as if revealing a secret of the trade, "I never take a leak before I go on. It gives me more of a sense of urgency!" He slapped Nestor on the back and let out the amplified laugh that could never belong to a taciturn New Englander, but only to the native New Yorker he was: "HAH HA HA!" He threw a twenty on the table and paused; gazing into some middle distance, his features assumed the stern and reflective mask of what Nestor knew must be an aged Herman Melville. His voice grew deeper, and resonant with a vague wonder:

> *Why upon your first voyage as a passenger, did you yourself feel such a mystical vibration, when first told that you and your ship were now out of sight of land? Why did the old Persians hold the sea holy? Why did the Greeks give it a separate deity, and own brother of Jove? Surely all this is not without meaning. And still deeper the meaning of the story of Narcissus, who because he could not grasp the tormenting, mild image he saw in the fountain, plunged into it and was drowned. But that same image, we ourselves see in all rivers and oceans. It is the image of the ungraspable phantom of life; and this is the key to it all.*

Eddie threw his arms out wide and grinned. "Good shit, eh? But I need my fuckin' beard to be Melville!" He danced away, laughing and repeating, "The ungraspable phantom of life!" No nerves at all. Eddie was a pro.

Now Nestor listened to the New Yorker's smooth banter with the tattooed woman as he ordered his coffee. "We got *Hamlet* coming up!"

"He's the 'to be or not to be' guy?"

"You got it! Phenomenal! Don't miss it!"

Nestor smiled and looked out the window. He imagined the people on Market Street frozen in a *tableau vivant*: the gray-haired Hispanic with paint-stained fingers, leaning on a parking meter and smoking a cigarette, waiting; a professional woman in oversized sunglasses walking an Australian sheepdog with one blue eye; a Rastafarian with earphones on, listening to Bob Marley or Burning Spear while he sipped a cappuccino at a sidewalk table.

Nestor placed his book facedown on the table and stretched a hand out toward his friend Eddie, who had rejoined him. "Be thou a spirit from heaven or a goblin damned," he intoned.

"I'm tellin' you!" Eddie said.

But Nestor's eyes had gone wide. His back straightened as if he'd seen a ghost himself, and without a word he rose and flew toward the door, knocking against the table so that some of Eddie's coffee sluiced over the rim of his mug and wet the pages of Chekhov's stories.

Eddie lifted the book and threw a few napkins onto the puddle of coffee before looking up to see Nestor outside the shop embracing his wife, stroking her hair and whispering into her ear. The girl whose arms were a wizard's scroll came from behind the counter to the window and said, "I think she's crying." Eddie nodded, watching them, but for the first time since she'd known him, Eddie Saitz had nothing to say.

CHAPTER FIVE

I n the car, Minerva's sobs subsided, but her eyes remained round and vacant, and Nestor knew that she could see nothing but the face of her tormentor, and hear nothing but the awful words that had left her soul wounded.

Haltingly, she described the woman to him. He would like to have assured her that she was just one of the local street characters, but the description she gave didn't sound familiar.

"There was a poor woman they called Depot Dolly when I was a kid," he told her. "I heard her screaming at a guy downtown one day, saying she would cut off his penis and feed it to the dogs. You can't pay any attention to these crazy people."

It was clear that his words had no weight when set in the scale against the cruel malediction. As he turned onto Broadway, she said, "Stop at Market Basket. I need to get more candles."

The Broadway Market Basket catered to the large Hispanic clientele that lived in the Acre section of the city. Minerva always went there to buy her *arepas*, her *queso*, her *platanos* and, of course, her candles. Nestor followed her to the appropriate aisle and looked over the candles with her. There were the red candles of the Sacred Heart, the white of Saint Theresa, and the blue of the Virgin. A stock boy tore open boxes of Goya pinto beans nearby, his price gun clicking rapidly over the cans.

"Where is the Virgin of Miracles?" she asked him.

He stood and scanned the rows of candles. "We're out," he said. "There'll be more coming in."

"When? When they will be coming in?" Nestor saw the desperation in her eyes, and a sympathetic pain began to constrict his heart.

"Want me to ask the manager?"

"Yes, please."

"Thanks," Nestor said as the young man trudged off. "Min, listen. Here's the *Virgin de Altagracia.*"

"But I've been making my novenas to the *Virgin de Milagros*! I have to finish them."

He wanted to tell her that they were all just names for the same person—or saint, or idea—but he knew it would do no good. In other matters, she was a reasonable woman, but this was beyond the realm of reason. It concerned things that had lain in the human heart since our earliest ancestors felt the sway of unseen powers and tried to name and invoke the forces at work beyond the veil of appearances. She felt those forces, and who was he to say she was wrong or question what she knew in her own heart. As Hamlet had famously reminded his friend, "There are more things in heaven and earth than are dreamed of in your philosophy, Horatio." He could doubt, but he could not deny anything with certitude.

"Tuesday or Wednesday," the boy said when he returned, and Nestor took his wife's hand and led her out of the market. As he started the car, he saw her troubled eyes and knit brow; a shudder passed through her as if she'd felt a cold wind blowing over her soul, and he knew that in her imagination she had already held their dead child in her arms, and he hated the crazy bitch who had done this to her.

Their apartment, four rooms in the top half of a colonial built in the 1920s, had always been a sanctuary for them. The Acre was an old neighborhood, one where police sirens often sounded at night, but they had never been disturbed in this space that they had made their world. They planned to save for a house in a neighborhood with more trees, more space, more quiet. For now, though, it was home, and Nestor hoped Minerva's feeling of security would return now that they were behind locked doors. They brushed their teeth, Nestor prepared the coffee for the morning, and they went to bed early. They lay close to each other, she reading Marquez, and he, Chekhov.

The events of the day had worn on them both, and around 9:30 he heard her sigh and close her book. He closed his, too, turned off the light, and kissed her. She nestled into him and he held her in his arms, trying to pass some confidence or strength into her. "I'm here, Minerva. Everything will be fine."

"I hope so," she whispered.

"Everything will be different in the morning."

They kissed again, and then they were still, falling into the gentle confusion that precedes oblivion. In sleep, Nestor was aware of a presence. It seemed to hover above, or through, his dreams, without interrupting them, until Minerva's cry tore the net of somnolence. He sat up, and immediately had to duck—he heard a flutter of wings and a creature, a darker stain moving through the darkness of the room, passed just over his head. A bat was circling their bed.

Beside him, Minerva huddled under the blankets, crying out his name.

"It's just a bat!" he said. He grabbed a sweater out of his drawer and swung at it, missing the animal in the erratic path its webbed wings cut through the air. He swung again, but the bat had found the doorway.

He ran after it, knowing he had to get it out of the house, for Minerva's peace of mind. Slowly, he stalked the rooms, waiting for it to fly again. Switching on all the lights, he hunted for it everywhere, behind pictures on the wall, in the curtains, under the furniture, behind bookcases. It was gone.

Minerva came out of the bedroom, a blanket pulled tightly around her. He explained that in these old houses, bats nesting in the eaves or in attic recesses sometimes get confused and find their way down. "By next month they'll be hibernating, and there will be no sign of them for a long time."

"But where did this one go?" Her eyes scanned the room warily, and

Nestor knew she was connecting this winged visitor to events earlier in the day.

"They can squeeze into tiny places. I'll find him tomorrow. In the meantime, we can close our bedroom door. I'll stick books under the bottom of the door so he can't get back in."

"*Dios mio*, they're awful."

"They're just mice with wings," he said dismissively, but he saw her shiver and wished he'd said something else.

He closed the door and slid his book barricade into place. When he had gotten back into bed, she gripped his arm and said, "Why tonight this thing comes into our room? Why tonight?"

"Most people in old houses get them from time to time," he said, but he knew that she did not believe it. She lay with the blanket over her head, and clung to his arm until she fell back asleep. Nestor spent Sunday morning in an exhaustive and determined search for the bat, but he never found it, and had to content himself, and he hoped Minerva, with putting weather stripping under the door that led to the attic.

Nestor got out of school at 2:15. The priest had agreed to meet him at St. Brigid's Church at half past three. Though the Irish had built it, most of their descendants had moved out of the Acre, and now the church served mainly Hispanics and various groups of Asians. From what he'd heard, it might soon close altogether.

He got out of his car and gazed up at the gothic spire, the immense stretch of slate roof, the flying buttresses, the gray stones of this earth. Across the parking lot was the brick school where he'd once sat trembling under the stern gaze of Sister St. Michael. He walked up the stone steps of the church and found the door unlocked. Ah, the tranquility of this sanctuary; the silent vaulted space, outside of time, recalled the certitudes of his youth amid these pillars, arches, stained glass windows and stations of the cross.

Now he only appreciated the religion in so far as it was a beautiful representation of hope, a uniquely human perspective of a universe in which humans really played such an insignificant part. He suspended his disbelief when he read Philip K. Dick, but he could not suspend his disbelief when Father Leahy said, "We who believe in Christ will never die. We will live forever." For when the priest concluded his homily, he always heard Mark Twain's voice in the back of his mind saying, "Faith is believin' in what you know ain't so." Still, he occasionally attended the Spanish Mass with Minerva because it made her happy, though he felt a silent hypocrite among the believers.

Sometimes he was filled with the nostalgia for the time that Matthew Arnold had described in "Dover Beach," when "the Sea of Faith was at the full." He felt that it was a good thing that there were people of faith in the world. And there was always the distinct possibility that he was wrong, and that the four evangelists were right.

Through the glass door, he saw a stooped Jack Landry struggling up the stairs. He was an old veteran who helped Father Leahy with the collections on Sundays and with odd chores around the church. Three Asian men walked behind him. One of them was carrying a bucket; the other two had boxes. Jack stopped to shake Nestor's hand at the rear of the church while the other men moved toward the back stairway to the basement. "The Vietnams are tiling the floor downstairs," Jack explained, and then followed them with his limping gait.

Nestor walked up the side aisle of the church, admiring the stained glass windows. There stood the bearded Saint Patrick before an angry King Laoghaire and the druids and warriors of Tara. Spearheads and an unsheathed sword glinted around him. Patrick leaned on the "Bachall Iosa," the Staff of Jesus, that later, Nestor had read, was burned by the English under orders of Henry VIII. The image was unusual in that the saint wore a red cape instead of a green one; he held no shamrock, but pointed toward heaven.

He moved past the rows of pews, ghostly in their vacancy. The scale of the edifice—the cavernous ceilings and the great marble pillars—made a man feel small. "God's house," the nuns had called the church, as surely the seat of power as any earthly palace. Nestor stopped again at what he'd always thought was the most beautiful of the windows, a representation of the Annunciation, one of the five Joyful Mysteries. The archangel Gabriel seemed to be in the act of landing before the Handmaid of the Lord. One scarlet wing was folded, the other outstretched. Gabriel was usually depicted holding a white lily, symbolizing the purity of Mary, but here he held a wand that looked suspiciously like the caduceus, the staff of an earlier messenger, the Greek god Hermes. The Holy Spirit, in the form of a white dove, hung in the air above Mary's head, shedding rays of golden grace, and presumably impregnating her with the child whom Gabriel tells her shall be named Jesus.

Such silence pervaded the church while he pondered these images that he heard clearly a rapid footfall on the stone stairs outside. A moment later, Father Leahy's imposing figure darkened the arched doorway.

"Sorry I kept you waiting," he said as he approached. "A young man showed up at the rectory after lunch. He's a mess—on crack. I was on the phone to some of the shelters, and finally gave him a ride to Middlesex Street."

Father Leahy never struck Nestor as a priest. He was broad-shouldered and bearded, powerful, virile looking. Women must still find him attractive, Nestor thought, and he wondered how he found the strength to push them forever out of reach. To live without the hope of a woman's love, without Minerva's warm body beside him, her embrace, her kiss, her solace…

"You're a good man, Father."

"Well, I know how it is. Before I became a priest, Nestor, and I don't make a secret of this, I took drugs. I sold drugs. I did a lot of things. Enough for a lifetime of penance."

"What happened?"

"I guess you might say I was knocked off my horse on the road to Damascus. I woke up one morning in a filthy room on Flatbush Avenue in Brooklyn with a woman. I didn't even know her name, and I started to cry. I began to pray for the first time in years and, well, here I am."

"Maybe her name was Grace."

He smiled and stroked his graying beard. "Maybe it was, Nestor, maybe it was."

"Since you mention women, Father, how do you… I mean is it very difficult? Celibacy? If you don't mind my asking."

"It's a sacrifice. I suppose that's the point. But there is a peace, a lightness that compensates one." He took Nestor's arm and said, "Come with me. We'll talk in the bell tower. Good exercise, and you'll enjoy the view."

He followed the priest up the narrow, winding stairs. Arrived there, they surveyed the city, breathing deeply. Across the dark canal shone the gold Byzantine dome of the Holy Trinity Greek Church. And beyond that, the clock tower of Lowell City Hall rose in its nineteenth century solidity, a golden eagle perched at its apex. In the distance, the mills crouched along the river, and Nestor remembered the words of Jack Kerouac, "the city where the smokestacks rose higher than the church steeples."

The priest half sat on the inset stone of a window. The crucified Christ, hanging from his neck on a black cord, peeked over his arms, which were folded over his black cassock. "You said on the phone that you were concerned about Minerva?"

"Father, let me ask you this. Does the Church believe in curses?"

"Yes, I would say that the Church regards curses as real. Curses are mentioned in the Bible several times. Let me see, in Deuteronomy and Ephesians. Christ's curse withered the fig tree, you'll recall."

Nestor shook his head, "But Father, a curse is just words."

"Just words… well, I should remind you that the world itself was created by words. But tell me what kind of curse concerns you."

Nestor looked out along the long, pale green copper ridge cap of the roof and saw clearly what was not evident from the ground. The building itself was laid out in the form of a giant crucifix. Slowly, loathe to repeat the witch's filthy words, he recounted the story of what had befallen Minerva at the shrine the week before.

Father Leahy listened, nodding his bearded head gravely, his hands folded as if in prayer before his lips. When Nestor was done, he cleared his throat and said, "Two things. First of all, when the archdiocese foresaw what the new congregations here and elsewhere would be, they sent me and many others to learn Spanish. I went to Peru for three years to minister to the poor there. I can tell you that these things are taken very seriously in South America, as they were among the Irish years ago, and that, naturally, if you believe something is real, well, then to you it is real."

"That's the problem, Father. She does believe it. It's eating at her. She got upset because the candles of the Virgin of Miracles were all gone at the supermarket. I guess there are a lot of people looking for miracles."

"Well, let me get on to my second point, which is the more important in this case. There is no reason for Minerva to fear this thing. First of all, a curse cannot touch a person who is redeemed in the blood of Christ."

"You have to tell her that, Father," Nestor interjected.

"I will certainly tell her that. Also, she did nothing to bring this so-called curse on herself. She is an innocent. Heaven knows her unborn child is innocent. Even the pagans knew that a person had to do something wrong to be cursed."

"Yeah, like the Red Sox trading Babe Ruth," Nestor said, feeling suddenly hopeful that the words of the priest might lift the fear and melancholy that had taken root in the mind of Minerva Herrera.

"Other than this, is there anything wrong with her? Physically, she's all right?"

"Yes, she's still working at the insurance office. I'm just afraid that it's going to make her sick. She used to laugh a lot. Now she's become quiet. I can see it weighing on her mind."

"It's a great shame that she had to run into this woman, who is also to be pitied."

The priest agreed to visit their apartment that evening after supper.

"Father, I really thank you, and I don't mean to insult you, but I know

Minerva. The more candles, prayers, blessings and holy water, the better she'll feel."

Father Leahy laughed and gripped his arm firmly, saying, "All of what you would call the *hocus-pocus*, eh?"

"Well, my natural inclination would be to appeal to her reason, but I know it's beyond reason, and if I had to choose a priest to wrestle with the devil, it would surely be you."

This amused the burly man of the cloth. His laughter filled the tower and resounded in the steel hearts of the pendent bells. "Ah, the devil. I sensed him nearby this afternoon, trying to destroy that poor drug-addled wretch. Oh, I've wrestled with that crooked fellow all right, many times."

His eyes moved over the city stretched out below them—as if they stood atop Olympus—the city of brick and stone, of timber and slate, of steeples and smokestacks, of miracles and maledictions, of aspirations and addictions. The priest scanned all of it and repeated wearily, "Yes, yes, many times."

On the way home, Nestor stopped at the Market Basket on Broadway and was relieved to see Minerva's candles had arrived. He bought a box of twelve. Perhaps he would have one lit when she returned from work, but then he thought she might want to light it herself. He wasn't sure, and he began to grow exasperated with the whole matter.

At the corner of Broadway and School Street, a woman sporting a tank top and a raffish mop of orange hair had double-parked an SUV. Her hoop earrings bobbed as she wagged her finger in the face of a frowning man slouched against the plate glass window of a cell phone store. As he drove around the SUV, Nestor lowered the window on the passenger side. He noticed a tattoo in florid cursive over the small of her back, the words half-hidden below her frayed shorts—a message reserved for the privileged. The man had had enough. He drew himself up and leaned toward her. "Get outa my face, bitch! Get the fuck home!"

She was not taking orders. Nestor would have heard her piercing reply with his window up. *"Cágate en tu madre, cabrón!"* The man drew a hand back in a threatening gesture, but turned and stalked off, muttering, head bowed, hands in pockets.

Nestor chuckled. *Go shit on your mother.* Not a bad insult. But not as good as the Greek insult Nick Betsis had once translated for him. "I will take the candle that will be burning at your wake, and shove it up your ass." The Greeks understood epic, and that was an insult of epic weight, maybe a curse, with its suggestion of impending death.

He took a right onto Wilder Street and pulled up in front of his mother's house, the solid colonial in which his family had lived since he was a boy. His mother was alone there now, since colon cancer had taken his father two years ago. As he got out of his car, two young men came up on the high handlebar bicycles that they called "Sting Rays" when he was a kid, only these riders were not kids. They whizzed by him, so close that he was pinned against his car.

"Jesus Christ!" he shouted, smelling the cigarette that dangled from the mouth of the one in front; the other looked back with glassy eyes and a chip-toothed smile. "Four in the afternoon and already drunk as lords," he thought. Though he had been brought up in the Acre, he could never quite comprehend the lives of some of its inhabitants. He saw them as the denizens of some other world, parallel to his own. They didn't recognize society's demands or plan for tomorrow. They were not troubled by scruples or worn by responsibility. They played by their own rules, but Nestor was damned if he could figure them out.

Three keys hung on his key ring, and he opened his mother's door with one of them, calling to her in one of his stock Greek phrases, *"Kalí mi téra apógev ma!"*

"Kaló apógev ma o gios mou," she responded from the kitchen.

They embraced, and Nestor said, "Mama, you have got to move out of this old house. The neighborhood is worse than ever. There's a couple screaming at each other in the street down on Broadway, and two drunks on bicycles almost ran me over out front."

She shrugged. "Eh, it's America. Listen, before you sit down, Nestor, can you go over to the house of Mrs. Mastakouris. In the back is a grapevine."

"Yes, on the arbor."

"Her son is going to build a deck there, and he must destroy the vine. She tell to me to come take the grape leaves, so that I can make *dolmades*."

"How many do you need?"

"Bring fifty big ones." She produced a cloth sack from the pantry and handed it to him.

Nestor stood under the arbor in the dappled light picking the leaves, feeling like a child once more, recalling the afternoons he had spent helping his mother clean the grape leaves, remove the stems, stuff them with rice and beef, and roll them. He would put four in each mason jar, and pour in the brine mixed with lemon juice. It was usually on a Sunday afternoon after Mass; she would never let his father help with the dolma rolling. She said that he worked too hard during the week, and he needed to rest, but it was more than that. Greek women of his mother's generation never wanted to share the kitchen with a man.

Nestor saw this when, from time to time, his father would decide to make some "boxty," or potato pancakes. Daphne Laganis McCorley would look on as he grated the potatoes, her eyebrows raised in open skepticism. When it was time for her to cook, she waved him out of her kitchen, "No, no, you go and take a rest." Eamon would smile and retreat to the living room to read the newspaper or his history books.

When Nestor returned, his mother was preparing the rice. She smiled as she examined the leaves. There were creases around her eyes, but her face was still smooth and retained some of the glow of youth; he hoped he had those genes. Her dark hair was shot with gray, though. His aunts and his sister, Alena, urged her to color it, but she only said, "Who I am trying to impress, eh?" She had come to this country at the age of sixteen, learning English at the high school at night and, she said, from his father, but she would never lose the Greek accent, and verb tenses would forever be a problem. She wiped her hands on her apron, poured him a glass of orange juice and sat down at the kitchen table beside him. "How is your work? Good?"

"Yeah, it's fine." He wouldn't complain to her in any case.

"How is Minerva? Still she is upset?"

"Yeah, you can imagine. About the last thing a pregnant woman wants to hear is a curse on her unborn child."

"Poor Minerva. She is a love. I like to put my own curse, the *katadesmoi*, on that woman that say those horrible things to her, but Nestor, she must be crazy, eh? We have to have pity on the crazy ones."

"I suppose we do."

"Why they let the crazy people out on the street like that to bother the decent people?"

"It's America, remember?"

"Yes, that's right, so you don't pay attention to those people."

"No."

"They crazy." She waved a hand to dismiss them all, then smiled and said, "You know what you like to name the child? What if it is a boy?"

"Well, not Nestor!" He laughed, but her brows lowered over her brown eyes, and he repented his joke.

"Nestor is a good name," she protested, "the best name."

"Oh, here we go," Nestor said, wearily.

She ignored his sarcasm. "He was one of the Argonauts, a man of sweet words, a strong, clear voice, and the Greeks they listen to him more than to anyone. He is the hero of my city of Pylos. So you have your father's last name. I tell him you can go to the Catholic school, and even I go to the Catholic Mass, yes. You are raised as Catholic boy, but I say give him the name of this Greek hero, my father's name, to remind him he has Greek blood, too."

"I'm only kidding, Ma," he said, feeling sorry to have offended her. "I'm very proud of my name." He should have learned long ago not to kid her about these things. Nestor, the Gerenian horseman, was no joke to anyone from Pylos. "We don't know if it's a boy or a girl," he added.

"What you want?"

"Well, as Woody Allen said, 'I'd like a boy, but a girl is my second choice.'"

She seemed to hold her breath for a moment, still and pensive, then smiled and said, "Oh, my second choice. I see. That is very funny. My second choice." But these were serious matters, and she continued, seriously. "The first one—is better if it's a boy. After that, a girl is OK." She put a hand on his forearm and said, "When you were born and the doctor say to me, 'It is a boy!' Oh my God, what joy! I kiss his hand. This is my Nestor, you see."

"And suppose he'd said, 'It's a girl.'"

She imitated a forced smile and said, "Yes, thank you."

He shook his head. "You're such a Mediterranean."

"But the second time I was very happy with your sister. It's only the first one you want to have a boy. Then it's all right."

"Was it difficult for you and Dad? The cultural differences?"

"Why, is difficult for you and Minerva?"

"Not for me. I hope not for Minerva."

"You speak her language. That is good. Your father knows only a few words of Greek, but he like the food, he like the music. Maybe some things he don't understand, but what is important is you share the same values. Your father and I we both believe in hard work, in education for the children, in family, in being good to the other people."

"That makes sense," he said.

"And I become expert on the Irish."

"What did you learn about the Irish?"

She smiled knowingly. "They are most happy when they sing about all the ones who die for their country, and when they tell the wild stories and sing sad songs." His mother was quiet for a moment, and then she added, "I tell you true. They say is the Italians and the French who are the romantic men. Oh, they talk like Casanova, but usually doesn't mean anything. But the real romantic heart you see is the Irish. Listen to the songs like your father sing, to the poetry they say, look at their story. They don't talk like French about the love, but they feel it more than anyone. Sometimes too much."

He had never heard his mother assess the Irish character, but her analysis was perceptive. He recalled the words of Prendeville: "The worst kind of romanticism. Ye must be Irish. Soon you'll want to go die for Cathleen ni Houlihan."

His mother got up to lower the gas flame under the rice, and drew out a large pan from the cupboard for the ground beef.

"Do you want me to help you with the dolma rolling?"

"No, Alena is coming over. You go take care of your wife. I give you some lentil soup I made yesterday. I don't put too much salt because it make the pregnant woman to swell up."

While his mother poured the lentil soup into a plastic container, he looked at an icon of the Virgin that had hung in their kitchen for as long as he could remember. How many images, how many incarnations of Christ's mother were revered across the Christian world? This image, which had fascinated him as a child, portrayed the haloed mother with arms raised to bless the beholder; her womb was visible in the form of a large transparent egg. Inside it, a tiny Jesus robed in red and white held a scepter and a globe. She saw him studying the icon and said, "The *Theotokos*, the God–bearer." She handed him the soup and kissed his cheek. "I was very happy with your father, Nestor." Her eyes looked off somewhere, into memory, and she shook her head slowly, smiling. "You remember the song he used to sing me?"

"There were a lot…"

"About marrying an Irishman?"

"Oh yes."

"How is it?"

He knew she wanted him to sing a verse, and he couldn't begrudge her.

Standing in her kitchen with the bowl of soup in his hands, he sang softly,

Oh! daughter, dearest daughter
What's this you are going to do?
To fall in love with an Irishman
A man you never knew

Well he'll work for me and he'll toil for me
He'll do the best he can,
And I know I'll never regret the day
I married an Irishman.

She nodded and rubbed his forearm gently as he kissed her cheek. "Never I regret that I marry him. Eamon was good to all of us."

"Yes, he was."

He was about to leave, but on an impulse he put the container of soup down on the entry table and mounted the stairs to his old room. It was much as he had left it years ago; the yellowing poster of Jimi Hendrix above the bed, a few dusty sports trophies on the bureau, the chess set his parents had given him for Christmas one year on his old desk, and against the wall, a bookcase full of the works that had given birth to his imagination, maybe to his soul. There was *War and Peace,* with its fierce Cossacks rushing out of a blinding snow to pick off the weary, retreating soldiers of Napoleon's rearguard as the shrewd, one-eyed General Kutuzov drove the Grande Armée back across the Berezina River. Stevenson's *Kidnapped,* which he read three times in seventh grade, Kerouac's *Doctor Sax,* Rahula's *What the Buddha Taught,* Heller's *Catch-22,* Clavell's *Shōgun* and the three volumes of Tolkien's *The Lord of the Rings* that had transported him to Middle-earth and deep into the dread Mines of Moria. He sighed and thought there is nothing to remind one of the passage of time, of the closed chapters of a life, of former selves, like an old bedroom and the bookcase of one's past.

He picked out one of the volumes of *The Journal of Henry D. Thoreau*, and sat in the rocking chair by the window where he had read on wintry high school afternoons.

February 28, 1857. It is a singular infatuation that leads men to become clergymen... in the clergymen of the most liberal sort I see no perfectly independent human nucleus, but I seem to see some indistinct scheme hovering about, to which he has lent himself, to which he belongs. It is a very fine cobweb in the lower stratum of air, which stronger wings do not even discover..."

He closed the book, and his eyes, and rocked gently in the chair, considering singular infatuations and independent human nuclei, whose *stronger wings* carried them through the gossamer webs of human *schemes*. Weren't Thoreau's words reminiscent of what James Joyce had written of the independent spirit? "When the soul of a man is born in this country there are nets flung at it to hold it back from flight. You talk to me of nationality, language, religion. I shall try to fly by those nets."

He went downstairs and kissed his mother once more, picked up the lentil soup, and reentered the present as he closed the front door. For this house would always be a time portal, haunted with icons, *dolmades*, his father's empty chair, the books of his youth, and some part of that former self.

In the car, he slipped into the player a CD of Seamus Connolly, the All-Ireland fiddler, with Joe Derrane on button accordion. Connolly was another Clare man, like his father. He lived in the Lowell area now, and had been friendly with his father. Nestor thought about his mother's life, and his own, all so incumbent on accident. Eamon McCorley and his brother, Colm, had been working in construction in Chicago for a couple of years. When they had saved enough money for a bit of land back home, they bought an old Buick, patched up the radiator and headed to Boston to catch an Aer Lingus flight to Shannon. But the car's water pump gave out in western Massachusetts. They left the unregistered car by the side of the road and hitchhiked to Lowell, where Colm had a friend from Ennis.

The plan was to stay for a few days, but the friend asked them if they wanted some good work hanging drywall for George Betsis, a Greek builder who ran Acropolis Construction. They signed on, and the Irishmen were quickly immersed in Hellenic Lowell.

He remembered his father, tall and lean, with his broad face and square chin, his wiry, russet hair sticking out from under a crooked wool cap, telling him the story of those days. It was near Christmas; he and Colm were cutting and nailing Sheetrock when a Greek framer came up and said in his best English, "Hey Irish! You stop you work!" And throwing open his arms, he added, "*Kala Kristouyena*!" Merry Christmas. He handed each of them a glass of liquor, and waved for them to follow him. The garage was framed, but still open and unroofed. They were almost blinded by the sun glinting off the crystallizing snow and by a fragrant smoke that hung in the air. The Greeks were turning a lamb on a spit in the open bay. George Betsis came over and shook their hands and told them to eat up and then to go home for Christmas holiday. "Well now," his father had said, "I turned to Colm and I told him, 'We're in God's pocket here.'"

All this was family lore, as was the fact that a Greek friend, Christos Manolopoulis, invited them to a party where, for the first time, Eamon McCorley saw Daphne Laganis dancing the *syrtos*, leading a circle of women with her right hand free in the air, snapping her fingers, angling her body to the right and then to the left, stepping so easily with and over the music, leaning forward and scuff-kicking the floor, bouncing backward, twirling, holding high the hand of the woman who followed her. "I loved it all right away, Nestor. I loved the music. I loved the people, and I was captivated by that woman, for as the old song says, 'I thought that she could be no mortal, but an angel that fell from the sky.'"

Yes, maybe the Irish were the real romantics, as his mother had said. How strange to remember those words now, because Nestor recalled the sight of Minerva Herrera the first time he'd seen her, swaying like some exotic tree in the wind, and moving her hips into the rhythms of a *cumbia*, feeling something very much like what his father had felt so many years earlier.

Eamon McCorley married Nestor's mother the following spring. And Uncle Colm returned to Ireland alone. The Shamrock Shore. Nestor's best memories of his father were from the two weeks he spent with him in Clare in 1989, and he remembered those days as the car, and his being, filled with the strains of Seamus Connolly playing the slow air "The Coolin." He liked to recall those days in Ireland, rather than the hospital days, later, as the cancer chewed at his father's intestines.

Clare was another world. He was only seventeen, but no one seemed to mind when the pints were pulled. With his father and Uncle Colm, he visited homey pubs off winding country roads where, of an evening, the men and sometimes the women took turns singing songs or reciting poems. Luckily, Nestor had memorized many of the poems he loved. Poe's "Annabel Lee" was always greeted with generous applause. He recalled one night talking to a young man who told him he was a mechanic, and yet after a few pints he began to recite a long passage from a poem translated from the Irish called "The Midnight Court." The songs were occasionally original compositions: "Dis is a song I wrote about me trip to Gougane Barra. It's called 'The Trip to Gougane Barra.'"

Often the songs told of days gone by, of doomed love, and of martyred heroes. "Mawkish, melancholy, maudlin, and melodramatic," his father said once, "all those horrible M words the elite use to disparage the sentiments of the working classes." If he hadn't read the poetry, if he hadn't grown up with his father's songs, if the sense of tragedy had not been bred in his bone, then perhaps he would find the songs trite or effusively sentimental, but he didn't, especially there in the west of Ireland.

There were Irishmen, too, who would scoff at it, who were understandably tired of the endless speeches from the dock and the *Shan Van Vocht* and the Land of the Heart's Desire. "To hell with the Celtic Twilight," Declan Prendeville had once pronounced, "give me the Celtic Tiger."

But the old strain was undeniable, at least in his father's generation.

They loved to sing of the heroes who'd failed, the rebels, Robert Emmet, Wolfe Tone, Kevin Barry, Muiris Mor O Sé, Walsh and Lyons and young Dalton, too, the Bold Fenian Men and the Wild Geese that "spread the grey wing upon every tide." The Minstrel Boy, the Borstal Boy, and the Croppy Boy—O shed a tear for the Croppy Boy, and it was a hard man indeed who would not, for they fought for old Ireland, and their ghosts were always close, a denser white in the fog that blurred the yellow gorse, lingering round the ancient dolmens that stood like timeless portals of stone; they whispered in the rafters of the dimly lit rooms where men in slouch caps took their jars of stout and listened to the singer in silence, nodding gravely.

Fire smoldered in the bowls of their pipes and danced over the black bog peat, burning the wood of ancient forests. They listened while a thin, white-haired man closed his eyes and sang one of the many ancient and forlorn songs that chronicled the history of the island:

Long, long we kept the hillside
Our couch hard by the rill-side
The sturdy knotted oaken boughs our curtain overhead.
The summer sun we laughed at, the winter snow we scoffed at
And trusted in our long steel swords to win us daily bread.

Till the Dutchman's troops came round us
With fire and sword they bound us
They fired the hills and valleys till the very clouds were flame.
Yet our sharpened swords cut through them
In their very hearts we hewed them,
Ah, but Sean O'Duibhir a Ghleanna,
We were worsted in the game.

Here's a health to your and my king
To the monarch of our liking

And to Sarsfield underneath whose flag
We'll cast once more a chance
For the morning dawn will wing us
Across the seas and bring us
To take our stand and wield a brand
Among the sons of France.

The past was always alive in Ireland, and the ghosts so close, nourished with sighs and tears for their names. When it was his father's turn, he loved to sing of the adventures of "The Rambler from Clare," who at one point was thrown in prison for deserting from the British army.

My poor innocent mother got a woeful surprise
And my loving brother his shouts reached the skies.
"Brave boys," said my father, "your arms now prepare,
To rescue my darling the Rambler from Clare."

His father showed him the sights of the county, the strange moonscape of the Burren, where *Poulnabrone*, a megalithic dolmen, or portal tomb, rose from the limestone bedrock in mute testament to the lives of some long lost tribe, a huge, flat tilting capstone laid over lichen-stained pillars. Archeologists had dated the site to 3800 BC.

"What does *'Poulnabrone'* mean?" he had asked his father.

"The Hole of Sorrows," he answered, which struck Nestor as a peculiarly Irish name. They saw the Cliffs of Moher, the ragged edge of Europe as it had once been called, in a fog that hung over all as they approached the precipice warily. This must indeed once have seemed the world's edge, beyond which lay the abyss, a bottomless white void. They visited the ruins of the castles of the O'Briens and O'Connors, and had lunch in Liscannor, where a rheumy-eyed local historian proudly informed them that it was the home of John P. Holland, the inventor of the submarine.

Nestor pulled into his driveway. He turned off the engine and sat listening to the music. Shortly before they left Ireland, he and his father went on a fishing trip to Doonbeg Bay, near the White Strand. Nestor leaned back and closed his eyes, remembering; he tasted the salt air, saw the broad bay and sensed his father beside him, humming an old song. His rod bent sharply, and after a good fight, he pulled in an Atlantic salmon.

"Ah, Nestor lad," his father said, "you've caught the salmon of knowledge!"

"Why do they call it the salmon of knowledge?"

"Well, I think originally it may have come from the fact that they are wise enough to know how to live in salt water and in fresh water. But the people say that the salmon of knowledge have eaten the nine hazels of wisdom."

"From where?"

"From the Well of Segais at the world's end—the source of all knowledge." He laughed in the sun and said, "Ah, they're great for the stories, Nestor."

He had pulled the hook from the salmon's mouth, and admired its silver-blue length, its gleaming back mottled with black spots. In his bare hands he felt it, slippery, still pulsing with life, drowning in air, struggling to twist power into tail and fins. It was a beautiful creature, and he wanted it to live. He leaned over, holding the fish. When its body touched the water it flew from his hands; the broad tail flicked twice and the salmon was gone—silver flashing into obscurity like a bright coin falling through a deep well. Clouds, white and gray, edged in blue and violet, charged over the bay. The water was dark here, and sunlit there, the breeze ruffling the outer bay beyond the cove where they fished, reflecting broken shards of light.

"Well, you'll never be as wise as Finn McCool, who ate the salmon of wisdom," his father said, but then he added, "Ah, well, there never was such a thing, Nestor, nor any nine hazels to be found in a magic well. No, wisdom comes from reading, from thinking, from talking to those who know, and listening, and I think especially from living, from greetings and partings, from suffering, from seeing those you love suffer, and in spite of it all, and though you remember, you find a way to sing, and laugh, and live the life you've been given to the full. That's wisdom. That's Irish wisdom anyway."

The plaintive air was drawing to a close when a knock on his car window made him jump. It was Minerva. Her earrings hung beside her cheek as she leaned forward, like large silver tear drops, reminding him oddly for a moment of the lure he'd used to catch the salmon in Doonbeg Bay. He turned off the music and hefted the box of candles on the seat beside him. They went into the house together.

CHAPTER SIX

When she learned that Father Leahy would be coming, she began to organize the apartment, and got the coffee ready so she could set it to brew when he arrived. Nestor was relieved when he opened the kitchen door and saw the powerful figure of Father Leahy mounting the back stairs in his dark clothes and Roman collar. Minerva pressed the button on the coffee machine and welcomed the priest. They spoke in Spanish, and he told her that he had heard that she was concerned about the incident at the shrine. Her eyes dampened immediately at those words and she bit her lip. He told her that as Saint Declan had assured us, a person of faith was under the protection of Jesus Christ, and immune to curses and to the powers of evil.

"But Padre, do others have the power to put a malediction on us?"

"*Si, m'hija*, we have the power to bless each other, and the power to curse each other. But as I told Nestor, you have done nothing wrong, certainly nothing to deserve a curse, and you are protected from its evil by your faith in Jesus Christ. I suggest we pray together to put your mind at ease, and to turn the curse into a blessing."

He placed his great hand over her bowed head and said, "In the sacred name of Jesus our Savior, let no evil touch this woman or her unborn child. Let the grace of Our Lord Jesus Christ fall upon them and fill them with blessings. We ask this in the name of the Father, the Son and the Holy Spirit."

He blessed her as she and Nestor made the sign of the cross; then he reached into his pocket and took out a small plastic bag. "This is blessed salt," he said, "throw some around the house. It's a very old Christian ceremony to ward off evil, but rest assured, Minerva, that neither your body nor your soul, nor the body or soul of your child, can be touched at all by this so-called curse."

They said a decade of the rosary, and lastly they prayed the creed together in Spanish. Minerva was much relieved when all this was done, and she poured the coffee while Father Leahy told Nestor about his plans to refurbish the old church.

"Where do you get the money, Father," Nestor asked, "from the archdiocese?"

"No, no. An old Greek gentleman, he must be in his eighties, has made a contribution of one hundred thousand dollars to carry out a lot of the needed repairs."

"What's his name?"

"Your father worked for him. George Betsis. Used to run Acropolis Construction."

Later, Nestor walked the priest out to his car and shook his hand. "Thanks very much, Father."

"I'll call you if I need help at the Bean Supper?"

"Fair enough. Nice touch with the salt." He looked up at the lit windows of the apartment. "She must be tossing it all around up there now."

Father Leahy shook his head and said, *Hombre de poco fe!*" Man of little faith.

"Sorry, Father."

Peace descended on their home while autumn ran its course. On weekends, Nestor and the old man who lived downstairs raked the yard and bagged the leaves, and the landlord knocked some money off their rent, which was welcome because he and Minerva had now saved nearly enough for a down payment on a house. When Nestor came in, his wife would often be making a *sancocho*, the Colombian equivalent of an Irish stew, or his mother's Greek *stifado*. A stew steaming on the oven was always welcome, especially when, as New Englanders said, "the frost was on the pumpkin."

Halloween passed, the night when his father used to say that the door between this world and the other was open, and spirits might wander onto paths we mortals trod. A silver pin worn inside the lapel, or somewhere about the person, would ward them off, but the smile in his father's eyes told him he believed in this no more than in the nine hazels. Children dressed as super heroes, pirates and little horned devils rang the doorbell and then shouted, "Trick or treat!" Sometimes they stood mute and wondering until Nestor would ask, "Aren't you going to say anything?" Parents holding flashlights out on the sidewalk smiled and shook their heads. "What do you say, Ricky?" And young Dracula would mumble, "Trickatreat."

"That will be us with a little monster in a few years," Nestor said.

"*Si Dios quiere*," Minerva said. That ubiquitous Colombian phrase, "If it pleases God," expressed the firm conviction that it was bad luck to make any plans without acknowledging that the Almighty could easily blast them all. Her Christian god, like the old Greek gods, always struck at hubris.

The trees stood naked against the pale sky of November, and Minerva's graceful walk had turned to a comical waddle that made him love her even more, and in some way feel sorry for what he'd done to her and for what she must endure. He went with her to the doctor's toward the end of the month, and through some machine heard the diminutive heart beating, and he laughed because it sounded like someone banging on a tin barrel lid. The ultrasound technician smiled as she slid the mouse over her swollen belly and said, "Oh I see something there. Do you want to know if it's a boy or a girl?"

Minerva's eyes widened. She bit her thumb and then shook her hand nervously, loose at the wrist the way that Latinas do. "Should I, Nestor?"

"Well, I have to know whether to paint that little room blue or pink," he said.

"All right, what is it?" she asked.

"It's a boy," she said. "See the little penis?" She placed her pinky against a spot on the screen, but all Nestor could see was the white, grainy outline of a head floating in a dark world, tiny arms bent up to his mouth, as if he were sucking his thumb. And he was moving, squirming, stretching his gathering body in her encompassing womb, and Nestor recalled the icon of the Virgin in his mother's kitchen—the child in the transparent egg.

"A little boy!" she cried, and then she squeezed his arm hard as he stood by her side. "Oh Nestor, I wish you could see your face! It's lit up!" He was glad that she could see his joy, and she would not have to ask him, "Are you happy?"

"You were hoping for a boy I take it?" the technician asked.

Nestor almost quipped, "Yeah, but a girl was my second choice," but it didn't seem to be the time for quips. "I would have loved either. It's just that knowing the gender makes it suddenly more real. *It* has an identity now. He's a baby boy."

"I always wanted the first one to be a boy," Minerva said.

"Have you been talking to my mother?"

In the car, she called her sister, Marina, excitedly to tell her the news, and asked her to call Father Leahy and let him know. Nestor suggested they go down to Café Paradiso so that he could buy her a hot chocolate.

Minerva pushed a CD into the slot and forwarded it to the track she wanted. It was her current favorite song, "Te Busco," by Celia Cruz, and she sang along with the mournful voice of the woman searching among dreams for a lost love. "And they say the Irish songs are sad," Nestor said.

At the café, they discussed names while she sipped her hot chocolate and Nestor sipped his beer. Now that they knew they would have a boy, they could eliminate the hypothetical female names.

"Remember that it has to go with McCorley. Carlos McCorley—that's as bad as Nestor McCorley for crying out loud."

"Is there an Irish name that my family could pronounce?"

"How about Roddy McCorley, like the hero of the old rebel song?" He leaned toward her and sang softly.

See the fleet foot host of men that speed with faces wan
From farmstead and from fisher's cot, along the banks of Bann
They come with vengeance in their eyes, too late, too late are they
For young Roddy McCorley goes to die on the bridge of Toome today."

Her brows lowered over indignant eyes. "You want to name him for someone who is going to die on a bridge? That's an awful name, Nestor!" She rubbed the swollen belly beneath her coat as if to protect the child from the name of the martyred rebel.

Too late, too late, he realized he'd made a gaffe, especially in light of all that had happened. He moved on quickly. "How about Christy?"

"Christine?"

"Oh, brother. Forget that one." He poured the remainder of his Molson Ale into the clear, tapered glass. Golden in the late autumn sun, a head of pure white froth. He read the label. *An honest brew makes its own friends.* Good words. He sat back, holding the beer contemplatively before him. "It's a hell of a thing to clap a name on someone that they have to carry all their days." He shook his head and thought of the awful names that had been given to some of the students he'd had over the years. "I had one poor girl whose mother named her 'Latrina.'"

Minerva put down her coffee so she wouldn't spill it and laughed. "*Como una letrina?* Does it mean 'toilet' in English, too?"

"Exactly."

"*Ay, Dios mio.* Yes, the poor girl." She sighed and said, "It's an important decision. But I think we will find a good name. We have to think about it."

He smiled. *Abow-teet.* "Well, we have time." They sat for a while, relaxing in the sun, watching people pass in the street while she gave him the news of her family in Florida. He held her hand in his, feeling the gold circle of the wedding ring.

"I want to get you a diamond."

"I don't care about a diamond."

"I know you don't. But I want to get you one anyway."

They left the café, walking close to each other. Nestor put on his sunglasses and thought that this was another of those golden moments that would adorn the gallery of his memory. He felt his wife stop short, and looked at her. She seemed to be in pain, her hand once again protectively under her curved belly. "What's wrong?" He thought for an instant that she might be going into premature labor, but he saw that her gaze was fixed ahead of her. Her fingers gripped his arm tightly, and he heard the first words of a Spanish prayer as he turned and saw a tall, gray-haired woman approaching, wool coat open, lifted in the autumn breeze. She was talking to herself loudly and rapidly, nothing he could make out—her eyes riveted on Minerva.

Nestor pulled his wife close and said, "Ignore her, *mi amor*, she's crazy!" but he felt his own heart picking up its pace as he stood between the two women, one chanting a stream of incomprehensible syllables, the other praying feverishly in Spanish. He guided Minerva along, trying to evade and pass by the madwoman. But when she had drawn within a few feet, she stopped and let out a loud, snake-like hiss, lips curled back from yellowing teeth.

"Fuck off!" Nestor growled.

"You tried to *expunge* it, didn't you? You tried to take it off, but oh, no, no—it's stuck on your baby! The master heard me, and there is no priest on this earth can get it off!"

At that moment, Nestor hated the shouting woman with an intensity that nearly equaled his love for Minerva. He whirled on her and said, "Shut your filthy mouth you crazy old bitch!"

Her eyes narrowed and she spat back at him, "It's working now. I can see the mark on her and I can see the mark on her son!"

"Shut up!" Nestor clutched her face in his hand and threw her backward against the brick wall of the old firehouse. He heard Minerva's voice, choked with sobs, "Nestor, no!" The madwoman staggered and went down on a knee, still grinning at Minerva. Nestor saw a stain of bright red on the faded bricks; his rage began to subside as other voices shouted in his head. The voice of his mother, saying, "We have to have pity on the crazy ones." The voice of conscience, saying *you can't attack a woman who's lost her mind for mindless words.* But he could not bear the sight of his wife being hurt so, knowing what those words meant to her, and thinking that none of this was good for her or for the child they had not yet even named.

Minerva was leaning heavily against a parked car, sliding toward the gutter, trembling, still repeating, "No, Nestor, no." A small crowd had gathered. They fixed questioning or accusing eyes on him as he lifted his wife to her feet. One man was on his cell, and Nestor realized that the police might be there soon. A soft chuckle rose from the throat of the madwoman and burst into a self-satisfied cackle. And Nestor thought, *She's succeeded. Her intentions have begun to materialize, to have real power in the world beyond her twisted imagination.*

"It's working now!" she crowed. "You can't get it off!" Minerva let out a long and forlorn cry, a bitter howl, and Nestor, powerless and ashamed, led her away.

"I'm so sorry, Minerva. We have to ignore her!"

"How does she know I have a boy?"

"She's just ranting! She's crazy!"

"No," she sobbed, "*No es una loca! Es una bruja!*"

She's not a crazy woman. She's a witch.

CHAPTER SEVEN

At home, it took Nestor a long time to comfort and calm her. In the end, he could not be sure whether she was calm or just emotionally spent. It was difficult for him to accept the fact that his wife now believed that they had been cursed by a witch. He remembered the *Mercado de las Brujas*, the Witches' Market in La Paz, where people went to buy dried llama fetuses, herbs, and tiny figurines that had power in the Aymara world of spirits, gifts and propitiations for the goddess Pachamama. The market was interesting from an anthropological point of view—with its vestiges of pagan belief and ritual—but now he had to deal with this spirit world as if it were the shadow of some reality beyond our senses.

After dinner, Minerva went into the bedroom with a book while Nestor poured a shot of Jameson over ice and went reluctantly to his desk, where he drew a set of colored folders out of the battered black bag he toted back and forth to school every day.

He had essays to correct, but he had a hard time getting himself motivated. He tried to put his mind on the writing. God, didn't anyone teach penmanship anymore? As he attempted to decipher a page covered in an awkward scrawl, the face of the madwoman floated before him, hard-eyed and hateful.

You can't get it off!

He saw the thread of blood trickling down the brick wall and shuddered with shame as he recalled his actions. How could he have allowed himself to lose his temper like that?

Once, in the city library, he'd thumbed through the *Bhagavad-Gita*, a Hindu scripture, examining its stylized and colorful illustrations. He never forgot one in particular, which depicted a man in a chariot led by five horses. On the forehead of one horse was drawn a finger, on another, an ear, on the third, an eye, and so on. The notes explained that the horses represented the five senses; the reins were the intellect, and the driver the human soul. In the illustration, the driver had lost hold of the reins and appeared to be screaming as the horses careened out of control, leading him, no doubt, toward the precipice—danger and folly. That was the image of the rage he had felt toward this witch. Rage—*rabia* in Spanish, which sounded aptly like "rabid."

He gave up on the illegible scrawl of the first paper, writing simply, "Keth, you'll have to read it to me. I can't read it." These papers were not from the Honors English class, which could be bad enough, but from his lower level classes, what one of the old teachers who'd retired used to call "Bonehead English." The assignment was to "write about a person who has had a strong influence on your character or ideas." He moved on to the next paper.

At first I went to USA I was nervous because I don't know nobody they look different from Puerto Rico. Some people were my cousins Luisito, Tito and Pablito. They are not important people but they are good cousins because I liked to play basketball with them they always played with me. Luisito showed me how to play and Tito like to hear music and trade card and spinning top. I remember in school from Puerto Rico a teacher named Mr. Berrio in gym class we were outside in the court and the kid true somthin at me then Mr. Berrio hit the kid hard. In my country people like to trade basketball card or chicken fight. And you can sell card you alway see people walking the street with card only in pina comerio. And I always like chicken fight and I remember that my grandfather gave me a chicken but my father gave it to a man I don't know why. And in pina the light always gone in all area and

I never go outside and people too because is dark. And water always gone and you need cube to get water in the truck. A hurricane was beginning and get a wood to close the window and the door I saw three time hurricane a year. And my chicken die, and they told me that is chupacabra I saw animal dead with blood because the chupacabra.

Nestor shook his head, remembering the slim, haunted Ariel Rivera. He should not be in a regular English class, but because he had been in the country more than three years, he would have to pass the state-mandated test. He had been pushed along into Nestor's English class, where he was lost most of the time, and where, with twenty-two others demanding attention, Nestor could never find the time to sit with him for even fifteen minutes.

Nestor had spent four years teaching ESL when he returned from Bolivia. Classes had been smaller, and he could spend a lot of time with students like Ariel, reviewing and practicing the strange hierarchy of grammatical structures and slowly reading aloud *Sarah, Plain and Tall* or *The Blue Bottle.* Poor Ariel. He would have to find some time to try to help him, and yet there was something suggestive and poetic in his expression. *My father gave it to a man I don't know why.* Those words summed up the boy's quiet disillusion; Nestor suspected that he had been disillusioned many times, and never knew why. God bless Mr. Berrio, who had hit the bully hard. You couldn't do that here, of course. Yes, poor Ariel, unable to quite comprehend the mystery of the motivations of those around him or how to explain his losses.

Someone had slaughtered his chicken and told him it was the *chupacabra*, the "goat sucker," that roamed the mountains, a fanged biped with egg-sized eyes and hard, curling claws; the mysterious beast that raided the animal pens for blood in the still Caribbean night, leaving fly-blown carcasses swelling in the warm morning air.

Nestor held his green pen in the air above the paper for a moment, then wrote, "Good effort. Come after school. I'll go over it with you." Right now, Ariel could not do any better, and so he wrote 70 at the top of the paper. He hoped it was high enough not to discourage him, and low enough that he could see that more was expected.

He paused and sipped the Jameson, thinking back for a moment to the days when he was a student. What joy it was to listen to Brother Sean declaiming *Catch-22*, or to read Keats' "On First Looking into Chapman's Homer" in some quiet corner of the old Pollard Library. There were stained glass windows there, too, and maybe that was his real church. In some ways he was very much like Minerva; she would never doubt her faith, but hold fast against all proofs to the contrary. He would continue to believe in the power of words to lift the soul, trying year after year to open Keats' "realms of gold" to students who were not struck with awe by Homer, but sore with boredom and eager for the bell. Nevertheless, like Minerva, he would never lose faith in the idea. Art might never fill the void left by a lost religion, but it was the next most redemptive power.

He continued to correct papers, trying to read more quickly, to think less. "Write in sentences!" he wrote, again and again. He circled the same errors he'd circled a thousand times before. Endlessly. "Divide your writing into paragraphs!" Some of the sentences were so convoluted that he hardly knew where to begin. Reading them was like trying to untangle a one-hundred-foot garden hose that had been thrown in a heap in the garage for six months.

He didn't mind helping the Ariels, anyone who cared—who had just a modicum of motivation or respect for education. He had gone through about four classes out of six when he began to feel the mental fatigue. He tucked the papers into the color-coded folders; he rested his head in his hands for a moment, rubbed his eyes, and turned out the light. The lamp was still on in their bedroom, but when he went in, he saw that Minerva was asleep with a book resting under her chin. Garcia Marquez. *El Amor en Los Tiempos del Cólera*. She had read it before, but she could not resist stories of what she called "impossible love."

He thought about a column he'd seen in the paper that day. "Love Not Enough To Make Marriage Work, Study Says." He hadn't read it. *Omnia vincit amor.* Love conquers all. He preferred to believe that, whether it was true or not. And, he thought, we believe what we want to believe.

He picked the book up carefully, replaced the bookmark, and turned off the light, thanking God that she appeared to be sleeping peacefully. Later, though, he awoke to her labored breathing. He was frightened by her panicked gasps, her breath rattling in her throat as if she were choking. He stroked her face gently and said her name several times before she opened her eyes and stared at him for a few seconds as if he were a stranger.

"*Es una brujería,*" she said.

"There is no such thing as a witch's spell, Minerva! You were having a bad dream, that's all."

"I heard her laugh and I felt her sitting on my chest so I couldn't breathe."

"That was the book on your chest. She has no power, *mi amor*! Only the power you give her."

Still only half awake, fretful in the lingering nightmare, she asked, "How did she know we went to the priest? How did she know the child was a boy?"

"You're trying to explain an irrational person rationally. That's the point. She says all kinds of things. She has no reason. Or maybe there is method to her madness. Maybe she realized that the kind of person who would be lighting a candle to the Virgin would be the kind of person who would go to a priest if someone said those horrible things to her. I don't know. But let's get real, Minerva. You're going to have a baby, our baby. She can't make you sick, but you can make yourself sick."

"So now it's my fault? You are going to blame me for what is happening?" she cried.

"Nothing is happening, goddammit! I thought you were religious! You're just superstitious! You sound like this crazy kid at school who believes in the *chupacabra*!"

"Maybe you're crazy. You don't see that there are many forces at work in the world of the spirit," she said.

"But you have the biggest and most fearsome on your side! Isn't that the whole idea? Didn't you hear the priest? I mean, if you have to be afraid of witches and curses and spells, what is the point of your faith? Is your God that useless?"

"God is not useless! You have no right to attack God! How can there be blessings on a house where God is attacked?"

"I'm not attacking God! I have no quarrel with God! I don't care one way or the other about God!"

"There! You have said it! You don't care about God! No wonder the *bruja* can do what she likes! She can walk through this godless house in spirit and crush me while I sleep!"

"You think a witch is walking through our house?" He threw his hands up, exasperated. "What did I get into? I married a fucking lunatic!" He jumped out of bed and left the bedroom, wanting, and not wanting, to say more. Finding his way to the kitchen, he opened the refrigerator and cracked a can of beer. He drank half of it in one long guzzle and put it on the table, where the candle of Our Lady of Miracles was burning low, flickering, so that light and shadows leaped about it.

She had followed him out. "If you don't believe in anything, why did you marry me in the Church? Didn't you swear—didn't our marriage begin at the altar of God?"

"Your mother would not have let us marry outside the Church."

"It's not my mother's fault! It's your fault! I am punished now, and maybe our child, with some bad thing I can't fight it because you don't have any faith in *anything*!"

"No, and I won't go through life scurrying away from curses hurled about by crazy, menopausal, schizophrenic shrews, and lighting candles made in China! I'm the captain of my soul, Minerva!"

"You're the captain of nothing! You're the fucking lunatic!" she cried. His jaw was tight, and blood pounded in his ears. He saw the candle casting its unsteady light over the room, and it became the symbol of some power that was constricting and impeding him.

He swept an arm across the table. The flame gutted before the candle struck the wall. The glass cylinder shattered, cracking the plaster, leaving a trail of spattered wax that began to run and quickly harden, like blue tears, down the wall. Minerva staggered backward, leaning on the kitchen table, her eyes wide, her hand over her mouth.

"I defy augury!" he shouted. "Let Satan send all the witches and the damned souls and the devils of hell! Come and get me!" He spread his arms as if to embrace the sinister horde. "Come on! Empty hell! I'm waiting for you, you bastards!" In the dim light that the street lamp cast between the curtains, he recalled the screaming rider at the mercy of those wild horses. He had let slip the reins once more, and was suddenly afraid of their charging hooves. What was happening to him? Nick Betsis' words came back to him. *The dangerous half.*

He heard Minerva's cry, soul-stricken and anguished, and felt her striking him on the shoulders and chest, but he didn't care. He collapsed into a chair at the kitchen table and buried his face in his hands and absorbed her blows.

"I pity the poor immigrant," Bob Dylan had sung. He would never know, Nestor thought, the pain or the hope in the immigrant's heart. Yes, both his parents were immigrants, but he lived in the familiar landscape of his birthplace, steeped in local memories and landmarks that held his ground, like anchors to his being. He understood every nuance of language, idiomatic expression, regional accent, the weight of words and the intention of inflections. He got every joke, caught the wit in every quick retort, knew the origin of arcane words, and could read the poets of his everyday language in their subtle depth.

For Minerva it was different. She had fluency in the language of her people, but was not completely at ease in the language of her adopted country. "What is the difference between *el fondo* and *el botón*?" she would ask.

"*Botón* is *button*. *Fondo* is *bottom*."

"Ah, they sound the same," she would say.

Her family was far; in Miami and in Medellín. No wonder her faith, the only familiar thing, the only root that reached the water of her source, had become her Ironsides. He had once been touched by the simplicity of her devotion. Whether or not he believed in it, it spoke to him of his own childhood, of innocence, and of the desire of good people to transcend their imperfections.

He had chosen the wrong path twice: first by attacking the mad woman and then by attacking Minerva's beliefs, however illogical they might seem.

He wished, even as he had spoken the words that hurt her, that he could reel them in, as he had reeled in the salmon from Doonbeg Bay, pull them back to live a brief life in thought, and then disappear into the region of the unuttered and forgotten. But spoken words could never be recalled. It was Minerva who had reeled them into her own mind, and there they settled into the deep waters of her psyche to swim forever. His father's voice again, quoting Yeats: *Words I have that can pierce the heart.*

In the hospital, his father had entertained the nurses with ever-flowing poetry and song. At first, none of the family realized how serious the illness was, that it was cancer, but Eamon seemed to know, because on his first day in the hospital he began to remind Nestor that he would have to take care of some of the things that he'd always done. "Make sure there's water in the boiler. There's a glass gauge, you have to clean it once in a while so you can see the water level. It should be midway up. And every couple of weeks when the radiators are running, drain the rusty water into the silver bucket by the boiler. In the fall, make sure you put weather stripping around the windows upstairs, and pour some water into those trays that hang behind the radiator. Your mother doesn't like the dry air."

In the days that followed, the doctors broke the truth to them, not the whole truth, never the whole truth, never such words as, "There is no hope."

The doom they foretold was communicated sometimes in gestures; a shrug and a downturned mouth, raised eyebrows and a tilt of the head.

What words they used were indirect—veiled words that struck like hard objects at the glass of their serenity, sometimes with an alarming crack. In the car riding back from the hospital, his mother said, "Probably your father will not tell you he loves you, but you know he does love you."

"Yes, I do know."

"Nestor, he's not going to be better. He has a bad disease. His skin it look gray. He will die soon. We have to face that." The powerful emotion of her anguish was lashed down, deep in her soul, as Zeus himself had once been restrained by the Titans. Daphne Laganis McCorley was not ready to yield her tears to Death.

A few days later, Dr. Bertram tried to operate. "We just sewed him back up again," he said. At last he let the truth flow, and it struck Nestor like a torrent out of a crashed dam. "He's full of cancer," he said. "There's nothing we can do."

Nestor locked himself in a hospital bathroom and cried hard for five minutes before he washed his face, tried to remind himself of all the virtues they'd taught him at school, and went out to face the new reality with what courage he could muster.

When Eamon McCorley knew for sure that the end was near, he began to talk a lot about Ireland. Nestor visited him early in the morning before work, and his father would tell him about the strange dreams he'd had, the red-winged angel that flew in through his window, the small black child who stood at his bedside, warning him that half of the city was on fire, or how he had seen Charlie McGrail, who directed St. Brigid's choir years ago, clear as day, standing in front of Poulnabrone, singing "Shall My Soul Pass Through Old Ireland?" He would shake his head and say, "They're all so real. It must be the drugs they're givin' me."

Uncle Colm arrived, no longer the young man in the photo on the mantel, but balding, graying, sad eyes peering through bifocals. He wore a tweed jacket and a University College Galway tie, and sat by his brother's bed for hours talking softly. On a dark afternoon in late November, Nestor overheard this conversation as he stood outside the downstairs room where his father's bed had been set up.

"Well, Eamon, you always were a very good Catholic. Said your prayers every night and went to Mass even when we were hung over. I expect you'll go to heaven express."

His father's voice was thin, as if the base had fallen out of it. "You told me once, Colm, that you think there's no such place…"

Nestor heard his uncle pause, as if it was difficult for him to say the words. "I hope there is, Eamon."

"The way I see it," his father continued, "if I was right all my life, then I'll join all the ones we loved in heaven. And if I was wrong, and there is no such place—well then that's all right. The religion helped me through this life…"

"It was a good life," Colm whispered.

"So what did I lose by believing?" Nestor heard his father's voice fading as some painkiller overtook his spirit, but before he drifted off he said, "Sure… I lost nothing at all."

He never complained, really. Only once. When the woman came to cut his hair, he caught a glimpse of his pale, drawn, haggard face in the mirror and said bitterly, "I'm an old man now."

He died at home, a few days after Christmas, and left a note for them, written in a faltering hand on piece of note paper stuck into the copy of the book he read for consolation, Thomas à Kempis' *The Imitation of Christ*. "Daphne, Nestor, Alena. I love you all so much." Below that, he had penned his farewell:

For the sails are all set, and the wind it blows fair,
He's gone and God be with him, the Rambler from Clare.

Ever the showman. Nestor had Al Landry, the monument man, incise the final line into the granite of his headstone. After the funeral and the trip to St. Patrick's Cemetery, they came to his house, the Greeks, the Irish, and everyone who'd known Eamon McCorley. They brought food, Mass cards, brandy, a three-gallon coffee urn, and their stories. Greek men in black neckties and women in black scarves offered their condolences, *"Silipiteria,"* or the simple blessing, *"Zoi se sas."* Life with you. And when they had left the house to Daphne, Nestor and Alena, and to the absence that pervaded it, Nestor took off his suit jacket and went down to the cellar to check the level of the water in the boiler.

After their fight, Minerva would not speak to him, would not even look at him. The house was thick with silence, and he felt the foundation on which he'd built this new life crumbling beneath him. It shook not only his happiness, but his confidence, his core. And he worried that it was unhealthy for Minerva, too, and for their unborn child. He felt sure that she could not keep this up much longer, and one night he went to her as she sat on their bed reading a letter. His heart welled with pity and love because he could see that she was crying.

"Minerva, let's put all this behind us. We love each other, and we're going to have a child."

"I don't want to have the child alone. But if that's what God wants. If that's what I have to endure for Him, I will do it."

"No, *mi amor.* God doesn't want that."

"How can you know what God wants?"

"I know that God is supposed to be love."

"And faith." She wiped her eyes with her fingers and looked into his face. He pulled a Kleenex from the night table and handed it to her.

"You're emotional right now. That's normal. I made it worse. I know. I'm sorry."

"Nestor, I've been talking to someone."

"What do you mean?"

"I've been talking to Father Felix. He says…"

"Wait. Wait a minute, Minerva. Father Felix?" He could not say the words that were in his heart. That had been his first mistake. But it was hard not to strike back when he felt as if furious blows were beating him into a corner. As calmly as he could manage, he asked, "All right, what does Father Felix say?"

"He says… he says that when you married me, you made me to believe that you were a Catholic…"

"I never pretended to be anything but what I am."

"At least that you were not an enemy of the Church."

"I'm not an enemy of the Church."

"He says that it's easy to see you are, and that our marriage must be… *anulado*."

"What? Annulled?"

"He says this marriage is very bad for me and for our child, and I must get out of it. That if I… if I was married to a real Catholic man, the devil would have no power over us."

"The devil! So this whining hypocrite, the one who said, 'What God has joined let no man tear asunder,' has now taken it upon himself to do exactly that?"

"He's thinking of my soul, of the soul of our child…"

"You know what I'm thinking of? I'm thinking of getting on a plane and flying down there and dragging his cassocked ass out of the rectory and kicking it all the way to Jacksonville!"

She began to sob. "There you are starting again!"

"What do you expect?" He let out a cry of frustration toward the ceiling. "I have to fight an enemy that is… *nothing*, and now some sanctimonious fool is turning my wife against me!"

"He's not a fool! He was my priest almost all my life! And now it is all these terrible things are happening and I can't ask his advice?"

"Oh, he's a great adviser." He sighed and pressed his fingers into his forehead, trying once more to quell the anger that pushed his heart against his chest. "Minerva, can't you tell him that we love each other?" He watched her for a moment, drying her eyes and putting on the resolute look, the armor of God, her chin raised as she looked away. "No, you can't," he said.

He left the apartment and walked down toward the river and across the O'Donnell Bridge, where in the darkness below the river foamed white over outcroppings of rock, churning and swirling in its timeless surge to the sea; he pressed on through the dark hours like a man pursued, northward into Dracut, past old horse farms and nearly up to Pelham. As he returned before dawn, a cruiser pulled up beside him on Mammoth Road and a Lowell cop leaned out the window and asked if he needed help. "No, I'm just walking." He felt a fool then, because tears were running down his face. "My wife is leaving me," he stammered.

The cop shook his head. "That sucks," he said, "but life will go on. And I'm telling you that from experience, pal. You'll be back on your feet." This unexpected kindness affected him so greatly that he was unable to even say thank you, and only nodded as the cruiser pulled away. When he returned home, he had just enough time to take a shower and go to work, feeling very much a shadow of the man who had been Nestor McCorley.

The dreadful silence continued, enclosing each of them in a separate and impenetrable field. Nestor was always trying to think of some way to tear the heavy curtain, some way to find the lost pathway to her heart. A few nights after the Father Felix revelation, and after Minerva had made her predictable retreat to their bedroom, he sat in his armchair. A novel by Carlos Ruiz Zafón was open in his lap, but he could not focus on it. He was recalling how his mother, at Easter, would give him a red egg in accordance with Greek tradition. She explained that the red represented the death blood of our Savior, but the egg itself represented new life. What could he give to his wife that would make her see good arising out of evil, the hope for a new life beyond this fearful emptiness she felt? Was there anything?

The book slid from his hands, and at the same moment a window in their bedroom seemed to explode. He heard, all at once, Minerva's scream, shattered glass falling to the floor and the thud of something hard striking the oaken floorboards and rolling across them. He shot a glance into the bedroom as he ran toward the stairs; a rock lay amid shards of glass on the hardwood.

"Son of a bitch!" he cried as he shot down the stairs and out the front door. He saw no one, but as he stood for a moment listening, he heard what sounded like the rattle of the chain-link fence in the neighboring yard, and he ran in that direction, up the long driveway that fronted a row of condos. At the end he saw a figure, a man who had just landed on the other side of the fence and was heading down the hill toward Broadway—the parking lot at UMass Lowell. Nestor reached the fence and leaped at it, landing halfway up and scrambling to the top and over. He sprinted toward Broadway, and from the rise above the street caught sight of the man in the middle of the parking lot, running between cars.

"You'd better run you son of a bitch!" he shouted as he set off after him. Once Nestor was among the cars it was difficult to see the man, but he heard an engine start up somewhere in the lot, and the chirp of tires.

Nestor knew that the man could not get back out through the Wilder Street entrance; the gate only rose for incoming traffic. The bastard would have to exit onto Broadway, and then Nestor would have him, or at least have a look at his face and his plate number. He knew who he thought it was, but he wanted to be sure. He ran to the exit gate and waited there, but after a few seconds he heard a revving engine and a loud, splintering, crack. He'd broken out through the entrance gate. A minute later, Nestor arrived at the Wilder Street entrance. All that was left of the gate was a foot or so of lumber. The rest lay splintered on the ground.

A couple of Asian kids with skateboards were standing nearby. "You guys see what kind of car just broke this gate?"

"We din' see nothin'."

Acre kids aren't stupid, Nestor thought. "I don't want to know your names and I'll never mention I talked to you." He reached into his pocket. "All I have on me is a ten. What kind of a car was it?"

The taller of the two, in a Bob Marley Rasta knit hat, said, "You tryna kill that guy or sump'n?"

"Hell no, do I look like a killer? I may bust his nose. Bastard smashed my window."

Rasta boy looked at the other, shrugged, and approached. He took the ten and said, "It wasn't no car. It was a Ford pickup, red, not new, kinda beat up."

"Thanks, pal."

When Nestor returned to the apartment, Minerva was gone, as he knew she would be. A note on the kitchen table said, "I cannot stay here. I'm going to Marina's." He looked at her handwriting and remembered how once he'd been thrilled to see it on the back of an envelope in his mailbox. Now, the turn of every letter twisted his heart.

A message taped to the rock said, "HELL IS WAITING FOR YOU." Beautiful. Minerva must have fallen to pieces. He grabbed his car keys and left, carrying the rock. A couple of times he had given Ian Casey a ride home after track practice when he missed the bus. Nestor crossed the O'Donnell Bridge and drove along the VFW Highway to the Centralville section of the city. He turned onto Bridge Street and climbed the steep back of Christian Hill toward Beacon Street. It took him a few minutes, but he found the house.

A faded red Ford pickup was parked in the driveway. He pulled over a few doors down and walked back, carrying the rock. He put a hand on the truck's hood; the engine was still warm. He was about to launch the rock through the lit front window when he recalled that Ian had two younger sisters. And, of course, a mother, who, he reminded himself, had been through her own hell when her boy had fallen dead on the track in the flower of his youth. He set the rock on the hood of the truck in front of the driver's seat and returned to his car.

The next day he came home from work to find that Minerva's things were gone. She had left another note. "I will stay with my sister. When is born the baby I will call so you can see him, but I cannot stay here. I cannot live with you. *Lo siento.* Minerva."

I cannot live with you. Just like that. *Lo siento.* I'm sorry. One day they love you—the next they hate you because of a stupid argument, fantasies, bats in the attic, a crazy bitch, a fool with a rock. Maybe the old Irish ballad was right. *The devil take the women for they always lie so easy.*

His cell rolled out the sad organ notes of "A Whiter Shade of Pale." It was Eddie Saitz. "Nestor! My man! Can you come down and read for the part of Hamlet at the Old Court tonight?"

"Hamlet? Jesus, uh, yes I will." Maybe it would take his mind away from the life in which he was trapped.

"You OK?"

"Wife problems."

"Cah-mahn! Everyone has those! I'll see you at 8. Get there about 7:45. Ann Whitmore will be there. Wellington is going to measure the space for lighting and see what he can do about scrims and gobos."

"What's a gobo?"

"He produces these cutouts that he puts over the lights to project different images. Dude, with the right lighting and Wellington's gobos, that little stage will become the tower of fucking Elsinore. You'll hear the sound of waves crashing against the cliffs below! It'll be great!"

"OK."

"Cah-mahn! Cheer up. She'll get over it. They almost always do! The fucking Prince of Denmark, baby! Focus!"

CHAPTER EIGHT

F*ocus*. Not on Hamlet, but on his job. The job he was paid to do, and that he had always taken pride in doing well. A metallic crackle broke in on his thoughts, followed by the daily command, always delivered in exactly the same tedious tone over the scores of loudspeakers throughout the all the rooms and hallways of the vast building: "All students report to homeroom. All students report to homeroom immediately."

"Immediately" was understood by the students to mean within the next ten minutes or so. He heard the platoons of adolescents marching up and down the corridor outside his door and tried to shake off the weariness it produced in him today. His mind was not here, where it had to be. It was on his wife, or his ex-wife, whatever she really was now, and the son they would have. If only he could spend a week or so with her, quietly, away somewhere, where she could see the good husband he could be, the good father he was bound to be, but he knew such hopes were futile.

The witch insanity and Minerva's departure had left him spent, empty in some deep place, feeling, as an old friend used to say, that there was "a hole in his aura." Before the day was over he would teach three double periods of English, about ninety minutes each, along with a half hour of duty monitoring the "in-house suspension" room.

The students milled in. They pressed their problems on him. *Mister I need a pass to pay my senior dues. I need my coat in my locker my homework is in it. I gotta get a temporary ID. Mister I gotta see the nurse.* "Sit down and let me take attendance," he said. He wrote some passes while bus evacuation procedures were reviewed; the bells rang again, and they shuffled out. Soon he heard their raucous voices in the corridor, and new students began to fill his room for first period.

Later, when the bell sounded for his prep period, he left his room and passed quickly along the vast corridors, cinder block tunnels punctuated with metal doors. He descended the concrete steps to the cafeteria for a coffee. It was closed. The sign said that the staff was preparing for the annual Scholarship Dinner, a gala affair designed to raise money for deserving students. Nestor's head was throbbing.

Where could he get a coffee? He decided to do something he'd never done before; technically, a teacher was supposed to have permission to leave the campus, but by the time he found Emma Bergeron and explained the situation, he'd lose fifteen minutes. He felt for his keys in his suit coat pocket and passed out through a little-used exit, inhaling the spring air gratefully, like a deep diver breaking the surface.

He rode along the river for a few minutes to a Portuguese bakery near the Pawtucket Bridge, where he bought a fresh roll and a coffee to go. On the ride back up the boulevard, he flicked on the car radio, which was tuned to "Jazz in the Morning" on the local university radio station. The DJ sounded like an old-timer, one who remembered the jazz classics he spun when they were new. "And now," he said with unfeigned enthusiasm, "Ella Fitzgerald, from her 1974 *Ella in London* recording, singing, 'There Will Never Be Another You.'"

He tore his handkerchief from his pocket and, pushing back his sunglasses, wiped at his eyes. *Never.* As he approached the light at the Rourke Bridge, he considered pulling over to Boomer's and knocking back a shot of Jamie, but drinking while on the clock wasn't his style. Not yet. That would be the beginning of a long, steep slide. *Pull yourself together, man.* Instead, he took a left at the light and turned into the parking lot at the river boathouse.

He sat on a bench and sipped his coffee, watching the river move toward the Pawtucket Falls as it wound its way to the sea. The expanse of gently flowing water calmed him. He remembered the verse that Jack Mahoney, an old Irish friend of his father's, used to recite.

The bridle is no burden to the prancing steed
Nor is wool to the fleecy breed
The water with ease bears the floating kind
And Nature does not aggravate the mind.

He finished his coffee, and a few minutes later, feeling calmer, headed back to the school. Bells rang, corridors filled, and it was time for in-house suspension duty, where he was to sit for twenty-five minutes with students who'd been caught smoking, or told some teacher to go fuck herself, sucker-punched someone, downloaded pornography onto a school computer, or any of the other schoolhouse crimes that would land them in the cramped, windowless room for a day or two or three. They sat in sullen silence throughout the day, heedless of the sounding bells, outside the orbit of the rest of the school. If they claimed to have no work, they were given the school rule book to copy or class texts to study. They were taken out at set intervals to the bathroom. The female hall monitor took the girls; Mr. Broulette, the in-house supervisor, took the boys. Lunch was brought to them. Some faces changed, but certain ones always returned. It was good practice for jail, which was where some of them were headed, Nestor thought.

Broulette sat with these kids day in and day out, his voice booming over the bowed heads. "You have nothing to do, José? You want me to find something for you to do? Jared, get your head off the desk."

Broulette had a tough job, but he did it well. He had to be a bit of a Bligh, because if the pack in that room sensed weakness you'd be a goner. But Broulette had a heart, even if he didn't wear it on his sleeve. And often, when Nestor opened the door at 10:20 for his stint, he'd hear him helping some kid with his homework, or talking to him about the choices he'd made, and giving him some advice in avuncular tones. Nestor respected him for that, because it was a balancing act, and Broulette had figured out how to walk the line.

Still, every day when Nestor came in, Broulette would rise and say, in the same voice he used to announce school football games from the booth above the nearby field, "All right, Mr. McCorley. I'll be back shortly. Everyone has work to do. Anyone gives you one iota of crap, you let me know and I will take care of it. Thank you."

When Broulette was gone, some of the students put their heads down on the desks, but Nestor never bothered them. Let sleeping dogs lie. This was their break, too. And it wasn't a bad duty, really. He generally corrected papers, but today he picked up the *Boston Herald* that was lying across Broulette's bag, and stared at it tiredly.

"I gotta go to the bathroom." He looked up at a girl, slim and pale, lost in baggie black pants, her lips blackened and her face pierced with metal studs.

"When Mr. Broulette gets back you can go."

"I'm gonna pee in my pants."

"You'll make it." If they thought they could get out while Broulette was on break, they'd spend a half hour roaming the building or smoking butts and then concoct some story that involved stomach aches or diarrhea, or a long conversation with some teacher whose name they didn't know. Broulette had a bathroom system, and they got regular breaks. Nestor didn't want to let anyone go anywhere unless it was an emergency. He'd dealt with high-schoolers long enough to know that this was no emergency. The girl had waited until Broulette was out of the room to play her card.

When he began teaching high school ten years earlier, he was always giving kids the benefit of the doubt. He found it difficult to believe that a student would lie brazenly to his face. He remembered the girl, a senior, who told him her father had died, and that was why she'd been absent so much. Like a fool, he'd been ready to change her grade from failing to passing with little makeup work. And when he called the house to express his condolences, her mother said, "Her father is sitting right here watching *Family Feud*."

There were the kids he surprised in the bathroom with clouds of smoke rising from the stalls as their cigarettes hissed into the toilets. "We weren't smoking." It was the O.J. syndrome. You never admitted that you were guilty. Never.

He turned the pages of the *Herald* slowly, stopping to gaze over the photos of some American soldiers crouched with M-16s beside a stone wall in a desert landscape. *Not much older than these kids*, he thought. There had already been one alumnus of the school killed in Iraq. How do you go, in just a couple of years, from bathroom passes and hiding from Mr. Keough to shootouts with martyr brigades?

He heard chair legs scraping against the floor. Several of the students had jumped up, and were shouting, "What the fuck?" They grabbed their backpacks and hauled them off the floor, pointing under the desk of the girl with the black lipstick, where a puddle was slowly spreading. "Yo, thass nasty!"

"I tol' the fuckin' guy I had to pee!" she declared. She looked at him with a hint of a smile, and it was almost as if he could read the words *fuck you* written across her forehead.

"Shee-it!" someone cried, and they laughed like hyenas. What was it Holden Caulfield had said, that whenever you saw a bunch of people laughing like hyenas, you could bet that it was something that was not funny. The girl was not laughing. He knew that mentally she was preparing her defense; no, not her defense, her attack on him. And no one could ever prove that she didn't have to pee so badly that she went in her pants. He foresaw advocates, then maybe lawyers. She was a victim, and so she would win.

He could never prove that she was nothing but a manipulating liar, but for now he thought quickly what his next move would be. At the same time, listening to the half-stifled laughter, watching the leering eyes, and the smirk on the girl's face, he felt the anger, the dangerous half stirring, and he forced it down, because he knew that in the mental state he was in, anger was liable to explode into rage, and he could easily say something he would regret, and that way, too, she would win. What the hell did it matter anyway? Why get into—the phrase "pissing contest" came to mind—with a girl who had no class, no clue, and no self-respect. Nothing but issues, and a need to drag him into them.

He stood and picked up the phone, punching the extension of Dave Keough, the dean of discipline. He got the recording, but he pretended to have the dean, and said aloud, "Mr. Keough? Mr. McCorley. I'm sending down a girl who just had an accident." The students laughed louder, bent double and crying, "Oh, sheeit!"

"An accident! You know! No, I'm not calling from child care. I'm down in in-house. OK, I'll send her down."

Her name was written on the daily seating plan on Broulette's desk. Angela Purtel, and beside it: "three days—bullying." He scribbled a blue slip, wrote on the bottom "offensive behavior" and held it out to the girl, saying, "Report to the office. See Dean Keough."

"It's not my fault," she said.

"Of course not. You're a victim. That's why you're in in-house in the first place. Someone is picking on you."

"I told you I had to pee!"

"Go to the office now!"

She addressed the other students. "Didn't I tell the fuckin' guy I had to pee?"

He could feel the blood pounding in his head, but he would not be drawn into an argument with a sixteen-year-old girl about her bladder.

I have a son now who depends on me; that's all that matters.

"Go!" He followed her into the corridor and said, "I see you're in here for bullying, Angela. You seem to enjoy making other people miserable. You're not going to bully me. You can keep piling up your detentions, your in-houses, your suspensions. I don't know what you get out of it, but it doesn't affect me."

She gave him a smirk, and waved the blue slip at him with her middle finger raised as she turned and sauntered off—as if the whole scene had bored her.

He went back into the room to settle them down. So much for sleeping dogs. "The show is over. I'll be taking names and adding days. Never mind the puddle of urine—sit up and get a book out. If you don't have one, I'll get you one. Mr. Broulette has every textbook used in this school in that bookcase!"

The room was quiet again, though some of the students still laughed quietly behind their hands, shaking their heads. Broulette came back with a coffee in hand and spotted the vacant seat and the desks of the students nearby pushed away from it. "Any problems, Mr. McCorley?" His tone suggested that someone was going to pay if there had been.

Before he could answer, the phone rang, and Broulette picked it up and said, "Yes, he's still here. Right." He hung up the phone and said, "Dean Keough wants to see you." He stepped into the hallway with Nestor and asked, "Angela?"

"Yeah, she pissed in her pants."

"She's a piece of work. I'll call Ricky and tell him to bring a bucket."

"Wish we could make her mop it up."

"And violate her civil rights? I'm shocked, Mr. McCorley."

"See you tomorrow."

He stopped by his class and asked Mr. Kent in the class next door to keep an eye on his students if he wasn't back before the bell rang, then he ran down to the dean's office. He knocked on the door and heard Keough's voice, deep and official, "Come in." The girl was in tears, looking very much the distressed maiden now.

Mr. Keough, a big Irishman with curling hair and a grandiose mustache, asked, "Mr. McCorley, could you explain to me what happened down there this morning?"

"Angela told me she wanted to go to the bathroom. I told her that she should wait until Mr. Broulette got back."

"Which is what I've asked you to do. Thank you, Mr. McCorley. Go on."

"She said she was going to pee in her pants. I told her I was sure she could wait a few minutes until Mr. Broulette returned."

"Which I am sure she could have. Go on."

He paused while the girl had a loud fit of blubbering, and continued. "About thirty seconds later, a commotion ensued in the room, when the students alerted me to the fact that Angela had urinated in her pants."

"Yes, and you sent her to me, as you should have. Anything else?"

"Yes, Dean Keough. She referred to me as 'the fucking guy' on the way out."

"A serious lack of respect, Mr. McCorley." He nodded gravely and the great mustache nearly encircled his pursed lips.

"That's a lie! What really happened was…"

"Whoa! Whoa! Wait a minute, Angela! I don't need you to tell me what happened. Mr. McCorley just told me what happened. He's been here in this school, helping kids like you for ten years, without a single complaint against him in all that time. You've been here for two years, and your discipline folder takes up half my goddamn drawer! Do you really think I need you to correct his version of the story?"

He picked up the phone and punched an extension. "Mr. Broulette. What time did these kids go for bathroom break? Nine thirty-five. And did Angela go with Ms. Dawson at that time? She did. Thank you, Mr. Broulette."

As Keough hung up, Nestor heard the bell. "Broulette took the boys at 9:20, and Ms. Dawson took the girls at 9:35. What time does your duty start, Mr. McCorley?"

"It starts at 10:02 and ends at 10:27."

"Miss Purtel, you've been in in-house…" He picked up the folder on his desk and slipped his glasses on. "Thirty… let me see, twenty-seven days this year. I believe you know the bathroom drill. Do you have any medical problem we don't know about?"

"No," she said. Her tears had been ineffective, and they were drying up like last night's rain on a July morning.

"I have a class, Mr. Keough." Nestor stood up, gazing at the photos on the wall of a different Keough, before a Christmas tree with his daughters and wife. At a golf tournament with some teachers and a school committee member.

"Thank you, you may go, Mr. McCorley. We won't be needing you further."

As Nestor opened the door, he heard the girl, slouched in the chair to his left, say, "Just because he's been here for ten years doesn't mean he can grab my ass."

He closed the door and whirled on the girl. "What did you say you little fucking liar—"

"Mr. McCorley! Calm down!" Keough was on his feet, arms spread, pushing the air repeatedly as if in this way he could dissipate Nestor's anger.

"Calm down? Did you hear what she said?"

"Let me handle this, Mr. McCorley." He took a deep breath, one hand rubbing his temple. "Miss Purtel, that is a serious accusation. You had better think very hard before you throw something like that out there."

"He followed me out of the room and he said, 'Are your pants wet?' and he felt my ass!"

Dean Keough, seeing a small problem that had just become a big problem, looked suddenly weary. As calmly as he could, Nestor said, "I followed her out of the room to speak to her briefly about her behavior."

"Naturally," Keough said.

"I never have, nor would I ever touch a student inappropriately, and I'm at a loss to understand why she would..."

Angela Purtel laughed out loud at this and rolled her eyes. "Well, you grabbed my ass. I'd call *that* inappropriate."

"Dean Keough," Nestor said, "I'm leaving before I get very upset. The girl is a liar."

"A *fucking* liar, right? That's how *appropriate* he is."

"I'm going back to class."

"Angela," the dean said, shaking his head sadly, "wouldn't you like to take back this accusation before this thing…"

"Why should I take it back? It's true."

The big Irishman followed Nestor out and whispered, "I know it's bull-shit, Nestor, but I'm going to have to send her up to guidance to file a…"

"I know, and people who don't know me better may think it's true. Dave, in the corridor I told her that she was not going to get to me. So she thought of something that *would* get to me."

"It'll be fine, but you have to keep your cool."

"Aren't there any cameras down there?"

He shook his head. "No, not in that corridor."

"I don't need this right now, Dave. I mean, you never need something like this."

"Don't worry about it. The truth will come out."

"Jesus, I hope you're right." He walked up the stairs and along the dismal corridor, feeling well and truly cursed. Why would she say such a thing? And he knew that a lot of people would probably conclude that where there was smoke, there was fire.

CHAPTER NINE

L ate in the afternoon he drove through the city with no particular destination in mind, just trying to put off his return to the empty apartment. Once again, Shakespeare was apt: *When sorrows come, they come not single spies, but in battalions.* He was trying to put so much out of his mind: his wife, now his job. What would be left? He thought he'd go have a beer at the Worthen, listen to some loud songs on the jukebox and try to relax. As he drove along Broadway, though, he had another thought, and banged a left onto Quincy, heading down the old cobbled street toward St. Brigid's Rectory.

Mrs. Riordan, an older woman in a dress that looked like it was patterned after some wallpaper from the forties, opened the door. Her face was washed of color, pale and time-worn. "Is Father Leahy available, Mrs. Riordan? Does he have a minute?"

"I'm sure he'll make a minute for you. Come in, Nestor." She knew him from the days when she sang in the choir with his father. There was nothing he enjoyed more as a little boy than to follow his father up into the loft and watch the Mass from that airy perch. Máire Riordan was from Youghal Harbor in Cork, one of the few Irish immigrants left from the days when the parish had been home to so many from "the oul' sod."

"How are you, Mrs. Riordan?"

"Oh, I'm keeping well enough. I plod along like the old gray mare. And how's your mother this weather?"

"She's a trooper. You know, she never complains."

"It doesn't do a bit of good, does it? We all miss your father somethin' terrible, though. Such a lovely man. And his voice was—well, I often said to him, 'Eamon you could have been a professional!' Not like yours truly! Ah, it's been said before but it's true, Nestor, his like won't be seen again."

Nestor felt his eyes begin to sting as she spoke of his father, and he was relieved when she turned to usher him along the hallway. It was all dark mahogany and faded wallpaper and gloomy sacred artifacts. Long dead saints and founders of the order, expressionless, stared out from under glass. A heavy banister rose along the stairs to the forbidding and lonely rooms. She opened a door and he stepped into an office. There were well-stocked bookshelves on either side of a fireplace. Wing chairs, flanking a glass coffee table, were angled toward the hearth. The scene reminded him of a room where Watson might confer with Holmes at 221B Baker Street. "Please have a seat while I get the head honcho. I'm just after putting the kettle on, and I'll bring yiz tea, so." She closed the door behind her.

He began to peruse the books that lined the shelves. *The Doctrine of Grace, Sacraments, How Catholics Pray, Meditations on the Cross.* There was something sterile and depressing in all of these meanderings through the desiccated paths of medieval doctrine. You can experience a mystery; you can't explain a mystery. He imagined these solitary scholars with initials like S.J. and O.M.I. after their names writing their treatises in spartan, musty rooms like those he could picture upstairs, where the Beatles' Father McKenzie might be writing a sermon that no one would ever hear.

Amid these unreadable works, he saw *The Poems of John Greenleaf Whittier*, and thought that he might find something human there, even if it was out of style. He slipped the book out and sat in one of the wing chairs. He browsed the titles in the table of contents, "Snow-Bound: A Winter Idyl," "The Eternal Goodness," "The Changeling."

A page was marked with a yellowed envelope addressed to some long-departed priest: "The Wreck of Rivermouth." He scanned the introduction to the old ballad, which mentioned local coastal landmarks, places that Nestor had often visited: Hampton Beach, Boar's Head, Rye and Star Island among the Isles of Shoals. He thought it strange that he had opened to this work, since it dealt with the story of Goody Cole, who in the 1600s put a curse on a fishing vessel as it sailed out of Hampton River. When it was caught in a squall and went down with all hands, she was whipped and imprisoned.

> *"Fie on the witch!" cried a merry girl,*
> *As they rounded the point where Goody Cole*
> *Sat by her door with her wheel atwirl,*
> *A bent and blear-eyed poor old soul.*
> *"Oho!" she muttered, "ye're brave to-day!*
> *But I hear the little waves laugh and say,*
> *'The broth will be cold that waits at home;*
> *For it's one to go, but another to come!'"*
> *"She's cursed," said the skipper; "speak her fair:*
> *I'm scary always to see her shake*
> *Her wicked head, with its wild gray hair,*
> *And nose like a hawk, and eyes like a snake."*
> *But merrily still, with laugh and shout,*
> *From Hampton River the boat sailed out,*
> *Till the huts and the flakes on Star seemed nigh,*
> *And they lost the scent of the pines of Rye.*

He finished the poem and shut the book, inhaling its dusty breath. He heard, but could not comprehend, a low conversation between Father Leahy and the housekeeper, while the words "She's cursed" reverberated within him like a bell rung in an empty room. He put the book down on a side table and rose as the burly priest entered and took his hand in his stone mason's grip. "You got my message?" the priest asked.

Nestor was surprised. "No, I just decided to stop by."

"Hmmm." Father Leahy took a seat and extended an arm for Nestor to do the same. "Yes, well, I had left a message on your home phone earlier."

"About?"

"A couple of things." The priest looked tired. He paused and leaned over in his chair, his elbows on his knees, rubbing his eyes with his fingertips. "I don't know how to say this to you, Nestor. It's ugly."

"Fire away. I've heard a lot of ugly things lately. And said a few myself. You know what happened between Minerva and me?"

"Yes, in part. Regarding Minerva, all I can say is that when people see the world in terms of good and evil, you can't say things that put you on the side of evil."

"You know that her priest in Florida told her that our marriage was a fraud and that she should try to have it annulled?"

He sighed dismally. "Yes, I told her that I thought he was wrong about that."

"Thank you."

"Nestor, I think she'll come around, or I thought she would come around."

"You thought? What happened?"

"It's the woman. The crazy woman."

"Oh, God. What about her?"

They heard footsteps and a rattling of cups and saucers as, Nestor guessed, Mrs. Riordan tried to balance the tray in one hand and open the door with the other. He sprang up and opened it. Mrs. Riordan came in with a silver tray, on which were two cups, a china teapot, a creamer, a sugar bowl and spoons.

She set it down on the coffee table. "Lovely, Mrs. Riordan, thank you," the priest said, but when she'd left, he whispered, "She makes me enough tea every week to fill a swimming pool. I've never had the heart to tell her I'd just prefer a cup or two of coffee. But she's a highly intelligent woman, and I always value her advice. We have long talks, and she always makes sense." He poured the tea and continued. "The day after I was at your apartment, Nestor, I got a call from Father Murray, the pastor at St. Patrick's in Lawrence, a close friend of mine. A woman fitting this madwoman's description showed up down there. There's a statue of the Virgin Mary beside the rectory. The woman was striking it in…" He used the Spanish words for some reason, spreading his hands over his own stomach, "*en el vientre,* with a rock."

"Trying to strike at her womb?"

"So it would seem. Anyway, Murray went out to stop her. She shouted at him, 'You tell Father Leahy that he can't take my curse off that…" The priest paused, shaking his head in disgust. "… off that bitch." He put his teacup down and ran a hand over his graying beard. "She had knowledge, Nestor. I don't know how she had it."

"Who knows, Father, who knows? But why do we care? I'm just trying to forget the crazy old harridan."

"It's just that I think you really need to steel yourself in spiritual armor, Nestor. That may not make sense to you, but… especially now that you've tried to defy this power without God on your side. In fact, you've banished God from the game."

Nestor was looking out the window, across the parking lot, toward the two-story red brick school where the sisters, some of the sisters, had filled him with terrifying accounts of the tortures of hell, and the cunning of the serpent. A vague fear of all that, he knew, would always remain in some recess of his mind and cower his spirit. That was why he had never wanted to see *The Exorcist*; he had no desire to awaken the old monsters that slept below conscious thought.

He shook off these sentiments, reminding himself that he was no longer a boy; he had chosen to be a man of reason and not a man of superstition. "Father, when you talk like this, it reminds me of people who thought, not long ago, that the stars were pinpricks in the blanket of night. It's crazy. I just won't allow myself to be intimidated by… a witch."

Father Leahy blew an exasperated breath. "Nestor, she said to Father Murray, 'Tell Leahy to go back to New York to his drugs and his whores!'"

"You told me you didn't make a secret of your past."

"She said that Thomas is in purgatory! Thomas is... was my brother, Nestor! He died two years ago in New York. Now how did she know that?"

He felt something sinking, dropping like a stone falling through some dark lake within him at the priest's words, and the two sat in silence for a moment. Finally the priest said, "I'm not afraid for me, Nestor, nor for Minerva or your child. I'm afraid for *you*. Arm yourself, my friend, with the light and the truth. Put on Christ's armor." He reached out to the younger man, who was shaking his head and looking toward the coal-stained hearth, and gripped his forearm. "Listen to me. Didn't you tell me that you would choose me to fight with the forces of darkness?"

"I meant that metaphorically."

"This is no metaphor, Nestor. This is war."

"I can't see it."

"Then you're blind."

Nestor recalled Raftery, the blind Irish harper, *with sightless eyes and undistracted calm*. He essayed a half smile and said, "Well then, I'll just grope my way to the exit."

The priest did not smile. "When darkness falls, you need the light of the true faith."

"There's also the light of reason, Father. Anyway, I'm getting used to the dark."

The priest sat up, letting go of Nestor's arm as though he might catch this virus of faithlessness. "Say no more, please. I will pray for you. That's all I can do. I feel you harbor some deep resentment toward the Church. I don't know why."

Nestor was silent. The priest tugged at his Roman collar and cleared his throat. "When is the baby due?" he asked.

"In a couple of weeks. Minerva says she'll call me and let me know, like I'm some damned inconvenient uncle."

The priest wrung his hands earnestly. "In times of crisis, people of faith look to religion as the glue that holds them together. Differences in beliefs at those times become more critical—magnified."

"Father, I respect Minerva's beliefs, and yours. Why can't anyone respect mine? I'm a good person. But I didn't sign up for this. I just want to live my life as well as I can, and I'll take whatever comes when I die. Religion has produced great things, the architecture, the art, the music, the icons, the Christian philosophy of brotherhood… but I won't be at the mercy of curses and candles and sanctified salt. Yes, I lost my temper with Minerva. But I'm not *evil*."

The priest leaned forward once more and spoke softly, his tone imploring. "The art, the architecture, the music—these things are nothing if you don't *believe*…"

"What? That I'll be tortured in some fiery hole for eternity because I'm disposed toward reason, which brought us science?"

"Science *describes*, Nestor, but it doesn't *explain*. There are other ways of knowing, and another world to know."

Nestor sighed. He remembered the words of Henry Thoreau. "One world at a time, Father." He felt, as he often did with Minerva, somehow mean in rejecting the beautiful philosophy that she and this good man professed. "Look, I understand the need for the faith. I respect it. Just don't disrespect me because I don't share it."

Father Leahy shook his head, the movement and the graying beard lending gravity to his words. "You respect the faith, and I believe sometimes you feel its truth, and deny it."

"I feel the attraction of its simplicity. I feel its beauty. I never feel its truth. I wish I did. Life would be much easier." He looked directly at the priest so that he would know he was speaking sincerely. "I'm sorry, Father. That's what I feel. Does that make me bad?"

"Of course not, but then why did you marry Minerva? Didn't you know this would present a conflict?"

"I married Minerva because I love her. She loved me. I thought that would be enough. She knew I was not a true believer."

"Nestor, she did not know you were a mocker. That you harbored an animus against the faith."

"I told you I lost my temper. For that I'm sorry. I don't hate the faith. It's part of what made me. I hate the situation that we've gotten into, this artificial war with some unseen world. It's ridiculous."

"You can't see the wind, Nestor, nor the power of love, nor feel the turning of the earth, but all of these things are all real, not ridiculous."

"And curses are real?"

"As real as blessings, and I bless every day."

Nestor picked up the book of Whittier's poems and pushed it into the gap on the shelf. "When you believe in witches and curses, you end up flogging and hanging crazy old women. To walk in a faith that's blind is still to walk in darkness." He remembered the streak of blood on the bricks as the madwoman sank to the sidewalk, and felt the shame burn again. How had he ever given her words that much power? Only because Minerva had. If he saw her again, he would try to apologize, no matter what she said, to clear his conscience, which was real, and existed without heaven or hell.

Father Leahy stood and extended a hand. "We're on different frequencies, Nestor. I have to go, but I hope you won't mind if I say God bless you." He made the sign of the cross in the air before him, and kissed the crucifix that hung from his neck.

"Not at all, Father. And if I can't bless you, accept my sincere good will and my wishes for your health and happiness."

"That's what a blessing is, Nestor. The only difference is that I call God to witness it."

That night, as he lay on the couch, examining the familiar cracks in the plaster ceiling, the priest's words came back to him. *She didn't know that you harbored an animus against the faith.* He didn't, did he? In spite of Sister St. Michael, and the other one, Sister Theresa. What a sad case she was—pathetic, really. There was a woman who must have had reason to resent the Church.

In the seventh grade, the two coed classes that had existed since Nestor McCorley was in first grade at St. Brigid's were regrouped by gender. All the boys went into 7A, and all the girls into 7B. The sexes were separated by a door of rich-grained solid oak, under which the girls immediately began to slip notes, announced by two quick knocks, whenever the sisters from the adjoining rooms were conversing in the hallway. When Nestor asked why the boys and girls had been separated, Sister Cecile said simply, "Hormones." From her tone of voice, he gathered that hormones were highly suspect things.

Sister Cecile taught the boys; she had a face like a bulldog. Sister Theresa taught the girls; she was young and had a pretty face. The cross that hung from her waist on a length of beads swung back and forth across her legs when she walked. Nestor was not the only boy who had wondered what she would look like without her veil, and Roger Shea had said as she passed, "She don't walk like a nun," and swore that she "swung it" even more for Maurice, the janitor. The girls said she was strict, but Nestor had spent a couple of afternoons painting scenery with her for the Christmas play last year, and they had talked together easily and laughed a few times, too.

In late October, last-minute preparations were underway for Parents' Night, and both seventh-grade teachers took some students from each class to help set up the stage and practice the songs they would sing that evening in the school hall as a preview of the Fall Talent Show. In the meantime, the other students were left with a pile of rags and a wash bucket and told to clean their desks, wash the blackboard, and organize the reading books.

There was some competition among the two groups of boys who had suddenly been thrown together after six years, since each class had its own leaders, its wise guys, and its outcasts. They knew each other, but they had mixed very little, even at recess, in previous years. Now that they'd been left alone for the first time, Ned Twining was attempting to show the new, larger group that he was still the most audacious. He went to the blackboard and picked up a piece of chalk. He addressed himself to a new boy named Manning who had arrived at the school a week earlier from Ohio and appeared somewhat of a rustic to the other boys.

"Manning!" Twining said. "Eyes up here, boy! Let me explain what you need to know. He drew what looked like two big U's on the board. "These are tits."

The class laughed, a sort of choking laughter; they knew enough to keep their noise down. "I know what tits are," Manning said in a professorial tone, pushing his black-framed glasses farther up the bridge of his nose.

"And this, Manning," Twining continued, drawing what looked like a Popsicle above a rounded W, "is a dick!" Nestor McCorley laughed to himself, admiring the daring of Ned Twining, who wasn't even checking to see if Sister Cecile was about to return, though Mike Flynn was keeping a lookout.

The oaken door between the rooms opened, and Vera Noonan, Dolores Price and Sheila Greene tumbled in; they moved in a loose and bouncing circle.

"Are you the *teacha*, Neddy?" Sheila called out.

"I was just explaining the facts of life to Manning," Twining said to the girls. "He's from O-HI-o."

"I already know the facts of life," Manning insisted doggedly, but Twining continued his lesson, drawing a circular face, topped with triangular ears, and sprouting long whiskers. "Here—we have a pussy, Manning. Soft and warm and fun to pet."

At this the boys forgot themselves and laughed loudly while the girls' circle tightened; they spoke with their hands over their mouths, their hair falling about their faces, choking out incomprehensible phrases amid a swelling tide of giggles. Someone threw a rag out of the other room that struck Dolores Price in the head, and they all giggled some more while Dolores hurled it toward Ned, who now drew a large, curvy ass on the board and said, "This here is what we call *the backyard*, Manning."

There was a photo portrait of Mother Teresa taped to the blackboard, her saintly head bowed in prayer. Vera Noonan ran up and picked a piece of chalk out of the tray. She began writing something under the photo of the holy woman. She stood aside to show the girls her work when Flynnie, from his post at the door, called out, "Sista's comin'!" The girls flew out of the room, the oaken door closing on ghostly hinges behind them while Ned Twining swiped his illustrations clean. All began to busy themselves about their desks when Nestor spotted the crude message that Vera Noonan had scrawled under Mother Teresa's portrait. Hearing the footsteps echoing along the hallway, he bolted toward the board. The eraser was in his raised hand when he heard the voice.

It was Sister Theresa. "Stop! Nestor McCorley?"

He turned, trying hopelessly to block the chalked letters. "Yes, Sister?"

"What are you doing, Nestor?" She was approaching, but not directly. She circled to his left, like a wolf, detecting not blood, but shame. He could not keep moving to block out what was written there. She would know. She knew. Their former, pleasant association made Nestor more embarrassed, as if he had somehow fooled her before and now she could see his true nature.

In the ensuing silence, all eyes focused on the dynamic triad—the boy, the sister, and the portrait of Mother Teresa, below which were written the words: "NEVER HAD IT. NEVER WILL."

"I was going to clean the board, Sister."

She drew closer, so that she stood between him and the class, her back to the rest of the boys. There was something in her eyes that disconcerted him—not the cold, hard stare the sisters generally cast at the student caught in the act, but a knowing gaze that was vaguely complicit, as if they were cheating at a card game together. Her tone and her words were less ambiguous. "Yes, do clean it—it's quite filthy. And see me after school, Nestor McCorley."

The cries of the students leaving school had faded with the last groups crossing Quincy Street. Nestor sat in Sister Theresa's room, alone, watching the second hand wind out the long minutes of the afternoon. Maurice, the custodian of the keys, in his unchanging blue, with his unchanging stride, passed by in the corridor, pushing the wide mop-broom over the pale green tiles, silently marking the passing time like a figure that emerges from a cuckoo clock at intervals and disappears again.

He imagined Sister Theresa pulling his parents aside at the Parents' Night and saying sadly, "I need to speak to you." It pained him to imagine the look of disappointment in his parents' eyes; he knew how hard they worked to pay his tuition. Sister Winifred would know, too, and her good opinion had always been important to him. He saw a tiny bit of paper crumpled on the floor and picked it up, spreading it between his fingers. "Is DL a good kisser? You know! HAHA!"

He heard footsteps, the unmistakable click of a nun's black heels on the tile floor. Sister Theresa spoke briefly to someone farther down the hall, and in a moment she was in the room. He steeled himself for the preamble—the grave explanation of the seriousness of his crime, the need to come clean and apologize. But at recess he had promised Vera Noonan that he wouldn't squeal on her, and he knew this refusal was likely to irk the nun, though it would gratify Vera. That was the only good thing about this mess.

There was no preamble, though, no lecture. She pointed to a crate by the window, in which were four large potted plants. "You're a big, strong boy. Carry that across to the convent for me. Make sure you keep your hands under the slats on the bottom." She picked up a smaller open box from the windowsill, in which were a few small plants with purplish, star-like flowers. "African violets," she said, "aren't they beautiful?"

On the way, she explained that she was the one who took care of the greenhouse at the convent, and how with the cold weather coming, the heat rising from the radiators by the window would kill the plants. Nestor nodded, all the time wondering, was he in trouble or not?

"You know," the sister said as they walked along Quincy Street, "I was taught that the man always walks on the outside. It goes back to the days when the horses used to splash mud up on the people passing on the sidewalk." Confused, Nestor slowed and passed behind the long, pleated habit. Head bowed amid the plants, he saw the slight curve of her swaying hips below the rope cincture and the short, sleeveless cape. Roger Shea was right; she didn't walk like a nun.

"Thank you. You *are* almost a man, you know."

"Yes, Sister," he said, but he certainly didn't think of himself as a man. Thirteen years old was not a man.

The emptiness of the greenhouse, which was behind the convent, made Nestor nervous. As she removed the plants from the boxes and set them on planks supported by cinder blocks, she asked him who had written the offensive words on the board. "You really must tell me, Nestor."

"I'm sorry, Sister. I can't squeal."

"Are you willing to take the blame for that nasty piece of work?" She folded back her sleeves and began to pour a thin stream of water from a silver can into the shallow earthen pots. "Hmmm?"

Slowly, he answered, "I suppose so, Sister."

"Well, you are a good friend. I admire that. Do you really know how to keep a secret, Nestor? It's so hard to find a person who can keep a secret— tell no one, ever, and take that secret to the grave many years from now."

Nestor swallowed. Did she want to tell him a secret? Why would she tell him? A fly made repeated and hopeless buzzing charges against a cloudy pane. "Look," she said, bending over the plant, "the little leaves are hairy. Feel how soft they are."

Nestor touched the leaves quickly and nodded.

"Sometimes people need a good friend they can tell deep secrets to, but they don't know who they can trust. I had one friend like that when I first came here, but she left, and I have no one like that now. How can you find that person who can keep a deep secret? How can you be sure about a person?"

"I don't know, Sister. You can't tell what people are thinking."

Her voice was just above a whisper. "That's exactly it. But if someone were to tell *you* their secrets, do you think you could keep them safe—forever—just like the name you're keeping from me now?"

"If I promised I would…"

"Would you make a promise like that?"

The boy's heart was pounding. This was all upside down. The sister was too close to him now. He could see a wisp of blond hair that had escaped from her linen coif. The heavy scent of the flowers in the greenhouse, the African violets, geraniums, and he didn't know the names of the others, they were making him drunk, and all at once he recalled Twining at the board, pointing to the curvy lines and saying, "This here is the backyard."

"Never had it, never will," Sister Theresa said. "A young woman, and I am a woman, Nestor, doesn't want that to be her. I've never kissed a boy, Nestor. Never. Is it wrong to want that one beautiful thing? I think God would understand, but you have to promise, and it has to be a very deep promise. I would have to deny it, and we would both be hurt, and you would probably be tossed out of the school. We would hurt each other, and I don't want to hurt you. Can you make that promise?"

Nestor was excited and somehow sick at the same time. The nuns were God's brides, and what punishment, what hell might be in store for a boy who roused the jealousy of God?

"Do you promise?" she whispered again.

"I promise," he said, but his heart seemed to beat in his head and their lips had hardly touched when he felt the black veil of the nun fall over his face—a panic seized him, and he pushed by her, knocking some pots off the sagging planks; he flew out the door, running behind the convent, under the drooping boughs of pine trees and over a fence onto the next street.

He never stopped running until he reached the stairs to his back porch. He told his mother and father he wasn't feeling well and went to his room right after dinner. By the time they returned from Parents' Night, he was already in bed, pretending to sleep, but reliving the scene in the greenhouse, feeling sexual excitement, the fear of sacrilege, and a pity for the sister, who appeared so tortured with her secret desires. To do anything with a nun—even one that was young and pretty, that would throw a heavy weight over his soul—it would be a secret that would suffocate him and hurt him, and yet he could not stop thinking of her lonely struggle with her passion.

It took several days to get a moment alone with Sister Theresa, and when he did, at recess, he said quietly to her, "I'll never say anything, Sister."

She was toying with the long, heavy rosary that hung from her belt. "About what, Nestor?" She closed her fingers over the crucifix as her hands disappeared into the wide sleeves of her habit.

"About what happened."

Her brows lowered and her head drew back as if she were puzzled. "Nothing happened," she said. She spoke without looking at him. "I wouldn't bring up any dirty sexual fantasies you've had. No one would believe you, and you'd be a laughingstock, and be tossed." She smiled, seemingly content, and with her hands still tucked into her sleeves she walked quickly away, leaving him standing there, hearing the shouts of his classmates, but feeling suddenly too old for schoolyard games.

Nestor felt that he had grown up in that moment. He saw Sister Theresa not as a tortured woman forced to live a life without love—desperately seeking the kiss she'd never had—but as a manipulator of children; her expression and her voice projected the assurance of power and the will to control her victims. Someone else must have discovered her nature, too, because there were only vague excuses given for her sudden departure, months later, before the school year had ended.

Nestor thought she must have confessed her attempt to make him do something wrong, because shortly after she'd left, Sister Winifred called him into her office. She appeared to Nestor to be tired, pale, and even older looking than she had been.

"Are you all right, Nestor?"

"Yes, Sister," he said.

She stared at the withered hands she held clasped in front of her as if in prayer. "What happened was not your fault, and you should ask God to blot it out of your mind. It was unfortunate, but everything will be mended and God will forgive you and we will move on in His grace."

It was all very vague, and Nestor did not understand why he needed forgiveness if what had happened was not his fault. He thought it better to say as little as possible. "Yes, Sister."

"You haven't said anything to anyone it seems. Not even to your parents."

"No, Sister."

"You can always talk to me."

He nodded. "I know, Sister."

"Sister Theresa began as a very good member of the order. But sometimes people change. I don't know how or why. For some, the nun's life... well, they were not meant for it, or came to it for the wrong reasons, and it... it..." She seemed to be struggling to explain something to him, but her shoulders sagged and she stopped short and Nestor saw that her eyes were brimming with tears. "In any case, she is gone and will not be back." She smiled weakly and said, "Nestor, you're very young to have such secrets, and I would not normally tell you to keep secrets from your parents, but I think you have done the right thing." He felt a blush spreading over his face and wished he could leave.

"If you had spoken about it, the name of St. Brigid's would be disgraced and all the good work, well, it wouldn't matter." She sighed and shook her head. "Do you know what I'm trying to say, Nestor?"

"Yes, Sister. I never want to talk about it—with anyone. It's wicked embarrassing, Sister."

"It would be my responsibility you see, and it is I who would be..."

"Sister Winifred, I never told anyone and I never will. Like I said, it's real embarrassing."

She nodded gravely. "Yes, I'm sure it is, and I regret more than I can tell you... the way she behaved. You may go back to class, Nestor. If anyone asks you why I called you here, just say that I wanted to tell you what a wonderful job your father did in the choir on Sunday, because that's true."

On the way back to class, the boy considered the conversation. Sister Winifred had admitted that Sister Theresa was a bad nun, one who tried to get others to sin. There was such a thing then, and he swore that the days he had spent in fear and awe of the holy sisters were over, and his conscience was clear when, on the last day of school, Vera Noonan rewarded his silence with a long kiss down in the stone stairwell that led to the basement entrance of the church.

The nagging pain he felt now was not due to anything he had done then, but to the fact that he himself was now charged with an act of such an insidious nature—to abuse his position by groping a student under his supervision. It was the student, and not the teacher, who was now the manipulator, and he comforted himself with the hope that those who knew him and her would get to the truth.

Path—the Greek root meant feeling or suffering. *Pathos, sympathy, empathy.* And it seemed to Nestor, by some linguistic coincidence, that feelings could always be traced back along some path to a source, evident or concealed in some forgotten event. In his current state, there were too many feelings, too many paths winding backward from the dim room where he lay awake into events and consequences that often seemed to have no explanation. Yet there was one path that he could easily follow back to its source of sorrow from those days at St. Brigid's. It led through memory to a dark, rainy day in June, when Sister Cecile told them, just before she burst into tears, that Sister Winifred had suffered a terrible accident; she'd been found at the bottom of the stairs in the convent, dead.

CHAPTER TEN

t was just after 5:30 at the Old Worthen, yet most of the small crowd seemed to have been drinking for a while. *I went into an ale house I used to fre-quent.* The old Irish ballad was running through Nestor's mind as he sat at the polished mahogany bar drinking a draft beer. He hadn't come here much in recent years; he no longer recognized any of the patrons or the bartender, which was fine, because all he wanted to do was drink his beer and think.

Some of the men near Nestor wore work clothes and hammer holsters. They were discussing something with a plus-size woman who bore a tattoo of a smoking snub-nosed .38 over each substantial breast. Lost in his own thoughts, he heard their words as white noise, like the clatter of a passing train. *And I told the land-lady me money was spent.*

The ballad fled from his memory as the jukebox got going. "Maybe I'm Amazed." He listened to it while he looked at a picture of Bette Davis over the bar, head inclined, knowing smile and, of course, the Bette Davis eyes. A hometown heroine. She'd spent the first decade of her life in a house just a mile and a half from here.

Nestor had watched a lot of her movies again with Minerva. At certain scenes in *Now, Voyager* or *Dark Victory,* he would hear Minerva beside him in the gray light, beginning to sniffle, and then pulling a Kleenex from the box on her night table, so endearing. That was before all of this. When they were happy. She had said it herself: *Your hormones go crazy.* Maybe that was it, and things would be better after the birth of their son.

Just then, a disquieting thought occurred to him, and in the mirror behind the row of bottles opposite him he recognized the stony cast of worry on his face. *If he were healthy.* What if there was a problem? Sometimes babies were stillborn, or struck with some inexplicable disease, deformity or mental debility. It happened all the time. Then Minerva would believe that his lack of faith had invited the evil, or that his stupid call to hell had opened the gates to a Trojan horse full of devilry. She would blame him and hate him forever, even if she didn't want to.

"God, please don't let that happen," he prayed. And he pondered his own inconsistency, or was it hypocrisy? He didn't know anymore. In rational moments he rejected it all, but the tribal man inside, the man who stalked some unexplored hinterland with every sense alert, the man who saw images in the fire, who respected amulets and magic, the man who feared all the forces he could not control, who carved his totem into the shaft of his spear and felt the strength it gave him—that man lived within him, and prayed to unseen powers for protection. *Deliver us from evil.* Evil existed, whether or not it was coordinated from below. How else to explain the impulse that would lead this Angela to concoct a story that could destroy his reputation? He pushed the thought aside, telling himself again that it would certainly be straightened out. How far would she be willing to push a lie like that? It didn't make sense. But then, nothing made sense anymore.

He heard Paul McCartney on the jukebox bemoaning his loneliness. In the middle of something he couldn't understand.

"Christ, do I know the feeling," he thought, and he laughed out loud, lifting his glass. One of the construction guys turned toward him, nearly cross-eyed with drink. "What the hell are you laughing at? He is the gray-est, the greatess baskaball playa ever lived."

"What?"

"So, what? You don'... you don' 'gree with that?" He was sporting a three-day beard, a blue bandanna around an unkempt head, and a black gap where one of his front teeth had been.

"I don't even know what the fuck you're talking about, pal."

The drunk swiveled on his bar stool to focus on Nestor. "Larry Bird I'm fuckin' talkin' about. Larry Bird is probally, probally no, probally—*is*, he *is* the grayest fuckin' baskaball playa fuckin'... *evah*!" He raised his glass, but paused, holding it tilted before his mouth, and shouted once more toward the smoke-stained tin ceiling, "*Evah*!"

A sudden disdain for the ignorant creature gripped him. He couldn't fight with Minerva, and he couldn't fight with the madwoman, but he was just in no mood to listen to this guy's drunken bullshit. "Larry Bird sucks," he said.

To Nestor's surprise, the men with gap-tooth began to laugh, but the drunken Bird fan seemed not to have heard him as he warmed to his topic. "Fuckin' free throws, passin'... jump shot, the fadeaway..." He made a motion with one hand as if he were swatting a fly, which Nestor supposed was meant to represent shooting a basketball.

"He sucks."

"And for pure fuckin' hustle, man, the fuckin' intanga-brulls, Larry Bir... Larry Bird..."

"—sucks."

His semi-inebriated companions were slapping the bar, arms draped on each other's shoulders, laughing uncontrollably. The drunk looked at Nestor with unfocused eyes, wavering like a flame in a guttering candle, finally registering the insult, puffing out his lips as he considered his reply, probably realizing he was too drunk to fight and that he didn't really give a fuck about Larry Bird. He waved his bottle of Bud and shrugged. "Whatevah."

One of the men wiped his eye, and repeated, "the fuckin' intanga-brulls. You are a piece of work, Jimmy. Another round here, Liz. You want another beer, buddy?"

When he minded his own business he was in a world of shit, and when he looked for a fight they bought him a drink. "No. Thanks." He leaned toward the slumping figure beside him, feeling suddenly like he'd been a prick. "Jimmy, listen. You're right about Larry Bird. I was just bustin' your balls." His bandanna slipping over one eye, Jimmy was tired of the effort of speaking, but he raised a hand in what Nestor thought of as the old hippie handshake, as if he wanted to arm wrestle. Nestor shook his hand and gave him a friendly slap on the arm. "Thas coo'," he murmured.

It was six o'clock. Minerva would be home from work, if she was still working. He finished his beer and went outside. He dialed her sister's number. "*Hola* Marina, this is Nestor."

In the silence that followed, he imagined his sister-in-law looking at his wife questioningly, watching her shake her head. "I'm sorry, Nestor. She's here, but she doesn't want to talk to you right now."

"Tell her I'd like her to come home, will you, Marina? I miss her."

"I will tell her."

"Is she all right?"

"Yes."

What else could he say? Tell her I love her, like some dopey, pathetic song. "Not right now, huh? Maybe I'll call later."

The woman with the tattoos and a guy with a scraggly beard came out to smoke. "Whoa! It got fuckin' cold," the guy said. Nestor slipped his phone into his pocket and zipped up his jacket. It had gotten cold. And it was getting dark earlier. At city hall, the spotlighted American flag flapped in the gusting wind. Craning his neck, he looked at the great faces of the two glowing clocks on the visible sides of the stone tower, and higher, to where an eagle alighted from the darkness with spread wings onto the golden ball at its apex.

Minerva. The name conjured the image of the goddess, with war helmet raised, one hand on the shaft of the long ashen spear, the other bearing the aegis, the shield on which was mounted the head of the Medusa, a gift from Perseus.

Minerva Herrera. The name Herrera suggested "iron." He believed that *herrero* indicated an ironworker of some kind, a blacksmith. Now he saw that there was something of iron in the character of his wife. "She's here, but she doesn't want to talk to you right now."

He stopped at his car and picked up the copy of a scene from *Hamlet* that Eddie Saitz had left in his mailbox. Hamlet's part was highlighted in yellow. He tucked it under his arm, put his hands in his pockets and set off walking to the Old Court, remembering what he had said to Minerva. "Empty hell!" Stupid. Stupid. Stupid. He had hoped to dispel this world of demons by showing her that he was not afraid of it, but in her mind he had invited the hosts of hell into their lives, and now he imagined himself crossing Dutton Street trailed by a procession of imps, hobgoblins, hippogriffs, succubi, incubi, pixies, Ariel's fanged *chupacabra* and one tall fellow, red in hue, with curling ram horns, reeking breath, a sly smile and great pterodactyl wings fanning the noxious miasma that fizzled and steamed from his scaly body.

He chuckled at the image, but whirled about rather quickly when he heard what sounded like a scraping step behind him. The wind-driven lid of a rubbish bin scudded along the empty street.

The upstairs of the Old Court was vacant when he arrived, just a barren stage, a stretch of hardwood floor and a bar, a few tables and chairs piled at the back. He took a seat at the bar and began to look over the scene, but he was so familiar with it that he eventually pushed it aside and began to turn over the pages of a *Boston Herald* that lay on the bar. "British Scientists Say They've Made Human Sperm." Just what we need, a Frankenstein for the new millennium. There's some real witchcraft for you.

Eddie Saitz arrived carrying two pints of Guinness from the bar downstairs, and handed one to Nestor. He was followed by Ann Whitmore carrying a script and a glass of red wine. She wasted no time on formalities. She gave Nestor a quick peck on the cheek, pulled out a table from the back, and dragged it to the middle of the floor. Nestor and Eddie pulled out some chairs. "OK. Casting for *Hamlet* by William Shakespeare the Bard of Avon. Nestor McCorley. Take it from page 12, Act One Scene Four. Eddie is Horatio. I'll take Mar... cellus." They sat around the table, and Nestor began.

HAMLET: The air bites shrewdly tonight; it is very cold.
The guy outside the Old Worthen flashed into his mind. Whoa! It got fuckin' cold. A cold Christmas without Minerva.
HORATIO: It is a nipping and an eager air.
HAMLET: What hour now?
HORATIO: I think it lacks of twelve.
MARCELLUS: No, it is struck.
HORATIO: Indeed, I heard it not. It then draws near the season
Wherein the spirit held his wont to walk.

Even without sets or lights, the words began to dissolve the reality around him; he inhaled the salt air, felt the mists rising from the sea cliffs, and the cold breath emanating from the stones of Elsinore. A familiar ghost gathered shape among the deep shadows of stone bastions and battlements.
HAMLET: Angels and ministers of grace defend us!
Be thou a spirit of health or a goblin damned,
Bring with thee airs from heaven or blasts from hell,
Be thy intents wicked or charitable,
Thou comest in such a questionable shape
That I will speak to thee: I'll call thee Hamlet,
King, father, royal Dane: O answer me!

Eddie, too, had entered fully into the scene. He no longer saw his friend Nestor beside him, but a wild young prince of the royal house of Denmark. The mind does not choose to believe, Nestor thought, the mind accepts the world the story creates under the spell of words.
HORATIO: It beckons you to go away with it... Do not, my lord.
HAMLET: Why, what should be the fear?

I do not set my life at a pin's fee;
And for my soul, what can it do to that,
Being a thing immortal as itself?
It waves me forth again: I'll follow it.

HORATIO: Be ruled; you shall not go! *Eddie reached out, reflexively, to clutch at Nestor's sleeve.*

HAMLET: My fate cries out… unhand me gentlemen!
By heaven I'll make a ghost of him that stops me!
I say away!

He felt the prince's hard determination surging in his blood, and flung off Eddie's hand with such force that it struck the pint of Guinness, half full, sending it skittering across the barroom floor. There was silence for a moment, and then Ann said, "Well, Sir Laurence Olivier has nothing to worry about, but that wasn't bad."

"Sorry about the Guinness," Nestor said. He went to pick up the glass, and found a rag behind the bar.

Eddie pointed to the script that lay closed on the table. "He was already off book," he said to Ann.

"You haven't played the part before?" she asked.

"You do it five periods a day for several years, you get to know it." And, he thought, it was refreshing to become another character, especially right now, this one who stood fearless before blasts from hell and goblins damned. Wasn't that why people drank and drugged themselves? To become, for a while, someone else—someone pursued by different ghosts.

Ann laid her glasses on her script and picked up her wine. "Thank you, Nestor. We'll let you know," she said, but Eddie winked at him and gave him the slightest of nods. In the meantime, two other prospective Hamlets had arrived, and paced in the alcove, murmuring immortal lines.

CHAPTER ELEVEN

The emptiness of the apartment mirrored the emptiness he felt inside. He was tired, but had no desire yet to go and lie in the cold, empty bed. Ten o'clock. A bit late, but he dialed Marina's number.

"Nestor?" It was Minerva's voice, and it made him ache.

"It's so good to hear your voice. Listen, I was crazy. This whole thing has stressed me out." He chose his words like an artisan searching an overflowing box for the right tool. "We're going to have a son together. We can't let this madness, this so-called curse, come between us now."

"It's not just about the curse, Nestor."

"Let's work it out, Min. I love you."

There was a long pause. He closed his eyes and squeezed the telephone, seconds crawling by as they would for a man waiting for a diagnosis of some potentially terminal illness. Finally, she said, "I don't think that love is enough, Nestor. I'm sorry."

"Love is always enough. You want to break up our marriage because we had one bad fight? What about the vows we took?"

"I have thought about that, very much. But you insult the things I believe. You insult the Virgin and invite the devil to our home. I feel that I can't let you near my soul. How I can be married to a man who is a danger to my soul? Now you talk about the vows, but you say you don't care about the God who was the one… that we make the vows on His altar."

On the kitchen table, he saw a headline in *The Lowell Sun*. "Telescope Captures Colorful Image of Stellar Nursery." He and she, their unborn child, so infinitesimal, so brief, and yet to him, the whole world and all eternity. He wondered if there were any words he could find that would make her see he harbored no evil, that he was no danger to her spirit, that the whole thing was ridiculous. But that was the heart of the matter. It was not ridiculous to her. He recalled the words of Father Leahy: *We're on different frequencies.*

"I want to be a father to my son. You won't try to…"

"Of course not. Only I ask that you don't tell him is not true what I teach him about God."

"I wouldn't in any case. I've told you that before. I'm not the Antichrist, Minerva."

"I did not say you were."

"I lost my temper."

"I'm so sorry, Nestor, but I think with us it was a mistake. There are some things you can never take back."

"You can't take them back, but you can put them aside."

"I think… I'm sorry. We are not good for each other."

"There is no good and bad here. It's just the way you're choosing to think about it."

"There is good and bad."

"Yes, but believe me, not in this. Accept my apology and no one is really hurt."

"God is more than something I just think, Nestor. I do hope we will be friends."

"*Friends?*" He wanted then to shout "Fuck you!" into the receiver, but he hauled on the reins of those horses for fear they might trample his son. He took a deep breath. "We'll have to be, for the sake of… we never did decide on a name."

"Do you mind if we call him Joseph—José?"

"Sure, that's all right." He held the silent receiver. "Joseph what?"

"Joseph McCorley."

"Joseph Herrera McCorley."

"Joseph Andres? After my father?"

"That's fine."

"This is not easy for me. The baby made me realize that our differences..."

"You don't have to keep explaining, Minerva."

"I'm sorry."

"Yes. Well, that's comforting." He hung up the phone and tried to come to terms with the fantastic idea that his marriage was over.

His parents, of two different cultures, languages, and religions had made it work for so many years, but he had lost his wife out of a moment of frustration—with what? Some denizens of invisible realms? Another headline stared out at him from the national news roundup: "Ohio Woman Accused of Beating Fawn to Death." *There's a metaphor for our crazy world. They always kill the Christ figure.* Tears gathered in his eyes for his lost Minerva, for their son, whose family had broken asunder before his birth, and for the innocent fawn.

He took a bottle of Jameson from the shelf and poured a double shot into a squat crystal glass. Sipping it, he gazed at the wall where the blue wax of the Virgin's shattered candle was still visible. He opened the drawer beside the sink; it was full of toothpicks, miscellaneous power cords for long-discarded tools, business cards, warranties for products he no longer owned, old receipts, and cans of hardened shoe polish. He put down the drink and pulled the gold ring from his left hand, holding it for a moment above all the useless junk before he closed his eyes and let it fall with a soft clink. He closed the drawer and drank his whiskey.

He'd taken to sleeping on the couch, because the bedroom was too depressing. He awoke before the alarm went off, with the memory of a dream still vivid. In front of the small band stage at the Athenian Corner, his mother swayed to the music, arms above her head seeming to stir the air or conjure spirits as a bouzouki player picked out the staccato sixteenth notes of "*To Tragoudi Tis Xenitias.*"

His father, who stood near him, smiling as he watched her dance, had said something to him, but the words escaped him as the dream dissolved. Seeing his father, even in a dream, rekindled the feeling of loss. Alone at the table where he had shared breakfast with his wife, he ate his toast and drank his coffee. He remembered Fischer, his old Airedale, named for the great chess master; the dog had died a few years earlier. He was as good as a human friend. Better in some ways. And more loyal than his own wife had been. He thought that maybe he should get another dog, but hell, there would never be another Fischer. And there would never be another Minerva.

His boss, Emma Bergeron, called him into her office as he signed in. "Nestor, you look really down. The administrative team had a meeting about the Angela Purtel situation. No one believes her story. I'm confident that the truth will come out. Don't worry about it."

"Yeah," Nestor said. "Don't worry about it. Right."

She cleared her throat and essayed a smile. "Your wife must be expecting the baby soon."

"Very soon."

"That's so exciting!" When he said nothing, her smile faded. "Is anything wrong? Anything else?"

He sighed. "The baby is all right. Everything else is wrong. Minerva and me. Emma, sometime when you have about an hour I'll tell you about it, but I can't get into it right now."

"I'm sorry. I hope things work out."

He nodded and swallowed hard. "Thanks."

"Listen, I wanted to tell you that one of your students, Ismael Trinidad, was arrested for armed robbery."

"Great."

"He's been suspended, but of course we have to offer him tutoring at home. Presumed innocent. Do you want to tutor him after school? It's twenty-five dollars an hour."

"Sure. I'll do it." He hadn't even worked out how his financial situation would change. He and Minerva had been saving for a house, sharing the bills. He would have to think of those things soon.

"His number and address are on the computer roster. Just give him a call this week and set something up. Say three, four hours a week. I'll get work from his teachers and leave it in your box. Give the completed work to Marianne. She'll get it back to his teachers."

Ismael hadn't done much when he was here; Nestor doubted he'd do much while he was suspended, but he'd give the tutoring his best shot. His course load was split between Honors English and lower level classes for students who didn't speak English at home, which was where he'd met Ismael.

As he was about to leave her office, she added, "Nestor, you're not the first to have a run-in with Angela Purtel. She's a troubled kid."

"My trouble now."

"No one believes it."

"But I still have to deny it."

She smiled encouragingly once more, and rubbed her hand over his back, as if she were trying to transfer some of her own positive energy. "Things will get better."

When the bell rang he headed for his classroom, where he was teaching an honors class, a course called "Masterpieces of World Literature." The students didn't really like the material, but they knew they had to do it, either for college or to please their parents, and in general they attempted the work with good grace, but it was heavy going. Today they would try to finish Sophocles' *Antigone*. They took parts. Fittingly, he gave the part of Antigone to Elisse Vassilakhos, a Greek girl. The students liked to take parts because, Nestor suspected, it kept them awake.

"Can I be Creon, Mister?"

"Right, you're Creon, Jeff."

"Diego, you're Tiresias."

"The blind guy? How can I read the part if I'm blind? Right?"

"You got me there, Diego. Michelle, you're Ismene." He assigned the other parts and said he'd take the chorus to move things along.

They read stiffly, without emotion, giving each word the same weight. Painful, Nestor thought, but he reminded himself that they were very young. Michelle, an Asian girl, or young woman at seventeen or eighteen, was nearly inaudible as Ismene. He stopped. "Imagine, Michelle, that you have a volume control on your voice. It's now set at, say, 2. Turn it up to about 10. Much louder. Try those lines again." She read them over at about 2.5. To say any more would probably embarrass her, and he would never get her to read in anything approaching a stage voice.

A voice from the back: "I still can't hear her."

Elisse read Antigone's lines as if she were reading a grocery list, and yet still those words held power for Nestor. "O you mock me! Why in the name of all my father's gods…"

They plowed on, the words gnawing at something inside him—his conscience? "Protect your rights? When you trample on the honor of the gods?" As he read the closing lines of the chorus, Nestor felt as he had when he heard his own voice in the empty and desolate apartment that he'd once shared with Minerva—it was the echo of his grief. "Wisdom is by far the greatest part of joy, and reverence toward the gods must be safeguarded. The words of the proud are paid in full with mighty blows of fate, and at long last those blows will teach us wisdom."

Why did we need horrible divine retribution to teach us wisdom? If only, like Finn McCool, he could have eaten the salmon of wisdom. The students closed their books, passive, unimpressed, as if they had just read the directions for changing a tire, while their teacher continued to stare hard at the page, looking as if he were in pain. "Mr. McCorley? Mr. McCorley, are you all right?"

He felt as if he were slipping into the hole of sorrow. God, or the gods, or fate had rocked his house to requite him for the pride that Sophocles had warned us of more than five hundred years before the birth of Minerva's Savior. His own arrogance, his fury, had destroyed all that was dear to him. Certainly they could have been happy if only he'd had more patience. What price, wisdom?

"Are you all right, Mr. McCorley?"

"Yes, I…" They were looking at him strangely. "I have a headache. Copy the question on the board and answer it in your notebooks for tomorrow. 'Which is more important in Sophocles' world view, fate or free will?'"

"How long does it have to be?"

"I don't care how long it is as long as you show me that you thought about the question."

"What are we gonna read next?"

He looked over the syllabus taped into the back of his book. "Dante's *Inferno*. I think I'll skip that for now and go to Chaucer, if you don't mind."

They didn't mind. They stretched, yawned, and began to talk about important things while they waited for the bell.

After work, Nestor drove on a whim out to Carlisle, to the frozen cranberry bogs on the edge of a bare New England forest. He popped the trunk, hoping he'd left a sweater there, but there was nothing, and he pulled up the lapel of his suit jacket and set off. The day was gray, one of those early December days when the earth seemed to hold its breath under a pressing sky, waiting for snow. He walked the raised paths through the bogs, past the lake where, soon, deer tracks would cross snow-covered ice. Today the lake was still a black mirror reflecting towering pines, bare oak and maple, and, in the shallows, the high tawny bulrushes stiff with frost.

There are seasons inside us New Englanders, he thought, seasons in our blood that reflect the seasons in nature and turn with them. Each has its own beauty, but none is as beautiful as this. *The sedge has withered from the lake, and no bird sings.*

No bird sang in the barren trees; no curlew cried from the thickets; no bees sailed out from the box hives that were placed at intervals around the bogs. All was silence, save the low gurgle of a narrow stream flowing out of the lake into an irrigation ditch that ran through swampy land where small islands of dried grass stood like shaggy, straw-colored sheepdogs in the black water.

Fruitless, desolate in some ways, but not sad, not really. He took the path away from the lake that led up through the woods. White flecks, a few at first, and then the air was charged with them. *Not as single spies, but in battalions.* A stone wall crawled away between the pines into some dim, hushed eternity. He drank in the healing, crisp pine-laden air like a tonic, and remembered Thoreau's words: "Time is but the stream I go a-fishing in."

The Bach-like organ of "A Whiter Shade of Pale" rolled into the stillness. "Hello?" His voice sounded small in this space.

"Nestor, this is Ann. We'd like to offer you the part of Hamlet."

"Were the other Hamlets that bad?"

"Oh yes. What do you say? Will you commit to it?"

"Yeah, I'm a little nervous, but I'll give it my best."

"You'll be fine. Eddie will drop off the rehearsal schedule and our working script. We won't put it on until the end of July. Congratulations."

"Thanks." She was gone. Ann didn't waste words. Hamlet! My God. The thought of taking such a part, as an amateur, to try to bring to life on the stage the greatest creation of the most limitless imagination in literature; it was a frightening prospect. But he thought it was good to make himself do things he was afraid of doing. And he needed it to occupy his mind if Minerva would not come back. He picked up a stick and swung it against a tree trunk. "What may this mean," he cried, his breath a white fog, "that thou, dead corse, again, in complete steel, revist'st thus the glimpses of the moon, making night hideous; and we fools of nature so horridly to shake our disposition with thoughts beyond the reaches of our souls?"

From the corner of his vision, a dark figure rushed out of the swirling snow directly at him. A burst of adrenalin shot into his bloodstream; he stepped back, reflexively raising the stick. A great black Newfoundland, dusted with snow, ambled toward him. He relaxed and lowered his arm. The shaggy tail wagged a salute, and the dog sniffed the air near him. A woman appeared then on the woodland path. She wore a blue knit hat and scarf that accentuated her blue eyes, bright in the wintry air. Blond hair fell over her shoulders. Her cheeks were tinged with red. A leash, looped into circles, hung from her gloved hand.

"I'm not crazy," he said. "I'm in a play. *Hamlet.* Just rehearsing some lines. I thought I was alone out here."

She smiled tentatively. "That's all right," she said. "Break a leg," and called to the dog, "Come on, Sheba."

He inhaled the air when she had passed, detecting the scent of some shampoo or fragrance. Nosing the air, like the Newfoundland. He remembered Declan again. "The word you didn't want to say—*animal*!" He watched her move away, the bear-like dog loping along before her. He would like to have spoken more with her. He missed a woman's company. But out here, in this solitude, he was afraid he would frighten her. "Once more adieu!" he said to himself, "the rest let sorrow say!" She looked at him once over her shoulder, and smiled. A woman's smile. Wasn't that how all his problems had begun? But there just wasn't anything more beautiful in the world. He walked along the path, twirling his stick, softly singing one of his father's old songs:

> *I met my girl near Banbridge town*
> *My charming blue-eyed Sally O*
> *She's the queen of the County Down*
> *And my flower of Magherally O*

Not until he reached the path that opened onto the pine-covered peninsula before the second lake did he begin to realize that the day would soon give way to dusk, and that he was cold. He had managed to forget everything out here, and feel at peace with the world. Now though, he allowed himself only a moment to drink in the beauty of the dried rushes standing in the snowy silence. The lake stretched out like a Flemish painting, a dark glass under a low sky, a few red berries still bright among the naked bramble. He turned and began to trot back along the path.

In sight of the bog road where the wheel ruts of the tractors were filled with black water, he saw the woman with the dog about to enter a path that led through the woods toward the vast preserve of Great Brook Farm. He waved, and she paused when she saw him again. "Aren't you cold?" she asked.

"Freezing, actually. But it's so pretty out here."

"I won't keep you, but where are you playing in *Hamlet*?"

"Small local theater company. They're putting it on... we're putting it on upstairs in the Old Court, a pub in Lowell."

"And who are you?"

"In the play?"

"Well, yes, who are you in the play?"

"I'm Hamlet."

"Really?"

"Well, it's a small company, as I said." There was a moment's pause in which he was at a loss for something to say, thinking only that if he were a painter, he would like to try to capture the blue of scarf and hat and eyes, the flush of her cheeks, the vapor of her breath, the dark loop of the leash hanging from her hand, the great black hound stalking near her.

"Could I come and see it?"

"Yes, of course. I mean it won't be a Broadway production." The dog edged closer and sniffed at his pant leg. "It's not for a while, July something. We haven't even started rehearsing. What's your name?"

"Abby, Abby Griffin."

"I'm Nestor McCorley." He pulled a pen and a bank deposit slip from his pocket. "I'll give you my number and you can call me for the information." After he'd handed her the paper, he considered asking her for hers, but he decided to leave it as it was. He still harbored the hope that he might be able to reconcile with Minerva. At that moment, his phone sounded again. It was Marina. "Nestor, we're at Lowell General. Minerva is having the baby."

"I'm coming." He tucked the phone back into his pocket. "I've got to go. Nice meeting you, Abby." It might sound more than a bit strange, he thought, to add, "You see, my wife is having a baby."

He called his boss to tell her that he would not be in the next day, and left instructions for his substitute. The snow cast a hush over the city. By the time he reached the Pawtucket Bridge, the light was draining from the sky as if a plug had been pulled in the West, but through the swirling white haze he could see the Pawtucket Falls, and hear its low roar. Bare tree limbs caught on the dam wall reached out like dark, crooked arms above the churning water. The scene filled him with a sense of foreboding, and he shuddered as he remembered the cry of the crazy woman. "You tried to take it off!"

He understood his wife's desire, her need, to shield her frail human hopes in the blue folds of the robe of Our Lady of Miracles. He took a deep breath, and pressed play on the CD player. It was Paul Scofield's *Hamlet*, but it was Marcellus who spoke to Horatio and Bernardo after seeing the ghost on the battlements of Elsinore. The crowing rooster of dawn was thought to banish wandering spirits.

> *Some say that ever 'gainst that season comes*
> *Wherein our Saviour's birth is celebrated,*
> *This bird of dawning singeth all night long;*
> *And then, they say, no spirit dare stir abroad,*
> *The nights are wholesome, then no planets strike,*
> *No fairy takes, nor witch hath power to charm,*
> *So hallow'd and so gracious is the time.*

No witch hath power to charm. Put on Christ's armor. What comfort there must be to believe in such a panoply. The question that Nestor had banished from his mind crept back. How did the madwoman know that Minerva had seen Father Leahy, or that the priest's brother was Thomas? He turned up Varnum Avenue toward Lowell General Hospital, trying to shake off his misgivings; his reason must never allow a capitulation to necromancy. There had to be more to this story. How did the woman know?

The labor was long, and Nestor became exhausted just witnessing it. He could only imagine what Minerva was going through. The two nurses spoke loudly to his wife, urging her to push. "For five seconds! Five seconds now! One-two-three-four-five!" But she hardly seemed to hear them. She gripped a fistful of Nestor's shirt, pulling him close. "Tell him to give me a C-section!" she said through nearly clenched teeth. But Dr. Abaza, her Egyptian obstetrician, who, Nestor thought, must be near retirement, said, "I cannot do that yet, Minerva. I think the baby will come."

Nestor felt the dull ache of helplessness as Minerva began to sob and beg for the surgical remedy to her pain. He inclined his head toward the doctor's ear and said, "Can't you give her the C-section, Doctor?"

"I'm sorry to say, but there are two things she needs. More time and more pain. That's just the way it is. Tell her to breathe, and tell her she must push when the nurse tells her to push."

"But she's so tired, Doctor."

"I'm not ready to give up on this labor yet. I'll be back."

"Push now, dear," the smaller nurse said. "Just five seconds of pushing! One-two…"

"It's not working!" Minerva shouted. Her eyes were desperate and her dark hair clung to her damp temples. "Nestor! Tell them! *Ave Maria, no puedo mas!*"

He looked at his watch. It was 3:20 a.m. By 4:30 the nurses had tried all their strategies, all of the various positions they knew, and their exhortations were beginning to lose conviction while Minerva, wracked with contractions that did not produce a baby's head, cried, Nestor knew, in the bitter belief that the birth was cursed. Light was beginning to filter through the curtains of the hospital room when Dr. Abaza returned. He held a brief consultation with the attending nurses, nodded decisively, and said to Nestor, "I'll see you in surgery." One of the nurses handed him a set of green hospital scrubs with a surgical mask and cap.

"Maybe I should wait outside," he said.

"Let's go, Dad. No wimping out now."

After the long, terrible hours of Minerva's travails, the C-section was remarkably rapid. Silver instruments flashed above his wife's opened belly. He had wanted to wait outside, but Nestor was glad that he'd come in when Minerva took his hand and squeezed it hard. Soon the doctor held a baby, purple, trailing a glistening cord, waving tiny arms in the air of the new world and then suddenly bawling in startlingly loud bursts. Minerva craned her neck as a nurse held the newborn aloft.

"Please, is he all right?" she cried. The doctor cut the cord and the nurse placed the infant under a warm lamp as the purplish hue faded and the pink flush of life diffused throughout his tiny writhing body. Dr. Abaza's eyes smiled above his surgical mask. "You have a healthy son. With lungs like a trumpeter."

"A healthy son." The words she had prayed for so many hours to hear. A cry of joy welled out of her, and as her head fell back, she let go of Nestor's hand to bless herself and say a prayer of thanks. He listened to the squawking of the newborn, and to the click of the staple gun closing her wound. His eyes streaming tears that seeped under his facemask, he offered his own prayer, as the poet had once done, "to whatever gods may be," that this might be the beginning of closing the other wound, the one that the madwoman had ripped open in their marriage.

Back in her room, Minerva was asleep, pale, as drips of liquid ran through the clear plastic tubing into her bruised arm. She did not stir when Nestor kissed her forehead. He stopped at the nursery to see his son, swaddled in white, a blue knit cap perched on his head, as near to miraculous as anything could be.

"Do you know what you're going to call him?" a plump and friendly nurse asked.

"His name is Joseph."

She pulled a paper drawing of a teddy bear from a drawer. "Hello!" it read. "My name is..." She picked up a blue magic marker and printed JOSEPH across its belly. She taped it onto the front of the open plastic box in which he lay. "There you are, Joseph, your own name," she said. "And may you carry it through a long and healthy life."

"Thank you," Nestor said, and for some reason he was overcome with sadness and he began to cry once more. "I don't know where that came from," he said, embarrassed, wiping at his eyes with his fingers.

"It's a very emotional experience," the nurse said, kindly.

He drove home and, sinking onto the unmade bed, fell into a deep and dreamless sleep until he was awakened by the sound of a snow plow scraping the street, the yellow light on its cab flashing dismally through his room.

Back at work, piles of papers were stacked by class period on his desk. Substitutes hand out all the work in the "sub folder," but they correct none of it. He reviewed what the sub had done, her notes regarding discipline problems, who was naughty and who was nice.

While he waited for homeroom, he checked his email. A brief message from Lindsy Tamaril, the guidance counselor whose job it was to investigate accusations of sexual harassment, asked him to put his version of events in writing. The words depressed him further. Not what happened, but *his version* of what happened. It was CC'd to the head of guidance, the dean of discipline, and the superintendent. *If I believed in prayer,* he thought, *now might be a good time to kneel.*

PART III:
THE STRONGEST GATE

CHAPTER TWELVE

The following Saturday he found himself on a street in a run-down section of the Acre where he felt he should keep his wits about him and an eye out for trouble. So far, the winter had not been severe. Low snowbanks lined sidewalks littered with empty nip bottles and losing scratch tickets, and the unshoveled stairs of the tenements were coated with icy footprints. Though the air was cold, the front doors were open to reveal rows of mailboxes in graffiti-covered hallways. It was his first tutoring session with Ismael Trinidad, and Nestor carried a stack of books and a few "learning activity packages." Ismael hadn't done much when he was in school. Too many absences to ever get rolling, but he had struck Nestor as a bright student. Probably another kid who could have been something else if he'd had the right home. And the law said that while he was awaiting trial for armed robbery, the school must provide a tutor.

He walked up the stairway, inhaling the heavy scent of fried food, and knocked on a door, patched with plywood, on the third floor. A dog began to bark, and he heard the sounds of people arguing in Spanish, though he couldn't make out the words. He knocked again, and heard faint movement and a pause in which he imagined an eye checking him from the peephole.

The door opened. It was Ismael, slim, lost in his usual oversized T-shirt and low-hung pants. "Hey, McCorley, wassup?" He rubbed a hand over his shaved head. A lion wearing a five-pointed crown was tattooed across his forearm, along with the phrase *Amor de Rey.*

"It's *Mister* McCorley."

He shook hands and entered. The argument he'd heard was televised. Two couples stood before a sour-looking TV judge, replete with black robe and gavel. One man was saying, "Of course I intended to pay her, little by little," while a woman on the other side wagged her finger in the air and said, "*Mentiras! Mentiras!*" Lies.

In the kitchen, a pit bull strained on a short chain attached to a table leg. He studied Nestor with distrustful eyes, barking and growling until Ismael swatted at him with an open hand and said, "*Cállate pendejo!*"

Nestor got the young man to put the dog in a bedroom and turn off the TV. They sat at the table and he spread out the books. After fifteen minutes of Andrew Jackson and the Battle of New Orleans, there was a knock at the door, and Ismael rose. The dog renewed its barking in the bedroom. Three men entered, two Hispanics and an Asian, shadowy faces under the visors of baseball caps that protruded from the hoods of their sweatshirts. They nodded at Nestor, and Ismael said simply, "My teacha from the schoo'." He did not introduce the newcomers by name. "My boys," he said as they took a seat on the couch, turned the TV back on and tuned in to the cartoon channel. The young men seemed oblivious to the barking of the dog; they sat mute and motionless, nestled in folds of loose clothing. Nestor said, "Ismael, I'm going to go, but from now on we meet in the Pollard Library downtown."

"Where's the liberry at?"

Nestor was watching a cockroach creep up the wall from behind the refrigerator. "The big stone building next to city hall. I'll see you there at the main desk... how is Tuesday at 6 p.m.?"

"Tuesday?" He nodded. "Yeah."

He left a battered history book and a couple of pages of homework, without much hope that Ismael would do any of it. As he was descending the stairs, Ismael came out and leaned over the banister. "Yo, thanks McCorley."

"*Mister* McCorley!"

"My bad. Hey, ain't you gonna ask if I robbed that nigga?"

Nestor winced. "That's an ugly word, Ismael. Do you have to use that word?"

"Word don't mean nothin'," he protested.

"Every word means something. Anyway, no, I'm not gonna ask. And I'm not gonna ask if you're in a gang, either."

"Yo, I ain't in no gang," he said in a hollow tone. From inside the apartment they heard Ismael's "boys" laughing as SpongeBob shouted, "One Krabby Patty coming up!"

Nestor pointed at the young man's arm. "I don't think the Latin Kings would appreciate you wearing that tattoo if you're not a member." The young man looked away and shrugged. "If I thought it would do any good, Ismael, I'd give you a little lecture about life. Anyway, don't keep me waiting on Tuesday."

"I be there. Lawyer says I got to."

Words, words, words. Long had Nestor dwelled on the words that would bring her back to him. He felt that those words existed and that he must be able to pull them up from the lexicon of his heart, from his mind, maybe from the Well of Segais at the world's end, from the air—and if he could, find them and let them sink into her heart and entwine themselves in her thoughts of him. *Words I have that can pierce the heart.* Then she would see him as he really was, a good man. A man who sometimes spoke before he thought, who sometimes blustered in anger, but not a violent man, not a man who would hurt her, ever. A man who loved her.

Through long nights, as the clock on the coffee table beside the couch glowed the sad hours of his vigil, he searched for the words. Surely he could make her see that his soul was not stained with hatred or rotten with sin. Ah, but what is sin, he wondered. If not to share her faith was a sin, if reason itself was an affront to God, then there were no words, finally, that would reach her, unless the words he said were lies. The spiritual armor that she had donned to shield her from evil thwarted the words he had spoken in truth and sincerity, and turned them aside like arrows glancing off the steel, cross-embossed breastplate of a conquistador. They pierced nothing, but oh, he felt her words pierce his own thin armor like Toledan steel: "I'm so sorry, Nestor, but I think with us it was a mistake." There were no words. There was nothing, and he had to accept what she had told him. Their plans, their dreams, his vision of a happy family—it had all been a misunderstanding, a mistake. Just one of those things.

But he had a son. He picked up the baby every other weekend, and spoke with Minerva amiably, affecting the carefree smile of the drop-in dad. Sometimes when he talked to her, he thought she did look at him with love, but then he'd see her look away or shake her head slightly and he felt that it was not love but pity. She believed in the wrath of God, and she pitied a man who had summoned the devil out of hell. He knew that she believed sincerely that if he would not repent, he would have to pay, and Nestor was sure she took no pleasure in the knowledge.

The long internal discussions with Minerva that never resolved a thing began to give way to thoughts of the boy who at two months old had begun to study him with eyes as serious as an old man's. *Joseph, my son.* For now, he did not need to explain the events that had broken his parents' bond, but someday he would, and Nestor did not know what words he would find for that, either. When Joseph stayed with him, he recited *Hamlet* while the dark-eyed boy sucked his thumb and watched, with an intense absorption, the declamations of this strange man. And seeing such a grave spectator, Nestor would stop and pick him up, laughing, and hold him high and dance him around until a toothless smile spread across his face and broke into a long ooooooohh. And Nestor loved him with a tenderhearted ache that he had never felt for anyone or anything in his life.

On a Tuesday night in December, Nestor sat at a table in the Pollard Library, reading *The Boston Globe*, waiting for Ismael to show up for his fourth tutoring session.

A pale blue packet entitled "The Battle of New Orleans" with a red B minus on the title page sat on the table beside a biology book. At 6:20, he folded the paper, swore softly to himself, tucked the packet into the book, and was rising to leave when he saw Ismael sauntering toward him. "Six o'clock, Ismael. You got a watch?" He recalled then that no one under twenty had a watch; they all used their cell phones for the time, and few could even interpret the moving hands of an analog watch.

"I gotta talk to you, McCorley."

"*Mister* McCorley, goddammit."

"My bad."

Nestor sighed and sat back down. The young man took the seat beside him and pulled off his baseball cap. From his backpack he hauled out the history textbook and a copy of *To Kill a Mockingbird* and pushed them across the table to him. "Look, I 'preciate you tryin' to help me."

"Well, I am getting paid. But to tell you the truth, I always thought you had potential, Ismael, even though you do some dumb-ass things. A lot of dumb-ass things."

"Yeah, well, I don't know. Can I tell you somethin' that you can't tell nobody?"

"Sure, I can keep a secret. Just don't tell me you're gonna commit a crime and ask me to be quiet."

He shook his head. "I gotta go back to P.R. or I may not live to go to trial."

"You robbed the wrong guy."

"It ain't got nothin' to do with that. It's somethin' else."

"How much bail are you going to lose?"

"The bail was five thousand."

"Who paid it?"

"My uncle put down a thousand. When I disappear, he gotta pay the rest, but he tol' me to go. He jus' gonna pay it. He feel bad for gettin' me into this."

"Into the gang?"

"I said all I can say, Mr. McCorley. But I wanted you to know."

"Well, I don't know what you did, but I hope someday you can make things right. Good luck." He shook his hand and they walked out together, down the granite steps. Ismael crossed the street with him as he headed back to his car on Worthen Street.

"I'm gonna lay real low in P.R. Gonna try to start over."

"You have someone there who can help you get on the right path?"

"Yeah. I got in with the wrong people here. My uncle tryda warn me, 'You don't wanna be like me.' But I always look up to him like an O.G., an Original Gangsta, you know what I'm sayin'?"

A metallic blue Honda with darkened windows had stopped at the top of Worthen Street, not at the red light, but in the middle of the intersection. Nestor heard the quick chirp of tires as the car turned and accelerated toward them. Ismael was still imagining a brighter future: "I be on a farm fo' a while, in the *campo*, away from…"

The Honda's windows lowered as it approached, and the headlights went dark. All at once adrenalin flowed into Nestor's chest. He dropped the books he carried and threw his body at Ismael, knocking him to the ground in the alley beside the Old Worthen just as shots, five or six, cracked the calm of evening. Nestor rolled away and scrambled deeper into the dim space between the old wooden clapboards of the Worthen and the brick wall it faced. Three more shots sounded, closer, and Nestor saw that Ismael was crouched at the mouth of the alley. His backpack was open beside him and a gun had appeared in his hand. Jesus Christ. There were more shots as they traded fire. Glass shattered, and then the tires screeched again. In the silence that followed, Nestor felt the drumming in his chest and heard his own sharp breaths.

Ismael looked at him, wild-eyed, breathing hard. Nestor pointed to the Battle of New Orleans packet and the books on the ground near the boy. "Stick that stuff in your bag! Your name is on them!" Ismael gathered it all up quickly and thrust books and papers into his bag. He flashed a peace sign, and was gone. Nestor stood on trembling knees; he staggered to the chain-link fence at the far end of the alley and clambered over it, still ready to dive for cover. Around the block then, eyes darting in every direction, and back to his car. The Worthen had emptied, and he saw the crowd that was forming in front of the bar as he drove by. He pulled over on Broadway as first one cruiser and then another flew by him, sirens wailing, blue lights pulsing, heading in the direction of the Worthen. His heart did not begin to slow until he was back in his apartment, where he pulled a beer from the refrigerator, collapsed onto the couch and said to himself, "Thank Jesus he's going back to P.R. Who brings a damned gun to the library?" When he thought about dying, it was the image of a fatherless son that frightened him now more than anything.

He noticed that the tiny red light was flashing on the answering machine, but it was a few minutes before could rise. He remembered Winston Churchill having said that nothing was so exhilarating as being shot at without result, but it was not a thrill he'd seek to repeat. Finally he got up and pressed the button on the answering machine. It was a woman's voice. "Hello, Nestor. It's Abby Griffin. Do you remember? I met you in the woods a while back. I know you said your play isn't until July, but I thought we might get together before that if you're free. You can call me at 603 883-1807."

It was a New Hampshire area code. What had she been doing in Carlisle late on a weekday? "If I'm alive," he said aloud. The second message was from Father Leahy.

"Hello, my friend. I've been thinking about you. I hope you're well. I know it hasn't been easy. Call me and we'll have coffee downtown in the next few days."

CHAPTER THIRTEEN

Declan Prendeville's house sat on a high bank overlooking the Merrimack River. It was a veritable museum, though a strange one without any particular theme. Spanish breastplates stood by the fireplace; swords were mounted on crossbeams; bookshelves sagged under the weight of innumerable tomes and folios; an extended table overflowed with curios, prints, reference books, and an ornate Russian samovar. Above the low couch was the print that he had referred to at the Old Court—Don Juan de La Mancha, a book in one hand and a raised sword in the other, a cloud of menacing figures encircling his head, and the French phrase Declan had translated: "His imagination filled with everything he had read."

Under another framed print of a shouting Brendan Behan within the outline of a map of Ireland, a jeweler's loop sat on top of a thick coin album, and in the corner—Prendeville's prize, the complete uniform of a French Hussar of the Napoleonic era hung on a clotheshorse, sky-blue breeches, a scarlet jacket cross-braided in gold, and an enormous bearskin shako draped with gold cord and topped with a white cockade.

The Irishman handed Nestor a glass of Jameson and the two of them stood for a moment admiring the uniform. "Crazy bastards they were, Nestor. General Lasalle once said, 'Any Hussar who is not dead by the age of thirty is a blaggard,' though he made it to thirty-four."

"*Blaggard*. That's a great word. You never hear it anymore, except in old books." Nestor loved to visit Prendeville, and the Irishman, in turn, enjoyed having someone who appreciated his finds.

The bearded collector sipped quickly at his whiskey and said, "Look at this." He unfolded a felt cloth on the table and produced a silver serving spoon. "I found this at a small secondhand shop in Hollis last week. The woman said she wanted forty dollars."

"That's a lot for a spoon. Did you talk her down?"

"Talk her down indeed. I almost hurt meself gettin' the money out."

"Why?"

"Do you see nothing of interest on the spoon?"

"It looks old and worn... some initials here on the back... B-E-J. Doesn't mean anything to me. Some other little markings here I can't read."

"Jasus, yer hopeless. That's the hallmark punch!"

"Hallmark?"

"The mark of the silversmith!" Declan picked up the loop from the table and handed it to him. "Here!"

Nestor looked through the lens. The tiny rectangular block of letters suddenly became large and visible. REVERE. "Not Paul Revere!"

His Irish eyes were smiling. "The fuckin' British are comin'!"

"Is it real?"

Prendeville enjoyed this part the most. "You're damned right it's real."

"So it's worth a hell of a lot more than forty dollars."

"I'll have to have it appraised at Skinner's, but my guess would be about ten thousand."

"That poor woman in the secondhand shop."

He shrugged. "That's the game. You must know what you have or you have nuthin'."

Declan's phone rang, and Nestor held the spoon in his hand, imagining the famous Paul Revere marking it with his block stamp two hundred years ago. He could hear his friend in the kitchen describing a signed photo of Jack Dempsey that the caller was apparently interested in purchasing. Nestor sipped his whiskey and began to look through the titles of the books that lined the great bookcases. They were in no particular order, it seemed, though Declan probably had some kind of method to this madness. One title caught his eye. *The Art of War*, by Sun Tzu.

Who had mentioned this book to him? Yes, it was Minerva. She had said that Marquis Alicea was always studying it. He turned business into war, she said. Nestor sat down with the slim book. Soon he was quite absorbed, his body absolutely still, save for his eyes, which moved over the lines with a sudden and keen sense of their relevance. *All warfare is based on deception*, he read. *Know your enemy's weaknesses and attack them.* Some realization was beginning to dawn on Nestor—perhaps realization was too strong a word. A suspicion. *Sometimes an enemy's strength is his weakness. He will not defend the strongest gate.* He closed the book and sat back, considering this.

Yes, Minerva's strength was her weakness. Someone—could it be Marquis Alicea?—had attacked the strongest gate, the iron door of her faith, and broken it open, creating a breach for a host of doubts and fears to rush in. Prendeville returned and asked Nestor to carry their drinks out to where a pair of Adirondack chairs sat a few feet from the edge of a steep drop to the river. "I'll be with you directly," he said.

All was peace here on the high bank above the moving water, but somewhere in the tall pines that traced the river's edge he heard the shrill cry of a hawk. He put down Declan's whiskey on the flat armrest and sipped his own. Prendeville emerged from the house carrying a wooden box, and Nestor saw the trademark "S&W" imprinted on the side.

"Let's do a little shooting," the Irishman said. He lifted the lid of the box and withdrew a pistol, smiling proudly. "Nickel finish, walnut grip. The Model of 1917—.45 caliber military six-shot revolver. Hand-ejector model. Very few of them made between '52 and '66."

Nestor put down his drink and took the pistol in both hands. "It's heavy."

"Thirty-six ounces. I just picked it up for three hundred dollars from a guy who didn't want a gun in the house. Kids and all that horror."

"What will you get for it?"

"Nine hundred. A thousand if I'm lucky."

This was one of Prendeville's favorite occupations. Whenever he "picked up" a new pistol, he was fond of showing it off to Nestor. He would usually light a cigar as they took turns firing at coffee cans on a plant stand or debris floating in the river. Once he had produced a Mauser bolt action rifle and fired at a log floating by in the river. The log seemed to explode.

"By the way," Nestor said, hefting the .45 in his right hand, "you have a permit, right?"

"For the love of God, how would I deal in guns without a permit?"

"Do I need one to fire a gun?"

"Jasus, you worry more than an old woman with her porcelain plates," Declan responded. "Here, load the .45 while I light me Felipe Dominicana. And if you see a policeman in a canoe, hand the gun to me."

Christmas decorations hung at intervals across Merrimack Street. The massive granite tower of city hall was outlined in lights, and below the great clock the words "Season's Greetings" were spelled out in glowing white bulbs. A Nativity scene with life-size figures sanctified the plaza below. The dutiful Joseph, staff in hand, and the loving Mary looked down upon the Christ child in the manger. The colored lights of the surrounding decorations played over their faces, and Nestor noted that the artist had captured both their love and their sadness, as if the future had already cast its portentous backward shadow over the joyful event, or maybe it was the viewer's knowledge that lent sadness to their tender gaze, or maybe there is sorrow in all love, as Yeats had said.

He walked on toward the center, stopping again to lean against the bridge railing above the Merrimack Canal. The eaves of the long brick gatehouse were strung with lights, casting red and green rays across the snow-encrusted canal bank. Three arched waterways, ice-ways now, were dark, stone mouths in the foundation on which the gatehouse sat. The canals had been dug, and the walls constructed, by the Irish immigrant workers whose image could be seen under plastic in an old black and white photograph on a nearby plaque, standing with their bowler hats and suspenders and great sweeping mustaches beside wagons, pulleys, and slabs of rock—picks and shovels in their hands. He smiled as he examined the image of a broad-shouldered man in a slouch hat leaning on a long iron pry bar, recalling a song his father used to sing:

I'm as strong as any lion. I was reared on eggs and ham
I'm a terror to all fightin' men around the Mickey Dam.

He breathed the chill air, feeling the gathering wind that ruffled a narrow lane of dark water in the center of the canal. By morning, he thought, the canal would be frozen completely. His mind turned back to his meeting with Abby. She lived in Nashua, where he'd met her at an Irish bar called The Peddler's Daughter. She wore faded jeans, a white sweater, and a black and white houndstooth scarf.

"Your eyes look sad," she said. He didn't want to dwell on his problems, or bore a woman he hardly knew with the details of a failed marriage, but he told her in outline what had occurred in the last year. He had begun to reconcile himself to the separation from his wife, but the separation from his son was a psychic burden that he was still learning to cope with.

She listened, her silver-ringed fingers on the base of her wine glass, turning the stem slowly as he spoke, sometimes sighing or biting her lower lip or making those low sounds that women make to express sympathy. Finally he paused, and decided it was time to change the subject. "What about you, Abby?"

Her mother lived in Carlisle, which explained why he'd met her in the bare December woods there. I'm a clinical nurse psychologist—a psychiatric nurse."

"So you're an RN with a specialty in that area?"

"An RN, yes, with a master's in psychiatric nursing from UMass Lowell."

"Did you always want to be in the medical profession?"

"No, I wanted to be a harpist. That was my passion."

"A harpist? Really? *The harp that once through Tara's halls the soul of music shed...* for the Irish, you know, the harp is the queen of all instruments. What happened? Why didn't you...?"

"I auditioned at the University of Oklahoma for admission to their program in Harp Performance. I just wasn't quite good enough." She gave a sort of "what can you do" shrug and sipped her wine.

"That's too bad, Abby." He felt sorry to hear of such a beautiful passion thwarted.

"Oh, it's fine. You have to be born to be a concert musician. It's one in a million. Like, you know, some great singer, like Maria Callas. When she was born, God just stretched out his arm and touched her throat. And she had it. But I still play. And around that time my brother was on drugs—it got bad, and he was being treated by a psychiatric nurse who helped him a lot. I started talking to her, and I decided it was something I'd like to do."

"Speaking of voices, your voice is very calming. You're a calming person to talk to." He hadn't felt so relaxed in some time. "No boyfriends?"

"Nothing serious. I was dating a guy last summer until I realized the main thing he wanted from me was to try to cop a prescription for Xanax."

"What a dope," Nestor said. He found himself asking how she felt about religion.

"I suppose I believe in God, but..."

"Not really."

She laughed, running spread fingers through her blond hair. "Well, I don't worry about it. Does that make me a bad girl?"

"That's the kind we men love."

"Now your eyes look happy."

"I'll bet."

Nestor smiled, remembering the date. Life would be so much easier if he could forget Minerva, with her candles and her prayers and the invisible spirits that haunted her world, or tried to guide her through it. But he could not forget her. He sensed her presence, dark and beautiful, brooding at the edge of his consciousness. Glancing at his watch, he saw that it was time to move on. A few minutes later, he walked into Café Paradiso, where he saw Father Leahy reading a book and drinking a coffee, ironically, at the same table where he'd sat, it seemed long ago, with Minerva discussing baby names.

He bought a draft ale at the bar, admiring the curvy redhead as she pulled on the tap, and joined the priest, who put down his book and rose to shake his hand. Nestor sat down and looked at the book on the table. "*The Brothers Karamazov.* Haven't read that in many years. I must have read an abridged version. It wasn't as thick as that."

"The character of Ivan makes me think of you."

"Ivan… the doubter?"

"He chooses reason over faith."

"And winds up insane or something."

"Well, I haven't gotten that far yet, but let's hope you don't resemble him in that respect. He reminded me of you because he is basically a good person."

"Basically."

The priest laughed. "I didn't mean to qualify it. He is a good person."

"Thank you, Father. I sometimes feel I need reassurance on that point."

"I thought I'd left you feeling badly the last time we spoke. I know we disagree on some very important issues, but I do respect you, Nestor, and I believe in you. I want you to know that I've advised Minerva to try to reunite your family."

Your family. At those words, Nestor felt that sudden rush of emotion that sometimes caught him unaware. Blinking at the tears that blurred his vision, he thanked the priest. They spoke for a while of life, of love, of family, but not at all of the bawling hag who stalked the darkness outside the light of their friendship. While they conversed, Nestor saw Declan come in and take a seat at the bar, where he spread out a newspaper, ordered a Guinness and soon had the redheaded bartender laughing at his stream of banter.

When the priest left, Declan came over and sat at the table, setting down his own beer, and another before his friend. "Making your confession?"

"How I wish my problems could be solved with three Our Fathers and a Hail Mary. I'm so confused, Dec. All good people caught up in this madness." He had spoken with his friend from time to time concerning the strange events that had shaken his world and about what Father Leahy had told him of the words the crazy woman had shouted at the priest in Lawrence. "What happened to the life I knew?"

"Gone, alas, like our youth, too soon. You know these cross-cultural marriages are always difficult affairs."

"You think that was the problem?"

"Well, it didn't work out for Madame Butterfly, I know that."

A look passed over Nestor's face as if for a moment he were trying to solve a difficult math problem. Finally he shrugged and said, "Things just happened."

Declan shook his head in knowing disdain. "What's happened is that you've been targeted, boy. Think about it now. Crazy people don't appear and say one wild thing to one person, or related group of people, and disappear. They say crazy things to everyone. Now I've not seen this 'witch' character about the city at all. She performed all her carry-on with you and Minerva, and the priest, and then she's off like the fuckin' wild geese. Where the hell did she come from and where did she go? She was a hired actress. She did her job—and she made her exit." He leaned back and took a long drink of stout.

"Hired?" Nestor considered the implications of the word. Had Marquis Alicea deceived him into an easy friendship, and then struck at him, at his marriage, by attacking the strongest gate, where Minerva was vulnerable? Or could Robert Casey have paid the woman—trying to give him a taste of fear for his own child?

"Hired," Declan repeated. "Had to be. And your clerical friend confirmed it. Unless you believe the wild woman has some mystical powers, which you, and I, reject." The Dublin man leaned forward, his blue eyes magnified behind his glasses. "May I also say, Nestor, that the fact that Minerva bought into this so thoroughly suggests that perhaps someone knew she would. I mean, if some oul' blathershite were to throw a curse on me, I'd hurl a good Irish curse right back in her face, 'May you marry a ghost and bear him a kitten and may the High King of Glory permit you to get the mange,' as James Stephens put it. And I'd think no more about it."

"You're right, Declan. But of course, a woman in the act of lighting a candle—one might assume she was devout."

"Witches and curses. You might as well believe in leprechauns and banshees and that wee red prankster, the *far darrig*."

"A curse takes on power as people believe in it."

"Well, you know I believe in nuthin' at all, unless, as Joyce said, I can knock my sconce against it. But at least a leprechaun or a fairy is harmless. Whereas I've got a copy of the *Malleus Maleficarum*, known in English as *The Hammer of Witches*, first published in 1487, I believe. Not an original copy of course—Jasus, I wish it were. It was used for three hundred years as a manual for witch-hunters: how good Catholics should recognize them, do battle with them, and finally torture confessions out of them. It is the work of a completely deranged mind. Full of witches copulating with devils, and stealing the souls of babies, transporting themselves from place to place across the night sky with the pagan goddess Diana... pure insanity."

"Looks like this witch transported herself out of the city."

"Ah, she's holed up somewhere. Find the oul' harridan. Suss out her game. Who hates you enough to put her up to that? To be looking into the lives of you and your friends? What about the fella whose son died on the track?"

"Of course that thought has occurred to me. He said, 'I hope someday you find out how it feels to lose a son.'"

"There's your curse, reworded."

"You could well be right, Dec, but for some reason, Casey just doesn't strike me as the answer to all this. He's angry all right, but... oh, I don't know."

"Sure I don't know either, but someone hates you, of that I'm sure." He signaled to a waitress who was leaning at the end of the bar, pointing to his empty glass. "Another Guinness, please, Cindy. Nestor?"

"I'm good."

"Well, you know," he continued, "Winston Churchill was no friend to the Irish, but there's little doubt he was the man for the job in 1939. He said one thing I always remember, and I think you should remember it too, Nestor."

"And that is?"

Declan leaned closer, and with narrowed eyes and an air of determination, he said, "When you're going through hell... *keep going.*"

In the following days, when time permitted, Nestor searched the homeless shelters, the cheap rentals on Bridge Street, the mental health facilities; he spent hours walking the downtown and the outlying streets, talking to those who existed on the margins. None could place her. None knew where such a person might be found. There was no sign of the madwoman, and at length he began to think that it was just as well. He could not bring himself to confront Robert Casey or Marquis Alicea without evidence. He could be wrong about all of it.

Meanwhile, the Earth continued its orbit, and as the great bulk of the Northern Hemisphere inclined toward the sun, winter began its retreat and Eddie Saitz told him, "The fucking snow crocuses and the early daffodils are up!" He reminded Nestor that summer would be coming soon, and that he should focus unwaveringly on the Prince of Denmark. "Dude!" he admonished him. "Shit happens! Life's a bitch! Your problem is you don't know how to move on!"

"What do you mean I don't know how to move on? I moved on after the '86 Red Sox, didn't I?"

"Yeah, in 2004."

March 17, St. Patrick's Day, was sunny. Nestor took a pint of Guinness with Declan at a window seat in the Old Court, watching the parade of green-clad Lowellians marching along the sidewalks, making the annual pub crawl. The day always marked the beginning of spring for Nestor, a time of hope.

"Do you know you must have gotten me thinking about love and romance, Nestor boy."

"Is that right?" He picked up a napkin and wiped the froth of the Guinness from his mustache.

"Ah, there was this woman in Dublin years ago. Gina O'Healy—her people were from Cork."

"Gina? Doesn't sound Irish."

"Well there's no law that you have to be called Molly or Siobhan, for God's sake. Americans are always saying, 'Prendeville? That's not Irish.'"

"Norman Irish, right? Like all the Fitzes."

"Can I do the family genealogy another day?"

"I'm sorry. Continue."

"Jasus, you're a very difficult person to tell a story to." He cleared his throat and continued. "Well, anyway, she was out of my league as they say. Her hair was that reddish brown…"

"Auburn?"

"Auburn or russet, I don't know. And the bluest eyes. I know it's a cliché, but you could fall into them and drown, so you could. Well, she never took much notice of me. But one night a crowd of us students were out at a bar called Toner's on Baggot Street, a grand old pub, you'll have to stop in if you ever get back to Dublin. Anyway, she flashed this great warm smile, and cast those eyes on me. She took me arm, and just for that night—ah, women are strange creatures—it was as if she was suddenly mad about me. We retired to a snug and, you know, it was all very romantic believe it or not, as if she had just seen me, looked into me and saw—somethin' she liked. Ah, you smile, but I was young, slim, strong—who knows, maybe even attractive.

But after that night…" He shrugged and shook his head as if he had never quite resigned himself to the mystery. "I don't know what happened, Nestor, if I said something, or maybe she'd drunk too much and it was just a lark, but she never showed any interest again. She put me off.

"Well, the other morning, sometime around dawn, I was dreamin' about Gina. Jasus, but it was real. I was at Toner's once again, in the snug there, with the door closed and her in my arms. In the dream it was the same night, like a movie that had just been on pause. She was kissing me like she loved me, Nestor. I was young again and wild about her and happy, and then I woke up in the dawn and the vision flew and I was sixty fuckin' years old, in tattered pajamas with a house full of old books and the uniform of a dead Hussar."

Declan was slumping over his pint now, and Nestor patted him on the back. "Ah well, the Buddha says that unhappiness comes from desire. You want some alternate reality that you perceive as superior. Trying to remake the past, worrying about the future, instead of accepting the present as it is."

"Well, of course you want something else. What if you came into the Old Court tonight and Finbarr or Jerry said that from now on instead of serving Guinness we're going to serve orange juice. Would you accept that reality with good cheer and drink up?"

"So much for the consolation of philosophy."

Declan groaned and looked toward the ceiling, or maybe toward heaven. "Christ! Gina! *Long, long shall I rue thee, too deeply to tell.* Well, there's my confession. And that's why I scoffed at your romantic notions, Nestor. Every woman I met after, I was always tryin' to recapture that feelin', but I never felt about any of them the way I had about her."

"They were all orange juice to her Guinness?"

"Indeed. I had just one taste of that kind of emotion, and then—gone forever. Maybe that's why I'm such a cynical bastard. That's why I put those feelings down you see, and that's why I comfort myself with believing in Pavlov's dog and…"

"Tubes and pumps."

Declan nodded, and said without conviction, "Maybe that is all we are, Nestor. And that frightens me."

They heard a drone and a skirl of notes. A piper in a green kilt led a gaggle of young revelers down Middle Street. The older man sat up and raised his Guinness. "Ah, fuck it, Nestor. It's a great day for the Irish. Up the rebels and all that." The two men drank, Nestor wondering if he would awaken in some gray dawn of his sixtieth year still haunted by the image of the woman who had been his wife so briefly.

Greek Independence Day followed about a week later, and Nestor wore a blue shirt. Nick Betsis called to invite him to a party at the Hellenic American Academy. His mother said she would like to go, too. Once there, she quickly launched into long discussions in Greek with the other women she knew, some of them widows like her. A trio was playing a Greek song that Nestor recognized, but could not name. Nestor greeted Nick and some of the other men he'd worked with at Acropolis Construction. After a while, Nick took him by the elbow and said, "My uncle wants to talk to you."

He led him to a table near the back, where the old patriarch sat by himself, finishing a demitasse of Greek coffee. Nick presented him to his uncle, patted him on the back, and left him there.

"How are you, Mr. Betsis?"

"George," he said, and began to consider the question. "How am I?" He received the words not as a greeting, but as an earnest inquiry. "How am I? *How am I?* I don't know, you see?" he said, now turning his eyes thoughtfully toward the coffee grounds at the bottom of his cup. "I got arthritis in the hip, the knee, here, there. The whole body system start to fall apart. What you can do, eh? Can do nothing." He waved a hand hopelessly in the air, as if he were tossing this life away. "I think I like to go to Mount Athos, *Agion Oros*, you see, live as a monk, go there and eh, meditate, you see? Worship in my own way, because I am not Orthodox Greek, my friend."

"I thought you were Orthodox."

"The Orthodox Greeks they worship one God, you see? I worship twelve."

Nestor smiled. "You mean Zeus and..."

"Yes, of course, my friend. The Olympians. Why not? They were the gods during the golden age of Greece. They are good enough for Homer, then they're good enough for me. What the Greeks have done since they accept Christianity? Nothing, you see?" His slim shoulders shook as he laughed.

"I'm just teasing you, Nestor. What I am going to do with my wife if I go to a monastery, eh? They don't accept the women there! And probably I will even miss her." He raised open hands in a gesture that Nestor took to mean something like *you can't win*. The old man continued. "Eastern Orthodox, Roman Catholic..." He shrugged. "It's same thing, just different signs on the door. Peace to the men of good will." He raised his hands as if those words summed up all religious philosophy. "You remember the Pope John Paul, he ride in the, what they call, the 'pope-mobile,' meet all the people, you see? Then some crazy bastard come and he shoot the pope, eh? Why anyone want to shoot the pope, eh?" He shook his head, disgusted. "The pope, you see, he was nice guy. Crazy people, Nestor. What you can do? Can do nothing. It's the crazy people."

George Betsis was a friend not only of his mother, but of Father Leahy. He knew everyone, and nothing of consequence happened in the Acre that he did not know about. And so Nestor gathered that this last remark may have been a veiled reference to his own troubles.

"Now the Greek priests they make me mad. They want to say the Mass in English. They try to put us in the melting pot, and melt us, eh?" The two of them laughed, and George continued, leaning closer, "Look around, Nestor. Tell me, what is difference you see between, eh, the Greek party, here tonight, and when the Irish they have a party?"

"Maybe the Irish drink a little more?"

"The Greeks they drink…" He raised an index finger. "Only they follow the important rule… they eat first. But look, you see all the people here? Big crowd, eh? No policeman. The Irish they have party like this—have to hire two policeman. We don't need policeman, you see? We are civilized."

"That is true, George."

The old man laughed, amused at his own observation. "Listen, I like your father. Is good man, eh? Straight man. He's Irish, but that's all right, eh? We forgive him. Now already you go to Ireland see the old country with him. So I talk to Daphne, to your mother—she don't like to fly and she think, you know, is too sad to see the old home. Lot of people she know they die or they all gone. But she want you to see Pylos. I want to send you, whenever you ready to go, you tell me. I buy your ticket, everything. You go see, eh?"

Nestor was touched by the generosity of this old immigrant. "That's very kind of you, George."

"I make a promise to your mother, so you don't let me down. Within this year, eh? While still I am alive."

"All right."

"Now you make me a promise." He nodded and tapped a finger against his temple. "I don't forget."

He touched Nestor's shoulder and pointed to the dance floor, where he saw his mother, arms raised and hands clasped with the other dancers moving in the circle of the *syrtos*. How many days had passed since Eamon McCorley had watched a young Daphne Laganis turning in this circle and dreamed of her in his narrow bed.

George Betsis leaned close to him and said, "Always your mother she was good dancer."

CHAPTER FOURTEEN

The meeting over the Angela Purtel issue took place after school, late in May. They sat around the long rectangular table that was used for school committee meetings; Nestor, Lindsy Tamaril of the guidance department, Dean Dave Keough, Jack Crowley, a liaison from the Lowell Police Department, Angela Purtel and her mother, and Linda Starkey, a lawyer provided by the Massachusetts Teachers' Union.

Nestor sat with sweaty hands and a racing heart, feeling like a defendant in the dock, while Keough outlined the charges as well as Nestor's defense. Mrs. Purtel, an underweight blonde in a leather jacket who looked as if she'd had a hard life and wanted revenge on the world for it, interrupted to say that she demanded justice. She resembled her daughter, Nestor thought, except for the shadows under her eyes and the fact that her face was not studded with metal.

"We all want justice, Mrs. Purtel," Keough replied. He nodded toward Crowley, a crisp and official presence in his police uniform. The officer opened a folder and read, "All right... the bottom line... pursuant to complaint made etcetera etcetera... based on written affidavits from Nestor McCorley and Angela Purtel as well as interviews with others witnesses, examination of the facts around the case and relevant evidence etcetera etcetera... the Lowell Police Department does not find sufficient facts at this time to bring charges against Mr. Nestor McCorley."

"So what are you saying?" Mrs. Purtel demanded while Angela, elbows on the table, examined her split ends.

"I'm saying that an investigation was inconclusive," Crowley said.

"So this is your justice? A phony investigation?"

Linda Starkey interjected, "If we get real justice here, Mrs. Purtel, you may find your daughter charged with slander and malicious prosecution."

"And he called my daughter a fucking liar in front of the dean! Are you denying that?" She pointed the accusing finger at Nestor, who nevertheless felt as if a weight was slowly lifting off his heart.

"No, we're not denying that. Mr. McCorley will be given a three-day suspension without pay for that remark," Keough said, rising stiffly.

"A three-day suspension?" she said. "That's nothing for what he did!"

Attorney Starkey made a note on a yellow legal pad, and Crowley said, "Mrs. Purtel, think about it. Mr. McCorley was very upset by your daughter's behavior. We have numerous witnesses to that: all the students who were in the room, and Mr. Broulette. She, your daughter, obviously showed no respect for him and seemed to dislike him very much. So at this point, a teacher with no record of any such behavior… he chooses this moment to try to make some kind of sexual overture to Angela? Does that make sense to you? Honestly?"

"I wouldn't 'choose any moment,'" Nestor said, but his lawyer put her hand on his forearm and shook her head. As soon as Nestor had spoken, Angela spoke for the first time. Still poking through the ends of her hair, she said, "If you study anything about it, it's not about sex. It's about power. Or maybe he just kind of went crazy because his wife dumped him."

Nestor felt as though he had been punched in the gut. Starkey squeezed his arm harder, shaking her head slowly and resolutely.

Dean Keough said, "Well, though you may have watched a lot of Oprah, you're not a psychologist, are you, Angela? Once again, this meeting is over. Thank you for coming." Then, all at once he let the folder of papers he carried drop onto the table, and leaning over it, asked Angela, "What do you know about his wife anyway? I never hear him talk about his wife at all!"

"Word spreads," she said, smiling.

"Let's go," her mother said, "the newspaper will hear about this cover-up." She gathered her cell phone, cigarettes and car keys, muttering all the while about justice, and marched off, urging her daughter to hurry.

Nestor thanked Linda Starkey, who allowed herself the shadow of a smile. He asked if the newspaper would print the Purtels' allegations. "I doubt it. They could print that there had been an investigation of a teacher who was not charged. But they wouldn't print your name. This girl is a loose cannon if I ever saw one. Scary though, because she's as cool as a cucumber."

Nestor walked with Dean Keough out to his car. He put on his sunglasses and breathed the fresh air deeply, his suit jacket hanging over his shoulder. Summer was coming. "Thanks, Dave," he said, "thanks for believing in me."

"If I thought you were guilty, our friendship wouldn't count," he said.

"That's the way it should be."

"What the . . ." They stood in the administrative lot, which was near the entrance, but looking off toward the faculty lot, he saw only two vehicles. One was his own car, the other was a familiar red pickup. Its door opened and a man got out and cut across the swath of grass that separated the lots, walking purposefully toward them. He wore a dark sweatshirt, a Yankees baseball cap, and the scowl he could never seem to take off.

"This could get ugly, Dave," Nestor said. "Robert Casey."

"Shit, I don't have my walkie-talkie to call security."

"I don't see any weapon. Thank God for that."

He came up quickly, and ignoring Nestor, spoke to Keough, "Still protecting this piece of shit?"

"Your attitude is menacing, Mr. Casey. I'm advising you to get off school property immediately."

Nestor leaned against Keough's Crown Vic, waiting, for now, to see how this would play out, and wondering if it came to a fight, if he could take Casey. It might be tough; maybe it would come down to who was angrier, and Nestor felt he could at least match him there. He remembered the lines he'd been rehearsing the night before: *For though I am not splenitive or rash, yet I have in me something dangerous, which let thy wisdom fear.*

Casey was still speaking to Keough, but he jerked a thumb in Nestor's direction. "When he was responsible for my son, he killed him, and when he was responsible for Angela Purtel, he molested her. I want to know why you protect him. I want to know why he's still working here."

"Because in both cases he is innocent, Mr. Casey. It's that simple. And how do you know anything about Angela Purtel?"

"I know everything that concerns Coach McCorley. And I'm going to tell every parent in this school what he did to her..."

"That's harassment, Mr. Casey, and the court has already warned you about that."

"The rock you tossed through my window, Casey," Nestor said, "if it had hit my pregnant wife..." His own words were making him angry, and he was about to say, *you would have joined your son,* but he stopped himself. An image of his attorney shaking her head flashed through his mind. Besides, Ian didn't deserve to be brought into this mess. "You would have regretted it," he concluded, weakly.

"I don't know what you're talking about, McCorley. But as for your wife, she got smart quick and left you. How bad must a woman want to get away from a man to walk out on him while she's pregnant?"

Adrenalin surged with spite. Nestor pulled off his sunglasses and dropped his suit jacket, stepping toward Casey, but Keough moved between them, risking his bad back, and announced in the booming voice that for thirty years had dispersed crowds of students bent on a fight, "All right, that's it. For the last time, Casey, get off the school property, or I *will* have you arrested for trespassing."

"You're not going to get away with this," he said, and stalked off, looking back over his shoulder to glare at them.

Keough took a deep breath and turned to Nestor. "Well done. Well done, McCorley. I thought I was going to be calling an ambulance for the bastard. Not that he doesn't have it coming, just for wearing the Yankees cap, but that wouldn't be good." He shook his head. "Wouldn't be good," he repeated, and added, "more lawyers."

"You're assuming he'd be in the ambulance and not me," Nestor said. His hands were trembling with the excess of unused adrenalin. He'd have to go out to the woods for a run.

"Yes, that is what I'm assuming. Shit, I'm too old for this." They watched the pickup pull out of the parking lot and head out the back gate. "He certainly takes a keen interest in your affairs. I don't know how the hell he's connected with the Purtels. They must have talked to him after the meeting. He was waiting out here."

"There's probably an 'I Hate McCorley' page on Facebook." Nestor shook his head and picked up his jacket. "He's determined to make something out of Angela's allegation. And a lot of people want to believe the worst..."

The big man shrugged. "The people who matter don't believe it. The hell with the rest."

Nestor nodded. "I suppose. I'm just a little worn out, Dave."

"Yeah, by the way, I am sorry to hear about your wife. If there's anything I can do..."

Nestor shook his head, "No, but thanks, Dave."

"How the hell does Casey know about that?"

"I think he watches my house. He probably figured it out and told the Purtels. I don't know." He shrugged. Just one more mystery.

"Jesus. Well, the summer's here," Keough said. He opened his car door and was about to get in when he paused and asked, "And the bastard threw a rock through your window?"

"At the very least, Dave. At the very least."

The final days of the school year passed quickly. He scanned the list of works that he had ticked off on his honors syllabus: *The Odyssey, Antigone, The Inferno, The Canterbury Tales,* and *Macbeth,* before putting a check beside the final one, *Things Fall Apart* by Chinua Achebe.

The final bell rang on June 20th. He looked forward to the long days of summer, during which he could see his son. To have more time, he decided not to do drywall for Acropolis Construction. Instead, Nestor agreed to make home visits to incoming freshmen whose parents did not speak English, and explain the paperwork to them—bus schedules, free and reduced lunch forms, and orientation programs.

Most lived in the more run-down sections of the city, the projects—tenements that landlords rarely visited, where old furniture was piled in backyards, overflowing garbage bins soured the allies, and curtains blew out of open windows. All were poor, but many maintained their dignity. They kept their homes clean, often under the gaze of the Sacred Heart, and offered Nestor coffee, or a plate of *arroz con gandules*. Not unlike his father's people in Ireland. Others seemed to have given up, or given in to drugs or alcohol; traded ambition for a disability check and video games. Nestor had just come out of an apartment in the projects on the North Common, where he had spoken to an unshaven man with no teeth, or perhaps he could not be bothered to put them in. From the man's mumblings, he understood that the prospective student was not in, but little else, and was happy to finally leave. He handed the man the paperwork and highlighted a number he could call with questions.

As he walked out of the building, he looked across the street at his old school, St. Brigid's, still sitting like a red brick shoe box at one end of a large gray lot—the granite church with its Gothic spire at the other. He lingered there, gazing at the row of windows in the classrooms, and in particular at the windows of the room where he had been introduced to Catholic education.

He crossed the street, walked past his car, and found himself on the familiar old stairs, gazing up at the graven cross above the entrance. The door was locked, but there were two cars parked close to the building. He pushed the doorbell, and looking through a window up the interior stairs saw a stout, middle-aged woman peer around the corner of a doorway at him from Sister Winifred's former office. She paused for a moment, and then came down and pushed open the door.

"My name is Nestor McCorley." He explained to her, and perhaps to himself, as best he could, what he was doing there.

She smiled, perhaps a bit warily, and extended a hand. "Sister Veronica. And you'd like to see your old classroom?"

"If you don't mind…"

She wore a simple pale blue skirt. The small silver crucifix that hung over her white blouse was the only indication of the vows she had taken. The imposing black habit—tunic, veil, wimple and rosary belt—had been consigned to the history of the order.

He was conscious, as he stood in the classroom, of time as a river of days and years that flowed about the soul, shaping it as the flowing water had shaped the granite of the White Mountains, wearing smooth curving basins in one place, and breaking through in another. The days that had shaped him seemed to flow about him once again as he walked toward the tiny desk where he had sat in fear, and later in blessed calm. He reentered the river: the corner where he had been consigned his first day, the row of windows framing the North Common, the letters of the alphabet, upper and lower case, stretching out above the blackboard, the sad crucifix above the teacher's desk. He wondered what had ever become of St. Michael, Theresa, Cecile and all the sisters of those days at St. Brigid's.

As if she had understood his thoughts, Sister Veronica said, "I'm afraid there's no one left from the time when you were a student in this room. Mainly lay teachers now. Who was your teacher here?"

By "here," he knew that she meant this room. Perhaps she could sense the strong feelings the place had brought back. "Sister St. Michael, at first."

"How was she?"

"Since I have nothing good to say about her, I won't say anything."

"I'm sorry," she said, but the tone of her voice implied that she was not surprised.

"Do you know what became of her? Is she still alive? It seems she was transferred out or fired after my first day here." The thought crossed his mind that he would like to find her and tell her that she was no sort of Christian, and a bully of small children.

"She left the order. She's working with alcoholics and drug addicts now, as a counselor."

Left the order, or was tossed out, he wondered. How much had Sister St. Michael changed? Often he had tried to explain her behavior to himself. He'd heard that former alcoholics often worked with others who were struggling with the bottle. Maybe she had been a closet alcoholic; it was all a long time ago.

"What about Sister Theresa?" he asked. "I know she left this school years ago. Is she still in the order?"

Her averted eyes, and a slow movement toward the door, gave Nestor to understand that she was not keen on discussing the fates of former nuns. But he was taken aback as she continued tentatively. "I'm afraid she passed away."

"When?"

"Not long after she left here. I'm only repeating what I've heard."

"My God, she was young. What happened to her?"

"I… well, I don't know the details. It was before my time here."

"I understand." She appeared uncomfortable, and he wondered how much she knew. Nestor changed the subject. "Sister Winifred took over our class after Sister St. Michael left. She was wonderful."

Sister Veronica's face brightened. "Oh yes, she was indeed. Her death was a blow to the whole order. There's a photo of her in the lobby." They walked the vacant corridor together.

In Memoriam, Sister Winifred, S.H.F. Even in the black and white photograph, her eyes, amid myriad wrinkles, spoke to him of calm resignation to the travails of life in a world the sisters always referred to as, "this vale of tears." He touched the picture frame reverently. "Thank you, Sister Veronica."

"I'm always happy to meet an alumnus. Peace be with you."

"And with you, Sister."

He was descending the stairs toward the great doors when he heard someone coming up from the basement, where the school hall and cafeteria were located. A white head, blue work clothes, body bent forward as he lugged a bucket of what looked like tar up the stairs.

"Maurice?" Nestor asked. He could not believe that he still haunted these halls.

The custodian looked up. "Yes, it's me." He put the bucket down on the landing and pulled a stained handkerchief out of his pocket, wiping the sweat from his brow.

"I was a student here," Nestor said.

Maurice scanned his face and sniffed. "I remember you."

"Let me give you a hand with that bucket," Nestor offered, taking the tacky handle grip.

"No, no," the older man said, clutching his arm. "I have it." His tone was insistent, and Nestor released the handle. "I'm not an old man," he said, and Nestor reflected that though he looked washed-out and weary, he might not really be more than fifty.

Nestor imagined that the tar would be used to patch a leak in the flat roof. "I'm not saying you're old, but the bucket looks heavy. Let me help you get it up to the roof, Maurice. I don't mind."

The custodian shook his head. "It's my penance," he said. "Didn't the nuns teach you that you need to do penance? Every single day. I thought that was one thing everyone learned in this place." And with that he hefted the bucket and continued his slow ascent, mumbling words that Nestor couldn't make out, probably in French.

Performance night was drawing nigh. Ann called to remind him that the final dress rehearsal for *Hamlet* would be the next night, Wednesday night. Thursday would be a "dark night." She said she always believed in a dark night before opening night.

At home, he organized his paperwork and wrote comments on the home visits. His mind was elsewhere, dwelling one minute with joyful longing on his son, whom he would see this weekend, and the next on Hamlet. His lines ran like a recording on a loop through his mind continually, and he sometimes felt that every remark made to him in the course of the day could be answered with a relevant quote from the Prince of Denmark. And every time the tape in his head ran through Hamlet's question to Rosencrantz and Guildenstern—"Were you not sent for?"—he remembered Declan's words, "She was hired."

Thursday night, "the dark night," he spent with Abby. They drove to Concord and had a drink at the Colonial Inn, where an older woman played "Lady Be Good" with youthful dexterity on an upright piano. Candlelight glowed warmly over the rich mahogany of the tables, and no television with its incessant prattle disrupted the healing calm. Music, candlelight, a beautiful woman. *Now there's a holy trinity*, Nestor thought.

"Are you nervous about tomorrow night?" she asked.

"A little. I have a recurring dream that I'm on the stage and I completely forget all my lines, but that's a pretty typical actor's dream, or nightmare. Anyway, it distracts me from other problems."

She reached across the table and touched his hand in the way, Nestor thought, Minerva used to. "Will you stay with me tonight?"

It was only then that he realized that she must wonder what he had been waiting for. Maybe he had become accustomed to Minerva's attitude toward premarital sex. She had asked him once if it was important to him to marry a virgin. His answer had seemed to deflate her. "Not really. I wouldn't care if you'd lost your virginity, as long as you still had the box it came in." She didn't really get the joke, or maybe she just didn't appreciate a joke about something that was a serious matter to her. Looking back on it, he imagined it must be disappointing to offer a man this great gift, only to find out it really wasn't that important to him.

And now Abby was offering, not virginity, but intimacy, the solace of her body. He had enjoyed her company and friendship, and had imagined sex with her, but just hadn't done anything about it. She was waiting for an answer, and what answer could a man give, looking into those empathetic blue eyes, following the curve of her neck, the blond hair that shone in the candlelight. "Yes, of course, Abby. You know I'm sorry I'm not more... I mean I do like you very much."

"Ah, when a young man declares his dispassion."

"I'm glad you're smiling. I'm sure a lot of women would be annoyed. I'm just a little lost right now."

"I understand. But Nestor, no matter how you feel about me..."

"You're great, Abby..."

"You're only saying that because it's true." They laughed, and Nestor said, "It *is* true." She lifted his hand in both of hers and spoke with such kindness that something long closed in his heart seemed to open, and he wondered if he was beginning to love her, and if that would mean that he did not love his estranged wife. "It's sad," she said. "I know you loved, or you love, Minerva. You may be in love with her for a while. You love your son, and that will never change, but this bad thing has happened between you and her. It's not your fault, but you do need to move on at some point. It doesn't have to be with me, but you have to do it."

Softly she spoke, and with such earnestness that the words touched him. He didn't make any jokes about the '86 Red Sox. "You're right, Abby." He felt then like the little boy who was about to cry when his parents left him with strangers at St. Brigid's. "I'll be right back," he said. Thankfully, there was no one in the men's room. In the mirror, he saw that his eyes were red and glassy. He ran the cold water, splashed it over his face, and setting both hands on the sink, leaned toward his reflection. "Move on," he told himself.

He didn't want to have sex with another woman in the bed he'd shared with Minerva, and he was relieved when she said they'd have to go up to Nashua so she could let her dog out. The great bear of a Newfoundland bounded through the door, wagging not just her tail, but her whole body.

"Good girl, Sheba!" They waited outside while the dog sniffed about the yard and did her business. Arm in arm by the porch railing, they watched the time-lost stars burn, silent infernos in a black sky. Once inside, they kissed by the closed door. All that Nestor could think was that her kiss was different than Minerva's; her fragrance, different; the feel of her body, different, and he didn't know why he had to experience her only in comparison rather than simply as the beautiful woman that she was.

In the living room, photos of her parents and friends watched him from atop a bookshelf, and he was reminded of how very little he really knew about her, so absorbed had he been in his own difficulties. She led him on to the bedroom, where her harp sat like the golden wing of an angel in one corner. Above her bed hung a framed poster of a woman in shades of blue and white, her face half in shadow, her fingers running over the strings of a harp. "Catrin Finch, Carnaval de Venise, 2001."

"I'd love to hear you play," he said.

"Yes, but not now."

"No." Nestor tried to place this feeling that was flowing from his heart through his body. Excitement, yes. Nervousness, yes. And something else that he realized he had not felt in a long time, perhaps since he was a child— that he was committing a sin, staining his soul in some way, and he tried to clear his mind of it, because it made him feel ashamed and foolish. *This is where I need to be. This is where every man wants to be. You have to move on.* The room was lit only dimly from the living room, but Abby took some matches from a drawer and lit a candle on the dresser.

She let go of his hand and began to undress, pulling her sweater over her head, unbuttoning her blouse, unhooking her bra and letting it fall, watching his face, as women do, to try to catch a sign of approval or disdain. He smiled and whispered, "You're beautiful, Abby," and he remembered the first time he'd seen her, how he wished that he could paint her beauty, but a feeling of anxiety had begun to impinge on this appreciation, because the normal physical reaction he would have expected in himself had not occurred.

He took off his clothes and sat on the bed. She pushed his shoulders back against the pillows and straddled him, her blonde hair falling over his chest as she kissed him. His anxiety was turning to panic; he had never experienced this sort of failure, nor even given it a thought. He tried to focus, to shake off the strange discomfiture that had unsettled him. She arched her back as he kissed her breasts and ran his hands along the curves he had often admired, but his own body, in mutiny (against what?), remained completely unprepared for sex.

She was no doubt aware of his difficulty, and rising on her knees, slid a hand between his legs. Shame burned his face as she touched him. "I'm sorry," he said. "I just don't understand…"

"That's all right," she said in soothing tones. "It happens."

"Not to me. It's never happened. It's very embarrassing."

"It's psychological, Nestor. You're in a difficult place."

"I would have thought this is the easiest place in the world to be. I'm in bed with a beautiful woman I really like, and the elevator is still on the first floor."

Her laughter lightened the mood, and she said, "I'm sure there's nothing wrong physically…"

"It's like she put a spell on me."

"The witch?"

"No, Minerva. I know she's left me, but I still feel like I'm cheating on her. I mean, I'm supposed to get the divorce papers soon, but I'm still married. She says our vows meant nothing to me because we swore them before a God I don't believe in, but I do believe in the vows, or I did, because I gave my word. Maybe that's why…" She slid off of him and sat leaning on her elbow, listening in the dim light, her hair casting a shadow over half of her face. "I'm sorry, Abby, you don't want to listen to all this shit. You deserve someone… I should go."

"It's all right. It's all right," she said. "I can't blame you because you loved her too much." She comforted him as only a good woman can, with deep-hearted concern, a tender voice, empathy, and somewhere, beneath it all, strength beyond a man's. She kissed him twice and they lay back in silence and fell asleep, and Nestor was relieved to escape the shame of this surprising predicament.

When light began to filter into the room, he was deep in sleep, floating among the mangroves of Caesar Creek with Minerva. The water was still, life was still, the air hung with the delicate fragrance of the spider lily, and in the shadows of the overhanging boughs, the canoe drifted past wading herons while birds filled the pathless, impenetrable groves with their song.

Oh, her dark eyes stirred him as she pointed eastward and spoke of a passage to the sea. Her lids closed as he drew near, and he saw the shadows of the leaves on her face before he closed his eyes, too, and felt the warm welcome of her lips. When he awoke, the image of Minerva hung in the air before him as he stretched, but began to dissipate in air as he recovered his sense of place, in Abby's room.

She awoke as he did, and sliding a hand down his chest, stopped suddenly and said, "Well, the spell is broken."

Nestor was genuinely relieved. He pulled Abby closer and kissed her. His hand ran down the small of her back and over the perfection of what the urban dictionary aptly named *the marble peach*. At that moment he wondered how men ever convince themselves that anything else is important, anything but this warm proximity to a creature of soft heart and soft—soft everything.

"So soft," he said.

"What did you expect, sandpaper?"

He smiled, his face buried in her blond hair, though in one sun-dappled corner of his mind he still saw Minerva drifting, alone now in the canoe, those dark eyes downcast. *It wasn't my choice*, he told himself. *Live in the present*. He felt Abby opening her legs, and he lifted his body and slid between them.

"Happy Birthday, Mr. President," she sang in a throaty whisper in his ear, and he laughed aloud and thought, *Surely, if I could get my mind right, it would not be difficult to let myself love this woman.*

CHAPTER FIFTEEN

Nestor had told Minerva that he would pick up little Joe at Marina's restaurant, La Aguacatala, at ten o'clock, and bring him back at four o'clock so he could get ready for opening night. He planned to stop at home, shower and shave, then grab a coffee and newspaper at the Market Street Market and saunter over to the restaurant. He wondered if Minerva would be there to hand his son over to him, but then he told himself that it really didn't matter.

When he pulled into his driveway, he was shocked to see Minerva's blue Ford Taurus parked in its former customary spot under the basketball hoop. It was empty, but when he got out of his car, he saw her coming toward him from the steps. She was crumpling a piece of paper, perhaps a note she'd been writing, and stuffing it into her pocket. Their son was not with her. "Where were you?" she asked as they approached each other.

"I was with a woman I know."

"You were with another woman?"

"Yeah, it was either that or join a monastery. And as you know, I wouldn't fit in there."

She looked at the ground between them. He remembered his dream— the downcast eyes. "It did not take you long."

He steeled himself against the love he felt swelling in his chest. "Well, it sure seemed like a long time. Some of those nights in that empty apartment last winter seemed like years."

She nodded, and looked away, and Nestor saw something in the movement of her jaw, the way she used to purse her lips and seem to cover her upper teeth with her tongue when she was trying not to cry. "It's all my fault," she said, finally.

"Oh, I guess we both could have done better…"

"No, it was my fault. I brought it all on. I'm afraid I invited all the evil, without thinking…"

"You invited the evil? You were just lighting a candle, Minerva."

"Before that. Nestor, *te puse un hechizo.*"

"*Un hechizo*? A spell? You put a spell on me?"

"To make you love me, and then you asked me to marry you that day. So our whole marriage it was begin with this spell."

She'd always had trouble with the past participle *begun*. He began to laugh, and asked again, incredulous, "You put a spell on me?"

"My grandmother… Nestor, in Latin America religion and superstition get mixed up sometime, but I didn't mean any evil… I didn't really believe it. It was just an old thing, like you have the foot of a rabbit, but I did it."

"What did you do exactly?"

"I'm so ashamed to say. I made tea for you with the water that I poured over my breasts."

Later, he was not sure how it happened, but she was in his arms. The last time he had held her like this she had been pregnant, and he marveled at her body, now returned to the slenderness he'd known when they met. "Minerva, I loved you before that day. And I love that you cared enough to try to put a spell on me, but, come on, I was under your spell the night we met. What is love but a spell?" He would never believe in Prendeville's chemical reactions, his tubes and pumps. Prendeville didn't even believe in them. "All the madness that came after had nothing to do with your magic love tea."

"I don't know. I felt that I couldn't be strong in the only place I was always strong, because of what I did, and because of what you did, too. It frightened me. I was afraid my baby would be punished for it, and, Nestor,

I fell apart."

Nestor was thinking once again of *The Art of War*. Sometimes strength is a weakness. The strongest gate is undefended. He could not explain any of this to her now—maybe he never could. They stood close, holding each other's arms, and Minerva's voice was low, her head bowed toward his chest. "Father Leahy likes you very much, even though that you are..."

"A pagan."

"He didn't use that word. But he said that even if we do not share the same beliefs, we share the same values. That's true, isn't it?"

"Of course it is! So you'll listen to Father Leahy instead of Father Felix?"

"Yes, I think Father Leahy is right. Even Marquis Alicea says that you are a good man."

In some primitive part of his brain, the wolf lifted its head and inhaled the air that carried the scent of the hunter. "Do you talk to him?"

"Well, not really. I mean, I have now because he's in Lowell." She saw his widening eyes and hastened to add, "Not to see me! He's helping Marina with some kind of business plan for the restaurant, and he has some meetings in Boston. He is for a few days staying at the Radisson."

"So he knows what's going on?" He recalled the day they had gone to Café Paradiso after the sonogram reported that the baby was a boy. Hadn't she spoken with her sister on the way? Had she then spoken with Alicea? Was that how the madwoman, or the paid actress, had found them?

"Yes, since the beginning, because he was advising Marina... but he always say... *says* something good about you."

All war is based on deception. Since the beginning. "That's very kind of him."

"Maybe I have no right to ask, Nestor, but are you in love with this other woman?"

This morning he had thought that he could love Abby. Maybe he could have. Maybe he would even have been happier with her, in the long run, than with Minerva, but happiness didn't matter, only love mattered. With

Minerva once more so close he felt like a heroin addict who had just gotten a big shot of smack in the arm. Might as well be a spell, he thought. "I want my wife and son back," he said.

"Nestor, do you think we can make it work? Be happy, the way we were before?"

"I love you as you are, Minerva. Just accept me for who I am, and we'll be fine."

She frowned and said, "I can smell that other woman on you. You didn't really answer me when I asked you if you love her."

"No. I like her very much, but I love you. Still, let me talk to her and explain what's happened. I'll end it, but I need to explain it to her. She'll understand. She knows I love you."

"You're going to talk to her, but not make love to her again?"

"Are you coming home?"

"Yes, I'll come home."

"When?"

"Tomorrow?"

How long he had waited to hear those words. "Then it's over. I'll tell her tonight. She's coming to the play."

"Oh, your play is opening tonight. Are you nervous?"

The same thing Abby had asked. "A little bit, yeah. I have a recurring dream that I'm on stage and forget all my lines."

"That won't happen. Marina is watching Joseph at the restaurant. I didn't want to take him in case you went over there early. I'll go back. She may be getting busy."

"I'll just shower and shave and I'll meet you at the boathouse. We can walk him over at the river." Her face in sunlight and leaf shadow now had lost the tautness of worry, her eyes had lost their apprehension, and her smile had regained its lovely witchcraft. "My God, Minerva, it's so good to see you smile again."

He kissed her, feeling the spell, the love-drug running in his veins.

A wife returned, a son beginning a new life with two parents who loved him, and who loved each other. When she had gone, he went upstairs, and rummaging in the drawer by the sink, he pulled out the gold ring and slid it onto his finger. A new chapter was beginning, and he thought of the title that Charles Dickens had given to Book One of *A Tale of Two Cities*: "Recalled to Life."

The Merrimack River is born out of the Pemigewasset in the mountains of New Hampshire, and is fed by Winnipesaukee, the Contoocook, the Souhegan, and the Nashua. The Concord River flows northward to join the Merrimack in Lowell, where it bends and turns northeast, breaking over a spine of rocks, some sunken and others rising out of the river in outcroppings where stunted maples, Canada yew and shrub thickets sprout from mud-filled crevices. The river runs on through Lawrence and Haverhill to empty into the sea at Newburyport, one-hundred-and-ten miles from its source.

And there, in a crumbling Victorian home near its mouth, forty-four miles downstream from Lowell, Eileen Nash sat at a large mahogany table in a room on the second floor. A single window beside her looked out over Merrimac Street to the widening estuary of the Merrimack River. Between the near bank and Ram Island, a crowd of naked masts gleamed in the afternoon sun—the moored sailing vessels of the well-to-do members of the Newburyport Yacht Club.

Eileen Nash was not taking in the view. Her eyes were fixed on a pair of muslin dolls on the table. Beside them was a glue stick, some flat disks that resembled eyes, doll stuffing pellets, scissors, sewing materials, patches of various fabrics, and a copy of *The Lowell Sun,* the pages of which were beginning to stiffen.

She picked up the smaller of the two dolls; it was six inches long. Her jaw jutting forward as she concentrated, she rolled the glue thickly and set the dark eyes, the pink triangular nose and a hapless red smile. "And my big dolly, well, I already have a face for you." She chuckled to herself and mumbled a low stream of curses, "He'll get his comeuppance, oh, we'll see to that, him and his little bitch. His little god-fearing, candle-lighting bitch." She held the doll at arm's length and said, "What do you think?"

She was alone until she asked the question, and then she had company.

A man in a black-belted leather coat, now at the other side of the table, leaned forward. His pale eyes studied the doll, his thin, arching eyebrows rising; his lips puckering. A smile then broke over the broad flat face, and his large ears seemed to rise slightly upward. "Very nice," he said. "Lovely." Meditatively, he fingered a star-shaped military medal pinned on his coat and said, "They always say they've killed me, but I never seem to die. They always say they've defeated me, but I never really lose."

"They lie," she said. "That's what they're good at. That's what they do."

"Pretty lies for the sheep. Whereas I tell the truth! Isn't that backward?" He stretched his legs and smiled contentedly, his hands folded across his chest.

"I don't care about heaven," she said. "I want justice."

"Justice is my business! Two eyes for an eye! A set of teeth for a tooth." The two of them laughed, and the man's pale eyes, like ashen coals under a gusting bellows, glowed red. When she refocused her attention on her task she was alone again, though she continued to chuckle softly to herself.

Opening *The Lowell Sun* to a page marked "Wedding Announcements," she folded the paper so that a photo of a smiling couple was before her "Herrera—McCorley." Below it she read, in a mocking voice, "Andres and Barbara Herrera of Miami, Florida, announce the engagement of their little god-fearing, candle-lighting bitch daughter Minerva." She was taken with another bout of hilarity as she picked up the scissors, and had to wipe the tears of mirth from her eyes before she could begin to cut out the face of Minerva Herrera, leaving Nestor McCorley embracing emptiness.

Backstage, Nestor sat in the corner with a small glass of Jameson. He would allow himself one shot, no more, before he went onstage. The other actors left him alone. A part like Hamlet required concentration; no one wanted to jinx the role. He was like a pitcher in the seventh inning of a no-hitter; quiet and apart, and that suited him, because he wanted to take a few minutes to recall, to relive in his mind the walk along the Merrimack River arm in arm with Minerva, pushing Joseph in the stroller. With his family reunited and his wife beside him he felt the—what did they call them—the endorphins, flowing into his troubled brain, calming his nerves and soothing his spirit.

She leaned against him as they walked, and in memory he heard her words more clearly than the bustle of preparation and the low voices around him. "It hurt me so much whenever I spoke with you. Always you seem so sad."

"Oh, you noticed! I thought I was a better actor." The prince, his constant companion, cloaked in black, buzzed: *Seems, madame? Nay, it is, I know not "seems."* "My world was falling about my ears! And you say I 'seemed sad?' How did you expect me to…" She kissed him then, again and again rapidly and stroked his face, saying, "Let's not go back to that now. I love you… I know that now."

It was the fate of the literary man to have a mind resounding with the echoes of words, and as he embraced her warmly with a heart so full, Keats' famous line sprang into his mind: *La Belle Dame sans merci hath thee in thrall.* A pair of gulls wheeled above them clamoring and Joseph in his stroller held out a hand, opening and closing his tiny fist and saying, "Oh. Oh."

Nestor and Minerva broke into laughter and bent down beside the boy to watch the bright birds dive into a water-skimming glide over the river. They stopped the stroller at a bench in the sun and spoke of their new life. The image that came vaguely to Nestor's mind then was the worker painstakingly mending the crumbling foundation of a home.

Nestor stood and sighed contentedly at these memories and swallowed the last few drops of Jameson. What was not so pleasant to remember was Abby's call late in the afternoon. She was gracious and said that she would be selfish to have wished things to turn out differently. "I know you can't see me again," she said, and Nestor admitted that it was true. She wished him luck on opening night, but said that she would not go. And before she hung up, she added, "You deserve good things, Nestor."

He thought about those words. Before ever reading *Hamlet*, he had instinctively shared the prince's opinion: "Use every man after his desert and who should 'scape whipping?" Maybe none of us really deserved good things, but it showed something admirable in her character that she thought otherwise.

Eddie had done a thorough job publicizing his *Hamlet* on local radio and in the newspaper, and the upstairs of the Old Court was filled to capacity—about eighty people. On the other side of the curtain, Nestor could hear Alena, his sister, loudly telling a group of people that Hamlet was her brother, Nestor! She was proud of him, God bless her. His mother had planned to attend, but she was not feeling well.

Eddie, dressed as Horatio, gave his usual introduction, requesting that the audience turn off their cell phones and reminding them of upcoming productions by the Imagine Theater. Nestor could hear Ophelia doing vocal exercises in the ladies' lavatory/dressing room backstage, and the beat of some hip-hop music that the staff had cranked up in the kitchen below.

"And so, ladies and gentlemen, Imagine Theater is proud to present its first production of a Shakespearean play. Please sit back, and in just a minute you will experience the Bard at the top of his game in *The Tragedy of Hamlet, Prince of Denmark.*"

Eddie darted back between the curtains while the audience applauded, and nearly collided with a stagehand who was about to peek out at the house. "Jack! Go down the back stairs and ask them to turn down that rap shit in the kitchen! Jesus Christ! And tell Ophelia to shut the fuck up back there, we got the curtain coming up! Go! Kelly! Drop the dry ice now!" He looked left and right; expectant actors stood in the wings. "Places!" he gave a thumbs up and stepped aside as the curtain opened to reveal a platform before Elsinore, its crenellated walls and parapets projected by Wellington's gobo onto a scrim behind Francisco, the solitary watchman, and Bernardo, stepping out of the curling dry-ice fog to relieve him.

Nestor surreptitiously observed the audience from a gap in the curtain at one of the wings. He recognized a few faces in the first and second rows, but beyond that they faded into darkness, shadowy heads outlined in halos of light. Now Eddie joined the others on the stage, saying, "What, has this thing appear'd again tonight?" while behind the curtain, Jack Dacey, imposing in pale makeup and rented armor as the warlike ghost of Hamlet's father, put on his sternest face to prepare for his first visitation upon the night watchmen.

The actors all seemed more relaxed once the first scene had concluded without mishap, and Eddie circulated among them backstage, encouraging them like a halftime coach, "Better than in rehearsal!"

Nestor tried to empty his mind and let it fill with the character. Hamlet. Indecisive, haunted, needing proof of murder to avenge with murder. Not trusting his senses, the "honesty" of his father's ghost, who spurred him on to bloody revenge. Not trusting the love of Ophelia because he had seen the inconstancy of his mother's love for his father. Everyone "seeming." *Just play the part. Say the words. Speak the speech. Scholar and soldier. Anon he finds him.* He had spent so much time with Hamlet that he felt as though he was alive somewhere, or was brought to life every time this play was staged.

Just before he took his place for Scene 2, Eddie clutched his shoulder offstage. "You're gonna be a great Hamlet. Your own father died recently, right? That's all you need to feel. Just remember him." *Aye, while memory holds a seat in this distracted globe.*

The actors, as Shakespeare wrote, had their entrances and their exits. Nestor, through the strange metamorphosis of the theater, began to feel what the melancholy prince would have felt, to see the other characters and react to them as Hamlet would have seen them and reacted to them;

the loyal Horatio, the double-dealing Rosencrantz and Guildenstern, the long-winded Polonius, the treacherous king. It was no longer acting; it was responding as it was natural for this other self to respond. Only when he was offstage, when, for example, Polonius was giving his farewell advice to Laertes, did Nestor begin to think of extraneous things, of embracing his wife once again, of his son's smile, waving his tiny arms at the life that abounded on and around the river, and of Abby's classy reaction, but he let all of Nestor's thoughts fall away at his entrances, and picked up Hamlet's. Between acts, he considered the purport of the next scenes, and outlined his actions and speeches mentally.

Act III. The King has bellowed for light and rushed from the room, certain that the young prince is insane, or has knowledge of the secret murder he has committed. One hand on his sheathed dagger, Hamlet steps into the circle of light that Wellington had focused at the center of the dark stage:

> 'Tis now the very witching time of night,
> When churchyards yawn and hell itself breathes out
> Contagion to this world: now could I drink hot blood,
> And do such bitter business as the day
> Would quake to look on.

For a moment the audience was so still that Nestor could hear the faint hum of the refrigerated beer coolers behind the bar at the back of the room, and then he heard a voice, one he had heard before, one that burst through the surface of who he was on the stage and sank deep into who he was in life.

"Hell will breathe contagion on your house, Nestor McCorley!" He stepped out of the spotlight and raised a hand over his eyes, but he knew who it was. The house lights came up. "Hell's contagion and death!" He saw her gray hair, her hateful eyes—heard her scornful words. If she was an actress, she was a damned good one.

"Such bitter business! Ha! I'll give you some bitter business you son of a Greek whore!" Nestor jumped from the stage, but a crowd had formed around her, a circle of moving bodies jostling her toward the stairs. Wellington and the sound man were at its center, joined now by a bouncer who'd rushed up from downstairs. The door at the bottom of the stairs closed and the woman's shouts became less audible, and then stopped quite suddenly altogether. Nestor began to push his way through the crowd toward the exit when he was pulled back sharply by the arm.

"What the hell are you doing?" It was Eddie.

"I've been looking for her for a long time. I have to..."

Still gripping his arm, he leaned toward Nestor and spoke into his ear. "You have to get back on that stage. McCorley, don't do this to me, man. You're the show. I put the theater company's name on the line because I believed in you. Don't fuck me over." In a louder and suddenly lighter voice, he said, "Sorry about that, ladies and gentlemen! One of Lowell's many eccentrics! If you'll take your seats we can continue. Thank you. Thank you for your patience."

Nestor whispered, "Let me take a five minute break."

Eddie Saitz spoke through nearly clenched teeth, and Nestor realized that he had never heard him speak angrily before. "There's no five minute break in the middle of Act III! This is the fucking theater! Respect it! Gertrude and Polonius are in their places waiting for you. Don't fuck the entire cast! Take the stage! Anyway, what would you do if you caught her? She'll give you the same witchy bullshit. She ain't gonna explain anything to you! Then what? You beat the shit out of the bitch? Oh that's a good idea. Take the stage!"

The audience had taken their seats again. There was something in what the man said, he knew. Besides, an image had flashed through his mind of Eddie, alone after the show closed, packing lights and speakers and props into his station wagon parked in the alley, lucky to have made a couple of hundred bucks for the next production, but never complaining because he loved the theater so much. He couldn't leave him in the lurch.

In any case, he had his wife back; the crazy woman was irrelevant now. Reluctantly, unable to ruin his friend's production, and the work of so many, still unsure of whether he was doing the right thing, he remounted the stage. The house lights came down and the circle of light reappeared, but he was no longer the Prince of Denmark. He was Nestor McCorley doing his best to recite lines convincingly, and once in Act IV, when Gertrude asked him, "To whom do you speak this?" he stood mute, like a rank amateur for several seconds, transfixed by the sight of Hamlet's father's ghost entering through the audience.

Eddie fed him a line in a loud whisper from the wing. He stumbled on, but it was at that point, looking out over the rows of spectators turned toward the bloodless father, the ashen king now silently approaching, that Nestor was taken with an inexplicable feeling of dread, an oppressive weight that settled in his chest and grew heavier into Act V, when he said to Eddie's Horatio with utter sincerity, *Thou wouldst not think how ill all's here about my heart.*

The normal post-production opening night rush of relief, of tension flowing out of the body, of intense camaraderie with one's fellow actors; Nestor felt none of it. The other actors were circulating among the remaining spectators near the bar, discussing with each other the small glitches, blocking, who had skipped a line here or upstaged another actor there, and of course the crazy lady. "Who was she?" "Was she shouting at Nestor?"

"All right, all right, forget about it," Eddie was saying. "Like I said, another Lowell nutcase." Nestor gave his sister the same reassurances. "Anyway, you were very good!" she said.

"And you're completely objective."

Ann handed Nestor a bouquet of flowers, but he could see by her expression that her initial observation had been confirmed. Sir Laurence Olivier had nothing to worry about. He thanked her without registering whether the flowers were from her or someone else, and a minute later he slipped out of the crowd and was wandering down Market Street, the bouquet dangling from his hand. He pulled his cell phone from his pocket and turned it back on. No messages. He shivered with a kind of shame as he recalled his onstage lapse, at how he had let the madwoman unsettle him and get under his skin. *How all occasions do inform against me.* No, not all. Minerva was back, and Joseph. Nothing else mattered. Hang onto that.

But why such hatred? What had he ever done to call down this fury? Don't think that way—that's insane. Still, the dead boy sprawled on the track, Angela Purtel, this howling witch? They say things come in threes. Maybe it's over.

Lost in these thoughts, he was aware of, but paid little attention to the figure whose steps, behind him, were quickening. He moved aside to let the person pass, not turning to focus on him until he was aware of the other's proximity, and that he had slowed his pace to walk beside him. Nestor took an involuntary and rapid step backward. The man who faced him was well-built, older than Nestor, but much tougher, that was for sure. Hispanic. His shaved head glistened in the light from a street lamp. On his thick neck the numbers 978, the Lowell area code, were tattooed, and on his face, three black-inked tears seemed to roll out of one eye and down his cheek.

"*Me conoces?*" he asked. "You know me?"

Christ, here we go again. Someone else who hates me for some reason I can't understand. A comic image passed through his mind of himself beating the man with the bouquet of flowers, followed quickly by images that were less comic. "Were you one of my students in Adult Ed?"

The man pulled up his shirt. "You know this?" Across his muscular abdomen was another tattoo: the five-pointed crown and the letters LK.

"No," Nestor lied. "I'm sorry. I don't know you. *Buenas noches, amigo.*" He began to walk quickly away, but he stopped when the man called out, "I know *you* McCorley."

Oh shit. He turned to face the music. "How?"

"Damn, you saved the life of my sister's boy."

He studied the figure under the streetlight. "You're Ismael's uncle?"

The man came toward him and reached out, offering a small set of black and gold beads attached to a wooden cross. Nestor accepted them. Apparently this was some kind of tribute. "Listen. Ismael tol' me whachu done. Ramon Trinidad don't forget shit like that. So Ismael was talkin' to his boys up here. He say this bitch, Angela Purtel, she tryin' to take you down."

"She's just a crazy kid. It's all bullshit. Tell him not to worry about it."

"No, see I'm here to tell *you* not to worry about it." He held up a smart phone and pushed a button. Angela appeared on the small screen, crying. "I made it up. Mr. McCorley didn't do nothin'. I'm really sorry. The guy paid me to say it." Real, not tattooed tears, streamed down her face before her head hung low and shook with heaving sobs.

A pang of fear shot through his body. "What the hell did you do?"

He held the phone up and pushed another couple of buttons. "Deleted. We didn't give her the bullet she deserved, but she was damn scared. An' she better be. She gonna say she made it up—thassa truth anyway."

"My God. Why did you get involved in this, Ramon? It was nearly settled!"

"Well it's *all* settled now. Like I said, I owe you."

"You can't go threatening a high school girl! She's a kid for Chrissakes! What she did was wrong, but…"

"What, you gonna let some bitch ruin your fuckin' life 'cause she's a kid? She betta grow up 'fore she get herself in some shit she can't cry her way out of."

"If we threatened every high school kid that said crazy shit…"

"Look, I don't care how old she is, man. She betta learn words can be dangerous. You get yourself killed with words. She betta learn that fast."

Nestor took a deep breath. No one knew better than he how dangerous words could be. Trinidad was right about that. "Ramon. You know the expression 'with friends like you I don't need enemies'? Let me deal with my own problems." He tried to sound as stern as he could, but Ramon Trinidad was not going to be impressed with his stern manner, and besides, he was holding a fucking bouquet. "You might really mess me up big time." He sighed, "You didn't hurt Angela? You're sure?"

"Nah, we jus' let her know you got some fuckin' bad friends. You hear her say some guy paid her to say that shit?"

"Yeah. Was his name Casey?"

"Yeah, I think it was—you wan' me to pull a Rambo on that *chirujo*? We see how smart that mutherfucka is wid a trey-eight in 'is grill."

"No! No, thank you! Don't do that! And Angela's all right?"

"She's fine, an' you all set bro, believe me. She ain't stupid. You got any other haters fuckin' wichyou, you come look for me at Club 21. I don' know what made you try to take care of Ismael steada jus' savin' y'own ass, but I lay down my beads to you. Ramon Trinidad gotchu covered from now on."

"Ramon, I don't want your help!" he called after the retreating figure, but a black Escalade that had been idling down the street pulled up and he hopped in. Nestor watched the taillights slip away down Market Street. "Shit!" he said, and flung the bouquet onto the sidewalk, where it landed unbroken and intact with hardly a sound, dropping only a few of its red and yellow petals onto the granite curb.

CHAPTER SIXTEEN

At about the same time that Nestor was leaving the Old Court, Minerva Herrera was leaving La Aguacatala with Joseph in her arms. Marina had told her to take the baby home while she served the last customers and cleaned up. She thought of stopping in at the Old Court to see Nestor, but she knew that his new friend, the other woman, might be there, and she did not want to see her.

She pulled into the long driveway that looped around the back of the house where her sister had the upstairs apartment. Joseph was asleep in his car seat. Gently, she unbuckled the harness and pulled it over his head, lifting his slight, precious weight onto her shoulder. Nestor was right; these back stairs were too steep. She watched her feet carefully as she mounted the stairs, leaning forward, whispering soothing words softly to the child whose head was nestled in her dark hair. As she approached the top step, she felt with her free hand among the keys on her ring for the house key, which she knew by the shape of its head and the notches on its grooved stem.

On the landing she raised her head; her hand moved toward the lock, but flew backward as if she had touched a scalding iron. The keys clattered on the landing.

The face on one of the dolls that hung before her was her own; a long needle pierced the head of the child it held. Her cry was wordless, the cry of a wounded animal. Reflexively she pulled backward, but there was nothing behind her. For an instant she teetered at the top step. She could not reach with both hands for the wooden railing without dropping the baby. Her left hand flew out, clutching it, but she was already twisting and falling backward, and though she managed to hold on, the momentum of her body swinging outward carried her hard against the aged and wobbly railing. Long-rusted nails released their bite and the rotting wood gave way. The scream that the couple downstairs heard was cut short, and when they ran out their back door, no one answered their calls.

Nestor thought that he would have to talk to Dave Keough about the Ramon Trinidad affair. The gangster's intervention had deepened that particular pile of shit, but it didn't matter; he remembered Minerva's earnest expression as they sat on a bench by the river, conversing. He could face anything, anything at all, if the foundation was solid, if the anchor held. His cell rang as was getting into his car.

"Nestor?"

"Marina? What's up?"

She spoke in Spanish, but slowly and distinctly, as one would talk to a child. "Nestor, there has been an accident. You need to be strong. Very strong."

"No, no," he said, anticipating the hammer blow that he knew was coming. "What? What happened?"

She spoke of a *muñeca vudú* that had been hanging on their back door. Nestor's overwhelmed brain translated the term: *muñeca vudú*—a doll—a voodoo doll. "Minerva and Joseph… they fell from the back steps. They are at Saints Memorial …"

"Are they all right?" The engine turned over and he jerked the gear shift into drive. "Are they all right, Marina?" In the ensuing seconds of silence, he felt like a man sitting in an oarless rowboat drifting toward a gray horizon, and he heard the roar of the cataract beyond.

"Marina!"

"It's very serious… I'm so sorry. You have to come." He heard her voice break into sobs and couldn't follow what she was saying. He threw the phone down and concentrated on getting to the hospital as quickly as possible. His face streamed with tears, and for the first time since he was a boy at St. Brigid's, he was praying fervently—to any god who would listen.

The automatic doors to the ER seemed to open too slowly, and Nestor nearly ran into the glass as they slid apart. The small crowd sitting under a TV eyed him with casual curiosity as he spoke with the admissions receptionist. She didn't have to ask his name; he had known her since he was in Boy Scouts with her younger brother Vinnie. She did not attempt the normal small talk they made whenever they met. He thought he saw her glance at the computer screen apprehensively, keeping what his father had called a "poker face," though her eyes said something that he didn't want to know. She handed him the visitor's pass, and pushed a button that unlocked the door to the ER with a metallic buzz. No "good luck"—no words. Just sympathetic eyes. He could feel his rudderless vessel gathering speed as the edge drew near.

Marina hugged him, murmuring a desperate stream of Spanish prayers and invocations, words that increased Nestor's sense of helplessness and fear. It was clearly a case that she now felt was in God's hands, beyond the remedies of Man. Before he could question her, a doctor, an Indian full of professional gravitas who must have been awaiting his arrival, stepped out from the nurses' station, extending a hand. "Dr. Patel," he said. Marina stayed behind as he ushered Nestor into an empty room. They sat on plastic chairs. The doctor drew his chair close, and Nestor listened anxiously to the oracular voice. "Mr. McCorley. Your wife and son fell from a second story..." He paused while Nestor struggled to hold back a cry of grief. ". . . a second story landing. Now I could show you a lot of X-rays..."

He didn't want to hear the words, but he had to know. "Just... just tell me."

"Your wife is suffering from a cerebral hemorrhage. Her brain is swelling, and we have had to induce a coma to try to reduce the fluid in her body, because it creates pressure in the brain. For days, probably, she will continue in this condition. In addition, she has several cracked ribs, which is of less concern, a broken arm, which has been set. Finally, an ultrasound has identified some internal bleeding; it does not appear major. Often, Mr. McCorley, internal bleeding stops on its own, but I will be performing a laparotomy to be sure, and I will seal any leaking blood vessels with a heat probe. I have great hope that she will survive and recover."

Nestor clutched the doctor's arm. "Thank you. And Joseph?" He saw the doctor's eyes before he had even begun to answer; a painful foreboding twisted like a snake inside him.

"Your son was killed in the accident, Mr. McCorley."

Things became unreal after that. The doctor was very sorry. Words. Nestor could not connect the words to any real thing; he was afraid to connect them to all they signified.

"Would you like to see him?" The doctor wanted to know.

"See him?"

"Would you like to see your son?"

No, it was more than words. The reflection in a mirror was not the reality, but what it showed was real. His son was dead. He shook his head. The gray stiffening bundle with clouded eyes was real, but it was not Joseph. Like the old song. *No more, no more, no more forever, shall love or gold bring back MacCrimmon.*

"No, no thank you, Dr. Patel."

"I'm very sorry," the doctor said again.

"Thank you." *No more, forever.*

Someone, a nurse or aide, brought him to Minerva, masked with a respirator, immobile amid a tangle of wires and tubes, the room dim and silent but for the beep of a monitor that displayed in graphic digital lines the feeble pulsations of her soon-to-be-broken heart. "She must be prepared for surgery, Mr. McCorley."

"Tubes and pumps," he said, half to himself.

"I'm sorry?"

"That's all we are is tubes and pumps," he said, and he left the emergency room, past the hurrying nurses, the emaciated old man groaning on a stretcher, past Marina's tear-stained face, Vinnie's sympathetic sister, the forlorn figures pacing the waiting room of life, and outside, past the drowsy EMT smoking a cigarette beside a growling ambulance spewing diesel fumes, past the policeman at the parking lot gate who sized him up in some rapid forensic calculation.

He kept walking, beyond the lot, across the street, over the bridge and down an embankment to the river's edge. A waning half-moon sailing amid shrouds of mist shed a weak and watery light over the Merrimack River and the abandoned mill complex where the Concord River joined it. Those empty mills were ghosts in brick; the din of industry still hung within them, and the hopes of thousands seeped in whispers from the dark, empty frames of their innumerable windows. Roofs had collapsed under the weight of time and the bricks of silent bell towers had tumbled and lay in piles on rusted and buckling fire escapes. Bent trees grew out of the raceways where the river flowed through the old mill's heart, swirling around those still turbines—the massy wheels now settling into the undredged silt of years— seized where they stalled long ago. And from amid this ruin, haunting the confluence of two great rivers, a single smokestack—breathless now—rose out of a dark fist of brick and into the moony clouds like an accusing finger pointing toward heaven.

When you saw the left half of the moon it was waning, and when you saw the right half it was waxing. Such order without any apparent explanation. Stellar nurseries, Aldiss' *Galaxies Like Grains of Sand*, infinite time, infinite life, expansion, contraction—the electron orbiting the nucleus, the planet orbiting the star, the moon wheeling her pale course about us—and here below, a single mystified being overcome with the loss of one so new to this tenebrous shore, a loss that was of no account to this world. Thicker dark clouds were moving in to extinguish the moon.

The things we gather through life to let fall. Joseph had left only the small tokens of a child's life, those sad testaments that still littered Nestor's apartment: stuffed animals, plastic toys, cardboard picture books. None of the things he should have gathered to himself in time: dog-eared novels, hockey skates, a soccer trophy perhaps, a driver's license, a prom picture, a wedding ring. None of those things, nor friendship, a first kiss, nor the view from the branches of boyhood's trees. Nothing but the broken promise of his tiny body. A few pounds of flesh and bone, so small. *Wrapped in swaddling.*

Nestor leaned on the railing and cried, and the river rush sent up its own mists like a cloud of tears, but he knew the river gave up no tears for his dead son; the pathetic fallacy they called it, that our sadness was reflected in nature, a fallacy indeed to think the river cared, or the stars, or God. Of no account to this world. *A consummation devoutly to be wished?* Maybe that's all death was, a kink in the tube, a pump that seized—the turbine still, and peace as the river of time flowed on.

Tubes and pumps and fear—oh, the full complement of fear. The vicious bitch had won. A voodoo doll? So she had succeeded with such a trifle? Fear had trumped faith, or were they in part the same? A fucking voodoo doll. She had destroyed the sweet boy and his dear wife with a doll! And Minerva, if she recovered, would never love him now because it must have been his insult to the Virgin that had brought them through some mystical indirection to this end. Nothing else made sense, and Minerva could not live in this world of waxing and waning, of living and dying, of clockwork planets and turning tides, of greetings and partings—so many partings—if no divine will ruled it all. There must be some being infinite in power and infinite in empathy, for little Juanito and his mule, for the hopeless, and for the family that had just had its heart ripped out. Yes, infinite in mercy, but willing to brook no insult. Pride was punished. Pride has always been punished by the gods in the chronicles of men.

A tremor of rage coursed through his body, and for an instant a purpose kindled within him, to find and kill this so-called witch, but it flickered and smoked out with the renewed conviction that it didn't matter. None of it made sense, and worse, none of it mattered. There's the ultimate sorrowful mystery for you, Minerva.

He traced a lonely river path that led eventually under a bridge near the Pawtucket Falls, and leaning on a railing, wracked with suffocating despair, he lost himself in the roar of tumbling water. If he jumped, the mystery would be solved, or at least resolved. He wanted to become a part of the mist that rose from the river. A fog. A whiter shade of pale. Nothing. *O that this too solid flesh would melt, thaw, resolve itself into a dew, or that the Almighty had not fixed his cannon 'gainst self-slaughter.* The pain would end. In a few seconds, a few moments—it didn't matter. Would he hail some far shore where Joseph wandered lost, waiting for him—and where he could try once more to protect him? No, Joseph was gone. *Poulnabrone—the Hole of Sorrows.*

"Gimme your wallet!" He raised his head. A figure stood before him dressed in dark clothes, his face lost in the shadow of a loose hood. "Gimme your fuckin' wallet, now!"

Slowly, Nestor reached inside his coat and drew the wallet out. Ignoring the outstretched hand of the thief, he flung it far into the rushing river below, taking a grim delight in the look of disbelief in the hard eyes, and then the cold hatred. "I'll fuckin' kill you!" the hooded figure whispered.

"Go ahead, you piece of shit!" Nestor cried. "Do me a fucking favor! Here! You want the watch?" He tore it off and tossed it into the churning foam. "Gold wedding ring?" It flew into the mist. "Go get it! There! I have nothing! I have *nothing*! So kill me or *fuck off*!"

The man struck Nestor on the side of the head with his open hand, growling, "Asshole."

He never tried to block the first blow, but as the man drew back the hand that held the pistol to strike him with its butt, Nestor began to loathe the brutishness in the unshaven jaw, the pitiless gaze of the eyes, the coarse, loutish voice—and rage swelled within him. The horses in his head now charged forward with reckless abandon. In what seemed a single rapid motion, he stepped forward, knocked the man's arm aside, and lunged at him, using all the strength of his chest to throw his head directly into his face, as if he were heading a soccer ball into a goal.

Blood spurted from the man's nose as he tumbled backward, and Nestor heard his gun clatter across the asphalt walkway as he landed. The hood had fallen back from his head to reveal stringy locks, an astonished face running with blood, a gaping mouth. The man scrambled over the ground, feeling desperately for the gun, but Nestor saw its dark glint in the grass and kicked it out of his reach. He dove on it then and rolled over, finding himself sitting with the gun in his two hands aimed up at the looming body of his attacker. He squeezed the trigger. "Oh God!" the man gasped.

"God doesn't give a fuck about you!" he cried. He fired three more shots. The dark form staggered and dropped backward, hard, to the ground, his body convulsing. Nestor stood and turned the gun on himself. Tears welled anew in his eyes as he thought of Minerva, but they would never recapture their fleeting happiness. *O that the Almighty had not fixed his canon 'gainst self-slaughter.* The line ran ceaselessly through his head, but he had just killed a man in cold blood. Nothing mattered. His son stood lonely on that distant shore. He swiped at the blood that trickled into his left eye. The Almighty was having a good laugh at all of them tonight. *A consummation devoutly to be wished. The rest is silence.* He put the gun to his temple, roaring a cry that drowned out the sound of the falls. He pulled the trigger. *Click.* An empty chamber.

A wave of nausea overtook him; he fell to his knees as he sensed, in some parallel world, the bullet shattering his skull like a ripe pumpkin—blasting through the warp and woof of experience and memory—lead and bone fragments spinning through brain tissue, tearing asunder the delicate web of self and the hidden nest of sorrow and love. A trail of ruin, and by the dark river, two men whose lives had intersected in death.

The rain came while he knelt there, and in some way revived him. He stood weakly, trembling, and was about to toss the gun into the water, but his attempt on his own life had left him gasping, bewildered, and as the rain fell harder, somehow exhilarated, and now the horses were running with high hearts, snorting the very fire of vengeance. *Yes, by Saint Patrick.* By the rusting stanchions of the bridge, a martial ghost took substance in the curling mists, lending steel to his purpose: *I find thee apt, and duller shouldst thou be than the fat weed that roots itself in ease on Lethe's wharf wouldst thou not stir in this.*

Nestor McCorley had gone to the edge and peered into the abyss, but suddenly it seemed far better to drag the guilty with him into hell. He loosened his belt and tucked the pistol into his waistband. Bending over the dead man, he rummaged through his pockets and felt a small carton. He worked quickly. Blood was beginning to well out of the dark holes in his chest and mix with rainwater. "Gold Dot Hollow Point .38 Special 125 Grain Bullets. *A round to trust your life with.*" He jammed the ammo into his jacket pocket, lugged the mugger's guts to the precipice and rolled him into the churning rush.

Stumbling, the rain now washing streaks of tears and blood from his face, muttering vows of revenge, he followed the path back, conscious of the weight of the pistol, finding all he needed or wanted to express already written in his mind. *Is there a Divinity that shapes our ends? Providence in the fall of a sparrow? Yet I cannot choose but weep to think they would lie him in the cold, cold ground.* But a warning voice below the clamor of hooves whispered faintly, fearfully: *That way madness lies.*

Marquis Alicea was staying at the Radisson she had said. And how should he appear here at this time? He recalled Declan's words about the witch. "Hired. Had to be." If Alicea's hand was in this, he would pay with his life tonight. Returning along a low shore path by the corpse-bearing river, he saw figures like the wayward shades of Hades hunched beneath a great spreading oak in the flickering light of a fire that spouted a stream of sparks out of a corroded barrel. As he passed them, his soul overflowing, he bawled out, "Heaven hath pleased it so, to punish me with this, and this with me, that I must be their scourge and minister!"

"Go to hell!" someone shouted.

CHAPTER SEVENTEEN

Nestor pulled over under a streetlight. As the rain thrummed the car roof and blurred the windshield, he examined the gun, which shone dully in his hand. He was not an experienced gunman, but Declan had shown him how to load revolvers. He pulled a latch and felt the cylinder fall heavily into his palm. There was what Declan had called the ejector rod. He pushed it and one by one the empty shell casings fell out, five of them. The cowboy movies of his youth had left him with the impression that any handgun was a six-shooter. The new bullets slid into the empty chambers, one, two, three, four... he remembered Declan telling him that it was always better, when carrying a revolver, to leave the last chamber empty in case the gun went off accidentally. "There's no safety on a revolver," he'd reminded him.

It was approaching one in the morning. Nestor drove toward the Radisson Hotel. "I'm coming Marquis, and then you'll see the fucking art of war." Minutes later he pulled into a slanted space at the back of the hotel lot. He'd switched off his headlights when he left the main street so that no camera would record his license plate. In the glove compartment he found a napkin, which he ran over his wet face, dabbing the cut near his hairline. In the rearview mirror he saw the purpling skin around his left eye. He tucked the gun once more into his belt and donned a Red Sox baseball cap. Seeing his cell phone still lying on the seat beside him, he put it in his pocket, and with shoulders hunched against the rain, headed for the hotel entrance.

The clerk at the reception desk looked about sixteen, red-haired and freckled. Nestor read her name tag: DESTINY. He wasn't sure whether it was that portentous word or his wet clothes that made him shiver. Probably her first job out of high school, Nestor thought, but she was no fool. "I'm not supposed to give out information about who is staying at the hotel or what room they're in without the person's permission."

"It's an emergency. Could you call Marquis Alicea if he's here and let me talk to him?"

Nestor tried to look sincere as she considered this. "Well, I…"

"It's an emergency, Destiny. Please."

She glanced at the clock, 1:18, and looked him over once more, concluding that it very well could be an emergency. She went to the computer and clicked a desktop icon. "Mark Keys… what?"

He spelled out the name for her and she punched a number, biting her lip and leaning her knuckled hand on the desk as she waited, the phone tucked under her red curls. Nestor thought that he must not be in, but all at once she straightened and said, "I'm sorry to bother you, Mr. Alicea, but there is a gentleman here who says he would like to speak to you. He says it's an emergency."

Nestor, leaning into the counter to camouflage his movements, adjusted the gun in his waistband. Destiny nodded and looked at him. "Are you… McCorty?"

"That's right." The son of a bitch was expecting him.

"Yes, sir." She paused. "I will. Thank you."

"He's in room 227. You can take the elevator or the stairs at the end of that corridor."

He would take the stairs. He walked slowly, feeling like a man who was trying to put together the fragments of a dream, trying to turn them into a story that had a beginning, a middle, and an end. But the story would not form. He was left with a series of events, colored with strong suspicions, unable to say for certain how, or even if, they were connected.

His son was dead. That he knew. And in part, because of that a man was dead. That he knew, too. Another might die soon; that he felt. If Marquis gave him reason to—it must be more than to suspect—to believe, to know, that he was responsible for this, that he had hired some woman to play the witch, and cause the death of his son, then Marquis would pay with his life. And after that, let the cards play out as they will. The man would learn a lesson, however briefly, that he should have considered before he conspired against his wife and son. *Thou find'st to be too busy is some danger.*

He saw the number 227 on the door and approached, feeling the weight of the gun at his waist. He'd never imagined that he was capable of killing, and he did not want to kill again, but no one could set this whirlwind of horrible events in motion and sit at its center, untouched. No one.

Marquis opened the door quickly to his knock, taking Nestor's hand in his two hands, gripping it in seeming sincerity. His feet were bare, his shirt-tails hanging. "I've heard about the terrible accident. I'm so very sorry. Are you all right? Your eye is swollen."

"You've heard about it, you say?"

Alicea closed the door and looked at Nestor, his head turning slightly as if he'd heard a strange sound. "Yes, of course. If there is anything I can do…"

"Oh, I would think that you've already done quite enough."

"What… what do you mean?"

"*All war is based on deception.* Which is another way of saying that one may smile and smile and smile, and be a villain."

"You're not making sense. You've had a horrible shock, my friend. Here, sit down…" He began to clear a chair, but when he turned to offer the seat, he stepped backward, hands outstretched, eyes widening—there was a gun in Nestor's hand.

"What—?"

"Let's think about this, *my friend*. Let's go over it together. Minerva disappoints a wealthy man and marries another. Shortly after, a *witch* arrives out of nowhere on her broom, for no apparent reason, and begins to drive a wedge between Minerva and her new husband, using her own religious beliefs against her. Very clever. *Attack the strongest gate*—that's what your mentor, Sun Tzu, said, and that's what you did."

"Listen, Nestor…"

"You listen to me. And this witch knows all about me, the priest, everything that's happening. She knows that our son, Joseph, is a boy before he's born." Nestor was trembling, and at the mention of his son's name, he swallowed hard and swiped at his eye with the sleeve of his jacket. His palm was sweating and the handle of the pistol seemed to squirm in his grasp. "How does she know all this? Well, let's see, who else knew? Marina knew. And Minerva talked to her on her cell just after we'd had the ultrasound and the sonographer told us he was a boy. Marina knew that the priest had been to bless our house and to comfort Minerva. She knew everything. And this jilted wealthy man is in constant contact with Marina. All of a sudden he's taken a keen interest in everything that's going on here in Lowell, and on the night of the murder of my son, lo, he finds himself a thousand miles away from his home, here, where the final scene of the tragedy is played out. Now I've never served on a jury, but I am self-appointed to be heaven's scourge and minister in this case, you see? So there's heaven's case against you. Now you may present yours, and God help you if it doesn't make perfect sense to me. Can you explain all this, Marquis?"

Nestor heard a click and whirled to his right as the bathroom door opened. "I can explain it, Nestor." Marina, her face puffy and mascara-stained, her eyes red-rimmed, stepped forward. She spoke in Spanish. "Nestor, for God's sake, for Minerva's sake, put the gun down. Though the way I feel tonight, the way we all feel, death might be welcome." The tears streamed from her eyes anew. "But you're so wrong. The reason that Marquis has taken an interest in things here is because we are going to be married. Not even Minerva knew, because we were going to break the news at Thanksgiving in Miami, but tonight we decided not to wait."

"You're going to marry Marquis?"

"You're such a great detective! Do you not see that I'm wearing an engagement ring?" She thrust out a hand—the diamond he saw there, large and shaped like a vertical eye, filled him with doubt and confusion. She continued. "I asked Marquis to help me with the business, not long after Minerva broke off their engagement. Do you think I knew anything about becoming incorporated or making a business plan? Do you think the bank would give a loan to a woman with no restaurant experience who speaks bad English? He helped me, and we fell in love. This man has never been anything but good—to Minerva, to my family, and to me."

The hand that held the gun fell, and Nestor flopped into the seat that Marquis had cleared. He laid the gun on the floor between his feet and pushed off his cap, burying his throbbing head in his hands as if he were trying to hold together a cracked vase. He blew a long sigh of relief. The suspicions and suppositions that had been whirling in his head began to settle into the depths from which they'd arisen, and he shuddered at what he might have done. *I'll have grounds more relative than this.* Marina was now in the arms of Marquis Alicea. Nestor leaned back, suddenly very tired, and asked her, "Why were you hiding in the bathroom?"

"Minerva and I were brought up in the old way. To be found in the hotel room of a man in the middle of the night, even a man who is a fiancé, is a disgrace. But Nestor, to hear this crazy theory you invented... of what are you thinking? It's madness." *La locura.* The word hung for a moment in his mind, something more than a word—a house of many chambers, a laby-rinth of confusion, an idea alive with the weight of terrible possibility. *La locura...* madness. *I am but mad north-northwest.*

He picked up the gun and pulled himself wearily to his feet. "Maybe I am going insane. Maybe I am. I'm sorry, Marquis."

"Nestor, as I said, this is a terrible night for all of us, in particular for you. But don't do anything you will regret forever. Give me the gun."

He tucked the weapon back into his belt. "I was wrong about you, Marquis, and I may be insane, but one thing I know—someone has been fucking with my family for a long time. And now my son is dead and

Minerva… I don't know. I'm tired of being a victim and I just don't care anymore. Someone will pay for all this, even if I have to go to hell to find the bastard."

"But Nestor, you'll spend your life in prison!" Marina warned as he opened the door.

"The world's a prison, Marina."

He woke several times before dawn and after the light began to brighten the room's curtains, always with a jolting start, as the events of the previous evening and early morning landed on his soul like a boulder. His mind raced through everything that had occurred since Minerva had announced her pregnancy. He grappled with these memories, words and images, with the grave doctor informing him of Joseph's death, with the man by the river crumpling and falling, hard, as the bullets slammed into him—so hard, as if he'd been dropped from the sky. He fell again and again until Nestor's head spun, and out of sheer exhaustion he sank once more into a fitful sleep.

It was not the castle of Elsinore, where he found himself then, at the edge of the North Sea, but on the parapet of a stronghold of ancient stone on a moonlit plain. I was as if he were at the bottom of a bowl, hemmed in with a black silhouette of mountains—undulating ridges and star-eclipsing summits that rose from the edge of the plain. The ghost beckoned him forward, and there was no Horatio to hold him back. Under a stone archway the spirit drifted, trailing a curling fog through which Nestor pursued him, down winding stairs to a sunken courtyard where innumerable graven faces projected from a wall of hewn stone. He was alone for a moment, but then the mist gathered near a stele that stood in the center of the courtyard. Runic symbols were cut into its face. When the fog melted into the earth, his father was leaning against its length, dressed in his work clothes, "Eamon" stitched in red on his denim shirt, a gift from his mother.

"I thought you were dead," Nestor said, embracing him, crying tears of joy.

"Never better," his father said.

"But we buried you."

He laughed as if he knew a secret that he was not at liberty to divulge. "I'm here now, aren't I?"

"Yes."

A new awareness impinged on his joy—not yet knowledge, but an awareness of impending knowledge. Nestor felt that he could not be completely happy—not ever again. Something had happened, something real that his father's resurrection could not change. A memory gained substance and weight. "Joseph is gone."

"Listen here to me boy while I tell you." He was nearly chuckling, his eyes lit with amusement the way a grown-up looks at a child who cries when the string of the balloon he was holding flies from his grasp and shrinks into the sky, sailing into a space whose vastness he cannot comprehend. In this way did Eamon's smile light his eyes, indulgent and loving, as if he knew that Nestor could not see, or understand, the grand design that his father now saw.

The stone fortress faded, and all at once they were in Ireland—a rocky storm-swept shore. Eamon McCorley's open palms held what Nestor knew were the nine hazels of wisdom. He brought first one hand and then the other to his mouth, swallowing them effortlessly before he spoke to his son: "The salmon slipped from your hands so lightly in Doonbeg's water. Impossible to hold him. All we love slips from our hands." He raised his empty fists and opened them, spreading his fingers, as if releasing an invisible bird into ether.

Darkness fell and a stage lit itself by the shore. The brooding prince stepped into the light, arm-in-arm with his true friend, Horatio, but instead of Hamlet's lines, he repeated words from one of the Irish tales his father used to tell him as a boy: "If the dead leaves of the forest had been gold, and the white foam of the water silver, Finn would have given it all away."

The dream continued, growing more and more incomprehensible; a man with Elton John glasses arrived, carrying charts that were supposed to depict a sort of electrocardiogram of reality, or time. "When these two lines are parallel, something of great significance in the universe always occurs..." The latter part of the dream broke into muddled fragments, but he woke with the vivid recollection of his father's words; he wrote them down in his journal so they would not dissipate the way words heard in dreams quickly do, leaving nothing behind, for he thought it might be a message from his father or from his own subconscious approximation of his father, telling him how to deal with the pain that was lodged in his gut and between his lungs, twisting his heart. And below his father's words, he wrote his own interpretation of their message: "They only live who can endure all loss." He tried to recall if he had ever heard his father speak the dream words in life, but he was jarred from these thoughts by the sight of the blue metal of the gun on his dresser, draped with the wooden cross on its string of black and gold beads, the gift from Ramon Trinidad.

He put the gun and the remaining bullets into an empty Dunkin' Donuts bag and went outside. He opened the lid of the rubbish bin out under the back steps and put the bag in the bottom of it. The words that ran through his mind were: "The killer hid the murder weapon." On his way back up the stairs he became dizzy and sat down halfway up the flight. His mind was like a small room in which there were too many people, all shouting, confused, seeking something—an exit? Below it all the voice of the Indian doctor reiterated the tragic news. *Your son was killed in the accident, Mr. McCorley.* He saw Minerva so still in her hospital bed. *For days, probably, she will continue in this condition.* He must go and sit by her bed, and gird himself for the hate he would see in her eyes when, and if, she awoke. Yes, he would go there soon.

A brief time after this, a car pulled into the driveway. It was Marquis and Marina; they took him from where he sat on the steps and led him back into the house, saying soothing words to which Nestor could say nothing. His mother arrived with the inevitable lentil soup and other containers of food. His sister hugged him and pressed into his hands a copy of *When Bad*

Things Happen to Good People. He thanked her.

Friends called, not knowing what to say. They'd heard there was an accident, and they were sorry. *Thank you*, he said, *thank you*. His own voice sounded strange to him, like a murmur, a buzz, overheard from another room. Eddie Saitz called and told him not to worry about the play—it was canceled for the weekend. After that they might get a guy from Boston, but hell, it didn't matter. Just hang tough for Minerva. *Yes, thank you.*

The principal of the school called with condolences and word that Angela Purtel had dropped her accusations. Nestor listened with cold indifference as he explained. "She admitted she made up the story. Apparently was a friend of poor Ian Casey. Ian's father, for his own misguided motives, offered her five hundred dollars to make your life miserable, to destroy your reputation. She felt guilty about the lie and decided to 'fess up. You can decide later if you want to press charges." *No, no. I won't do that.*

"I know you have much bigger things to deal with, but you don't have to deal with this. We'll talk before September. We're all so sorry. I'll send you the number of the Employee Assistance Program. Take advantage of that, Nestor.

Yes, thank you.

"We're praying for you."

Very kind. Thank you.

And he wondered, *if you could see inside me, would you pray for me? If you knew what lay in a paper bag at the bottom of the waste bin, and what I've done with it?*

Later he recalled little of the events of the next few days. His mother, along with the soup, had brought him a prescription she had obtained from a family friend, Dr. Gionakis. He slept. His mother and sister were there whenever he woke, handing him an ice pack for his bruised face, for which he made some lame excuse, and trying to get him to eat lentil soup or *spanakopita*. Seeing the anxious looks on their faces, he tried his best. They spoke carefully of funeral arrangements, and Nestor insisted on a small family service, for several reasons, not the least of which was the horrible feeling that he would see the face of the bitch from hell among the crowd and try to lunge through it to strangle her.

In sunglasses and half-tranquilized, he buried his son. Don Andres and Doña Barbara came up from Florida, but they had nothing to say to him. He didn't blame them. He had taken their girl away and led her to this. On the way home in the car, Nestor heard on WCAP that some boys fishing in the Merrimack River near Lawrence had discovered the body of one Emanuel Rosario tangled in some brush in shallow water. A coroner reported that he had been shot several times. Nestor began to tremble. He pulled over at the Gorham Tap and ordered a Jameson. The bartender knew him from high school, but wisely left him alone.

CHAPTER EIGHTEEN

The following day, Nestor was called to the hospital. Minerva was awake. "What happened to your face, Nestor? Your eye looks swollen."

"I walked into the edge of a half-closed door in the dark…"

"Be careful!"

"It's not as bad as it looks."

They did not speak of what had happened. Though Dr. Patel had told her, he could not bring himself to say the name of their boy, and he feared, in her fragile condition, to put any emotional strain on her. He put the flowers he'd brought on her night table and clasped the hand that protruded from a hard cast.

"Thank you. They're beautiful," she said, though she had hardly looked at them.

He kissed her gently and asked if she was in pain. She shook her head. Helplessly, he looked for some way to comfort her. He got up and adjusted the blinds, held the straw to her lips, pulled a strand of hair from her eyes, which were set in dark hollows, and watched the fluid run in droplets through the clear tubing into her bruised arm. The hands of the clock crawled in slow circles while they sat in near silence until Marina and Marquis and Minerva's parents came, bringing more flowers, chocolate, a small teddy bear wearing a "Get Well" T-shirt, and Nestor kissed her once more and told her he would return later. Her eyes said something to him, something of immeasurable sorrow he thought—and of love, he hoped.

Her strength returned by degrees, and by the end of that week she was taking tentative steps with a cane in her good hand, standing for a moment to look out the window. And as she stood there, Nestor said, "I was afraid you would hate me for what happened."

"No," she said. "I could not hate you." She pulled a Kleenex from a box on the sill and pressed it to her eyes. "It's strange. I knew, even in the coma, that Joseph, that he was gone." She was looking at him now, but he turned away because her eyes were too sorrowful.

"Do you think," he asked, "that what happened was my fault? Due to something I did or failed to do? Something I said? Was there some way…"

"No. No. I need more strength to talk about it."

"All right. I won't speak about it."

"Nestor…" She sagged slightly as she exhaled and began to move back toward the bed, suddenly weary; with his right arm he encircled her waist and guided her.

"It's just, I need to know if we can survive this, or if…"

"I do love you, Nestor. But… help me lie down." She sat and he lifted her legs back onto the bed. Her eyes closed as her head sank into the pillow. She was quiet for a moment, and Nestor felt sorry for having spoken at all because he saw a tear flow from the corner of her closed eye into her dark hair. "You were not responsible for Joseph's death," she said. "I was responsible. I *am* responsible for Joseph's death."

"I know who's responsible."

"If you were carrying Joseph. If you saw… the thing I saw, would you fall? Would you be terrified and jump back like some stupid horse that sees a snake? No, Nestor. You would be angry, and you would rip it from the door, but you would never… you would never fall down with our boy."

He tried to find some way to reassure her. "People react to different things. She knew what would frighten you. With me it could have been something else."

"No. I don't believe that. So here is the problem. I say I have faith. And you say you have no faith. And we both want to protect Joseph. But what killed him…" Nestor reached out and gripped her hand because she had begun to sob. "… what killed him was not that you don't have faith, it was that… something in me, or something I did not have."

She shook her head and pressed a hand over her eyes. "So either I should be like you, or my faith, it was too weak. Just as you said, what good is my faith if I am afraid of witches and curses? You were right. You were right, and God did not fail me, but I failed Him. I should have been fearless in my faith and fearless to protect my boy… but I was not, and now he is dead because I was not brave and I can never forgive myself for that. Never."

They cried together for their son, and Nestor held her and tried to comfort her—to tell her that she had done nothing wrong, that he loved her, and that they would go on together—wounded, yes, an incurable wound perhaps that always gave some pain, but that would not kill them or kill their love. And in time perhaps they would become accustomed to the pain and learn to be happy in spite of it, like old soldiers who had lost limbs in some bitter struggle.

He told her that he had read how Henry Thoreau was shattered by the death of his brother until he asked himself, "What right have I to grieve who have not ceased to wonder?" He said that he still wanted to be with her, and together they would wonder at what was still left in life, and maybe have another child, not to take Joseph's place, but to give them another reason to live. He was surprised at his own desire to live and continue to love, and could not tell her that only a few nights ago he had tried to end his life in a fit of passionate grief.

"Nestor, I wish I could say yes. I wish I could forget what I have done. But what this proves to me is that my faith is imperfect, it's not a real faith, just as you once said, and I now must prove to myself and to God that I will perfect it—that it will be *real*. The only place I can do that, Nestor, is the convent."

He held his breath for a moment because he felt he had to be careful how he responded. He wanted to say, "Are you joking?" But he knew that she was not joking. "Minerva, whatever you think you did, I forgive you. Joseph was my son, too, and I forgive you. You were startled, ambushed, and you fell on some steep stairs. That's all."

"It was my fault. Joseph is dead because I am a coward and had no faith in God. And you can't forgive me for that, and I can't forgive myself. Only God can forgive me."

"All right. You're under a lot of stress. We'll talk about it later."

"Nestor, I'll have to go…"

"Go, then!" He rose and walked to the window, thinking how as a boy he had been terrified that a jealous God would punish him if he let Sister Theresa kiss him. He had run away, but God was going to punish him anyway—take the woman he loved into his dim sanctuary. The hills of Centralville rose on the other side of the river, and in the distance he saw the spire of a church rising like a spike against the wandering line of the New Hampshire hills. He nearly laughed to himself as he thought of another scene now completed in this tragicomedy. *Get thee to a nunnery, go, and quickly too!*

"It's strange," he said bitterly. "None of your prayers worked. None of them did any good at all. The only thing you did that worked, that really worked… like a charm, as they say, was the spell you put on me, right? Because God help me, but I do love you. Maybe you would have made a better witch than a nun."

"Nestor, I'm sorry. You should not love me… you have to…"

"I have to pack up my troubles in my old kit bag and smile, smile, smile."

"Everything is my fault, but it will be difficult for me, too. If I didn't love you, Nestor, there would be no sacrifice. And don't you see? I need a very hard penance."

"Oh yes, penance and sacrifice. It used to be human sacrifice the gods favored. Remember how God told Abraham to kill his son Isaac? And he was perfectly willing to do it, too, just to prove what a swell, God-fearing guy he was. I have no respect for that kind of piety. A true heart needs a touch of the skeptic, Minerva. I respect Doubting Thomas. You're damned right I'd want to examine the risen Christ's wounds. I respect the Irish hero Oisín. In the old legend he told Saint Patrick, 'Let your god come and meet my son Osgar on the plain. And if your god puts him down, *then* I will say he is mighty.' And if God had told me to sacrifice my son, I'd have met him on the plain and set my feeble strength against all his omnipotence until he blasted me into oblivion. But if there is a God, he has no use for such unholy sacrifices, nor does he have any use for the sacrifice of our love."

She was crying again now, and a dull throbbing beat like a dirge in Nestor's head. There was no use in saying more. "Nestor, I can't ever make you understand. I'm sorry. But all the great and wise men and women who died in Christ—they were not all fools. Some of us feel the presence of God, even if you don't. If I didn't believe I will ever see my poor Joseph again, I could not live at all."

Wanting it to be true doesn't make it true, he thought, but he said, "I understand your feelings." He also understood his own desire, the need to share with someone he loved his guilt for what he'd done, to save him somehow—with prayers, with love, with a meal taken together, even in sorrow, with consoling embraces.

Because what really frightened him was the thought that, as Marina had implied, he'd stepped over the line; that he was lost in the darkness of the shadows cast by Joseph's death, that he had ventured into the realm where madmen hunch in corners, chattering to themselves. And now he had found, not a wife who could pull him back from that awful precipice, who until death parted them would remind him of the connection that no man could tear asunder, but a woman who believed that heaven demanded their separation to placate a petulant God. Pull him back from madness? No, she was crazier than he was.

"I could not make you happy," she said. And it was with the pain of certain defeat after a long and tiring battle that he thought that she was probably right. He wondered how it was that the women who had no power to make us happy could so easily make us unhappy. How to stop loving her?

"Nestor, why does this creature hate me so much? Why does she hate my blood? How could she do it?"

Weakly, shaking his head, he answered with the same tired response he'd given her since the woman had appeared. "She's crazy, Minerva." But he knew there had to be some deeper answer that he could not give her.

He held her hand in silence for a while, until Marquis and Marina came in with fresh flowers and he began to choke on their fragrance, which reminded him of a wake. He told her he would return. Marquis walked with him out to the elevator. "Nestor, are you all right?"

"I don't know."

"I'm very worried about the gun. Where did you get it?"

"I bought it from a guy in a bar. I'm sorry I threatened you."

"Will you give me the gun?"

"I threw it in the river, Marquis."

"I hope you did, Nestor."

CHAPTER NINETEEN

t was late afternoon, and Nestor McCorley was leaning over the bar at the Old Court, working his way through his third pint of Guinness. He'd spent the morning and the early part of the afternoon calling credit card companies, the bank, and finally waiting in an interminable line at the Registry for a new license. Matters of life and death, good and evil, heaven and hell—none of it caused the slightest vibration in the machinery of the bureaucracy.

He leaned back and stared at the talking head on the TV screen perched above the ranks of bottles, trying to block out the mad swirl of pictures and voices that seethed inside his head: Rosario the thief falling, Ian Casey, too, tumbling to the ground, his son's tiny casket, his wife's eyes as the devil woman shrieked, "You tried to take it off! But you can't take it off!" Even Angela Purtel's sobbing voice on the little phone video that Ramon Trinidad had shown him.

His expression gained focus and his back straightened as the scene on the television switched to a reporter standing in front of the new Yankee Stadium. "As *The Post* reported earlier this week, Gino Castignoli, a Bronx construction worker and Red Sox fan, buried a David Ortiz game shirt in the concrete of the new stadium, somewhere behind home plate, as a sort of curse on the Yankees. We have just learned that after five hours of busting concrete, a jackhammer crew did locate the jersey at approximately 3:25 p.m. The shirt will remain at the bottom of a two by three foot hole until it can be removed in an extraction ceremony—what some have called an 'exorcism.' Regarding Mr. Castignoli, Hank Steinbrenner has been quoted as saying, 'I hope his coworkers kick the crap out of him.' The cost of removing the number 34 Red Sox shirt and the so-called 'Curse of Big Papi' was forty-five-thousand dollars."

Higgins, the bow-tied barman, shook his balding head and said over his shoulder to Nestor, "Are people fuckin' stupid or what? Curse of Big Papi my arse. A load of shit is what that is."

Nestor nodded and drank off the rest of his pint. A year ago he would have agreed enthusiastically. *I defy augury.* That was what he'd said to Minerva. "The thing about curses, Higgs," he said finally, "is that if you believe they're real, then, by God, they're real."

The barman frowned and repeated, "My arse."

Big Papi agreed. He was on the television now, saying, "I don't like all that curse stuff and voodoo stuff."

Nestor nodded. "I'm with you, David."

"Another stout?"

"And a Jameson. Left the car at home and I'm goin' down hard tonight, Higgs."

"Well, I won't say you got no reason."

Nestor took out his pen and began to draw on a bar napkin, names within circles, arrows between them and question marks. But he soon stopped because it didn't make anything any clearer. The barman's gold-ringed hand pushed the tumbler of amber whiskey toward him, while the half-poured Guinness settled below the tap. Brendan Behan had asked, "Did y'ever notice how much a pint a' Guinness looks like a Catholic priest?" He watched the white swirling foam rush through the dark cassock of the body and rise to the Roman collar. *Bless me, Father.* He closed his eyes and drank the whiskey. He heard the door open behind him and Higgins call out, "Hey, Finbarr."

"Hey yerself, Master Higgins." Finbarr, a native of County Cork and the co-owner of the Old Court, sidled up to Nestor, who raised his whiskey glass in salutation. The lanky Irishman, an unlit cigarette hanging in an unshaven jaw, placed a sympathetic hand on Nestor's back and said, "Very sorry to hear about your troubles. Very sorry indeed." He hopped onto a bar stool beside him. "How is your wife, Nestor?"

"Well, she's recovering."

"Thank God for that."

"I'm not sure if she does. But she says she's going to a convent to atone for… our son's death. She thinks it was her fault that she fell on the stairs."

"Ah, Jesus, Nestor. Life is full of tragic accidents. And there's not a damned thing we can do about it. Last fall a woman ran over her child in the driveway. He was hiding in a pile of leaves. Tell me how you live with that. A convent. Jesus, Nestor. That's not good news. A terrible waste if you don't mind me saying so."

Nestor shook his head. "I don't mind."

"What are you goin' to do?" He twirled the length of the cigarette under his nose, inhaling the scent of tobacco.

"Well, I was planning on getting drunk right now, and then I'll try to pull myself together later."

Finbarr nodded. "Sounds like a plan all right. Listen, I was hopin' to run into you soon. I've somethin' to show ye."

"And what might that be?" Nestor asked.

"Get me a soda water an' lime, there's a good man, Higgs," he said to the barman, and turning back to Nestor, "You know the old queer-hawk who interrupted your play?"

Nestor's glass of whiskey came down hard on the bar. He stood and leaned closer to the Irishman. "What about her?"

"Eddie says she's been houndin' ye, though you don't know her from Adam."

"That's right."

Higgins slid a soda water across the bar to his boss and the Guinness he'd topped off to Nestor. Before the barman could pick up his tab off the bar to add the whiskey and Guinness to the total, Finbarr pulled it away and said, "That's on the house, now." He crinkled the bar tab into a ball and tossed it into a waste basket behind the bar.

"Thanks," Nestor said.

"Come with me," he said. They passed through a swinging door and across the kitchen. At the back, Finbarr handed him his drink and unlocked a door.

"Step into my office, as they say." Inside, Nestor saw a framed map of Cork, and a poster of a smiling workman easily carrying a twenty-foot steel I beam on his head. GUINNESS FOR STRENGTH was the caption. From a drawer in the cluttered gray metal desk, Finbarr produced a manila envelope from which he extracted two 8-inch by 12-inch black and white photos. Nestor put the drinks on the desk and took the photos. They were grainy, but that face was unmistakable, and his jaw clenched as he studied it. "Of course," he said at last, "you have a video camera at the front of the bar. I should have thought of that."

"Maybe you could find out who she is, anyway. Put a restrainin' order on the old hairpin."

Nestor left his Guinness on the desk and was on his way out when he stopped, and raising the manila envelope, called back, "What do I owe you for the photos?"

"Ah, y'owe me fuck-all. We did a great business here for the Shakespeare." He paused and added, "He was Irish, you know."

And for the first time in weeks, the shadow lifted, and Nestor laughed.

On Friday afternoons in St. Brigid's, Father Leahy heard confessions from 3:00 to 4:00. There was a 6:30 Mass in Spanish, and he was a firm believer in confessions before all weekend Masses so that anyone who wanted to be absolved of sin to receive the Eucharist could do so, though few took advantage of the service. Inside the confessional, by the light of a small reading lamp, he studied his Book of Psalms: "Great peace have they who love your law, and nothing can make them stumble."

He switched off the light and leaned back, closing his eyes. Here in the dim stall of the confessional there was peace; he always felt humbled by the mighty power of the absolution that he was able to grant in the name of a forgiving God. *Te absolvo. I absolve you of your sins in the name of the Father and the Son and the Holy Spirit.* He counseled those who came, urging them to call upon the Lord for strength to resist temptation, and to become better men and women. He heard a penitent enter the confessional and drew back the slide. "Bless me, Father, for I have sinned…"

"Go on, my child."

"Father, I lose patience with my mother. I know she can't help it—she has Alzheimer's, but it's so hard, so hard, Father."

"We are weak, but Our Lord is omnipotent. Pray to Our Lord and His Holy Mother for patience, and believe me, you will be given the patience you need. With the help of Christ, you will bear the most unbearable cross as many before you have done in the power of his limitless grace. Know that your sacrifice will be rewarded and that this suffering makes your soul shine before God like a bright angel."

"Thank you, Father. Thank you." He could hear the relief in her voice as he comforted and absolved her and gave her the meager penance that would balance her soul's account in heaven.

After that, he was left in silence for a while, and peeking out over the church, he saw that it was empty. He switched on the lamp and returned to his psalms until he heard someone enter the confessional to his left; he slid back the grill and inclined his head to listen. "Bless me, Father, for I have sinned…" He was conscious of the imprecise outline of the woman who spoke in low tones beyond the wicker screening.

"Go on, my child."

"Well, let me see, Father, it's been, oh, a very long time since my last confession. Where to begin? I guess some would say I killed the McCorley baby, but that was beyond my hopes at the time." Father Leahy listened, still and silent. The heart he felt beating in his breast might have been a pulse at the center of a cold stone. "I must say I was not surprised, though. Because I remember what happened with Sister Winifred."

Sister Winifred. Father Leahy remembered her well. A kind old nun who had run St. Brigid's School for many years until she had fallen... "What happened to Sister Winifred?"

"She got what she deserved is what happened to her."

"I cannot absolve you. Go away, and come back when you truly wish to be forgiven."

"But my confession is not over, Father."

"You're not confessing, you're gloating over your sins, and I suspect you need a psychiatrist more than a priest."

"You know the curses the ancient Romans made? They've found them at Bath—at sacred wells all over Europe. Well, I studied those, and I wrote a curse on Winifred. I wrote it backward on a sheet of lead, a prayer to Hecate, Queen of the Crossroads, and the Lords of Hell..."

"Get out!"

"I folded it and buried it with a dead cat. It was a joke, really, done out of spite, but within a week the old bitch had fallen down the stairs! Dead! That's when I learned who really answers prayers!"

Father Leahy rose and threw open the confessional door as the woman drew back the curtain of her stall and stood facing him. He saw a repulsive combination of mocking triumph and hatred in her face. "Remember, you can't repeat what you heard in confession," she said.

The priest struggled to rein in an impulse that made him want to wipe the smile off her face with his fist. His words came slowly between hard breaths. "You made no confession, and no penance can serve you until you abandon your wickedness."

"It makes me laugh when a priest of the Catholic Church talks about wickedness. Whitewashed sepulchres! And you can tell your little Hamlet that I'm not done with him yet! I'll never be done with *him*, as he'll find out when we meet again."

He had seen evil at work in the world, but this was different. Such raw hatred shocked the priest to his core. Perhaps he was confronting a woman whose soul was now possessed by the devil she served. This was the one with mysterious knowledge, the one Father Murray had spoken of. She was possessed. What other explanation could there be? He made an effort of will to regain his calm. *Great peace have they who love your law, and nothing can make them stumble.* The woman began to walk away, throwing her head back in laughter that echoed from the vaulted ceilings, profaning the sacred calm of this space.

"Why?" he roared after her. "My God, why?"

The laughter ceased and its echoes faded into stillness. She turned on him with violent energy. "The Church never explains itself, and neither do I. Part of the terror all you good people feel is that my hatred is inexplicable, like one of your dirty sacred mysteries!"

"I have no terror of you. My faith is a rock you cannot shake or move."

"Hell sent me!"

"Neither you nor your master has power here!"

She spit in his direction. "Go fuck yourself with a holy candle, priest!"

To fly after her and catch her by her hair and throw her to the ground would be to surrender to the devil, he knew, and trembling, he dominated this urge. *Nothing can make them stumble.* He lifted the purple stole from his shoulders and kissed it, then slumped into a pew, and head in hands, began to pray for the faithless Nestor.

CHAPTER TWENTY

Once more, Nestor had taken to the streets, the homeless shelters, the cheap hotels, the bars where paychecks and welfare checks were cashed and spent, any place where the flame of madness would not burn so brightly as to attract attention, because he felt that must be where her face would be known. Unless she were mad only in craft, hired or "sent for." Then she would be harder to find, but he would find her, and then he would have to make a decision.

When evening descended on the city and bats flitted above the tree-tops, he drove by his own street. He followed the river, and when he found himself in Tyngsborough, realized that he was driving to Abby's apartment. What if she had company? If there seemed to be anyone there, he would leave. But he saw only her Subaru, and the Honda Civic he'd seen there before, belonging no doubt to the upstairs tenant. As soon as he got out of the car, he heard music—the harp. He climbed the porch stairs, quietly in case the dog was near, and sat on the floor by her threshold, his head against the back door, listening.

Music. It was wonderful how humans had learned to speak with this other voice—this extension and expression of the heart. The individual notes of the melody brought to his mind the steps of a man, pacing alone through empty rooms, and when at the end of a measure her hands swept the strings, the chords came like mournful ghosts surrounding that man, importuning him to remember. It comforted him in some strange way, but he understood the real, the longed-for comfort that had brought him here, and with a feeling that he had no right to it, he rose and left.

The following afternoon, Nestor was playing chess with Father Leahy in the rectory. He'd been thankful, somehow, to receive a call from the priest; he welcomed the distraction, and there was something in his presence that he found soothing, like Abby's music. It was a sentiment that he could not understand. If he rejected the idea of a deity, why did he sense something holy in this man? What did it mean, really, to be holy? What sort of spiritual comfort could the nonbeliever take from the presence or from the words of a holy person?

Leahy was a keen chess strategist. There was nothing wrong with his reason, and he usually won their games, but this afternoon he was distracted, and within ten minutes Nestor had his queen.

The loss did not seem to trouble him. He continued to scan the pieces, leaning toward the board, stroking his bearded chin with an index finger. The body language suggested total concentration, but his focus was divided. "So Minerva has made up her mind to join a religious order?"

"So it seems. Some Sisters of St. Francis in New Bedford."

"Franciscan Sisters of the Immaculate?" the priest suggested.

"Yeah, I guess that's it. She has to wait six months for the divorce. The director of novices told her she can be what they call a 'lay sister,' unless she gets an annulment, but I don't think she wants to deny that we were ever married."

"What do you think about it?"

Nestor shook his head. "I've stopped thinking."

"Hmmm. I understand," the priest said. He was quiet then as he took stock of the positions of the pieces on the board, his elbows on his knees, chin resting on his fists. He appeared disgusted with what he saw, and after a moment he sat up straight. "They say the great chess masters can look ahead twelve or fourteen moves," he said. "I read about Kasparov's match with the IBM computer, Deep Blue. He lost the first game badly, then won the second, fifth and sixth, and played the other two to a draw."

"So he figured out how the computer was thinking. Amazing mind."

"I wish we could apply that penetrating power to our problems. If only we could see two or three moves ahead." Father Leahy brought his knight out to face Nestor's ranks. "The woman... the so-called witch... whatever... she came to the church on Friday."

"Is that right?" Nestor tried not to let the other man see the hatred that he felt rising in his blood and flushing his face at the mention of this creature. "To the church? What, to howl and curse and terrify the young?"

"Ostensibly for confession..."

"Ha!"

"Well, she was not penitent, nor was she looking for forgiveness. I don't know if she is possessed or mad, but Nestor, you mentioned to me once that you thought she might be a paid actress, sent by some individual who doesn't like you. I can tell you that is not the case. She hates you. Personally. She seems to want revenge on you for... I can't imagine what. She went after Minerva to hurt you, I think. All she's done was part of a plan to hurt you, and she won't stop."

"And you just let her go?"

"I wanted to tackle her and hold her down, yes. But then what? If I call the police—well, what crime has she committed? She's yelled at people—hung dolls? And we don't even have proof that that was her. Is it a crime to curse someone? Maybe in the 1600s."

"My son is dead because of that bitch." And another, too, he thought. Because on any other night of his life he would have handed over his wallet and walked away. Any other night. The man might have shot him, but he didn't think so.

"Nestor, stay calm, please. I understand. I do. But think. Try to think twelve moves backward, or more, all across the past. Is there anyone who has reason to hate you like this?"

"Don't you think I've gone over this problem until my head is ready to explode?"

"Anything to do with Sister Winifred?"

"Sister Winifred? You lost me there! What did she say about her?"

"She just mentioned her. I thought maybe…"

Nestor remembered the photos. "I'll be right back, Father."

He ran out to his car and returned with the envelope Finbarr had given him. The priest was not even looking at the chessboard; he was gazing off into the cold, empty hearth. He started as if from a reverie when Nestor handed him the photos. "Just to be sure. That's her, right?"

He nodded. "Yes. Nestor, you have to promise me you won't do any violence to her if and when you find her."

"And what if she tries to kill me?"

The priest remembered the words she had spoken: *I'm not done with McCorley! I'll never be done with him!* He thought it was possible, with that kind of hatred, that she might try to harm him, physically, even to murder him. She had destroyed Minerva with words, and nearly destroyed Nestor, but if she was not done, it would take more than words to destroy Nestor. "Just remember what I'm saying. I'm… pardon the expression, cursed with the Irish temper, too. In my younger days I was vain enough to take an insult as a reason to beat a man. That was wrong. It is wrong. Don't let anger, hatred and vengeance rule your soul. You will regret it. And she will have won. The devil will have won."

Nestor laid the photos on the table beside the chessboard. "Well, I don't know about the devil." He shrugged and looked the priest in the eyes, speaking honestly. "You're a holy man. Me, I'm just a regular guy who's been messed with once too often."

"I'm no different than you. It's just that …"

"No, you are different. Your kind is rare in the world. But you don't know what it is to lose a son… and please don't tell me that God sacrificed his son for us. Because his son was a god anyway—he couldn't be killed, so it's no sacrifice. My son is gone."

"No, Joseph is with God and His son."

He shook his head. "I wish I could believe it. Anyway, there's hatred and vengeance and violence, but there's also justice."

The priest put his hand on Nestor's arm and spoke to him, not as a Father, but as a father. "Justice is not yours to mete out," he said. And in his heart, Nestor suspected that he was right, despite the war drum that pounded in his head whenever he saw the mocking face of the hellish woman.

"It's only that when I think of what our lives could have been without this nameless she-wolf…"

"I know. I know."

Mrs. Riordan knocked on the open door. "Hello, Nestor, how are ye keepin', dear? I'm sorry for your loss. I'm prayin' for you, and that's all I can do. It's a terrible thing."

"Thank you, Mrs. Riordan. I appreciate that."

"It's as my own grandmother used to say, we have to take what we get. Sure, what else can we do?"

"She was right. Thank you."

"Father, I bought a nice piece of haddock at Lowell Provision. It'll be ready at 5:30, unless you'd like me to cook it sooner?"

"No, that will be fine."

"Would you like tea?"

"You'll make it anyway."

"I will indeed." She seemed about to leave when the photos on the table caught her eye. She took a step closer, a quizzical look on her face. "Do you know her?" she asked, pointing uncertainly at the photos.

"Do you?" Nestor asked.

"Yes. Yes I do. That's Rosalind Cannon." She saw the look on their faces and took a step backward. "Mother in Ireland! Don't tell me that she's the one… the one that frightened Minerva with the curse business? It can't be! She said she'd been a nun as a young woman, but that she made a mess of her vocation. She didn't like to talk about it."

"How often have you spoken with the woman?" Father Leahy demanded.

"Is it her?"

"Yes, Mrs. Riordan, it's her. How often have you spoken?"

"We've become... I mean I thought we had become good friends. I believe I've mentioned her to you, Father. She used to come to my house with a pound cake or something and we'd have tea and talk."

"Have you spoken to her about what's been going on... with Nestor and his wife?"

"We spoke about all kinds of things, the way we women do. All of our problems, and..." Her eyes grew wide with realization and her hand rose to her mouth. "I'm so sorry, Father. I thought since she didn't know Nestor or Minerva, it didn't matter really. She seemed so sympathetic. She always asked, like she was very concerned. She said she would say a novena for them." Her voice was twisted with compunction and self-reproach. "Oh, what have I done?"

The priest rose and put a hand on the old woman's shoulder. "There, there, Mrs. Riordan. She's a very good actress. You're not the only one she fooled." He turned to Nestor. "It's my fault, too. I've always valued Mrs. Riordan's advice. We talk about everything, the same way she spoke with this Cannon woman. That's how she knew."

Nestor put the pictures back in the envelope. As calmly as he could manage, he asked, "Where does she live, Mrs. Riordan?"

"In Chelmsford—I don't know her address. She always said she would have me over when her house wasn't such a mess. She said she was doing renovations."

"How did you meet her?"

"I'm very involved in the Catholic Education Fund. We had a bake sale at the school. Sister Veronica introduced me to her."

"Sister Veronica? Is she a friend of hers?"

Her brow creased in thought. "I don't know, rightly. But I believe so, yes."

When Nestor left the unfinished chess game and the tearful Mrs. Riordan at a determined pace, he found that Father Leahy was beside him.

"I'm going with you," the priest said.

"What do you think, I'm going to attack Sister Veronica? I'm not a madman!"

"I'm going, and I won't argue."

There was something in the man's demeanor, or in his character, that made Nestor loathe to contradict him or disrespect him. He also knew that twelve years of undiluted Catholic education had planted deep in his psyche a deference to the Roman collar, as well as the other thing he never wanted to acknowledge—a fear of the devil. *I defy augury* a voice within him cried. But another whispered: *There are more things in heaven and earth than are dreamt of in your philosophy.*

The two men came around the rectory and walked quickly along the wrought iron fence of the churchyard, nearly running as they crossed the lot between the gray stone church and the red brick school. Sister Veronica had an armful of papers and was in the act of locking her office door when she heard the buzzer. Looking down the staircase, she saw Father Leahy's face peering through the narrow strip of glass beside the door. She came down the steps and pushed it open.

"Good afternoon, Father, and… what was your name again?"

"Nestor McCorley. Sister, could we have a word with you?"

"It's rather important, Sister," the priest added.

"Of course. Of course." She unlocked the office door and put the papers back down on her desk, and Nestor wondered at the strange circle of events that had brought him back here, to the office where he had met Sister Winifred so many years ago, on his first day of school. There were two seats facing the desk, and the men sat down like schoolboys in front of the principal.

"Sister," Nestor began, "do you know a Rosalind Cannon?" He handed her the photos. Her look was troubled, and Nestor was glad now that he had the priest with him, because she looked questioningly at him. Father Leahy nodded, indicating that she would be doing no harm by answering.

"Yes, well, I've met her recently. She's been up for various functions, trying to get involved again in some way—trying to help out with the Catholic Fund and various school projects. She said she preferred to keep her past in the past. Why are you looking for her?"

"Again? Why do you say involved *again*?"

"Well, she was before. Father, generally we don't discuss personnel issues without…"

"Personnel?" Nestor leaned forward in his chair.

"Sister, this matter requires my immediate attention. Do you know the woman?"

"Rosalind Cannon is… well, it was before my time, as I said to you, Nestor, but you knew her by the name of Sister St. Michael."

The Lawrence Alcohol Drug Rehab Center was located, fittingly enough, in a rehabbed mill building on Canal Street. The next day, Nestor and Father Leahy stood at a glass window, speaking to a weary-looking receptionist sipping a Diet Coke, part of what apparently had been a vain effort to shed some weight. Three men and a woman, all of whom looked like they badly needed a drink or a fix, sat near them in the waiting room, texting, looking at their cell phones, or idly watching the interaction between the receptionist and the priest. "Do you have an appointment?"

"No, I've come to…"

"Do you have group with Ms. Cannon?"

"No, I'm here on a personal matter. Something I need…"

"Who shall I say wants to see her?"

Nestor took a step backward, looking at a poster on the wall: "HOPE IS AS REAL AS DOUBT."

"Father Leahy, OMI, if I could just have a moment of her time." The receptionist slid the glass closed and struggled out of her chair. "Here goes, Nestor. Now listen. We'll inform her that we know who she is, where she is, that the police will be informed of her behavior…"

"Her behavior..." Nestor snorted.

Father Leahy raised a hand to quell Nestor's ire and continued, "... and that a restraining order will be taken out against her this afternoon. That's our only possible course of action here." Nestor, lips compressed and arms crossed, turned away and studied another poster on the wall. "ACCEPT YOUR FEELINGS AND LET THEM GO." The two men watched the door through which the receptionist had gone. Father Leahy leaned toward Nestor and whispered, "I just can't believe that she can hold down a job, let alone counsel people! She's completely demented... rabid... I would have said possessed—honestly."

The door opened and the receptionist lumbered through. "She'll be right with you," she said. A minute later, a tall woman in a black turtleneck and jacket emerged, redundant circles of pearly beads hanging at various lengths about her neck, rectangular silver glasses, gray-white hair parted on the side and swept back enough to show off a pair of discreet pearl earrings—every inch what one would expect of a professional woman.

Her raised eyebrows and clasped hands indicated an expectant curiosity. "How can I help you, gentleman?"

"We're here to see Rosalind Cannon."

"Yes, I'm Rosalind Cannon."

"No, that's not possible," Nestor began.

She reached into the pocket of her vest and pulled out an ID. "I should be wearing this, but I'm not usually questioned about my own name." Below the name of the facility and her photo, they read, Rosalind Cannon, NAADAC Addiction Counselor.

Nestor began to speak, but Father Leahy put a hand on his arm and asked, very softly, "Ms. Cannon, might I ask if you were once a member of the order of the Sisters of the Holy Faith, and if your name was Sister St. Michael when you worked at St. Brigid's School?"

Her chin rose and her expression became more solemn, as if she expected some onslaught that had arisen out of her past. "Yes, that is true. Could we talk in my office?" They followed her back through the door, along a corridor and into an office, much larger than Sister Veronica's, furnished with a couch, a wing chair, and several foldout chairs. The oversized windows of the old mill overlooked a stone-walled canal. There was a desk pushed against the wall, below a poster that said simply, "Using Sux."

"Before we begin, Sister," Nestor said, "let me say that you never should have been allowed to work with children." He stared at her, trying to re-create the cold hard look that he had seen on her face so many years before.

"You have no right to judge me," she said, just above a whisper.

"Did you enjoy terrifying little children?"

"Nestor," the priest said, "why don't we try to…"

"You don't know anything about me!"

"I know you banged a six-year-old's head against the blackboard!"

"Nestor! Stop!" The priest had his hand on Nestor's chest, his fingers pressing hard into his rib cage. "Stop!"

The woman who had been Sister St. Michael sat down and leaned forward, her face in her hands. "No, he's absolutely right. *Nestor.* I only ever had one student called Nestor. You were what Sister Winifred called 'the last straw,' weren't you?" She looked up at him, not with the cold hard eyes of the nun, but with an expression of contrition. "I'm embarrassed to remember who I was then. Sister Winifred advised me, or told me, to leave the order, and to seek help for my… issues. I'm sorry, Nestor… McClure was it?"

"McCorley."

She nodded. "All I can offer you is my apology. I wish I could apologize to all of them. If I tell you that I treated others the way I was treated? That I learned intimidation and physical abuse were the tools the powerful use to maintain control? That as a child I lived in fear? That my own father…"

"Sister… Ms. Cannon," Leahy interjected. "You don't need to go into this now. We're here for another reason." He shot a warning look at Nestor.

Rosalind Cannon continued, as if she needed to explain, or confess. "She,

273

Sister Winifred, thought at first that prayer alone could solve my problems, but at last she realized that I was beyond anything that convent had ever seen. Intensive therapy—and pharmaceuticals were what I needed." Nestor noticed that one of her hands was twisting the fingers of the other. There were nicotine stains on her thumb, and he was sure that she was dying for a cigarette at this moment. "I was bipolar, with anxiety disorders, all the unresolved emotional traumas you could imagine, or maybe not. Anyway, I was released from my vows. I did the therapy, a lot of counseling, and the meds, eventually pulled myself together and went back to school, and here I am, trying to help others who are dealing with similar things. I'm still a practicing Catholic, but of a far less severe kind. All I can say is I'm truly sorry."

Nestor sighed, almost disappointed in the sincerity of her plea. Over the years he had often imagined screaming into her face. *Now I'm bigger than you!* To make her as afraid of him as he'd been of her. But the menacing woman of his youthful nightmares no longer existed, and Father Leahy was right. This was not why they'd come.

"All right. Apology accepted." He drew the photos out of the envelope. "Ms. Cannon, do you know this woman?"

"It appears," Father Leahy said, "that she has been using your name while engaged in the worst kind of harassment, with very tragic results. She's still making threats. We're trying to get a restraining order, but we need to find out who she is, where she lives. She knows you, or knows of you. Does she look familiar?"

The woman studied the photos carefully. "She does look familiar, but…" She shook her head. "I can't place her exactly right now." The two men did not move while Rosalind Cannon continued to examine the photos. She took in a breath between closed teeth, shaking her head, as if the memory was somewhere within her mind's grasp, but she could not retrieve it.

Eventually, Nestor and Father Leahy exchanged looks of disappointment, and stood to leave. "I'm sorry I haven't been more helpful. It's too bad, Mr. McCorley, that our lives intersected at these two unfortunate instances."

Father Leahy searched his pockets and came up with a piece of paper, on which he wrote his number at the rectory. "If anything occurs to you… you looked as if you could almost remember."

"I'm stumped, Father, because at first I thought she was someone else that I knew, but it can't be…"

"Who?" Nestor asked.

"Well, I thought it was Sister Theresa—I forget what her lay name was. We were friends back then. I heard that she left the school quite suddenly. I sent her some letters through the order, but I never heard from her."

The mention of that name in connection with all this created a jarring seismic disturbance in Nestor's mental landscape. He was already reexamining the photos apprehensively, trying to recall the time-blurred face of Sister Theresa.

"It might be difficult for you to remember, since at school she was always wrapped in the white coif, bandeau and guimpe."

Nestor assumed that these were the names of the articles she had worn over her head, forehead and cheeks, all crowned with the black veil. He couldn't recall much of her face clearly, or associate it in any definite way with the photos. "Why *did* she leave? Was she transferred?"

"I only had one old friend from the school who used to write to me—Sister Julie—she's passed on now. She mentioned that Sister Theresa had gone. It seemed she may have been asked to leave, some problem—it was never discussed. There was never much discussion of things that were directed from above. The vow of obedience is not one that rewards curiosity."

"In any case, Sis—Ms. Cannon, Sister Veronica said that Sister Theresa had died."

"Yes, that's what I heard later," Rosalind Cannon said. "It can't be her. She's dead."

When they had exited the old mill building and were making their way back to the car, Father Leahy said, "A cul-de-sac, Nestor."

"Looks that way," he said, because he did not want to tell his clerical friend what he was thinking—not yet. It was all supposition. Yet the former nun's mention of Sister Theresa, the madwoman's use of the name of Rosalind Cannon, her appearance at the bake sale, and a reference she'd made to Sister Winifred combined to convince him that what had culminated in the death of Joseph McCorley had begun years ago at St. Brigid's School.

He put on sports radio, where the talk was about the latest Red Sox collapse, and pretended to listen. It was difficult, as the priest had said, to see several moves into the future, but it was equally difficult to look into an ever-receding yesterday. Memory is a land of shifting sands, where individuals gain stature or slip into oblivion, and events are transfigured, forming an evolving superstructure in which the original shape is lost.

Could any of this be related to the sudden departure of Sister Theresa? If she was dead, she could do no harm; if she was not really dead (was that possible?), she had no reason to hate him. Like the sisters themselves, he had never questioned her departure, but now two remarks, a quarter century apart, flitted about his mind and lingered there like a cloud of gnats. The first was the one made by Roger Shea long ago: "Sister Theresa don't walk like a nun, she really swings it for Maurice." The other was more recent: "It's my penance. Everyone who was here learned about penance." The words of the old custodian had a bitter chill about them. What could he have done to earn such endless penance?

Nestor felt that the chess pieces had been rearranged, and that if he could only see the whole board clearly, he might fly through some sudden gap, breach the enemy's gate for a change, knock down the queen of shadows and checkmate the king she served.

CHAPTER TWENTY-ONE

I t struck Nestor as he waited on Quincy Street for Maurice to pull out of the parking lot of St. Brigid's School that he did not know his last name. There were only two cars left in the parking lot, and one was Sister Veronica's; it was parked close to the door in a spot that was marked with a sign affixed to the brick wall: Principal.

His cell rang while he waited. Minerva's voice, sounding a little stronger than when he'd last spoken with her. "Nestor, I was released from the hospital this morning. I can't drive well yet. Do you want to come with me to visit Joseph's grave? Marquis and Marina can take me if you are busy."

At the mention of Joseph's name in connection with the grave, his breath stuck for a moment in his lungs, and in his mind he saw the dear boy in his high chair, picking Cheerios off his tray, delighted in his own developing dexterity as, patiently, he lifted each tiny circle between finger and thumb and pushed it into his grinning mouth. *No more. No more forever.* "I am caught up in something right now, Minerva. The truth is I haven't been there yet, since the funeral. I've been waiting until I feel I can face it."

"I understand," she said.

"Could we go tomorrow morning?"

"I have flowers to lay there, and a prayer I want to say for him. I'll go with you again tomorrow if you want."

"Yes, that would be good. You haven't changed your mind about... your vocation, have you?"

"I don't think I will change my mind."

"Minerva, it's up to you. I can't stop you. But you don't need to be forgiven for any sins. You're the *victim*."

"If love was enough, Nestor, I would stay with you."

The old impasse. He didn't even try to tell her once again that it *was* enough. "I'll call you in the morning. Stay strong."

At 3:30, the custodian emerged from the side entrance, locked the door, and got into his car. Nestor turned the key in the ignition and pulled out after him.

He followed Maurice's Chevy Cavalier a few blocks to the Canadian Social Club. He didn't know whether to follow him inside, or wait and try to talk to him alone, but not knowing how long he would sit drinking, Nestor decided to confront him in the club.

The place was not doing a booming business. A scattering of middle-aged men played Keno at one end of the bar, while a few others smoked, chatted in French and watched a poker tournament on ESPN. Nestor hoped that when he was in his sixties he would not be spending his days at the bar of a social club drinking the afternoon away. The only woman in the place was the bartender. Maurice had staked out a seat by himself near the center of the bar. He stretched out an arm and pulled an ashtray close; he was reaching for his cigarettes when he saw Nestor leaning on the bar beside him, his folded hands resting on a manila envelope.

"What do you want?"

"Those are bad for you. We need to talk."

"I got nothing to say."

The bartender brought Maurice a draft beer. "There you go, Mo," she said brightly.

"Thank you, Ann," he said, the gruffness falling away for a moment.

She flashed a pleasant smile at Nestor. He noticed the ample cleavage of a bosom that filled not only her brassiere, but, he was sure, the tip jar. "What can I getcha, Hun?"

He was always well-disposed to these solid women from Lowell's Acre,

Centralville or Pawtucketville neighborhoods who weren't afraid to call a man "Hun." They didn't mind being friendly because they had already heard and could handle all the come-ons.

"Cranberry juice and lime, please." Bars full of aging men, Keno, and poker tournaments always made him want to go on the wagon.

Maurice lit a cigarette and was doing his best to ignore him. "Let's have a seat at a table," Nestor suggested.

"Leave me alone."

A memory was surfacing in Nestor's consciousness from the days when he had first started teaching. Someone had set off a stink bomb in his class. He suspected a particular individual, but he knew if he asked, "Did you do it?" the answer would be "No," and he had no proof. Instead, he called the suspect at home and asked, "Why did you do it?" He at once, as Shakespeare put it, "proclaim'd his malefaction." With this in mind, Nestor decided to play the hand he had put together, card by card, in the last few days.

When Ann of Cleavage had brought his juice, he leaned close to the older man and said, "Listen… Mo… either you go and sit with me at a table and talk to me, or I announce to your fellow social club members that you once raped a nun."

It was a hand he had not been sure was a winner, but when he laid it on the table, he saw the look on the custodian's face. His eyes were wide. He cast nervous glances the length of the bar, grabbed his beer and cigarettes and headed for a table. Nestor picked up the envelope and followed him. When they sat down, the older man said, softly but emphatically, "I did not rape her. *She* came on to *me!* Hell, she was a nun—I know it was wrong, but she was still a woman! And I was young then; yes, a little older than her, but still young. I sure wasn't going to worry about hell when she was… you know… coming on to me."

"I can understand."

"So don't use that word *rape*. That's not the way it was at all! I would never…"

"All right, I believe you. Look, Maurice, I don't care if you and she had an affair. Much better two adults having consensual sex in the cloakroom than some frustrated, perverted celibate raping an altar boy. I don't care what you and the young nun did. It's just that someone seems to be…" He stopped and sighed. "God, it's a long story, Maurice. Just trust me. I won't involve you. At all. Sister Theresa … what was her real name, do you know?"

He nodded, head bowed, exhaling a plume of smoke. "Her name was Gretta. Gretta Nash. And we weren't always in the cloakroom, as you say, or the janitor's closet. We found ways to be together. We were in love. I was, anyway. I think she was. I took her for car rides—she'd have to cook up some excuse. Once we went up to Newburyport. She showed me her family home. Very nice. She loved the sea. It was in her blood, you understand."

"How long did it last, this affair?"

"A few months." His crushed his cigarette into the ashtray as if he had just realized that the taste of it disgusted him. "The best few months of my life." He unbuttoned the top of his shirt and pulled out a silver chain, on which hung a heavy miraculous medal that he held in the air between them. Nestor saw that he kept it shining, like her memory. "A gift from her. 'I have nothing else to give you—nothing but scandal.' That's what she said. I wear it every day."

"Maurice, Gretta Nash is dead, right?"

He pushed the medal back inside his shirt. "Yes, she's dead. That's the part I'd rather not talk about. The truth is I'm ashamed. I'm especially ashamed to tell *you*…"

"Listen, I *have to* know. Whatever you did with her is of no concern to me. My concern is something else entirely, but what happened back then is somehow tied in—a prelude. How did she die?"

Maurice closed his eyes; his hand formed a fist beside his ear and gave a short tug.

"She hung herself? But *why*?"

"Can't you guess?"

CHAPTER TWENTY-ONE

"She was pregnant."

He nodded. "She was pregnant, and she wanted to keep our child, but they forced her to give it up for adoption. In those days, they just wouldn't hear of anything else. A pregnant nun? That's a scandal all right, for us and for the Church. She tried to keep the baby—a boy, but her family, the Church… they were all against her."

"They would have done better to worry about the real scandals. So they took her baby away?"

He nodded. "And then Gretta… she hung herself." He wrung his hands for a few seconds, eyes downcast. Then he looked at Nestor and said, "That's the way it was." He drank some beer, and rubbed his forehead, tiredly.

Nestor wanted to ask, where the hell were you, you worthless bastard? Why didn't you stand up to her family and to the Church and everyone and claim your child? But he was afraid that the man would burst into tears and run out of the bar or shut down and he would not learn what he needed to know. "Maurice, when we met at the school, you said, 'I remember you.' Why do you remember me? Thousands of kids have passed through that school. And why is it that you are particularly ashamed to tell *me* this story?"

The old man groaned as if a knife blade was twisting his gut. His expression was that of someone who was becoming nauseated, and Nestor felt that his interrogation was cruel in some way, but he had to continue. He had to know. "Carrying buckets is no penance, Maurice. This is your penance. Tell me."

"First of all, she told me what happened in the greenhouse—with you. And then one day she came back into the school at recess. She had spoken to you in the school yard, threatened you, said that you'd be thrown out if you said anything."

Nestor made a face, as if the memory had brought a bad taste into his mouth. "I remember. She was smiling."

"She wasn't smiling when she came in, believe me. She was crying, and she had squeezed the crucifix in her hand so hard that blood flowed from a wound, there." He tapped his finger into the palm of his right hand. She kept saying, 'What have I become?' We had talked some before that, but that's when our, you know, our affair began. I was trying to comfort her."

Nestor sensed that there was more to the story. "Go on."

"I was engaged at the time… to a French girl, Louise Cyr. She worked at the Bon Marché. She was a good girl, and my family adored her. And I had gone and fallen in love with Gretta. But I couldn't very well tell my French-Canadian family, or hers, both Catholic to the core, that I wasn't going to marry Louise because I had met a nice nun. Maybe I would have done it. I tell myself I would have, eventually, if things had been different, if I'd had more time."

"Sure."

He ignored, or didn't hear the sarcasm. "Gretta wanted to protect me. She did protect me. She told me that she confessed to Sister Winifred that the father of the baby was a student, because she said that they would never do anything about that. The school would never want to admit that one of the boys under their care had been seduced by a nun, and they certainly couldn't say that a grammar school boy had seduced a nun! You know how the Church was—if the problem could be hidden, swept aside or covered up—then it never happened."

"Did she name the student?" Nestor asked, but he already knew the answer.

Maurice closed his eyes and took a breath, trying to get the strength to speak. When he opened his eyes, he was looking directly at Nestor. "She said the baby's father was you, Nestor McCorley." He raised his glass and tilted back his head, drinking deeply.

"Well, well. Wasn't *that* fucking lovely."

"Well, she was right, wasn't she, that they would sweep it under the rug? I mean, you never even knew! It didn't affect you!" He drank more, and set the empty glass on the table.

Nestor controlled his tongue with effort. *Didn't affect me? It may have cost my son his life! If she wasn't already dead, I'd kill her myself.* He said none of this. He pulled the photos from the packet. "Maurice, do you know this woman? Someone claimed it was Gretta Nash."

Wearily, the older man fished a pair of reading glasses out of his shirt pocket. "She does look something like her, older of course, but no, Gretta is dead. I went to her wake." He shook his head, and moved uncomfortably in his seat. "I saw her in her casket."

"And it was definitely her?"

"Well, she didn't really look like herself because of... you know. The funeral home did the best they could. Her lips were still blue, and..." He shuddered, and looked toward the bar, waving his empty glass at the idle bartender. "But yes, it was her. Her family wanted her to wear her nun's habit, but the Church would not permit it. They say that suicides go to... well, you know what they say. She wore a white dress with a scarf around her neck, a gold scarf to cover the rope marks."

His head sank into his hands. "*Ah, ma pauvre petite,*" he said. "I can still hear her mother wailing. She, her mother, didn't live long after that—a few years, and her husband followed her from what I understand. I never married Louise, and so you see, that's what happened, and that's why I don't think heaven will ever hear my prayers."

"Gretta didn't by any chance have a twin?"

"A twin? She never mentioned that. She had a sister. I don't remember her name."

"Maurice, that's who I need to find. When you went to the family home in Newburyport, do you remember where it was?"

"Yes, it was on Merrimac Street, right across from a marina or yacht club. It was on the corner of Merrimac and Ashland. I remember that because I thought it was a coincidence. There was an Ashland Street off of the street I lived on as a kid."

"Right on the corner?"

"Yes, a nice old stone wall around it. I don't know if the family still owns it."

Nestor stood and slid the photos into the envelope as Ann came with Maurice's beer and set it on the table, taking the empty glass. Nestor threw ten dollars on the table and said, "Thanks, Maurice."

"I'm sorry she used your name. Like I said, she thought…"

"I understand what she thought. She should never have done it, and you shouldn't have let her." He leaned over the table and said, "Didn't you ever think of taking responsibility for your actions?" At the same time he remembered Rosario shuddering as the bullets slammed into his body, a crime far worse than Gretta Nash's, and he had not taken responsibility. He straightened his back. Maurice was looking into his beer, where he saw, no doubt, all the lost years that had sprung from one wasted opportunity, one failure of nerve—from the fear of scandalizing all the believers with his sacrilegious love. "Maybe you're right, Maurice. We all need penance." He was going to ask his last name, but he decided it didn't matter; no one of his stock would carry it after him.

CHAPTER TWENTY-TWO

The Candlefish 16 skiff slid easily through the waters of the Merrimack River estuary. Sitting at the back with one hand on the tiller handle of the 20 hp Mercury outboard was Eileen Nash. She was alone until the other spoke: "A lovely boat, but the center of gravity is too far astern," he said. She had always admired a well-dressed man, and she smiled as she took in the dark, double-breasted jacket with its epaulets and double gold stripes at the cuffs—and pulled low and tight over his head, a white captain's cap, its peak emblazoned with crossed anchors under a human skull.

"The center of gravity might be farther aft if you had some weight," she told him. "Do you have any weight at all?"

"Atomically? Oh yes. The same as smoke."

Her smile widened and her eyes lit with mirth. "Did you see me with the priest?"

"You know I hate those places. But I heard you very well from where I was. With a holy candle! Brilliant!"

They laughed together, and as the sun emerged from behind a pillar of cumulus cloud, she pulled her sunglasses from the pocket of her windbreaker and put them on. Her eyes were the most expressive of her features, and with those hidden, the windows to her interior world were shuttered. The wake of the skiff rolled its perfect V as the shore panned by them. She scanned this waterway she knew so well: its channels, its tides and currents, buoy markers, the best spots to catch stripers and mackerel. As a child, she had plied these waters in sailboats and skiffs, often with her older sister, Gretta.

"Ah, the pines of the shore and the salt and spawn of the sea!" cried the man in the nautical uniform, slapping his chest and inhaling deeply. "Does a demon good!"

"Did I ever tell you about the time we, Gretta and I and little Skipper, our cousin, took a small fiberglass boat out in Plum Island Sound? We were heading back before dusk when a big boat came along and swamped us."

A yellow biplane lifted off from Plum Island Airport and passed overhead. Eileen Nash leaned back to watch it bank and soar out over the Atlantic, heading south toward Cape Ann. Her companion had been listening carefully to her story, tapping an index finger meditatively against his chin. "They say you are mad, but look how calmly, and with what skill you guide the boat."

"Yes, when you see more than others, they think you're crazy. And sometimes it suits me to be crazy—when I want to scare the sheep."

The other laughed, "Baah! Baaaah! So you were out in the Atlantic, near dusk, on a swamped boat. How did you survive?"

Looking out over the broad entrance to the Atlantic, Eileen shuddered and pushed the tiller handle to her right so that the boat leaned into a sweeping turn and began to move back up the Merrimack River.

"Go on! What did you do?"

"I didn't do anything. I was only thirteen or so. But Gretta was sixteen, very clever, always thinking. Thinking and praying." The sun had passed again behind a cloud bank, and she removed her sunglasses, revealing eyes that were brimming with tears. "She saved our lives that day, my sister. She told me later that in those moments before she found the answer she made a promise she had to keep. She was quite sure we would die, but she promised the Virgin Mary that if she showed her a way out, a way to save her sister and her cousin, that she would renounce the world and serve the Church. It was my sister that saved us, not heaven. But she would never break that promise, though she wanted to. That was the day Sister Theresa was made. Until Nestor McCorley and Sister Winifred betrayed her and drove her to an early grave. And then they say she went to hell? Well then, it's hell for me, too."

"The old nun paid. And McCorley will keep paying. Take his life only after he's lost everything else."

"Yes, then I'll take it. Oh, don't think I won't." She turned the throttle back, and the skiff settled into a slow crawl upriver. "What will I do when McCorley is gone? Life without hate will be empty again."

"You declare war first, and then you learn to hate the enemy. Whoever it is."

"But I can never hate anyone as much as I've hated McCorley and Winifred."

"There's Mother Church herself!"

"That's true. They twisted her and suffocated her and eventually they killed her, and they protected the boy they used. Nothing ever happened to him. Nothing ever would have if I had not found her diary. Do you know what that bitch Winifred said to her? *You must leave immediately. Nestor McCorley is but a boy, and the full force of the Church will be exercised to make certain that you do not keep the child. You are unfit for motherhood as well as for sisterhood. May God forgive you.* Hmph! And may the devil blast you, McCorley! All the filthy details of his illicit meetings with my sister must have been on the pages that were torn from the diary. He shamed her; they all shamed her into the grave. He thought he could go on with his life with never a tear for Gretta, never a wave to knock *his* little boat into the cold sea, and live in peace with his own happy family after he destroyed my poor sister."

"But Fortune's wheel spins, doesn't it?"

She spit over the side and laughed softly. "Oh, it certainly does. I made another trip up to the old mill town last night. One more nail for little Minerva's coffin, and a hammer blow to McCorley's core."

CHAPTER TWENTY-THREE

Did she still live in the family house in Newburyport? She certainly didn't seem to live in Lowell; she appeared in the city and disappeared like a ghost. Nestor was driving home along Broadway, considering his options. He watched the schoolboys and girls talking in groups or chasing each other along the sidewalk. He envied their innocence for a moment, but then he reminded himself what his years as a teacher had taught him: you never knew what a young person had experienced or endured. The steeple of St. Brigid's Church rose out of the heart of the Acre and towered above it. Nestor could picture Father Leahy up there, drinking his coffee, smoking a clandestine cigarette and surveying the landscape of his parish, a battlefield where good and evil were always at war.

The priest had set out the course of action, the only ethical one, he had said. He was right, no doubt. Nestor would get her name, report her whereabouts to the police, file a restraining order—that was all he could do. The knowledge of the gun he still kept hidden in his trash barrel and what he'd done with it sat like a stone on his heart. At times his anger rose from some dark place within him, and he longed once more to kill this woman. He felt once again the hatred he'd felt on the night his wife had been driven to fall with their son from the steep height. He had to get rid of the gun, because as long as he had it, it would be too facile an option.

He pulled into his driveway. Branches drenched in sunlight and housing innumerable sparrows swung their shade over the yard. From under the stairway, Nestor pulled out the trash bin and extracted a plastic bag. Then he tilted the bin so that the gun in its paper bag slid onto the ground. With the gun safely stashed under the car seat, he headed to Prendeville's house. He could stand on the bank there and toss it far into the deep channel of the river. Then he would take a trip to Newburyport.

He'd just crossed the Rourke Bridge when his cell phone sounded its "Whiter Shade of Pale." He heard Minerva's voice, but her words were incoherent. A vague panic seized him, and he pulled his car into the Brunswick Bowling parking lot. "What is it, Minerva?"

"She won't stop! Joseph is dead, and she won't stop!" Her voice trailed off into sobs, while Nestor kept trying to get her to speak clearly. "Where are you, Minerva? I'll come right away."

Marquis Alicea was on the phone. "Nestor, listen, Marina and I are here with her. She's very upset."

"What happened for God's sake?"

"We took her out to visit the grave. Someone has drawn things on the headstone."

"What kind of things?"

"Bad things, Nestor. An inverted cross, the number 666—other things I don't know what they are." His voice lowered to a nearly inaudible whisper. "And there is a hole dug over the grave, with what looks like a dead rat in it."

His breath faltered, and he gripped the phone tightly in his fist. Marquis' words seemed to crawl into his ear like a parasitic worm or like drops of poison from the assassin's lethal vial. "Please Marquis, get Minerva away from there right away."

"Yes, Marina is getting her into the car now, but she says we have to come back with the priest."

"Tell her that this is about to stop. I promise. I'm on this bitch's heels now."

"Be careful, Nestor. Don't do anything…"

He ended the call and tossed the phone onto the passenger seat; he re-crossed the bridge and got on 495 North toward the coast, while the glowing coal of hatred within him was fanned to flame with thoughts of his nd his broken wife. In less than an hour he was in Newburyport, a

ith century seaport town of red brick, from the center of which rose

iark white church steeple. He pulled into the city parking lot and

aged through his trunk for his Red Sox cap. He put it on and set off

y down Merrimac Street, carrying the Dunkin' Donuts bag in his left

. He found he was walking the wrong way, because Merrimac became

er Street before he had come to Ashland. He headed back toward the

n, passing Butler and Forrester; he saw Ashland on his left. He had

iagined, for some reason, a cape or small bungalow, but the house inside

ie stone-walled yard was a sprawling Victorian with a mansard roof. The

Nash family home. On the sea side of the street, a boatyard crowded with

hulls, some canvass-covered, blotted out the view of the estuary, at least

from this ground level.

As he approached the house, he saw that it was in disrepair, badly in

need of a paint job and a new roof. The chimneys leaned away from the sea.

He hoisted himself up to sit on the stone wall. He took off his cap, wiped

his forehead and looked out over the great hulls and tilted masts of the

boatyard, breathing the salt air deeply; meanwhile, he dropped the gun in

its paper bag down into the grass behind the wall. He lined up his position

with the mast of a sailing yacht, noting the name *Mist Runner* on the stern.

He left and walked up to the Grog for a beer. He chatted with some of

the locals, all the time hearing Minerva's voice in his head, and seeing the

ghastly face of the woman who had visited all this upon his house. When

the sun had set and the streetlights flickered on, he left the Grog and walked

ip the cobbled street toward the river. An offshore fishing boat, a gillnetter

iiling a cloud of gulls, churned upriver in the dying light, returning to its

oring. After it had passed, Nestor leaned against a railing, inhaling the

f of diesel that hung on the breeze and listening to the wharf creaking

st sun-bleached poles in the boat's wake.

uples strolled arm in arm through Atkinson Common and along the

edge. Nestor remembered his own walk with Minerva by this same river as it flowed through Lowell on the last day of his son's brief life. The nuns had spoken of the "sins that cry to heaven" in the Catholic catechism, and Hamlet had felt "prompted by heaven and hell" to his revenge.

Now he weighed once again the offenses this woman had committed. She had hounded Minerva into near insanity, put his son in an early grave, and pursued the innocent boy's body beyond it. He was sorry about Sister Theresa. He was sorry that this other Nash was out of her mind, but no restraining order would ever stop her. He had to kill her before she killed Minerva, or him, or others. His wife would be in a nun's cell and he would be in a jail cell and his son in the narrow cell of his grave and there would be an end to it all. The moon, his old friend on these werewolf nights, was rising over the port town like a grim lantern.

He crossed the street when he came even with *Mist Runner* and leaned over the low stone wall, pulling out the paper bag that was tucked in the undergrowth at its base. Seeing no one about, he pulled himself over the wall and walked uphill through the spacious enclosure, lost in a darker night below the spreading limbs and rich foliage of a copse of ash trees. Passing them, Nestor recalled the old folk song, *Jack O'Rion swore a bloody oath, by oak and ash and bitter thorn.*

Quietly, he mounted the back stairs onto a wraparound porch and peeked through the kitchen window. A voice reached him indistinctly. It was the television—Alex Trebek posing his *Jeopardy* questions. Light from a parlor or TV room beyond illuminated an antiquated kitchen of dark wainscoting and stained wallpaper. The table was covered with stacks of newspapers and old magazines bound with twine into bundles. All he needed to know was that she was home. He heard Alex Trebek say that they would be back for Final Jeopardy. Just then the kitchen light came on, and the woman who had mocked him in his dreams for too long stepped into his field of vision.

He turned the door handle once; it was locked. He took two steps backward and lunged forward, driving a furious kick into the old door, which flew open and crashed against the kitchen wall, shattering the pane of glass it held. He ripped the paper bag away from the gun and charged into the kitchen. The woman had stood still, stunned for a moment, but now she turned to run—not fast enough. Nestor gripped her from behind by the hair, dragged her backward and flung her to the floor. The shadow that the gun cast in the overhead light fell over her breast. "Where's the devil to help you now, bitch?"

A slow smile spread over her face. "The devil hath power to assume a pleasing shape…"

The shape that rushed into the kitchen was that of Abby Griffin, and for a moment Nestor wondered whether it was possible that a devil had translated itself into this body through some dark metamorphosis, but their eyes met, and he knew. It was Abby.

"My God," he said, "are you part of this? Tell me you're not."

Like some Medusa, the other rose and pointed a crooked finger. "She's the one I serve, fool!"

"Nestor, put down the gun!" Abby pleaded. "She's goading you!"

The gun trembled in his outstretched hand. "Why are you here?"

"I was watching your performance that night from the back of the room. I didn't want you to know I was there. After she came in screaming, I followed her and got her license plate. A friend at the Registry gave me her address and I came to see her. I've been trying to help her, to prescribe some meds for her." Eileen Nash's derisive laughter mocked the explanation that Abby offered.

Stepping closer to Nestor, Abby continued. "I didn't want to tell you, because I thought if she just went away and left you and Minerva alone, that would be the best outcome. Besides, there's patient confidentiality and all that. I thought… I mean she almost convinced me that she's better, but I wonder now if she's taking her meds at all. It's just part of this crazy, calculated scheme." She glared in the direction of Eileen Nash and said, "I've tried all these months to help you, Eileen."

"Oh she can weave a tangled web for you," the other responded. Her laughter filled the room now, laughter that Nestor had heard once too often. He aimed the gun. Abruptly, she was silent, but she raised her chin and fixed him with an icy look, almost seeming to gloat over the murder he was about to commit, though it was her own.

"Nestor!" Abby said. "You can't do it! She's not in her right mind!"

"Hitler was insane and we all sure as hell wish someone had shot him."

"But she hasn't killed anyone."

"Charles Manson didn't kill anyone directly. This fucking harpy has worked things in such a way that my son is dead and my wife thinks she killed him."

"Nestor, tonight she scares me, but you scare me more! Please put the gun down."

The laughter resumed with renewed vigor. He took a step closer to this woman, this devil out of hell, steeling his mind for the shot and all that would follow. The laughter stopped once more. "I dare you!" she whispered. "You don't have *the balls.*"

His mind was racing. He recalled Polonius nodding his grizzled head and muttering, "He is far gone, far gone." Another vision played itself out in his head: the gun firing and this fiend blown back against the wall. He wanted to feel the justice, the finality that would be in that. The hammer of witches. The scourge and minister of heaven. And then what? And now it was the priest who whispered to him, "If only we could see two or three moves ahead." He tried to see beyond that moment. Would there be any good there? He saw himself in a jail cell, his mother crying for him through sleepless nights. No more would he watch the moon sail out full in the heavens on the sixteenth night, or have a beer with Declan at the Old Court, or see love once more in a woman's eyes, maybe in Abby's eyes.

He knew that he would have suffered all those losses and more if any pain could have saved his son, but he could not give it all up for something that could never be changed with tears or blood or bullets. The price of vengeance was too high, and however just his cause, he would be not a man who killed an attacker once in a rage, but a cold-blooded killer, and he began to hate the gun he saw in his hand more than he hated the woman who taunted him.

Abby's hand was on his arm, pushing it down, gently. "That's what she wants, Nestor. Don't do it!"

"*That I, with wings as swift as meditation or the thoughts of love, may sweep to my revenge,*" he whispered. "Well, it wasn't so easy for Hamlet, and I see it's not so easy for me. Sweeping to one's revenge is much easier when you're insane. Maybe that's why she's so good at it."

He put the gun back in his waistband, and Abby whispered in his ear, "I think I peed my pants."

His laughter surprised him; he breathed deeply twice and said, "Let's get out of here."

"You think it will stop here? Oh, he didn't kill me. What a great man! I owe him my life! Thank you! Thank you, McCorley! You think I care about my life? I care about justice! Three eyes for an eye!"

"Justice? Listen to me, Eileen Nash—your sister, Gretta, of sacred memory, tried to seduce me when I was thirteen years old, in the greenhouse of the convent. I was scared shitless and I ran away! The child she had was never mine. She said that to protect someone else, a man, because she knew they wouldn't blame a boy. They would send her away and sweep the scandal under the convent rug. And that's exactly what they did."

Her face lost its twisted animation; the narrow eyes opened wider and the fire behind them flickered as the oxygen of motive for her undying hatred leaked away from the flame. "Swear," she said. "Swear that it's true on your boy's soul."

"By the souls of my father and my son, it's true. By all that's holy! By oak and ash and bitter thorn, it's true—and you know it."

Her head cocked to one side, she studied his eyes. "And the devil take your soul if you are lying?"

"The devil take my body and soul if I ever had a child, or if I ever had sex with your sister. She *lied*!"

"Eileen, it's over," Abby said. "You need help to get past all this once and for all. I'll get you checked into…"

Her gaze remained fixed on Nestor. "Then who? Who was the father?"

"That I'll never tell you. You've done enough harm, you venomous bitch."

She turned and flung open a drawer, pulling out a long serrated carving knife. "You'll tell me, McCorley!"

Nestor pushed Abby backward and in one motion picked up and hurled a chair at the armed woman. Before it struck her he had the kitchen table in his hands. Piles of old newspapers thudded to the floor, but as he raised his arms to throw that, too, he saw the knife on the floor and Eileen Nash huddled against the wall, groaning in pain.

Nestor pulled Abby by the arm out onto the porch. "I've got to get out of here, Abby. So do you, in case she comes around and picks up another knife."

"Nestor, I swear she was acting as if her delusions were under control. I thought I was helping you. She was talking to me like an eccentric, but a sane eccentric."

"No good deed goes unpunished, right?"

"What if she's hurt?"

"I don't care, but if it will make you feel better, call 911 on your way home. There was no gun. That's part of her craziness. For everything else, you can tell the truth. I came to confront her, but not to kill her. She pulled a knife. Can you tell that one lie? I'll dispose of the gun, and never get you in a mess like this again."

"All right, go."

"What about your pocketbook?"

"Shit, yes. My bag is in the TV room."

"I'll keep an eye on her while you get it."

They stepped back into the house. Abby ran into the other room while Nestor watched the wild woman, still slouched against the wall, shaking her head and muttering to herself, "You lied, you lied, you lied."

Abby returned. "My God, Nestor, where did you get the gun?"

"I'll explain everything later."

As they made for the door, Eileen Nash rose. Nestor pulled Abby back, but there was nothing to fear this time. She scrambled out of the kitchen, limping awkwardly. There was the sound of a rapid footfall ascending the stairs followed by a series of crashing noises overhead. The couple stared at each other, dumbfounded, as they listened to what sounded like bookcases tumbling, mirrors shattering, bottles, lamps, old photographs and whatever else lay on dressers and tables being swept away, and a voice shrieking through a fit of sobbing, "She was good! She was *good*!" Nestor felt an unexpected pang of pity for the woman he had been ready to murder a short while ago.

The heart in the woman who staggered from room to long-deserted room in the desolate manse was full of misgivings. Nestor's words had rung true, and her thoughts returned to the pages that had been torn from the diary. Why would Gretta have torn out the pages that recorded the events that led to her disgrace, and leave only the name of Nestor McCorley? The pages she had torn out held the true identity of the one who had made love to her and ruined her; that was the man she had protected, and his name was the secret she took to her grave.

Downstairs, Nestor pulled out his shirttails to hide the gun, and led Abby out of the house once more; they walked quickly to her car. They kissed and he hurried off toward the municipal parking lot. Halfway to his car, he heard the wail of sirens, and looking back from where he'd come, saw a column of smoke blotting out the stars. He ran the rest of the way to his car. On the way to Lowell, he pulled over at the entrance to the Moseley Woods and walked halfway out across the Chain Bridge. He tossed the dead man's gun into the Merrimack River. He did not stay to reflect on the serenity of the silently flowing water.

CHAPTER TWENTY-FOUR

B ut it did flow serenely, by Ireland Point, around Carr Island and Ram Island, past Mud Creek and Hate Cove, under the wharves of Ring's Island Marina, between the barnacle-encrusted pillars of the Bridge Road Bridge and on toward the sweeping beam of the Plum Island Lighthouse. The light was reflected in the eyes of Eileen Nash as she motored with the flowing tide toward it. She held the chart of the river and the surrounding coast in her mind. She could see it as clearly as she had when it hung on the wall of the bedroom she shared long ago with her sister, Gretta.

She could trace the innumerable inlets, small rivers like arteries flowing from the crevices of the earth, tidal basins, and spits of land thick with marsh grass where the tern and plover nested, all shielded by the sea barrier of Plum Island itself, stretching from the mouth of the Merrimack in the north to the mouth of the Ipswich in the south. Out beyond the lighthouse, beyond these unique landmarks and old reference points so familiar to her, the chart showed nothing but a pale blue expanse. That was where she was bound.

She was wearing the only thing she had taken from the house before she set fire to it: the musty habit that Gretta had not been allowed to wear to her grave. Eileen had thought to wear it to confession, one more time, and when the priest friend of Nestor's leaned forward to hear the timid sins of a nun, to plunge a knife through the screen and into his neck. Such glorious plans she'd had for the final scenes.

"But he wouldn't swear on his dead son's soul unless it were true," she

297

sobbed. "You know it's true and that's why you abandon me! He'll never tell me the name, and it was long ago, and how can I start again? They know me now. It's hopeless and I'm tired." Her eyes narrowed and the veins in her throat pulsated in her rage. "I hate you. You promised me vengeance and I got nothing! A comedy of errors with a riddle at the end! If hatred can kill on the other side I'll find you! *Liar!*"

Eileen Nash railed against her traitorous accomplice, but she remained alone in the skiff as the lights of shore and the glow of flames were swallowed in darkness. When the gas tank was empty and the engine sputtered and stalled, she picked up the bailing can and began to pour water into the boat. "This is how it should have ended long ago," she said. The boat settled deeper and deeper into the water, and she shivered as the cold numbed her bones and seeped into her core.

The wind kicked up a sea chop as the vast screen of the eastern sky turned from black to pale violet, and a bell buoy began to toll. "A knell to mine ears!" she cried. The boat foundered; the voluminous habit grew heavy about her. A keening sound rose from her throat for the woman who had been good before her soul was twisted by a promise into a life she was never meant to lead. Eileen's small forlorn cry was lost in the bitter, unchecked wind, and if there was a momentary glimpse of sanity or an ache of regret before she slipped though the water—if she asked God, or anyone, for forgiveness, no one heard. A dawn broke, two herring gulls alighted to inspect the scant flotsam, and the solitary bell tolled across an empty sea.

Minerva and Nestor sat in Marina's kitchen on an August afternoon, at the table where he'd asked her to marry him on a day that seemed long ago now, though really it wasn't. He had just related the strange events that had unfolded since Finbarr had given him the photos of Eileen Nash. An air conditioner hummed in one of the windows, and outside thunder rumbled in a steel gray sky. Minerva had listened in silence, biting her thumb, lines of anxiety still etched in her face. When he finished, she was quiet a moment longer, trying to take it all in. "So they think she's dead now?"

"Apparently the skiff she used to keep at a dock is gone. No one has seen it or her. It seems likely that she burned her house in a final act of rage, and then just went out to sea and scuttled the boat. It's over, Minerva. But I want you to know…"

Thunder cracked the heavens, and Nestor imagined the lightning shivering the sky above the steeples and smokestacks of the city, and maybe farther east over the sweep of sea where Eileen Nash had found a grave, blue and deep. Minerva blessed herself, murmuring, "I hate the thunder." The air conditioner stuttered and went off for a second, then hummed to life again, while the thunder boomed overhead. Through the open blinds, he watched the limbs of the trees surging and billowing in the wind, and then the rain came coursing down, pattering with a dull beat through the leaves, drumming on the roof, glutting the sagging gutters and the drainpipes of the old house.

"I wanted you to know, Minerva, that none of this was your fault. She was a madwoman who wanted to punish *me*, and leave me broken and alone, the way she'd been left."

"And Mrs. Riordan told her all about us?"

"Yes, without any bad intent."

"But we had just come from the hospital. How did she know already that we would have a son? She knew that, Nestor."

"Well, you spoke with Marina right after the ultrasound, and asked her to call Father Leahy. I'd have to ask Mrs. Riordan if she spoke with Nash immediately after that. It's possible, but she probably didn't know. Still, there are only two choices. And I think she believed we would have a boy because her sister lost, or had to give up a boy. So she believed that the devil was working everything out so that she'd get her so-called justice. That's my guess."

She nodded.

"She was a vicious lunatic, Minerva, and she almost made lunatics out of us."

"Nestor, when I saw what she did to Joseph's grave, I wanted to kill her."

He took her hand in his and tried to comfort her in silence for a few minutes while she cried. "I would not have blamed you," he said, "but it's over. What will you do now? Are you still planning to join that order in New Bedford?" The thunder began to roll on, sounding now more like the artillery of a distant battle.

"You remember that you said one time that if I joined a convent you would come and steal me away?"

He paused, recalling the vivid light of Miami, the witchcraft of her smile, and the enthralling gamble that was new love. "Yes, I do remember."

"Would you still do that?" When he did not answer, she continued, "Because Nestor, I don't know what's right."

"Minerva, I don't know what's right, either. I know you acted according to your beliefs, and they're good beliefs. You tried to be true to yourself, and it was confusing and difficult for you. There was a war inside you between love and faith; you were fighting battles where I couldn't help you because I couldn't even see the enemy. You know how much I've loved you—almost since I saw you. There is a hell, and I've been there. You left me. I was a danger to your soul."

"I'm sorry now that I said that."

"No, you were being honest. But you came back, and I'd never felt such joy. Then all the horror, and I knew somehow it was over as soon as I heard… about Joseph. You asked me to sign divorce papers, and I did. I know the circumstances were awful, but they were awful for me, too, and I had to force myself to accept the reality, all over again, that we could not be together. And I did that. But I couldn't go through all that torment, cross that dark place, again. It would have destroyed me. So I broke the love on some hard anvil deep inside. Maybe I couldn't break it all, but enough. I don't know how else to say it, Minerva. I'm not angry, but I'm worn out. I'm done."

"Are you sure that's the right thing to do? Are you sure, Nestor?"

"Sure? No, but a friend of mine once said that when you're trying to make a decision, trying to decide which path to follow, the right one is usually whichever is most difficult. I think that's probably true. That's what I'm going to do now." *How long ago it seemed now, that first dance with her, El Camino de Amor.*

The road of love is like the road the wanderer takes,
It is steep and full of dangerous turnings,
The wisest man does not know where it leads.

"Is it because I blamed you, and now, deep down, you blame me and you hate me for it?"

"No, no. I don't hate anyone," he said. "I'm a Christian... of sorts." They looked into each other's eyes and finally they smiled, wearily. He continued, "You have to forgive yourself, Minerva. 'All dogs have their day,' someone once said, 'even rabid dogs.' Eileen Nash was a rabid dog, and she had her day. You weren't... we weren't prepared for anything like her. Who would be, Minerva? Who would be?"

She wiped a tear away with her fingers. "Poor Joseph. Why did this have to happen to us?"

"I don't know." How to explain the strange crosscurrents, mistaken judgments, minds turned from any natural course... *mad as the sea and wind.* He shook his head, and tears filled his own eyes remembering the boy who was theirs so briefly. "We'll never understand such senseless and passionate hatred, but we can't let grief be our master forever. One thing I do know, Minerva, a time of trial will come again, just because we're alive. And when that trial comes, you will need your faith. That I know about you. If not in the convent, then with a man who shares those beliefs. You were right in the end, and I was wrong. Love alone is not enough. It's just not."

"Do you really believe that?"

"Right now I do. Tomorrow, who knows?"

The torrent ceased as suddenly as it had begun, and the ever-changing sky over the Merrimack Valley shifted from gunmetal to white. Neither spoke as light began to diffuse throughout the room—a saintly presence. Both were wondering at the events that had led to this day, this day when all the possible roads they might have traveled together—lovely roads beside bright waters or through greenwood shade, the multitudinous roads that once seemed to stretch out before them in every direction—had all somehow converged into one stark and lonely road in a rearview mirror, the road the old poet remembers when the shadow of a lost love falls across his page as the day dawns gray, the road where dreams die.

CHAPTER TWENTY-FIVE

nd then I heard that they found his body in the river. His name was Emanuel Rosario." When Nestor had finished his confession, not in the confessional, but over a chessboard in the rectory, Father Leahy was quiet, his head inclined, hand smoothing the dark beard shot with gray, a "sable silvered," as Horatio had said.

Finally the priest sighed and nodded. He looked up at Nestor with a certain resolution in his eyes, as if he had weighed the ethics of the matter in some scale in which he had utter confidence. "And you want what, penance, forgiveness, advice?"

"I killed the guy. I had time, seconds, but I had time to think. I did not have to kill him. I had the gun. He would have fled."

The priest rose. "Let's walk." The two of them left the somber rooms of the rectory and Nestor put on his sunglasses as they stepped into the early August light and walked out on the bridge over the canal where a century and a half earlier the Irish had driven back the Know-Nothings who came to burn their church, in the days when the Catholic religion was in the blood and bones of the Irish.

"I feel sometimes that his death will always hang over me," Nestor continued. "If someone came to you in confession and said he'd killed a man like that, you wouldn't offer him absolution unless he turned himself in, right?"

"Well, in general that's probably true."

"Do you think that for me to be really square with—I don't know, I almost said heaven—with moral law, myself and society, that I need to turn myself in and take whatever punishment is meted out?"

"I don't think I would urge you to do that."

"No?" The sun illuminated the dark green water of the canal, in which they saw small fish, what Nestor and the friends of his St. Brigid's days used to call "kibbies," moving in lazy circles.

"I'm not saying that I'm speaking *ex cathedra* here, but I don't see what good would be served by turning yourself in. You're not a killer. It was an extraordinary set of circumstances, and very bad timing on his part. And there's a good chance that he would have killed others had he lived, though that is not a moral certainty."

"Then I should just try to forget it?"

"Do you want me to give you the penance I would find suitable?"

"Yes, I'll do penance. Strange, I know, I say I don't believe in it, but I feel I need to do something."

"Then I would tell you to take some time each month and volunteer at a homeless shelter. Try to help the poor and the outcast, those brought low by drug addiction or the weight of their own crosses. You will find some very good people there, and you may also meet the kind of person that Rosario was, and try to help him. I really think that would be a better use of your time than wasting the taxpayers' money, if a jury would even convict you, which I doubt."

"All right then. I'll do that."

"But you can't do it yet." He pulled an envelope from his pocket and handed it to Nestor. "George Betsis gave me this to give to you."

An airline ticket. Boston to Kalamata International Airport, via London and Athens, and a half-inch sheaf of one-hundred-dollar bills.

The priest watched him, amused. "He knows you've been through a lot. He said he wanted you to go before the summer is over and you go back to school."

Nestor laughed in the sun, "An offer I can't refuse." Without warning, a shadow passed over him and checked his joy. The memory of Joseph, almost a presence. His smile faded and he asked the other man, "Do you really, *really* believe that our souls are immortal?"

"Do I strike you as the sort of man who would build his life on a lie? Who would pretend?"

Nestor shook his head. "No, no you don't."

"And you can't believe, in spite of all this?" He raised his arms and spread his hands in air to encompass the celestial dome, the world.

"I'm afraid I feel that Shakespeare is about as immortal as a human being can be."

The priest chuckled. "And what if I told you that there was no Shakespeare? That the words to all his plays just... oh, the wind just blew them together? Would you believe that?"

"I see your point."

"Anyway, I'm glad that you got a glimpse of your own brand of immortality, that at least for one night you were Hamlet."

"Yeah, I was Hamlet."

"Sorry I missed it."

A woman passing by on Broadway stopped when she spied Leahy's Roman collar and approached them. She was young and carried a backpack, probably a student on her way to UMass Lowell's South Campus. "You're a Catholic priest?" she asked. Her blond hair was pulled back from her forehead with a white headband. Thick curls, radiant in the sun, framed her face like an aura; her skin was smooth and beautiful, but her mouth curled bitterly downward, and her eyes were narrow with anger.

"Yes," he said, "I'm a Catholic priest."

"I grew up in your Church," she said. "Now I'm ashamed of it. Cardinal Law should be in jail for shuffling perverted priests from parish to parish, but instead they gave him a post in Rome. The whole Church is sick! Hypocrites!"

Nestor was studying the priest, trying to learn the calm he maintained, and the humility with which he finally responded. "I don't blame you for giving up on the Church," he said simply. "But don't give up on God."

She looked at him for a moment, and Nestor could see her features softening, just a little. Her anger was doused in his sincerity in the same way that Rosalind Cannon's sincerity had quelled Nestor's anger. "Well, I had to tell you how I feel," she said.

"You're right," he said, nodding humbly. "They were wolves in sheep's clothing." Father Leahy watched her with pensive eyes as she retreated, then looked at Nestor once more, shrugged sadly, and said, "What do you say we grab a quick beer over at Cobblestones?"

"Thy will be done," Nestor answered, slapping him on the back.

"Irreverent bastard," the priest said, and they set off together down Broadway.

A week later, Nestor sat at the Ionis Café in Pylos, sipping a Heineken. Earlier, the manager of the Hotel Karalis had warned him that the local beer would give him a bad hangover. The sounds of the Greek language he heard around him, foreign, and yet not foreign, soothed his mind, as did the light breeze and the sound of water lapping the nearby piers. The fabled waterway of the Ionian Sea lay before him, upon which Telemachus had once arrived seeking news of his lost father, Odysseus.

The sun was now sinking into the hills across the bay; the hotel manager had told him they rose out of a long, narrow island, but he could not recall the name, other than that it was difficult to pronounce. The island was not far—he wondered if he could swim it—three kilometers, they'd told him. No, he'd never swum that far, especially after two Heinekens and a calamari and artichoke salad. Still, as long as there was an ounce of life, you would never give up and just let yourself sink. He decided that we all might be surprised how far we could swim with land, however distant, in sight.

He asked himself whether he would be more surprised to meet Abby here than he had been to meet her at Eileen Nash's house. He decided it was a draw. He was keeping in touch with her via email on a computer at the hotel. She wished she was with him, she said. He wrote back that he wished she was with him, too, but he didn't know if that was completely true. Tomorrow or the next day he would ride out on Greek National Road 82 to Mycenae, see the Lion Gate, and the golden Mask of Agamemnon, and scan the Plain of Argos. It was a time for solitude and reflection, a time to pray, to whatever gods might listen, for Joseph McCorley, a time to gather strength, to read Kazantzakis in a roadside café, roam the strange streets of a foreign capital and listen to the timeless music of a Byzantine choir in some ancient stone basilica where the placid eyes of the icons watched the centuries pass. Yes, he would see Abby again, but that would be another time.

Thoughts of Minerva rose, too, but those thoughts were already the sort of memories one associates with the past, beautiful but ever-fading like the light of the dying day on the water before him, the pain of all their losses locked in a box deep in his heart, held in the sinewy grip of tough scar tissue.

A quartet had begun to play: an oud, a clarinet, a violin, and a handheld drum. Nestor inhaled the salt air; he sat back and relaxed in the soundstream of his mother's home. A man's voice wound through the piercing notes of the oud—insistent, pleading, and though Nestor could not understand the words, he felt he must be singing about death or parting or love lost. The plaintive voice rose and fell amid a skirl of undulating notes, as if the melody meant to net and ensnare his very voice. With greater urgency, the words tried to rise once more above the music—wounded birds struggling for the sky. All at once the patrons clapped their hands three times and the man continued his song.

Nestor leaned over and tapped the shoulder of a man at the table beside him. He had spoken briefly with him in the hotel; he managed pretty decent English. The fellow turned around with a pleasant half-drunk smile and kindly eyes that shone amid the wrinkles of a weathered face.

"Excuse me," Nestor said, "what is this song about? The guy sounds like he's in pain..." He realized he was a little drunk himself. "I mean, is it about lost love or death?"

The man's smile widened, the wrinkles deepened around his eyes and he leaned closer to Nestor. "No, no. Is not about death or bad thing. This man say, he say, I'm come home now from, eh… the journey, you see, and I'm gonna get drunk so clap your hands." As if to punctuate this explanation, the crowd gathered under this pergola by the sea clapped their hands again three times.

"*Efharisto*," Nestor said, and he sat back again, thinking, Jesus, wait until I tell Declan—they might as well be Irish. And so, all the mysteries were solved, Nestor thought, except the mystery of the stars, the moon, the sea, and us; all the questions answered except whether God watched us from on high, and whether Joseph was with Him as Father Leahy believed; all the spells broken except the inexplicable and tireless yearning to live and love forever. The sun had now set, but a rosy bloom still infused the stippled clouds above the wandering outline of island rock. He watched it fade as the lights of the land began to spread wavering fingers of yellow, white and red across the water, reaching into the deepening darkness from the shore of sandy Pylos.

ACKNOWLEDGMENTS

People always ask me how long it took to write this or that book. I'm never quite sure how to answer. In the case of this title, I remember my pregnant wife telling me the story of a chilling encounter she had at St. Joseph the Worker Shrine in Lowell with a woman, no doubt mentally ill, who hurled a horrible curse at her and our unborn child. That was twenty-two years ago.

I remember sitting in St. Patrick's rectory some years later with the kind Father James Taggart, better known at that time in the parish as Padre Diego, inquiring about the Church's opinion on curses. I began to think a lot about the widespread, perhaps universal, human fear of malediction, the power of words, the eternal struggle between good and evil, and the very different struggle between faith and doubt. It may be, as Tennyson wrote, that "there lives more faith in honest doubt, believe me, than in half the creeds." I will leave the reader to decide which characters in the novel were ennobled by their faith and which were twisted by it; both results are possible.

And so for many years I was working on this story in the way that Irish poet and novelist Brendan Kennelly once explained to his wife: "When I'm looking out the window, I'm working." Then, at some point five or six years ago, I began to put serious time into getting on paper the story that had begun to take shape in my mind.

I was fortunate throughout this period to have friends and relatives I could press into service, people who read and responded to various iterations of the story as it evolved, or with whom I discussed some aspect of the story. I listened to and considered all of their feedback. There was my sister Annie and her husband, Terrence Downes; my other sister, Ellen and her husband, Kevin Cavanaugh; Marianne Innis, a former English teacher with a sharp critical eye; Honey Music, a friend from my Catholic school days; talented writer Josh Shapiro; writer, musician (and my best man) Brian Hebert; and Malcolm Sharps, a brilliant Englishman I met in France in 1979 and with whom I've continued a long literary correspondence (between Lowell and Budapest). I should also thank Jerry Bisantz for his insights into the "small theater" elements of the story.

Later, there was *Merrimack Valley Magazine* and Merrimack Press editor and writer Emilie-Noelle Provost, and meticulous line editor, Steve Wilder, with whom I had long discussions about the finer points of comma usage, and much more. Novelist David Daniel has long served as a mentor and a sounding board for all kinds of literary ideas; I'm indebted to him.

I also appreciate the enthusiasm and energy of Glenn Prezzano, owner and publisher at 512 Media Inc., for deciding to launch his book publishing division, Merrimack Press, with the publication of this novel. I hope his confidence in me is rewarded. Publishing is a tough business, never tougher than today.

Many thanks to my mother, Elinor, who may not know that the greatest gift she gave me, besides life and her love, was a copy of Fitzgerald's translation of *The Iliad* for Christmas in 1972. Finally there's my wife, Olga, my son, Brian, and my daughter, Molly, the family who together give me a reason to join the battle every day.

Stephen P. O'Connor
Lowell, Mass.
November 2014